ATTACK FROM ABOVE!

The Lynx settled on the glacier surprisingly gently. Pross heaved a sigh of relief and was about to relight the engines when great shards of ice suddenly leaped into the air about fifty feet to the right of the helicopter — and a sudden scream came from overhead.

"What the hell!" he exclaimed, but did not waste time putting the power on. The twin Gems shrieked lustily and moments later he lifted the Lynx off the glacier's surface. He put her into a 360-degree jinking turn and searched the sky.

Pross knew the scream of a jet fighter when he heard one. He also knew about cannon shells. Someone was trying to kill him on this bloody glacier in deepest Switzerland. But who was he? *And where was that bastard?*

THE FINEST IN FICTION
FROM ZEBRA BOOKS!

HEART OF THE COUNTRY   (2299, $4.50)
by Greg Matthews
Winner of the 26th annual WESTERN HERITAGE AWARD for
Outstanding Novel of 1986! Critically acclaimed from coast to
coast! A grand and glorious epic saga of the American West that
NEWSWEEK Magazine called, "a stunning mesmerizing perfor-
mance," by the bestselling author of THE FURTHER ADVEN-
TURES OF HUCKLEBERRY FINN!
    "A TRIUMPHANT AND CAPTIVATING NOVEL!"
        —KANSAS CITY STAR

CARIBBEE   (2400, $4.50)
by Thomas Hoover
From the author of THE MOGHUL! The flames of revolution
erupt in 17th Century Barbados. A magnificent epic novel of
bold adventure, political intrigue, and passionate romance, in the
blockbuster tradition of James Clavell!
    "ACTION-PACKED . . . A ROUSING READ"
        —PUBLISHERS WEEKLY

MACAU   (1940, $4.50)
by Daniel Carney
A breathtaking thriller of epic scope and power set against a
background of Oriental squalor and splendor! A sweeping saga
of passion, power, and betrayal in a dark and deadly Far Eastern
breeding ground of racketeers, pimps, thieves and murderers!
    "A RIP-ROARER"
        —LOS ANGELES TIMES

*Available wherever paperbacks are sold, or order direct from the
Publisher. Send cover price plus 50¢ per copy for mailing and
handling to Zebra Books, Dept. 2733, 475 Park Avenue South,
New York, N.Y. 10016. Residents of New York, New Jersey and
Pennsylvania must include sales tax. DO NOT SEND CASH.*

JULIAN JAY SAVARIN

RED GUNSHIP

ZEBRA BOOKS
KENSINGTON PUBLISHING CORP.

For Kate

a Welsh princess

Prologue

"Sod off!"

Pross stared at Fowler angrily. He had entered his small office at the Cardiff airport terminal to find Fowler waiting.

Fowler said mildly, "That is your last word on the matter?"

"Do you think I'm crazy?" Pross countered. "I have a business to run. I have a wife and kids. Or have you forgotten?"

"No, Pross. We haven't forgotten."

"And I," Pross went on in the same angry tones, "have not forgotten what happened the last time you were here. Good God! You must think I'm stupid or something!"

Fowler stood up, adjusted his spectacles. "I understand how you feel."

"Balls!"

"Er . . . well, yes. As I said. We do understand. Sorry to have troubled you."

Fowler left the office imperturbably, walked down the short flight of steps that took him behind the check-in desks, sauntered across the reception area to the main doors of the terminal. He let himself out into the frosty December day, entered his waiting staff car.

Pross watched as the distorted image of the white Rover flitted past the security guard's window. Fowler had given up too easily. That made him very worried indeed.

"You bastards," he said quietly.

He mentally consigned Fowler and his shadowy Department to all kinds of unpleasant hell.

The helicopter tipped itself onto its side, plunged earthwards suicidally. The people watching anxiously from the ground felt their mouths hang open as they began to move surreptitiously away, backing like herd animals in the presence of an unknown menace. They moved cautiously, guiltily, because no one wanted to be seen as being afraid. As a result, they all moved together; a perfect orchestration of anxious bodies.

The helicopter continued to plunge.

It was an unusual machine, not at all like the stablemates that normally came out of the factory that had built it. It was relatively small and narrow, almost slab-sided, with a rakish profile that gave it a formidable and dangerous presence. From the curving hump of its rotor-shaft housing, the forward fuselage sloped steeply to a pointed nose that housed all manner of electronic wizardry. The sharpness of the forward inclination was marred only by the fighter-like bulge of the tear-drop canopy of the single cockpit within which the pilot sat, in a reclined, armoured seat. The rest of the fuselage tapered to a tail so slender, it seemed in grave danger of snapping.

But this was merely an illusion. The whole aircraft, constructed of composite materials, was immensely strong. Its underbelly was unblemished by either dangling wheels or protruding skids. Its undercarriage was retractable. Unlike other helicopters of its size, it possessed a massive five-bladed main rotor with specially fashioned tips that cut down effectively the giveaway throb of other machines. It moved through the air with a menacing sibilance that brought involuntary shivers to those watching its precipitous descent.

Recessed beneath its nose, in a faired housing that did not spoil the lines of its lower body, was a six-barrelled rotary cannon that could spew a deluge of 30 mm shells in the blink of an eye. The fuselage sides sprouted a pair of anhedral stub wings that sloped downwards and were swept back, and from which hung a full weapon load of eight air-to-air missiles.

A true predator, the aircraft was painted all black, with no national insignia.

It maintained its hurtling fall, its twin turbines screaming barely perceptibly, as if in terror. Then suddenly, its maddened plunge was halted. It was as if someone from the deep recesses of the upper sky had yanked at it with an elasticated rope, causing it to bounce upwards almost immediately, pivoting about its axis as it did so.

Without warning, a pair of sunbursts appeared beneath the stub wings. Two missiles curved away from the ship, marking their scorching passage with twin trails of white as they raced into the distance. On the ground, eager binoculars tracked them. In moments, a bright orange fire bloomed a good five kilometres away. No one had seen the target aircraft whose demise had come so swiftly.

But a new sound had now come upon the arena and already, the helicopter was turning, seeking out the intruder. The machine seemed to sniff at this fresh prey. It climbed rapidly, seeking an advantage. Its adversary was another helicopter, of a totally different design. For the next thirty seconds, there was a savage dogfight as the two machines tried to get the better of each other; then came the terrible rasping belch of the rotary cannon. The interloping helicopter simply disintegrated.

The people on the ground clapped enthusiastically as the black aircraft tipped onto its side before sliding downwards, wheels coming out of their hiding places and locking just in time for a perfect touchdown. The work of an artist who knew his aircraft inside out.

The man who climbed out the helicopter was tall, elegant in his black combat flightsuit. He had landed close to the assembled watchers. They came eagerly towards him, smiles of satisfaction upon their faces. He smiled at them in return.

His eyes did not.

Chapter One

The Ford Escort XR3i turbo cruised slowly along the lane that bordered the airfield. It was a cold February day, but the sun poured its rays brightly out of a cloudless sky, bouncing them off the gleaming dark blue metallic bodywork of the car, making it warmer inside than would have been expected.

Logan drove the car unhurriedly past a cluster of ragged-looking women huddled by the coal fire built into an empty petroleum drum. They glanced at her uninterestedly. She smiled to herself as a bend hid them from view. No one had recognised her.

The road dipped, taking her past one of the high watch-towers. A soldier marked the passage of the car with neutral eyes, it seemed. She was not sure. The tower was at the inside fence. The face to whom the eyes belonged might have been that of a dummy in a shop window. Brain locked in neutral. A short distance ahead, an officer and a squaddie were striding along the well-trodden ground between the outer and inner fences.

They did not even glance at the passing car, though it was the only one on the perimeter road. Perhaps they were cold, and bored. Logan idly wondered what would happen if an armed attack were mounted against the airfield. The watch-towers were vulnerable. Rocket-propelled grenades would demolish them in no time. As for the perimeter fences, they could be breached with the right firepower. Entry could be gained long before any patrols arrived.

She thought of this as she swung the XR3i round a wide loop of road, taking her onto a short straight that closed in on the runway, before moving out once more on a north-easterly heading. The narrow lane forked into a T-junction.

She turned right, continued her journey round the big airfield. A short while later she stopped, and parked the car in a rough space at the edge of the road. The outer perimeter fence was only yards away. A soldier with a manpack communications unit strapped to his back was slowly patrolling the space between the fences. He stopped to stare at the car.

Logan smiled at him, gave a little wave. She wondered what he would do if he knew she had a .357 Ruger magnum revolver in the handbag that lay on the passenger seat.

The soldier did not answer her wave. Instead, he surveyed her stony-faced, and spoke urgently into his radio.

"Humourless sod," she murmured to herself, putting the car into gear and moving off. No point getting picked up by panicky security patrols; especially not with a magnum in the car. Fowler would not be pleased.

As the XR charged away, she could see the soldier in her mirrors, staring in her direction, still stony-faced. For a brief moment, she felt a strange shiver, as if she had somehow found herself in a hostile, foreign country. The same kind of feeling had been mildly experienced during the past months of her cover; but this was the first time it had come so strongly. Before, it had almost been a game with the airfield police at the gates. With this solitary soldier, it had taken on an air of something much more ominous. The alienation had been total; on both sides. A good deal more than the mere width of a road had separated them.

Logan smiled with irony. If only the soldier knew. She could give orders to his commanding officer which, under certain circumstances, would be obeyed without question.

"We're on the same side, for God's sake!" she said aloud. But the feeling of alienation did not go away.

Logan was just approaching twenty-four, young for the kind of job she was in, considering she had only been working for the Department for just under two years. She was of quite startling attractiveness rather than simply pretty. She was tall, strong-looking, yet there was an elfin quality about her face that made her seem vulnerable; a mistake many had made, to their cost.

She had pale green eyes, and a pattern of freckles curved from the corner of one eye, down one cheek to traverse her face across the bridge of a strong nose that just missed being too sharp and long. It sat perfectly on her face. The freckles continued their march across her nose, curved upwards in a repeat pattern to the end at the corner of her other eye. When she smiled, she tended to look like a mischievous child. She was soft-spoken, with the barest hint of an Irish accent, and could look astonishingly elegant when she wanted to. Today, she wore an almost dowdy outfit of grey calf-length skirt topped by a white nondescript blouse, over which she had put on a grey, short jacket. On her feet were plain court shoes that looked expensive. It was her image for the time being.

Her reddish hair, cut spikily on top, was shortish and styled in a neat wedge. It gleamed with health, and shifted lightly about every time she moved her head. Her mouth was tucked in at the corners, as if she wanted to smile all the time.

She hummed to herself as she drove the XR fast and expertly down the slope that led to the junction with the A339 into Newbury. She turned right and up the hill towards the main gate to the airfield. She drove slowly past, just another motorist gawping at the tents and the protesting women gathered there. A group of reporters milled around, chatting up whoever was prepared to give an interview. Someone was carrying an outside broadcast camera. She saw a couple of Japanese faces. World news these days.

Then she was past.

She knew all about it. She had herself given interviews, using a different name, and looking quite unlike her present self. As she headed towards Newbury where Fowler was waiting, she wondered what all her time in the peace camp had been in aid of. What mission was Fowler running? Perhaps she'd find out today.

In Newbury, she found she had time to spare. She put the XR in the car park by the shopping centre, walked along Cheap Street to the open market. The bright weather had given way to a cold greyness that had brought a sniping wind with it.

She stopped at a fruit stall to buy some apples. The woman at the stall said cheerfully, "Hasn't it turned cold suddenly! Sunshine one minute, now this the next."

Something wicked within her made Logan say, "Perhaps it's all the radiation."

The woman's eyes narrowed into instant hostility. They glared at Logan, confused by the fact that her attire did not mark her out as one of the protesters.

"Don't be silly," the woman said in a manner of someone talking to an imbecile. "I've never heard of such nonsense. You ought to know better." She had obviously decided that Logan had an acceptable background, though was perhaps not too bright.

"I was only joking," Logan said sheepishly, paying for the apples. The Ruger flamed briefly up at her as she opened her bag to replace her purse. She snapped the bag shut.

"It was a silly joke," the woman said, having the last word.

Logan took her apples and left, as if defeated. What she had seen behind the hostility in the woman's eyes had astonished her. Like caged, bewildered animals, they had shown a bemused fear. It was no fun living at ground zero.

Logan returned to the car, drove off to the petrol station near the café where Fowler was waiting. She filled up with petrol. Just as she had finished, a battered Volkswagen estate with purple paint smeared over it pulled up next to her. A woman climbed out, barely giving her the most cursory of glances. She felt her insides freeze. It was a woman from the camp, whom she knew well enough. There was no recognition.

Logan went to pay for the petrol, returned, and climbed into the XR. The woman did not even glance at her this time. She drove off the forecourt, parked a short distance up the road, outside the café. She left the car, taking her bag with her, and entered the brightly coloured building. Fowler was sitting at a corner table, well away from the wide windows that are staple features of trunk-road cafés.

In his late fifties, Fowler's lean frame gave him the look of a much younger man. His neatly cut hair, showing no signs of thinning, was only just beginning to go grey. He was dressed in a sober, but well-made suit and spread in his

14

hands was the day's copy of *The Times*. He was studiously reading, glasses perched upon the tip of his ascetic nose. He did not appear to have noticed Logan's entry.

She thought he stood out like a sore thumb, but that was his business. She went up to the table. Fowler looked up then, made a great show of standing up for her, offered her a seat.

"Well?" he began immediately after they had sat down. He pushed his glasses back to the bridge of his nose, folded the newspaper and put it to one side.

"No one recognized me." Logan stopped as a waitress came up to them. "Coffee, please, and a ham sandwich," she ordered.

The waitress turned to Flower silently.

"Another coffee, please," he said.

"Two coffees, one ham sandwich. Thank you." She went away with the order.

Fowler said, "I don't know why I continue to drink this stuff."

"Is it any better at the Department?"

"When Arundel makes it, it's perfect." Delphine Arundel, widow of a colonel who had been killed in Northern Ireland, had been Kingston-Wyatt's personal secretary; she had stayed, not to work for Winterbourne, but for Fowler whom she regarded as the real Head of Department. Officially, she was Winterbourne's PS. Fowler was quite happy to leave things as they were. "How do you feel you've progressed so far?" Fowler went on.

"I think I've done quite well. I'm well established now. They think I'm perhaps a little dim, but that's all to the better. I saw someone at the petrol station just a short while ago. If anyone could have recognised me, she would. I was caught on the hop and still gave nothing away. That was a true test."

"The glasses were obviously a good idea."

"And the hair."

Logan had worn fake glasses for her disguise, as well as allowing her hair to become straggly and dull-looking. She had attired herself in decrepit jeans, thick walking boots, an ancient woolen baggy sweater, and a padded nylon jacket that had seen better days. She had made a large donation to

15

the camp, courtesy of the Department.

"Some of them still think I did it for reasons of guilt," she continued. "Daddy's ill-gotten money and all that."

Fowler permitted himself a small smile. An effective cover had been created for Logan. It had taken several months of careful work. The quarry was worth it, but everything still had a long way to go.

Fowler said, "The second phase is about ready."

"I'd still like to know the rest of it. I hate working blind. You know that." Logan spoke quietly, her green eyes seeming to pierce Fowler.

Fowler's own eyes were like blued steel. "All in due course." He allowed himself another smile.

They fell silent as the waitress returned with their order. Logan stared neutrally at her sandwich before starting on it unenthusiastically.

"You should not have ordered it," Fowler suggested.

"I'm hungry."

"You'll eat anything," Fowler said mildly.

"Do anything too, it seems."

Fowler's eyes were expressionless behind his glasses. "Would you like to resign?"

Logan was unperturbed. "Do I have a choice?" Fowler did not worry her.

"At this stage, no."

She finished off the sandwich. "As I thought. But it would help if I knew why it was necessary for me to spend the last three months nearly freezing to death outside the barbed wire, in mud and snow. I've been asked stupid questions by journalists, roughed up by policemen . . . even arrested once . . . and insulted by the locals, for what?" The green eyes held Fowler's.

"As I've said, all in due course."

"Has it occurred to you that they may be right?" Logan remarked speculatively.

"Who may?"

"The women at the camp."

Fowler studied her thoughtfully, noting the tiny smile on her lips. "I hope that some of it has not rubbed off on you."

"That would worry Winterbourne, wouldn't it?"

"Leave Winterbourne's worries to me," Fowler said evenly.

16

"What you should be concerned about, is causing me worry. Should I be?"

Logan's smile widened suddenly, freckles prominent. An impish child enjoying a joke at the expense of her elders.

She patted his hand briefly. "No, sir. You have no cause." The smile died slowly, but the eyes remained lively.

"Good."

"I do have a question."

"I shall answer it if I can."

"Have you been in touch with Pross?" The green eyes had lost their levity.

Fowler said nothing, and that gave her the answer.

"I see." Quietly. "I had hoped you would have left him alone."

Fowler said, "There was no choice."

Her expression showed quite clearly that she did not believe him.

He said, mildly, "You may not want to believe it, but it is true."

"I would like to think you're telling me the truth," Logan said. "I would like to believe that. Pross is not one of us. We conned him into that job he did for us in China, and he performed well; excellently. He stuck his neck out for me. Without him, I'd have died out there. Many people would have left me. A true professional would not have taken the risk of coming back. But Pross, because he is not like us, came back."

She paused, remembering. Pross had been fooled by the Department. In China, he had found himself in combat with two unmarked Russian helicopter gunships. They had been waiting. It had been a neatly set trap, but Pross had fought his way out of it while she had been hiding on the ground with the agent they had come to collect, in an area suddenly full of soldiers. But Pross had come back for her. She had not seen him since Hong Kong. She wondered how he was.

"I would like to believe you," Logan said again. If Fowler had been to see Pross, it could only mean another helicopter mission. What did that have to do with her masquerade at the peace camp? "I only wish I could," she added, almost to herself.

Fowler was looking at her keenly. "You two developed a soft spot for each other. There was something in your voice when you talked about his returning for you. I do hope I won't have to remind you of what involvement means in your line of work."

She returned his gaze levelly. "Have I ever given you cause for worry?" She knew he trusted her judgment. He had shown that quite clearly on the last job.

"No. And as you've so recently pointed out, I have none. We'll say no more about it." Fowler gave a sudden, quick smile. "You'll like Cardiff airport. Interesting place. See Pross. Tell him he'll have to talk to me. Someone's after him. I may be able to help."

Logan was staring at him.

After a while, he said, "No questions?"

"No," she said quietly. "No questions."

"That's what I like about you, Logan. Totally professional."

"I don't see the point in asking questions that won't be answered. When do I have to go?"

"Tomorrow. You don't look happy. I thought you'd be pleased." Fowler's eyes seemed to search deep into her, probing for something. A sign of weakness?

She said, "Will I be minding him again?"

"That depends on several factors. It's too soon to tell at this stage."

Logan turned her head slightly to stare at the traffic roaring past the windows of the café. She could just see the XR, parked where she had left it. No one was near. No car either. Who would be picking Fowler up? One of the familiar white Rovers of the Department, senior staff for the use of, was conspicuous by its absence.

She gave a mental shrug. Fowler's transport arrangements were not her worry. She turned once more to look at him.

"I wish you'd left Pross out of it," she said.

Fowler said nothing.

Pross stared at the luminous dial of the small clock on the bedside table, and wished he hadn't. Four o'clock in the morning, and he'd been awake for a good half hour. Next to

18

him the sleeping body of his wife Dee lay peacefully. She would sleep through an explosion, he thought drily. Yet the slightest whimper from behind the closed door of either of the children's bedrooms would have her up in an instant. He'd seen it happen often enough to know.

It was as if Dee and the children operated within a very special communications channel against which sleep was no barrier. Her perceptions were very acute. He called it her radar. He was surprised she had not yet found him out.

Sleep having irrevocably deserted him for the third night running, he climbed gingerly out of bed as not to wake her. He groped around in the darkness on the floor near the bed for his dressing gown, then crept out of the bedroom on bare feet, putting the gown on as he left. He paused briefly at each child's door. All quiet. The ghost of a smile fleetingly took up residence on his lips as he made his way downstairs. The Dawn Patrol he called them. They tended to wake up when everyone else rightly considered the hour to be still the property of the night. The real Dawn Patrol would have shuddered at such sacrilege.

He went into the spacious kitchen, shut the door behind him before switching on the light. He intended to make himself some tea and felt the noise of the boiling kettle might echo through the sleeping house. He did not want to wake Dee. You never knew with her.

He moved reflectively around as he got on which his preparations, not really thinking beyond each separate stage as it came up. When the leaves were in the pot, the mug waiting with its layer of milk, the kettle hissing to itself, he sat down wearily at the breakfast table and at last began to ponder upon the reasons for his insomnia.

David Pross was well past his thirty-third birthday, but a casual glance would fool the observer into believing him a good ten years younger. The boyish face which liked to smile readily, and the thick growth of dark curly hair, served the illusion. Two inches under six feet, his solid-looking body seemed fit. It was a body that had experienced rigorous training. A picture on the wall behind his desk in the small office at Cardiff airport told part of the story. The proudly displayed photograph was of an RAF Phantom, heavily armed. In the navigator's seat, behind the pilot, his younger face grinned cheerfully. It was the grin of someone who considered the world his oyster.

The face of the older man in the kitchen now wore a very different expression. It was an anxious face whose dark brown eyes now showed, apart from the evidence of lack of sleep, the stresses of running a two-helicopter firm. It was a face that showed worry, as well as bewilderment.

Pross looked slowly about him, and thought about the current state of his life. He had a large, comfortable house. He had a wife and kids who loved him. He lived in a peaceful little village. He had a business that was running sweetly, despite the pressures that had to be endured. By all the rules, he should be happy, contented.

By all the rules.

But last year, the rules had been bent. Nothing was ever going to be the same again. He had been sucked in once, and that had been once too bloody often.

The kettle stopped its hissing with a loud click, telling him the water was boiled for his tea. The noise startled him. He had been so wrapped up in his own thoughts, the sound had faded into the background.

He sighed, heaved himself up off his chair. Turning, he found he had company. Dee. He had not even heard her.

"Got enough for two?" she asked mildly. Radar.

He nodded, went to make the tea. He might have known it would not have taken her long. Even in her sleep, she would have sensed the empty space on the bed. They did not speak until they were sitting at the table with their full mugs steaming before them. Throughout, Dee had watched him, holding her dressing-gown tightly about her in an unconscious pose of self-protection.

Now, she stared at her tea as she said, quietly, "I made myself a promise that I would say nothing about it. I've watched and watched since December, refusing to give in . . . even when you came down here before, in the middle of the night. But I . . . I can't help it, David. I know something's worrying you. It's eating away at you. Is it the business? I thought we were doing quite well . . ."

Since December. She'd given him plenty of time, all things considered.

He said, "I didn't want to worry *you.*"

20

"Is it the business?" she asked again.

There was no point in stalling. He'd have to tell her.

"Fowler came to see me," he answered at last in a flat voice.

She put her head in her hands. "Oh no." Wearily. "Not again. Damn these people!" she went on, voice tight with a quiet anger. "Damn them, *damn them!*" She stood up, walked away from the table, turned, hugging herself. "What do they think they're playing at? You're a married man with children, for God's sake, with a business to bloody run!" The hazel eyes that he knew and loved were trying hard not to cry. "God knows it was bad enough the last time. You've done enough! They're not saying it's Gordon again, are they?"

Pross shook his head. "They wouldn't expect even someone as green to their ways as I am to fall for that twice."

But he still felt guilty about the whole episode. He had not told her the full story. He had not told her about how he had fought for his life, and Logan's, against two gunships and hostile soldiers on Chinese territory, nor had he said a word about Logan's own gun battles. He had not even told her about Logan. But the greatest guilt lay in something else he had kept from her: that when he had been fighting, pitting his wits against the pilots in the other helicopters, how despite his fear, he had felt the heat of combat pulse through him; how he had blended himself with the specially moulded Lynx as it had carried him to battle; how going back to the Jetrangers at Cardiff airport had been like leaving a racing car for a horse-drawn cart.

But carts were safe. You didn't have to fight gunships in them; not when you had a wife and kids, and should know better.

Pross's arguments with himself did not make him feel any less guilty. Somewhere in his mind, against his better judgment, the Lynx seduced him. As for the amazing Logan . . .

Dee was saying, "What did he want this time?" She was still standing a short distance away, withdrawn, arms tight about her, hating the people who had encroached upon her life.

Pross sighed, stared at the tea he had not touched.

"Fowler? He didn't say much. Only that they wanted my help again. I turned him down flat.'

Dee was nodding to herself. "I remember that day. You said nothing to me about it, but I knew there was something very serious on your mind. You closed yourself to me. You don't do that unless you think it's something that might frighten me. Like the time in the RAF when a Phantom had gone into the North Sea. It took you a week to tell me; a whole four days after I'd got it from one of the wives."

"That was because I thought you'd worry about my flying."

"Oh David," she said gently, "do you really think I can ever stop worrying about it? As long as you fly, I'll always worry. But I've got it under control. You know that. I'd never dream of asking you to stop. You wouldn't be the same David, and I don't think I want that to happen. But this is different. I'm no weakling, but these people . . . they frighten me."

No weakling. In her own way, she was very strong.

Despite the way he felt, he smiled, remembering how they had first met. The introduction had been made by Gallagher, to whom she had been a complete stranger. Pross had been eyeing the slim girl at the Mess Ball, surrounded as she had been by an eager group of pilots. Then he had been seized by Gallagher, and propelled through the admiring circle to be introduced. It had gone on from there. To this day, Pross was still surprised by the speed with which he had gone to work, after that helping shove by Gallagher, and the way in which she had responded.

Dee had now come up to him and was pushing at him gently, to make room for her on his lap.

"I know that smile," she said as she sat down and put her arms about his neck.

The heat of her body, the smell of bed about her, began to excite him. He felt a sudden sense of urgency.

He kissed her on the neck. "Perhaps Fowler will leave us alone. He hasn't tried again since that time last December."

She shut her eyes, held him tightly, enjoying his caresses. "You don't really believe that," she said. Radar.

"No." He admitted, wishing it were otherwise.

They fell silent until, presently, she said, "Let's not allow him to spoil everything. Let's go up to bed."

"What about the Patrol?"

She smiled wickedly. "We've got time before they wake up."

And for the time being, Fowler was forgotten.

Chapter Two

"Golf—Juliet Alpha Delta Echo. You are clear to land. Wind 320, 10 knots."

"Delta Echo."

Pross brought the Jetranger in, low from the southwest. The surface wind was nothing to worry about. Above him, the cloud base was just 800 feet away as he held the helicopter at a height of 200. He approached the airport along 03, the short runway, and could feel the slightest of tugs from the northwest breeze as he crossed over. He followed his usual pattern of turning above the large roundabout that fed traffic coming to the airport, before heading back to hover above the apron near the domestic pier. As he overflew the roundabout, he saw a small blue car negotiating it in what looked like a controlled drift.

Naughty, he thought. There was a speed limit of 15 mph.

He forgot all about the drifting car as he brought the Jetranger down with the light touch that was his hallmark. He was shutting down when he saw the stocky, bullish form of Terry Webb approaching. Webb, a former RAF Chief Technician whose last posting had been at St Athan, the neighbouring air force station, was responsible for the maintenance of the firm's helicopters; which usually meant he worked almost round the clock. His professional pride ensured that no ship ever lifted off unless it was totally serviceable. He had once grounded G-EUAN, the second aircraft normally flown by Pete Dent, the other half of Prossair's two-pilot team, because of a loose switch on the cyclic.

Loose switches usually worked themselves completely off during the most dire of circumstances, he'd said, even

24

though they would probably give hours of trouble-free service. They'd wait for the moment when you'd need them most. Sod's infallible law.

Webb was grinning as he came up, a solid shape in his pale blue flight overalls. The wind played with the thinning grey hair on his head. He still sported an RAF-style haircut.

Pross climbed out, stared at him. "Have you been at the cream again, Terry?"

Webb said, "You can talk. Customer happy?"

"As usual."

Prossair had landed a lucrative contract flying executives for a Japanese electronics company. This was the third month of the contract, with nine more still to go. The hours were sometimes long, but the rewards were very good. The executives flew everywhere, and Pross would remember for a long time a flight to Scotland during the past winter when he had almost been caught in a white-out. All points of visual reference had practically vanished in the encompassing whiteness. His passengers had been most impressed with his skill. The client had even mentioned the possibility of a second contract, this time for two years. At this rate, Prossair could probably look forward to a cautious expansion. But he was not going to hurry. Stretch too far and bingo, he'd be in deep trouble.

Webb was looking up at the cloud blanket. "What's it like up there?"

"Clag, clag, and more clag. Instruments down to 1000 feet." They began walking back to the airport buildings. "Alright, Terry. What's the grin about?"

"It's your lucky day. First you come in this morning looking as if *you'd* had the cream all night, then this afternoon there's a nice bit of crumpet waiting for you in the office."

Pross stopped. Webb, not expecting it, took a few steps on before pausing to look round.

"For me?" Pross asked, puzzled.

"Mentioned you by name." Webb's grin had been replaced by a knowing smile. "Lovely, lovely lass. Does Diane know?" he teased.

"Put your mind back in its sewer, you dirty old sod," Pross said without rancour as they resumed walking. "I'm a happily married man. What is she like?"

He had a very strong feeling he already knew and the feeling crystallised as Webb began to describe Logan with relish, and in fine detail.

Logan.

Pross found that his undoubted pleasure at the thought of seeing her again was muted by the fact that her presence could mean only one thing: Fowler. The day began to feel sour. He forced the unpleasantness out of his mind. It would be good to see her, no matter for what reason she had come.

Webb was saying, with a sigh, "All the nice girls love a flyer. Some people have all the luck."

Webb was only making noises. He was still madly in love with his own wife, Maureen, who had followed him all round the world on various postings, some of which, she was fond of saying, would have made a saint weep.

"Logan," Pross said.

"So you do know her. Aha! Is that her first, or last name?"

"Her full name's Sian Logan."

Webb glanced at him as they entered the building. "You don't seem able to decide, me old mate, whether you're pleased or not. Trouble?"

"Maybe . . . but not the kind you're thinking."

He had not told Webb all the details of the Hong Kong affair, but Webb knew enough to fit it all together.

"You're trying to tell me she belongs to the same bunch of bastards who caused all the grief last July?"

Pross nodded. "I'm afraid so, Terry."

"A girl like that?" Webb was amazed. "She looks like something out of Harrods. Not that it's my kind of supermarket."

"Don't let her appearance fool you. She can be anything she likes when it suits her job. She's a tough one too. Take it from me. I know what I'm talking about."

"Was she on that job with you, then?"

Again, Pross nodded.

26

"Bloody hell. Don't tell me more, boss," Webb carried on hastily. "I don't want to know."

"I wasn't going to."

"Good. You've just made me very happy. If there's one thing the RAF taught me, it was how to be among those who didn't need to know. Most of the time, I succeeded. When I did get to know, I used to wish I hadn't. Now I'm out, I want to stay like that for ever. I'm only here to keep these crocks flying."

The Jetrangers were hardly crocks. Webb kept them sleek.

Pross smiled. "Thanks, Terry," he said drily. "I knew I could count on you." Which was certainly true.

Webb said, "Is Diane going to have to go through that shit all over again?"

Pross sighed. "I hope not, Terry. I hope not."

"You know what hope did."

"Oh yes? What?"

"Give me time. I'll think of something. Do you want me to keep Cheryl out of the way?"

Cheryl Glyn was Prossair's very competent receptionist-cum-secretary-cum-everything else.

"Where is she?"

"Up in the restaurant having lunch."

"The restaurant? Why not the bloody buffet? Tell her to watch the bill." Pross smiled. "Keep her there till I have you tannoyed."

" 'Mr. Webb to the Prossair office, please,' " Webb mimicked the airport announcer with a wry grin. "What do I say to Cheryl about the bill . . . exactly?"

"Piss off, Terry."

"Yes, boss. I'll tell her you said piss off." Then the banter died. Webb was serious again. "Look David . . . I . . . I hope it's not what you think. Honestly. I remember what it was like the last time."

Pross gave Webb's shoulder a brief pat. "Thanks, Terry. But I think we both know already."

They had reached the airport main reception area.

Webb nodded, looked concernedly at his companion. "Take care, boss."

"Logan's alright. I'm safe with her."

"I was thinking more of her bosses."

As Webb began moving away, Pross said, "Hang on, Terry. Has Cheryl seen Logan?"

Webb paused. "No. But she took the call while you were up."

"Alright. Tell her nothing. The less she knows, the better for her."

"Just like me, in fact," Webb said with feeling as he turned to make his way along the darkly gleaming floor. He turned right beneath a yellow lighted sign with three arrows pointing diagonally upwards. The sign said "Concourse" in three languages, one of which was Welsh.

Pross waited till Webb had disappeared, then followed. He turned before he had reached the sign, to walk through the line of red check-in desks. One of the company emblems, pale blue letters with white borders, announced: PROSSAIR. Logan's face was looking out at him from behind one of the large square panes of glass. It gave him a jolt to realise that after a good nine months he had forgotten how stunning she could sometimes look.

She was smiling at him. It was a smile of undiluted pleasure.

He went up the short flight of steps, pushed the door open, entered and shut it slowly behind him.

He stared at her. "Well," he said.

"Well yourself."

She was wearing a superbly cut white two-piece, with black tights that showed off her quite magnificent legs. She had chosen to wear expensive low-heeled shoes. Pross could remember being told how the male staff of the Department tended to look upon her legs with something approaching awe. He could well understand Webb's description of her. She was the epitome of what a highly successful woman would look like. Logan the freckled chameleon.

She said, "Do we stand here all day? Or do I get a hug? It's been nine months, and I was nearly dying when you last saw me."

"Of course you get a hug," he said, and went towards

28

her.

She met him halfway, and they embraced tightly. She kissed him very briefly just beneath the ear, then they released each other. Pross moved back to lean against the larger of the two desks in the room. It had once been the only one. Where there had also been one low armchair, there were now two. Signs of Prossair's burgeoning affluence.

Pross said, as Logan took one of the armchairs, "Sorry about the crampedness of our quarters. We've got extra furniture, but the same office space. Can I get you a drink?"

"I could kill an orange juice."

The word "kill" made Pross glance involuntarily at the small shoulder bag she now held on her lap.

"Talking of which," he said, "do you still carry that cannon of yours?"

She gave him one of her elfish grins, snapped the bag open to show him. He saw the gleam of blued steel.

"Ask a silly question," he said drily.

"Same old Pross," she remarked, closing the bag.

"Same old bloody Logan." He smiled as he straightened to go to the tall fridge tucked in a corner between the two desks. An electric kettle was perched upon it. "I think I'll join you," he said.

He opened the fridge, took out a carton of orange juice. He took two glasses from a shelf just above it, filled them. He returned the carton to the fridge, shut it, then picked up the glasses. He handed one to her, then took his seat behind the desk.

"Your health," he said.

"Ours."

They drank. Pross put his glass down, half empty. Logan looked up at the photograph of the Phantom.

"The pilot's Gallagher, isn't it?" she said.

Pross glanced back. "Yes. Ever met him?"

She shook her head. "No." Then she smiled, ruefully. "I was detailed to follow him once, in my car."

"And?"

"He lost me."

"He is supposed to be good."

"Which is why the Department keeps trying to get him back."

Pross said, "I'd like to think you came down here at the tail end of February just to say hello. But I know better. He's not involved, is he?"

Again, she shook her head. "This has nothing to do with him. Pross, I'm really sorry. I can understand your being bitter. There is nothing more that I would have liked than to have come down to see you just for the sake of it. I asked Fowler to keep you out of it, and—"

"What do you mean keep me out? Who said I was in?"

Logan's green eyes were troubled. The freckles had become prominent. "Oh Pross. I don't know how to say this."

"You can always try."

She seemed to flinch at the harshness in his voice, and immediately he felt contrite. She was obviously hating every moment. It showed in her eyes. Pross felt his sympathy go out to her. Fowler was using her shamelessly, the bastard.

He said, "Sian. I'm sorry." He looked at her, suddenly remembering how she had nearly fallen out of the helicopter when she had been shot. He remembered all the blood, and how he had felt when he had thought her dead.

She gave a resigned, fleeting smile. "Oh what the hell. I'll get it over quickly. Fowler wants to see you. He says someone's after you."

Pross felt a sudden weakening in his stomach. He was stunned. "Me? Who would be after me?" His thoughts flew to Dee and the children, their safety paramount in his mind.

Logan gave a brief shrug. "That I don't know. He did not say."

"Did he send you because he thought you could persuade me?"

She nodded. "I won't deny it, but that doesn't mean I like doing it." The green eyes looked at him, seeming to ask forgiveness. "He wants you to go up to the house in the Cotswolds."

"The place they took me to before?" It was there he had seen her for the first time.

"Yes. I served you breakfast."

He smiled briefly. "I remember."

"I'm meant to take you there."

"When?"

"As soon as possible."

"What's that in plain English?"

"Today."

"No chance. In any case, what if I refuse to go? Will you shoot me?"

She was shocked. *"Pross!* How can you, of all people, say that?"

"Oh Christ," he said tiredly. "I'm sorry, Logan. I'm sorry." He passed a hand through his hair. "I didn't really mean that. I'm lashing out at Fowler, and you're catching it. I'd hoped I'd never hear from him again. But it's like blackmail, isn't it? Once you're on the hook, it's for ever." He waved a hand briefly. "Look at this office . . . new furniture, new fridge. I've also got a fully refurbished chopper to replace a sick one I had last year. Before that job I did for your lot, I had one overworked chopper, and one ready to fall out of the sky. There were two mortgages on my house, and I was almost staring liquidation in the face. Today, the choppers are A1, and there isn't even a first mortgage on the house. On top of all that, we have some good contracts. In short, we are doing reasonably well for a high-risk business like this.

"I don't have to be a genius to know that the hand of the Department has writ quite large in our remarkable recovery. But I stuck my bloody neck out for it, and laid the lives of my family on the line. I'm not doing that again. I owe the Department nothing; not a bloody sausage. And what is more, I am never going to be able to forget what nearly happened to you out there. I'm not cut out for your sort of game. So you can tell Fowler to stuff it."

Pross stopped, looked at Logan defiantly.

She said nothing for a while, then, "Thank you for the flowers. I had hoped you would come, but of course, they never let you see me."

It took him completely off guard. "Well," he began awkwardly, "my minder went and got herself shot. It was the least I could do."

"Were you really worried about me?" The question was almost teasing.

"Of course I was bloody worried." Pross said exasperatedly; then he noted her tiny smile of satisfaction. "And you can stop that. You're playing with me, Logan."

She shook her head slowly, looking her most elfin. He would never be able to keep up with the changes in her.

"I'm not," she said, quite seriously. "For what it's worth, I believe Fowler," she went on. "There are not many people I trust in this game, as you put it, especially in the present climate where one is no longer sure who's for whom. But I trust Fowler. I know him well enough; much better than you do. If he says someone is after you, then I'd believe it. Shouldn't you at least find out? If not for your sake, then at least for your family. You don't want whoever it is coming down here, do you?"

Pross shut his eyes momentarily, again ran his hand through his hair. "This is a bloody nightmare. What would anyone want with me, for God's sake? I'm not one of you. I've never been one of you. I have no intention of becoming one of you. You must have some idea."

"I've told you. I don't know, Pross. I don't know! Do you think I like this any more than you do?"

He stared at her. The pattern of freckles seemed to leap out at him. She was now looking vulnerable.

He sighed. "No. I suppose not."

A jet passed overhead, spooling down, coming in for a landing. On this the last day of February, it seemed a rare sound.

Logan said, "I saw you coming in."

"How did you know?"

"Even without the Prossair logo, the registration G-JADE was a giveaway."

"Oh I forgot. The Department would have all this in its files. But it could have been Pete Dent doing the flying."

Logan smiled. "No it couldn't. I recognised the style."

Despite himself, Pross smiled in return. "Where were

32

you?"

"At the roundabout. You passed above me."

"I see. It was you I saw trying to take off."

"I wasn't sure whether you'd be on the ground for long. I wanted to get here quickly."

"You remind me of a friend of yours."

Logan grinned at him. "So you haven't forgotten her."

Pross shuddered at the memory. "How could I?"

The Marchesa Grazziella dell'Orobianchi had once been of invaluable help, bestowing lavish hospitality upon them, as well as giving them the dubious experience of suffering a long drive in her Ferrari 400 on the highways of Italy. Though, to be fair, it was Pross who had suffered. Logan had enjoyed herself. To Pross, Grazziella dell 'Orobianchi was the kind of Italian driver who could make other Italian drivers head screaming in panic for the hills. No mean feat.

Logan was saying, "I've heard from her once or twice. She expects to see you again."

"As long as I don't have to be driven in that bloody car of hers. I don't suppose she knew you'd been shot."

"Naturally not. She came over from Italy, but was told I'd gone abroad."

"That was convenient."

"Yes."

They fell silent. At last, she said, "You know you'll have to go, don't you?"

Pross sighed. "Not much of a choice, is there?"

She shook her head, hair shivering briefly to the motion.

Pross said, "I could always fly up. That way Dee will think it's a normal trip. There and back in no time."

Again, Logan shook her head. "Fowler was specific. I am to drive you back."

"You mean he doesn't trust me?" Pross said with bitter irony.

"There's a more practical reason. The airspace in the area is restricted. You need a special clearance to overfly."

Pross's short laugh was without humour. "What have they got? Anti-aircraft missiles hidden in the shrubbery?"

"Among other things, yes." Logan was quite serious. Pross said, "Jesus. Ask another silly question."

"It's a safe house, Pross. We sometimes have people from places whose governments would like to have them back either for execution, or who would like to carry out the executions on the spot. Such a site has to be protected."

Pross said nothing to that, remembering how the last time the Department had given him protection, several of its own people had died and his house in Craig Penllyn had been entered, as calmly as you please, by the man whose operatives had done the killing. Pross did not have faith in the Department's ability to protect; but he trusted Logan implicitly. He still found it difficult, even after having seen her in action, to equate the ruthless efficiency he knew her to be capable of, with the vulnerable-looking young woman before him. Only Gallagher, he thought, was deadlier. Those two would make an unbeatable team. He wondered when the Department would come to that realisation; assuming Gallagher would be daft enough to let them rope him in again.

Pross said, "I'm not going today. Tomorrow will have to do, or it's no go. I have a business to run."

As if on cue, the telephone on Cheryl Glyn's desk rang. He stood up, went over to pick it up.

"Prossair . . . no . . . she's at lunch. Can I . . . Oh I see. Yes . . . yes. I'm David Pross . . ." He listened for some moments. "Well we can help you on . . . just a minute . . ." He leafed through a large book that was spread open on the desk. "How about Wednesday next? Yes . . . yes. We can do that. Fine. Thank you." He hung up. "Every little helps," he said to Logan, "even during good times."

"Lunchtime's over," she said. "I expect your secretary will be wondering what's going on." She stood up, tugged lightly at her skirt to straighten it. "I'll be on my way. See you tomorrow, here at nine. Will that be alright?"

"Well yes . . . I suppose so, but . . ."

"Yes?"

"What are you going to do? Where will you stay?"

34

"I'll sort something out."

"Look. You're welcome to stay with us . . ."

Logan shook her head, gave a little smile. "Oh no, Pross. That would not be a very good idea at all."

"Why not? You'll like Dee, and she'll like you."

"Do you really believe that? In her place, I'd hate me."

"Why, for God's sake? The last time, you kept me alive."

"And here I am, to take you away again. What wife could like that? Have you told her anything about me?"

Pross shook his head. Logan had moved close to him.

"That's the way I want it to remain," Logan said. "The fewer people who know about me, the better. Besides, she might misunderstand."

"Dee's not like that. There's nothing to misunderstand."

The green eyes were fathomless. "I know, and you know. She can't be expected to; not really." Logan reached forward to touch his arm gently. "Take care. See you tomorrow."

She slung her bag from her shoulder and walked out, leaving Pross staring after her. It took him some minutes before he decided to leave the office and go up to the cafeteria. Webb and Cheryl Glyn were at a table that overlooked the wide spread of the airport runways and aprons. A BAC 1-11 was just touching down. The low cloud base was still there, looking heavy with threatened rain. The day had gone even darker, and lights were on throughout the airport buildings.

Webb said, as Pross joined them, "Wot? No announcement? I feel rejected."

"For you, Terry, personal service. Cheryl . . . Mountjoy's just called. They want that survey job next Wednesday. Give it to Pete. Nine a.m. take-off."

Cheryl Glyn was from Cowbridge, the small market town only about three miles or so from the village of Craig Penllyn where Pross lived. She was slim, dark-haired and very pretty, and was the daughter of a friend of the Webbs, who also lived in Cowbridge. Her father was still with the RAF at St. Athan.

She nodded to Pross, and stood up. "Okay." She peered anxiously at the cloud base.

Pross said, gently, "Pete will be alright. He's flown in nastier weathers."

Pete Dent was an ex-Army chopper pilot whose skill had sufficiently impressed Pross so that Dent now held the unique position of being neither employee nor partner. Pross trusted him completely with the airborne well-being of Prossair's precious assets.

Two faint spots of pink had stained Cheryl's smooth cheeks. "I'll . . . I'll go and see to that booking now." She hurried away, a slightly selfconscious smile on her lips.

Webb watched her as she crossed the concourse, heading for the stairs.

"Don't know what the world's coming to," he began with mock resignation, "a sweet RAF brat like that going potty over a pongo."

"Cheer up, Terry," Pross said. "He might have been Navy."

They smiled at his weak joke.

"Talking of downhill," Webb went on, "what did the dishy lady have to say for herself?"

Pross said, "I've got to go away tomorrow, Terry." He spoke without enthusiasm. "The three of you will have to hold the fort."

Webb had round grey eyes and wild eyebrows of silver grey that tufted upwards at the ends. When he was worried, he tended to look like a startled owl. He was now at his most owlish.

"How long for?"

Pross gave a half-hearted shrug. "Maybe a few hours. Maybe a few days."

Webb swore softly for long seconds. He used choice words that only many years of military service could have taught him.

"I knew it," he said tightly. "I knew the bastards would want their pound of flesh."

"What do you mean?" Pross was curious.

"It's obvious, isn't it? All those juicy contracts we've suddenly landed. I mean, we're a good firm; but we're small — tiny. Even I can see that when an international organization like Uchida gives us an exclusive contract to

36

fly their brass all over the country, somebody with muscle has been putting in a good word. What happens if you refuse to play ball? Will it be the boot instead?'

Pross sighed quietly. "Who bloody knows, Terry? Who knows?"

Webb said, "I don't want to know what it's about."

"I wasn't going to tell you anyway."

"Good. Whatever they've dragged you in for," Webb continued after a pause, "don't go sticking your neck out. I need somebody around here to argue with; even if it is the boss."

Pross knew it was Webb's way of showing anxiety for his safety. "Don't worry, you old sod. Somebody's got to keep you in check. Pete can't, so it's up to me, isn't it?"

Webb gave a tight smile. "To think I gave the mob the elbow for a quiet life."

"Didn't anyone tell you? It's a nasty little world out here."

Pross found himself thinking bitterly of the irony of life. He had come to Wales, to the little village of Craig Penllyn, to find the peaceful haven that everyone searches for, and thought he had found it.

But something else had found him. He didn't know how he was going to tell Dee.

Later that night, Dee told him.

"They've been, haven't they?" she said to him in bed as they retired for the night.

"How do you know?"

"Oh David. It was all over your face when you came home. You've been preparing yourself to say something to me. When you get like that, I know it's not good news."

"I thought I'd had it pretty well under control."

She snorted at him. "The day I can't read your face I'll eat rhubarb." She had a passionate hatred of rhubarb that had endured from childhood. The Dawn Patrol loved it. She swore it was the rhubarb getting back at her. She even hated cooking it. "Well?" she went on. "What do they want?"

"Fowler wants to see me."

She lay unnaturally still beside him. "When?"

He was almost afraid to tell her. "Tomorrow."

Silence.

"They've sent someone down to take me," Pross carried on apologetically. He decided not to tell her why. "We're meeting at the airport at nine."

Silence.

Pross lay there awkwardly, waiting. At last, he felt her body begin to shake; little tremors that were almost unnoticeable. The tremors increased. He knew she was crying.

"In God's name!" she said in a fierce, strangled whisper. She sniffed a few times. "Why can't they leave you alone? *Why?* Last night, I tried to persuade myself it wouldn't happen. All day today, I tried. What kind of people are prepared to do this? They know you've got little children . . ." Her voice broke and she cried more freely now, though quietly. "I'm not weak," she said through her tears. "I'm not. You know I'm not."

"Yes," he said gently. "I know."

He put his arm beneath her to bring her close. At first, she resisted; then slowly, she relaxed and allowed herself to be embraced. She cried until she had fallen asleep.

Pross stared into the darkness and cursed Fowler in his mind.

Chapter Three

12:30, the Hindu Kush, Afghanistan.

The huge griffon vulture glided effortlessly at an unbelievable 25,000 feet on the ten-foot spread of its wings. It was on the 200th mile of a food patrol that could take several hundred more miles. It thought it saw something, tipped over onto a wing, fell earthwards.

10,000 feet below the falling bird, was another: its slightly smaller, more fancily plumed cousin, the lammergeier, on its own food patrol. They were having a lean day. Then the lammergeier also saw what its bigger relative had seen: three shapes scuttling far below across the arid backdrop of barren mountains. It too, fell towards the parched earth. They were both in for a shock.

They had chosen their intercept curves well. Perhaps hunger pangs had made them irrational. Perhaps the strange mobility of the flitting creatures had made them believe their intended meals were wounded and that it was only a matter of time before they succumbed and fell dying to the ground where they could then be eaten at leisure.

Whatever the large birds thought, they were not prepared for the sounds which now assaulted the peace of their environment, nor for the speed with which the three creatures had closed in on them. The instinct for survival pulsing strongly now, they began to take evasive action, great wings paddling at the air.

They were far too late.

The first thing the gunner in the front cockpit of the leading Mi-24 *Hind* gunship knew of the presence of the massive bird was when it smashed into the armoured glass of his windscreen. The glass remained intact, but the blood and entrails of the griffon vulture were smeared all over it. Feathers exploded in all directions, disappearing swiftly. Harsh thuds hammered like great lumps of shrapnel against the fuselage. The *Hind* jerked upwards suddenly like a frightened horse being given too much of the bit, before regaining its equilibrium. It had all happened in fleeting parts of a second.

"Birdstrike!" the gunner shouted into his mike unnecessarily.

"I know!" the pilot in the second, raised cockpit said with some exasperation as he brought the big helicopter back under control.

He glanced to his left, and did not like what he saw.

The three Mi-24s had been flying in a wide, shallow vee formation at an altitude of 10,000 feet — just 5000 below their service ceiling — and at a separation of two kilometres. They had been specially modified, and were on a high-priority mission. The birds had come close to jeopardising that.

Unlike the griffon vulture, the lammergeier's collision had been more devastating. Its avoiding action had not been quick enough and it had turned squarely into the tail rotor of the left wingman. The rotor had shredded the bird, but at considerable damage to itself. The long wings of the vulture had somehow managed to wrap themselves about the rotor shaft and the tail fin, seemingly glued there by the viscera of the dead scavenger.

The helicopter fell out of the sky.

Watching impotently, the pilot of the leading *Hind* called to his remaining wingman, "Go down with him!"

The pilot felt despair as the right-hand gunship obeyed swiftly. There was nothing anyone could do. Only the pilot of the stricken aircraft could save himself and the other occupants.

The gunner, peering through his blood-streaked canopy as his own aircraft now began to circle, saw the falling *Hind* grow increasingly smaller as, deprived of the use of its tail rotor, it rotated viciously about the main shaft. He could imagine the horror inside the aircraft as the pilot fought for all their lives; as the gunship plunged inexorably towards the jagged towers of ancient rock that jutted, eagerly it seemed, from the treeless, sand-coloured landscape.

He hated Afghanistan, and hated those who had sent him there; but he loved flying, and would not have complained even if he'd had the courage to do so. Besides, Mi-24 aircrew — particularly those on *Hind* Es — were considered elite. To be on these particular *Hinds* was an even greater privilege. So the gunner watched the coming death of his comrades with outward equanimity. He was already regretting his earlier atavistic shout when the big bird struck. He hoped the Colonel would not hold it against him.

He thought again about the bird. Where had that monster come from? There had been two of them, and now it looked as if the other had succeeded in bringing down one of the most sophisticated helicopters in the world. Had the Afghan rebels got the birds on their side too, he wondered with grim humour.

Down below, the tail rotor of the falling aircraft had been progressively chewing its way through its bindings of guts and feathers, fighting to regain rotational speed, to the accompaniment of horrendous metallic screechings that reverberated through the aircraft. Suddenly, the screechings stopped and a smoother vibration hummed through the fuselage. The pilot's hands and feet worked frantically with cyclic, collective and pedals. The wild rotation ceased, the *Hind* seemed to stagger, shake itself as if rising from beneath the surface of a stormy sea. It steadied. It began to climb. A jagged tooth of rock, rearing hungrily 1000 feet into the cold March sky, missed its naked belly by a mere hundred feet.

"Colonel," came a calm voice in the headphones of the pilot of the *Hind* circling high above, "I believe we are not yet ready to die. We are coming up."

Colonel Aleksandr Aleksandrovitch Anakov smiled in his mask. "We are waiting, Grigoriy."

The gunner had heard the exchange, and marvelled at the calmness of the voice of Grigoriy Kachuk, the Major who was second-in-command of the special unit led by Anakov, of which the three *Hinds* were part. He marvelled, also, at Kachuk's piloting skills and toughness of nerve. Not once during the long, dreadful fall out of the sky had a single cry come over the airwaves. Kachuk had lived up to his reputation as a hard nut; and he had saved his aircraft.

The gunner, his mind still disturbed by his own cry of alarm, had a burning ambition. He wanted to be a proper pilot. He'd had rudimentary instruction, because these particular Mi-24s carried a basic set of dual controls in the front cockpit; but they were for emergency only. He wanted command of his own aircraft — hopefully one of the new single-seaters the Colonel intended to bring into the Service.

Kachuk's *Hind* rose swiftly in company with the one that had gone down to act as shepherd, their stub anhedral wings giving them additional lift as they climbed. The second *Hind* stayed close, as if checking for serious damage. They began curving in a wide circle in order to formate on Anakov's aircraft.

Anakov said, "What is your condition?"

"My tail feels rough," Kachuk replied, "but I can handle it."

"Can you continue with the mission?"

"I will tell you if I can't. Just keep those Afghan birds away from me in future."

Anakov grinned. They had been at flight school together and understood each other well. Kachuk had previously served with the 16th Tactical Air Army in East Germany where he had commanded a squadron of Mi-24Ds. Then he had been sent to Afghanistan. His actions against the rebels' rocky strongholds — the notorious *sangars* — had left even hardened pilots gaping with disbelief. On several occasions he had flown his aircraft up the steep sides of rock faces letting loose a combined barrage of rockets and chin-gun that had obliterated gun positions and rebels alike. He had asked for, and received, authorisation to transfer Kachuk to his special unit.

The *Hinds* they now flew were testbeds, harbingers of

things to come.

Anakov watched critically as his two wingmen rejoined formation. Kachuk's aircraft appeared to be operating normally. But you never could tell with Kachuk sometimes. The *Hind* could be handling like a pig, but he would not give up.

Once more in position, the three gunships continued their interrupted flight and half an hour later they came upon a huge body of water 10,000 feet up in the mountains. They had gained height on approach so that they were now a thousand feet above its surface.

The lake was twenty kilometres long, and eight kilometres at its widest point. In places, its shores furrowed into valleys like a multi-pointed star. There was nothing whatsoever upon it; nothing marred its placid sheen. It was as if it had been dropped there and forgotten for centuries. No habitation, no trees marked themselves by its shoreline, and for miles in all directions, the ridges, valleys and plateaux were bare of interruptions save for the odd distant streak of lingering snow and ice upon the implacable face of a mountain. Nothing moved upon the pale biscuit landscape. It was hard to believe that any other world existed.

The three *Hinds* looked totally out of place, noisy aberrations of metal that desecrated the aloof silence of the mountain lake. Its unmoving waters lay like a deep blue sheet, waiting, it seemed, for something to happen.

The gunships lost more height until they appeared to be skimming the surface. The downwash of their rotors created a choppy, circular tide in the water that followed them like confused shadows across the lake. It looked as if underwater craft were keeping station with them.

At the far end of the lake, two massive rock columns, each a thousand feet high, stood like colossi out of the water, about a kilometre from the shore. Once they might have been part of a cliff face, but the effects of the savage attentions of the elements through countless centuries, and the pressure of shifting continents, had shaped and marooned them in this enormous mountain pool.

They stood close together, the narrow gap between them

giving the impression that a giant axe had been used to cleave a single structure from the very top, down to the icy water far below. The caps of the pillars were like small plateaux, roughly strewn with boulders, while their trunks, ringed with horizontal striations, looked pitted and crumbly.

The *Hinds* clattered through this domain that seemed without life.

But life there was.

In the cold, underfished waters, was an abundance of trout and giant sturgeon. They felt the strange vibrations from above and darted for the depths. Other forms of life were also aware of the presence of the *Hinds*. Keen eyes had surveyed their coming. No sounds were made, no actions taken.

Anakov, in the lead gunship, watched the pillars draw near. Before the helicopters had descended, one of the monitor screens in the array of advanced avionics that had been fitted to each of the aircraft had shown the heat traces on the tops of the pillars. He had expected to find them. He smiled tightly. The mission was vindicated.

Getting authority for it had not been easy. Those opposed to his commitment to the eventual deployment of a regiment of fighter-helicopters had seen his request as an unashamed search for an opportunity to try out unproved tactics and what they saw as suspect equipment. Others had merely been unconvinced, and therefore unnecessarily reluctant. But he'd had powerful support too. A lot of lessons were being learned in Afghanistan these days, sometimes very harsh ones. Lessons learned in one theatre could, with modifications, be applied to another. That was his philosophy, and the modified *Hinds* were the backbone of his strategy.

His quest for a single-seat fighter-helicopter was four years old now, almost as old as the Afghan war. Even as a brand-new young officer of the *Voenno-Vozdushnye Sily*, the Military Air Forces, he had felt there was a need for such an aircraft; an inevitable evolution of helicopter warfare.

But it was not until he had become a Major, commanding his own flight of seven Mi-24Ds, that he had discussed the matter with his then commanding officer, Colonel Igor Sogovyi. Sogovyi had already earmarked Anakov for rapid advancement, and when the Colonel had eventually been promoted to General and moved to the V-VS Armaments Directorate, Sogovyi had taken Anakov's idea with him, and had kept it alive.

After what had seemed an interminable time, Anakov, himself now a Colonel, had been summoned to present his ideas for the new requirement, and to justify it. This he had done, and had received Sogovyi's full backing. The requirement had then gone through a mind-frustrating series of stages — from the Directorate's own formal request through to scientific technical committees, the General Staff, the Military Council, the Defence Council, the Minister of Aviation, the Ministry itself, the Central Bureau, and so on — before he had got his hands on a prototype. He had counted no less than twenty-eight stages by that time. There were at least another ten to go before the first operationally cleared aircraft would enter squadron service.

But he had stayed with it all the way, and Sogovyi had stayed with him. Then had come the loss of one of the only two prototypes in an unauthorised combat with a British helicopter, in China.

Anakov was very conscious of the fact that his entire career was riding upon the success of the project. Sogovyi had already made warning noises. He expected Anakov to prove that the new helicopter could out-fly and out-gun opposing machines, and survive over the battlefield. It was also to have a ground-attack capability. This last was not what Anakov wanted. His gunship was to be a fighter pure and simple. But he was a realist. To get his helicopter, he accepted he would have to give it an attack capability. He didn't like it, but felt the design had sufficient leeway to enable him to pacify the faint-hearted.

As he stared through his armoured screen at the approaching pillars of rock, he thought grimly that today he would prove a few things to the doubters. The modified

45

Hinds were faster than normal for that particular version, and had been given flaps in the stub wings which acted both as lift-enhancers and airbrakes. They enabled the gunships to reduce speed suddenly and to turn even more tightly. He was about to find out if the addition had been worth the effort. They had worked in practice, but it was never the same as in the heat of battle. If they worked on the *Hinds,* they'd be a nasty surprise for an enemy machine taking on a single-seater in combat.

When news had reached him via Sogovyi that convoys on the stretch of road between Bamiyan and Naiak Shah Fuladi were being hit with unfailing regularity by what seemed like air-launched missiles, yet with no hostile aircraft around to do so, he had asked for a high-recce mission flown by a MiG-25. Sogovyi had arranged it, a convoy being sent as fodder to coincide with the flight. The unfortunate convoy had been plastered, but Anakov had got what he'd been looking for. The secret of the mystery missiles had been solved. No one believed him. Impossible, they said. But no one had a better idea. The convoys continued to take a pounding.

He asked Sogovyi to authorise his taking the three *Hinds* to Afghanistan on a special mission. The general agreed. He wanted his protégé to succeed. The desire was not wholly altruistic.

Anakov was under no illusions. If his gunship project failed, he would be dumped.

Anakov spoke to his companion aircraft. "This attack will be carried out by pilots only. Gunners are to take photographs of the engagement."

His orders were acknowledged.

He spoke again, this time to Kachuk. "Grigoriy, how is the ship?"

"My tail is still rough, but no worse."

"Then you will give us top cover. I don't want to lose you on one of these lumps of rock."

"With the Comrade Colonel's permission — "

"The Comrade Colonel says no. Top cover, Kachuk."

Kachuk accepted his role reluctantly. Anakov knew he would be fuming at being left out, but they could not

46

afford to lose an aircraft during a tight manoeuvre. No account of the damage done by the birdstrike would be allowed by the project's detractors, who would be only too pleased to ground it.

I am not going to give you the excuse, Anakov thought sourly. The loss of the first prototype was a mark against him that would not go away. It would be folly to add more and thus ensure the early demise of the project.

"Begin the attack!" Anakov barked suddenly.

The three gunships went into their well-prepared routine. They shifted smoothly into line astern and squeezed their way through the gap between the pillars. Anakov's gunner momentarily shut his eyes, certain the main blades were about to slice into both rock faces and smash them all into oblivion, but the helicopters slipped between them like threads through a needle.

Anakov and his pilots knew exactly what was to be done. Detailed reconnaissance photographs of the area had been taken. None had shown the slightest evidence of human occupation, but Anakov had not been deflected from his purpose. He had studied every feature minutely before planning the mission. Then he had rehearsed the crews and the mountain troops they carried—eight to each aircraft—in the Turkestan ranges, near the Amu Darya river. There had been no rock formations to compare with these, but the method of attack had been carefully worked out. It was essential that the waiting enemy continued to believe they were not the target. Otherwise the three *Hinds* would suddenly become extremely vulnerable to the hidden missiles.

As Anakov threaded his gunship through the gap, he pulled sharply round to the left to curve tightly round the pillar. Kachuk, following close behind, began a vertical climb, going up like a lift. Piotr Vanin, piloting the third helicopter, emulated Anakov's manoeuvre about the right-hand column. Vanin, a Captain whom Anakov had pried from the V-TA, the Transport Aviation, had proved himself to be an exceptional helicopter pilot.

The three gunships were now rising in concert, with Kachuk's lifting high to enable him to spot any return fire and thus warn the other two.

The attacks on the rock plateaux came simultaneously. The lower *Hinds* appeared suddenly at the lips of the plateaux and immediately, a deluge of S-5 52mm rockets from the underwing pods roared towards the unassuming jumble of rocks. Each *Hind* carried two pods on pylons beneath each wing. There were 32 rockets per pod. At each wingtip was a quadruple missile launcher, fully loaded. Additionally, there was the murderous six-barrelled cannon, intended as main armament for the new single-seat gunship.

The *Hinds* worked their way round the plateaux, noses in, rather like humming-birds circling nectar-rich blossoms. But instead of taking, they gave. And what they gave was death.

Rocks flew into the air beneath the devastating barrage of the rockets. Great lumps of boulders were blasted over the lips of the pillars to plummet the thousand feet down into the cold waters far below. They curved upwards and outwards before falling with seeming slowness, turning over and over as they did so.

The tops of the pillars each covered an area perhaps slightly greater than a football stadium. The *Hinds* continued to pulverise them with rockets until the air in the immediate vicinity was thick with hurtling debris. The aircraft kept well away from these eruptions. A flying boulder in the main rotor could easily mean an unwanted and catastrophic descent.

They kept their missiles sheathed. As yet, nothing seemed to have been hit by the rocket barrage except the barren earth. Then suddenly, something metallic was flung into the air, breaking in two as it did so. A missile; the kind that attack aircraft carried.

Anakov said to his gunner, "Are you getting this, Nikolai?"

Nikolai Dznashvili, busily targeting the strikes through his own head-up display and photographing them with the gun camera, said, "Yes, Colonel."

"Keep at it. We should be seeing some of our friends soon. As long as they were undetected, they were very safe. But they have built themselves into a trap. There is no way out but down . . . the quick way."

Anakov spoke calmly even as he continued to unleash his rockets. One had to admire the tenacity of these Afghans, he thought. To have first taken boats to the pillars, perhaps at dead of night, then to have scaled their treacherous surfaces with munitions, weaponry and other supplies; and to further build perfectly camouflaged *sangars* from which to launch their missiles — probably captured — deserved nothing but admiration for the sheer magnitude of the endeavour. It had paid off handsomely, too, and would have continued to do so had he not taken a hand in it. He wondered how they had got their hands on the launch and guidance systems. Captured? Stolen? Or supplied by the West?

He would not have been surprised. Had the situation been reversed, he would have expected the same of his own side. Anakov was very pragmatic about the Superpowers' politico-military jockeying for world position. He was no Party slave and saw himself simply as an efficient exponent of the art he knew best. Others knew it, and left him alone to get on with the job — as long as he did not make mistakes. The loss of the *Hind* and the new gunship prototype in China counted as a mark against him, but what he would do here today would compensate quite generously in his favour.

People were now beginning to run out of the inexorably collapsing *sangars*. Some were flinging themselves to the ground to point small arms at the gunships. Others lay immobile where they had fallen. Anakov was amazed that anyone could have lived through the devastation that still continued.

As if in a slow-motion film, he saw an Afghan calmly go down on one knee to raise a portable surface-to-air missile to his shoulder. The weapon was aimed their way.

Anakov switched swiftly to cannon. This weapon had a range of 2000 metres. It was meant for tearing other helicopters to pieces. The kneeling man was less than 400 metres away. Anakov watched calmly as the HUD framed the target. He fired. The cannon rumbled harshly as it revolved, snarled its massive rounds at the kneeling figure. The man seemed to dissolve. It had all taken the barest fraction of a second.

More people were running out now, out of the ground, it seemed. Suddenly, there was a massive explosion on one of the pillars. The entire structure appeared to sway. Bodies were flung into the air and over the side, writhing as they fell.

"We must have hit a stockpile," came Piotr Vanin's excited voice on the headphones. "What do you think, Colonel?"

"I think you're correct, Piotr. More of our friends are coming up for air. Switch to cannon, then we must leave some for the mountain boys. But be careful. These people don't give up."

Neither would I, Anakov thought reflectively, *if I were defending my own country.*

He felt a brief twinge of sympathy as he watched the bodies being hurled into the air. In the global game of chess, it was the Afghans' turn to feel the whip. It mattered little which side did the whipping. The weapons still killed.

He received Vanin's acknowledgement, watched as the other's helicopter began preparing itself to drop the troopers.

Watching also from his top-cover position, Kachuk marvelled at the destruction that was being wrought beneath him, and wished he had been taking part. When Anakov played, he played hard. Anakov was a deadly foe to an opponent.

"Come and keep the heads down for us, Grigoriy," came Anakov's voice. "We're about to off-load."

"Gladly," Kachuk said.

The topmost *Hind* swooped down like an avenging angel to add its own brand of hell to the mayhem.

While Kachuk danced his gunship round the pillars, spraying them with suppression fire, Anakov and Vanin brought their own aircraft close in to hover about thirty feet above the battered ground. The assault teams, each led by a lieutenant who had been through the harsh

50

sergeants' school, slid swiftly down slung ropes. In fleeting moments, each team had landed safely on their own objectives and were immediately in action.

As he heaved the helicopter upwards and backwards, Anakov saw a trooper throw up his arms and fall heavily. He did not move. He silently urged the team leader not to lose more men.

Now all three helicopters were engaged in judicious suppression fire while the assault teams went to work. Anakov called on Kachuk to land half of the remaining team on each pillar. The squads were so well trained they could operate as individuals or in any-number team groupings.

Kachuk acknowledged, and carried out his own landing under the cover of Anakov's and Vanin's fire. Then after some minutes of fierce boulder-to-boulder combat, it was all over. The end came suddenly with radio calls from each team that there was no further resistance.

The helicopters landed. Anakov went to inspect the remains of the larger of the two *sangars*. There were dead bodies everywhere, in some cases the flesh held together only by the shroud-like clothing of some of the victims. The hides had been dug to three levels, roughly, but with great forethought. Judging by the number of dead, the accommodation had not even been cramped. It must have taken several months of work Anakov reasoned, as he continued his inspection. Over the smell and dust of the recent battle came the faint aroma of cooking. They must have been eating when the *Hinds* had descended upon them.

One of the mountain troop lieutenants was accompanying Anakov. "Careful, Comrade Colonel," he warned as Anakov went down to a lower level. "There may be booby-traps we have missed, and I do not think the walls and ceilings are very stable now. They took a pounding."

Anakov paused in an enlarged chamber. "Primitive, but comfortable." He looked about him. "And certainly warmer than the tents our comrades use in open country . . . or around Kabul, for that matter."

The lieutenant was not particularly interested in comparisons. He wanted to get the hell out before a sudden rockfall buried them. He wished Anakov would get on with it. He did not voice his impatience. A mere lieutenant did not get impatient with a full colonel, especially not one with Anakov's power; at least, not within earshot, or eyeshot.

Anakov turned suddenly, stared at the lieutenant. "Anxious to leave?"

The lieutenant was short and squat to Anakov's tall elegance. Anakov possessed a handsome, well-chiselled face, a fact that made some Party hacks suspicious of him. He seemed almost decadent; that was until they looked into the cold grey of his eyes. The lieutenant, broad of face and rough of features, found himself in the cold chill of the cold stare. The lieutenant was no softie — anyone who had survived the sergeants' school would have had all softness pummelled out of him — but he found himself taking an involuntary step backwards.

"No, Comrade Colonel," he lied formally. "I await your orders."

Anakov gave a fleeting, wintry smile. "Come. Let's go up and see what's been found."

He made his way back up, followed by the lieutenant. They re-emerged into the light of the cold day. Plumes of oily smoke from the battle rose into the clear sky. The mountain silence had been shattered by the shocking roar of weaponry, and the howl and clatter of the attacking gunships. Now it was broken by the subdued whip of the rotors, the low rumble of the engines, the crackle of fires burning half-heartedly, the intermittent shout of orders. For Anakov, all of this merged into one jumble of background noise.

"They did well," he said to himself, looking around the scene of destruction. The sickly sweet stench of burning flesh came to him.

Someone had come up. "Who did well?" asked Kachuk.

Kachuk was shorter than Anakov; broader too, with the same sort of large face possessed by the lieutenant. Kachuk wore his black hair cropped very short; so short, it bristled. He had little eyes that seemed hidden in folds of skin.

The eyes always seemed to be amused. It was said that Kachuk had once killed a man with his bare hands, and the eyes had been smiling throughout. Kachuk had also been through the sergeants' school.

"These Afghans," Anakov replied. "They planned carefully."

Kachuk was dismissive. "The pigs took out a lot of convoys. They deserve what they get." The eyes smiled at Anakov. "Well, you proved you were right. I'd better be careful. You'll be a general soon, if you go on like this."

"Then I'll just have to see to it that you become a lieutenant-colonel." Anakov smiled at the older Kachuk with genuine warmth.

"Perhaps I'll be able to buy American jeans for my daughter at last." Kachuk looked around exaggeratedly. "You don't think anyone's listening, do you?"

They laughed briefly at the irony of the remark. Kachuk hated Americans. He offered no patriotic reason for this. They got on his nerves, he'd once said.

"Speaking of Americans," Kachuk went on, "the assault team found a damaged launch command unit. Our missiles, their launch unit."

"Not so surprising is it? We get the electronics from them in the first place."

Kachuk shook his head slowly as they walked through the debris. The assault troopers were shifting bodies, scavenging weaponry that seemed of interest, searching here and there for anything that might give useful intelligence. They moved swiftly in the smoke and dust, ghostly, ominous children of a future apocalypse.

Kachuk said, "If these pigs steal from us, and we steal from the West, and the West steals from us, I suppose one day I shall be flying a ship with instruments marked in English and be shot down by one of our own missiles fired by somebody using an American launch unit." He laughed loudly, walked on towards his helicopter. He was still laughing as he climbed in.

Anakov gave a vague smile as he watched his colleague settle himself in his seat. Kachuk seemed to continue to find humour in the situation. He was apparently still laughing.

Anakov walked slowly away from the devastated *sangar* until he was almost at the edge of the pillar. He turned full circle, taking his time about it. The world was a cliff-edge away in every direction. He moved closer, gingerly, to the rim. Here the ground was crumbly, dangerous. One slip and it would be a very long fall to the lake below. Playing chicken with himself, he peered over. The sheerness of the drop took his breath away. Again, his admiration for the hardness of the dead Afghans returned. There was nothing wrong in showing respect for a stubborn foe, even if you have to kill him.

"Comrade Colonel," came a cautious, almost fearful voice.

Anakov stepped away from the abyss carefully, turned. It was the lieutenant.

"It's alright," Anakov said. "I'm not going to throw myself over."

"Comrade . . . I did not . . ."

Anakov smiled. "Of course you didn't. Are you finished?" he went on.

"Yes, Colonel. So are those on the other column. All the charges are set."

"Very well. Tell them to board, then get your men into the ship."

"Yes, Comrade." The lieutenant began speaking into his radio as he left Anakov. They would be taking their dead comrade, the only casualty, back with them.

Anakov went back to his gunship, climbed in. Dznashvili had remained in the aircraft throughout, and could have taken off if anything had happened to Anakov. Whether he would have made it back to base was open to question.

Anakov smiled to himself. It would not have mattered.

A minute later, he spoke into his mike. "Is everyone loaded?"

"I'm ready," Kachuk said. He had already picked up his other four troopers from the neighbouring pillar, and was hovering some distance away.

"So am I," came Vanin's acknowledgement.

54

"Alright. Let's go." Anakov lifted the *Hind* smoothly off the ravaged ground. As he did so, stark images framed themselves fleetingly upon his mind's eye: the trooper throwing up his arms for the last time; an Afghan being blown over the side, minus legs and arms; another Afghan lying dead at the ruined entrance to the *sangar*, not a single mark upon him; the man on one knee, squarely facing up to the formidable frontal aspect of the gunship, before being minced for his pains; and so on. The images flashed like flickers on a TV screen.

Anakov led the helicopters two kilometres away from the rock columns where they did a quick stop to the hover, then pivoted round to face the pillars once more, in line abreast.

"Arm your missiles," he ordered the other two ships. He armed his own weapons, watched as the HUD lit up. He would put the right load into the right-hand column, the left into the other. The missiles would not detonate on impact. "Descend," he ordered.

The three aircraft executed a vertical descent until they were only 100 feet off the surface of the lake. They hovered in perfect formation, great ominous insects with a seeming life of their own.

"Release!" Anakov barked into his mike.

Twenty-four fires bloomed at the wingtips of the hovering ships. Twenty-four missiles streaked towards the columns. Twelve embedded themselves in each, in a perfect horizontal line. There were no explosions.

"Let's go up," Anakov said.

He led them to 1000 feet and a further kilometre out. Again, they turned towards the columns, and waited. He eyed the glowing digital timer on the lower left-hand quadrant of his HUD.

"Detonate!" He spoke quite calmly as the readout showed him three zeros and squeezed a button on the cyclic, knowing the other two helicopters had the same readout and that Kachuk and Vanin were squeezing the detonators at exactly the same moment.

On the distant rock columns, great gouts of earth erupted in a precise line right across a belt of striations a

55

few feet above the water. Simultaneously, massive explosions took place deep within the tops of the pillars. A multi-tongued bellow rolled and roared its way across the lake. The shockwaves reached and buffeted the suspended gunships, making them dance skittishly as their pilots compensated with judicious movements of the controls.

At first, nothing seemed to happen to the columns after that. There was a pause, not unlike the advent of an earthquake. Even the mountains appeared to be waiting.

Then little cracks began to show at the tops of the pillars. Hesitantly at first, then with an awesome rapidity, the cracks ran down towards the water, splitting the columns open like sticks of celery. They swayed drunkenly towards each other, collided in a rising explosion of rock and dust that radiated outwards like a sunburst.

They began to topple. It was an astonishing thing to behold. As if bending from the waist, they curved together, their shattered tops swooping downwards. The momentum thus attained ripped them from their moorings like felled trees, all along the line where the missiles had slammed into them. They roared as if in pain, and the enclosed lake echoed their voices. Great slabs of rock hurtled through the air as they plummeted towards the now raging water. A rolling thunder had begun to fill the world it seemed, like a creeping barrage.

At last, the falling blocks began to slam into the water, which received them with a fury that sent foaming spouts reaching into the sky. A tidal wave radiated outwards, rushing towards the land. Parts of it rushed back, pouring into the spaces created by the tumbling slabs that had smashed into it with a noise like the waspish crack of a tank gun.

And then it was all over. The disturbed water settled. Where the columns had been, only their shattered bases remained, barely peeping through the surface.

"Think of all those fish," Kachuk said laconically.

Anakov was not thinking of fish. Ordering Kachuk and Vanin to circle and wait for him, he took his gunship back to where the columns had been. He circled once to survey the destruction he had masterminded, and to allow

Dznashvili to photograph the results.

"Do you know, Dznashvili," he began conversationally as they headed back towards the waiting *Hinds*, "what Hindu Kush means? It means Hindu Killer," he went on, answering his own question. "It kills other people too. Over to the east, Nepal nearly drowns during the monsoon—which is not so far away now, incidentally—but here, the rains hardly ever come. Yet we have this enormous lake in a barren landscape. Contradictions, Dznashvili. Contradictions."

The gunner, not knowing what to make of this impromptu lesson in history and geography, said nothing.

"You are confused," Anakov said. "You're wondering what my words mean and what they have to do with what has just happened. To know your adversary, you must study his environment and in turn, this helps you to understand what motivates him. The Afghan is a contradiction, as other nations have found out long before us. We caught him today because we behaved in a way he did not expect. His normal instinct is to do battle at every opportunity. Yet today he was prepared to allow three fat targets to go unmolested because he wanted his precious missiles to remain undetected. He did not expect an attack. If you want to be a pilot, Dznashvili, remember this. Never do what is expected of you. That way, you just might survive."

The gunner was silent for some moments. "What killed the Hindus, Comrade Colonel?" he finally asked.

Anakov waited until he had rejoined formation before replying. "Afghanistan," he said.

The three *Hinds* rose into the cold sky, their bulbous tandem canopies, protruding chin cannons and probes giving them the air of malevolent, prehistoric insects as they made their way back towards Kabul.

Chapter Four

It was 08.30, four and a half hours westwards. David Pross drove his white Jaguar XJ6C out through the wide, low wooden gateway to his home and onto the single narrow road that was the village's artery. He turned right, to drive slowly, heading for the A48. A short distance later, he passed the village pub, off to his left. The landlord was outside on the sloping patio, already preparing for the day. He waved as the car drove past.

Pross waved in return. It was their daily routine.

As the pub hid itself behind the next bend, Pross reflected that this was what his life had become. The thought that day after day Barry Jones would be outside his pub to wave was somehow comforting; as was the drive to the airport, listening to Terry Webb's irreverent remarks, laughing at Pete Dent's tales of army life, being amused by Cheryl Glyn's blushes, and waking up to Dee and the Dawn Patrol. He had made himself his niche, and he was happy with it. He cursed Fowler for having ensnared him in the first place.

"Bastard," he said as he stopped at the junction with the A48.

There was not much traffic. Only one car passed, going towards Bridgend. He turned right onto the main road, taking the same route. He put his foot down and soon caught up with the other car. He passed it easily and streaked ahead. The driver flashed him, perhaps in annoyance. Some people hated being overtaken.

Pross left the A48 soon after and took the road to Llantwit Major. Then it was on to St. Athan and the airport. He arrived at the roundabout to see a blue XR coming up fast behind him. He knew it was Logan. It sat in his mirror all the way into the reserved car park in front of the terminal. She parked next to him.

She climbed out, came over to lean on the Jaguar. Today, she was in tight jeans and a floppy sweater.

Pross looked up from his seat. "What have you got in that thing, anyway?"

"A turbo," she said, grinning at the sudden wariness in his eyes. There was nothing on the car to betray this. Even the standard badging had been removed. Its fat special wheels and the rear spoiler on the chopped tail were the only giveaways to its difference from the run-of-the-mill Escorts. "I promise not to scare you," she added.

Pross climbed out, locked the car. He did not look convinced. "I've got to check things out with Terry Webb, then we'll be on our way." He glanced at the XR critically. "Let's go in my car."

Logan shook her head. "Nice try, Pross, but no."

"Don't tell me," he began drily. "I need clearance to drive up there."

"I wouldn't put it quite like that, but you've got the idea."

"Jesus, Logan, how can you work for these people?"

The green eyes challenged him. "Gallagher worked for them."

"He got out."

"He thinks."

"What do you mean?"

Logan changed the subject. "What did your wife say?"

"Don't duck the question, Logan. Is he involved?"

"I've told you before. He isn't. You can believe me."

"You've got to be joking, of course."

They stood silently for a while. The day was cold, and as cloudy as it had been twenty-four hours before. Logan put her arms about her for warmth. A moderate wind swept the car park.

She said, "You're very hostile, Pross." She looked slightly hurt. "You haven't asked how I slept."

"I'm sure you were well catered for."

"I slept very badly."

"Then join the club. My wife cried a lot last night."

Pross walked away, leaving her standing there, staring after him. She waited until he had entered the building before turning pensively back to her car. She slapped a

59

palm exasperatedly against its roof, then opened the door to climb in behind the wheel. She settled down to wait.

Fifteen minutes later, Pross reappeared. He approached the XR, pulled open the passenger door and climbed in. He drew at the seat belt, clipped it on.

"Logan," he began, "I'm sorry. I keep taking my anger out on you. It's Fowler I want."

"Well," she said, "you'll soon have your chance." She started the car, put it into reverse.

To Pross's mistrustful ear, the engine sounded ominously powerful.

Logan eased the lever into first and drove slowly out of the car park. She behaved herself until they were well away from the airport area. Once on the open road, she floored the accelerator. The XR spun its front wheels viciously and the nose seemed to want to go its own way briefly before the fat tyres bit and the car hurled itself forwards.

"Bloody hell, Logan!" Pross shouted. "What are you *doing!"*

Instead of replying, she ignored his outraged stare and drove the little car with a verve that made him swallow nervously. The forty-mile-an-hour stretch that led to the huge roundabout near the Harlech TV buildings was taken at ninety. The XR seemed to swim round the big circle, going right to join the south Cardiff by-pass. She shifted gears upwards with hardly a drop in engine revolutions.

Pross watched the streaming ribbon of asphalt and decided he had been trapped with a madwoman. What the hell had got into her?

The by-pass was coming to an end. Logan didn't seem to be slowing down.

"Logan! For God's sake! I've got a wife and kids!"

Pross felt his feet pressing hard against the footwell. He was certain Logan was not going to be able to stop in time. After years of flying and even after experiencing combat, he thought bitterly, he was going to be totalled in a car by a maddened female. He waited for the inevitable.

But Logan was braking, dangerously late it seemed, going down through the gears swiftly as the engine screamed richly in response. At any other time he might have enjoyed its music.

The XR was decelerating strongly, inertia reels of the

seatbelts locking as the speed bled off rapidly. The car was barely crawling by the time they'd reached the end of the by-pass. She'd done it, with room to spare.

Logan turned left into the traffic as if nothing had happened. The silence in the car remained for several minutes. Pross stared pointedly out of his window.

At last, he said quietly, "Now what the bloody hell was that all about?"

She took her time about it. "Next time you're angry with Fowler, don't take it out on me." She threaded the XR through an impossibly narrow gap in the traffic.

Pross resisted the temptation to close his eyes. "I said I was sorry."

"Even so."

"I don't understand this," he said exasperatedly. "Aren't you spies supposed to be responsible superbeings keeping civilisation safe and all that bullshit? What happened to the cool-as-a-cucumber Logan I knew so well?"

"I wouldn't call blowing people away responsible. But that's what I do. It's my job. You've seen me at work." Logan spoke tensely. "And I'm not cool, as you put it."

Pross frowned, looked at her. "Why are we fighting, Sian?"

She sighed. "Oh . . . I don't know. I don't like the feel of this. Fowler's not saying much to me, I don't like his having dragged you into it, and I don't like being used to it."

"I thought you said he told you someone was after me."

They were heading out of Cardiff now, and making for the M4.

"He told me. I don't *know*."

"Well," Pross said. "We can sort that one out very quickly. Take me back."

"You know I can't. They'd only send someone else."

"Who wouldn't be as nice."

"I didn't say that."

"It's implied."

Logan said nothing as she took the XR onto the M4 and accelerated towards Newport.

Pross said, "If it's another con —"

"There's not much you can do about it." She tightened her lips briefly, smacked the steering wheel once with a frustrated palm.

"Terry Webb thinks," Pross went on slowly, "that we could quite suddenly lose all our nice contracts, particularly the one with Uchida. I happen to believe him."

Logan shrugged, and again said nothing.

Great.

Logan drove fast along the motorway, the XR sitting squatly as it ate up the miles. After the Severn Bridge, she took the M5, heading north. No one appeared to be following them. The only police car they saw was a patrol going the other way. Pross decided with a wry smile that they would have left Logan alone anyway.

They came off the M5 at junction 14, took the B4509 and headed deep into the Cotswolds. Logan drove along a series of B-class roads as if she were practising for the Round Britain Rally. Pross kept his trap shut as the XR did impossible things round corners.

Once, he spoke long enough to say, "You're still angry, aren't you?"

She held on to her grim silence as their destination drew closer. At last, the blue car pulled into the long drive of the small Georgian manor Pross remembered from the last time. He stared at the two-storeyed, bay-fronted building as Logan drove towards it. Impressive in its own right despite its relatively small size, its large bay window on the upper floor was supported by four massive Ionic columns. The grounds, Pross remembered, were extensive and well-kept, and were even traversed by a small stream somewhere. The place was sited in one of the most beautiful areas of the Cotswolds, and belonged to Fowler. Fowler had loaned it to the Department for its own mysterious use. Pross could never understand why.

As the car drew to a halt in a crunch of gravel, Pross almost felt like a returning schoolboy, albeit a very reluctant one.

Logan said, "This is where you get out."

He peered through the windscreen. "There doesn't seem to be anyone around."

Logan gave her a brief smile. "If you were a hostile . . ."

"A hostile?"

"What did you call hostiles when you were on Phantoms?"

Pross said wearily, "I keep forgetting you people talk in code. Alright. If I were a hostile, what then?"

"I doubt if you'd have made it to those columns alive."

Pross looked at her. "Who would have done the shooting?"

"Don't look at me. I wouldn't have had to do anything. This is a very unhealthy spot for the uninvited."

"For the invited too," Pross remarked sourly. He climbed out, went round to her side of the car. "Are you taking me back?"

She shook her head. "I think not."

"I'd have preferred you to."

"What about my driving?"

"Sod your driving."

She gave him one of her impish Logan grins, but it died quickly. The green eyes were withdrawn. "Look after yourself, Pross."

She had kept the engine running. Now she put the XR in gear, did a fast turn about, and shot back down the drive in a spray of gravel. She did not give him a parting wave.

"You too, Logan," he said quietly as he stared at the neat tail of the receding car.

"The drive has to be tidied every time she comes here," a mild voice said from behind.

Fowler.

Pross turned slowly. Fowler was dressed like a country squire out for a stroll in his grounds.

Fowler said, "Care for a walk?" And promptly took up his own invitation. "Good for the appetite."

Pross had no option but to follow.

"You're looking well, Pross," Fowler went on when Pross had joined him.

"But not pleased."

"No," Fowler admitted. "Certainly not pleased. It could not be helped. You had to come . . . for your own sake."

"Is that a threat?"

"Not from me, old son. Not from me," Fowler glanced at Pross, glasses flashing briefly in the weak, hesitant sun. "My job is to counter that threat."

"I'm that important? You flatter me."

Fowler ignored the sarcasm, glanced up at the sky. "Rain, do you think? Funny old weather we're having," he continued, not waiting for, nor requiring, an answer. "The promise of an intensely wet spring to be followed no doubt by a dry summer. Then everyone will cry drought, and panic. It never ceases to amaze me how we, who must inhabit one of the wettest pieces of turf in the world, manage to suffer a scarcity of water. We'd never survive an Israeli or Arabian summer." He smiled suddenly, more to himself. "But we do have our other victories."

They were walking down a rich green slope which led to the stream. Because of the recent heavy rains, it was fast-flowing. Pross could hear it as they approached. When they had reached it, he found it was much wider than he had at first thought, and had cut its way quite deeply. The bank was a good four feet high.

Fowler stopped, looked up and down the rushing water. "We've got a fine stretch of fishing further up. Some of our guests tend to take advantage of it. It helps them to forget."

"Forget what?"

Fowler glanced at Pross, and smiled. "Logan did her convalescence here."

"Did she fish too?'

Again, Fowler smiled. "Oh dear. We are angry."

"What did you expect?"

Fowler said, "Care to walk along the bank?"

"Do I have a choice?"

"You can stay where you are." Fowler walked on.

Pross reluctantly joined him. "Why are you trying to needle me, Fowler? First Logan behaves like someone with a bad hangover, now you're playing games. What's going on? Why have you dragged me away from my business and my family with a cock-and-bull story about my being some mythical person's target?"

Fowler stopped, looked hard at Pross. The eyes were steely behind the glasses. So hard were they that Pross began to wonder whether Fowler wore fake spectacles. The eyes behind them certainly did not look weak.

Fowler said, "There is no mythical person. He is very real, and *you* are standing between him and the success of a dream he has had for some years."

"Me?" Pross stared at him disbelievingly. "I don't know any such person."

"I should have been very surprised if you had," Fowler remarked calmly.

They walked on for a minute or two, Fowler apparently deep in thought, Pross impatiently wanting to know what was going on.

"The man's name," Fowler continued, as if he hadn't paused, "is Anakov. Aleksandr Aleksandrovitch Anakov."

"A *Russian?"* Pross exclaimed, more bewildered than ever. "I don't know any bloody Russian. Not my normal circle. You know how it is."

"You've just performed the unique trick of sounding both worried, and sarcastic."

"It takes talent," Pross said grimly.

"Anakov," Fowler went on smoothly, "is a Colonel in the Soviet air force and at the moment, is the bright boy of the helicopter procurement section of the V-VS. His rapidly rising star came to a rude halt last year. To be more precise, in bad weather across the Chinese border." He glanced at Pross. "I believe I'm beginning to detect dawning comprehension on your worried features, Pross."

"The chopper I shot down," Pross said gloomily. "The one that looked like a single-seater."

"The very same. You killed Comrade Anakov's baby. His career and his star, was hitched to that machine. Luckily for him, there were two airworthy prototypes. He has a second chance to make good. The fighter-helicopter was his idea, and he has virtually been given total responsibility for its success. Of course, the other side of the coin also means that failure is equally his total responsibility. Over here, we don't shoot people for failure — yet — but Anakov knows the penalty that's waiting for him. His priorities are therefore quite clear: the new helicopter must eventually be accepted by the air forces, which means he has to prove that it works. He can hardly do that if it keeps getting shot down. Are you following this?"

"I'm riveted," Pross said at his most sarcastic.

Fowler smiled to himself, continued, "Naturally, he wants to know what was responsible . . . and who. Then he'll obviously attempt to make quite certain it does not happen again."

Pross felt his stomach lurch. "Are you telling me that this man . . . this Anakov is *here* in England with a bunch of Russians, with the intention of knocking me off?"

Fowler was at his most soothing. "There is no cause for alarm. In the first instance, Anakov is not here . . ."

"Then —"

"But he will be coming."

"How can you tell?"

"I know. Take my word for it."

"Oh yes. Your word."

"I can understand your bitterness, Pross, but believe me, we are trying to help."

Pross kept his silence, anger in his stride as he walked with Fowler.

"At first," Fowler carried on, unperturbed, "we thought that Anakov might have got your identity from Ling. Remember him?"

"How could I forget?"

Ling had been the top Chinese agent who had caused him many hours of terror for the safety of his family. Ling had been a killer, and Logan had got him. Good old Logan. Poor old Pross, caught again. Sod it.

Fowler was saying, "But of course, despite the current game of footsies, Ling gave nothing to his Russian comrades. China will give nothing, either to the Russians or to the West, unless she expressly wishes to, for her own purposes, naturally. It is something our masters would do well to bear in mind. Don't misunderstand me. I'm no Sinophobe. This is a pragmatic evaluation. In their place, I'd do the same. Once one has made that intellectual jump, it becomes far easier to deal with them."

Fowler stopped again as they came up to a part of the bank that curved outwards. On the opposite side the land did the same, widening considerably so that a good-sized pool was formed. It was at least a hundred metres before the banks curved in once more, narrowing into a tiny neck by comparison, so that to Pross it seemed it could be easily crossed by a well-judged leap. In the pool, bordered by a profusion of reeds, the water was almost still.

Fowler said, "It's quite deep here." He peered down, searching. "Ah ha. There's one of them. Fair size, I'd say."

As Pross watched, something long and sleek powered its way just below the surface in a swift dash across the pool. Pike, he thought.

"Pike," Fowler said. "He'd give a good fight." He began walking again, not waiting for Pross whom he knew would have no choice but to follow. "Think of Anakov," he went on mildly. "Now there's a pike for you. And we've got to land him . . ." Fowler's eyes were now on Pross. "Before he lands you, of course." He smiled briefly as he looked away.

Their walk took them as far as the neck of the pool, which Pross saw was much wider than he'd thought. Anyone attempting to leap across would have got his feet very wet.

Pross said, as they turned back, "Logan tells me this place is very secure. Yet I've not seen anyone who looks like a guard. I've not seen anyone. Period."

"We are being observed. You can take my word for it. If you were the kind of person who was a hostile — assuming you would have made it this far — and you decided to make a move towards me, you'd be dead before you had completed your move."

Pross found himself shivering involuntarily. Fowler had spoken as if he'd been discussing the landscaping of his grounds.

Fowler said, "Don't worry. They are quite aware that you're friendly."

"That's nice to know."

"Gallagher, of course, would have spotted them," Fowler remarked musingly. "Instincts of a wild creature, that friend of yours. Exceptionally good man. Pity."

"Pity?"

"He doesn't like working for us."

"I wonder why," Pross said, the bitterness back in his voice. "Well, I'm not Gordon Gallagher, so I don't know any of the little tricks you people have taught him . . . for which I'm eternally grateful. And I'm not one of you, thank God."

Fowler said, "But you're a top-class chopper pilot, and for the purposes of this mission, that's just what we need."

Pross stared at him. "I thought you said you were going

to protect me from what's-his-name . . . Anakov. Where does chopper flying come into it?"

"Just about everywhere, Pross. Not only do we have to prevent him from getting to you, we want his other prototype too; in one piece if possible, but if not, totalled. In short, it must not be seen to work."

"I bloody knew it. And where is it this time?" Pross queried sourly. "Inside Siberia? You can think again if you believe you're going to drag me to Russia. Get one of your suicidal super-secret agents. Leave me to my sleepy Welsh village."

"Super-secret agents?" Fowler said with painted forbearance. "What have you been watching on the telly? I would not dream of sending you to the Soviet Union."

"Where then?"

"Somewhere very nice. Switzerland."

"Switzerland?"

"Come on, Pross," Fowler said in his mild way. "Let's go up to the house. You must be quite hungry by now."

Fowler set up a brisk pace. Pross tagged along, even more confused, nostrils stinging from the sharpness of the Cotswold air.

After they had eaten, Fowler took Pross into a large study that had one double-glazed french window overlooking the stream, and laden floor-to-ceiling bookshelves that took up all the available wall space. In one corner of the room, which Pross had no doubt was an original. Behind the desk was a high-backed, richly upholstered chair. To one side was a comfortable-looking armchair, and opposite that was a recliner, partially extended. The floor was itself expensively carpeted.

Had Pross visited Fowler's office at the Department, he would have marvelled at its spartan contrast.

Fowler flicked a switch by the door and light from a small eighteenth-century chandelier, suspended from the high ceiling by four strong chains, flooded the room. Its six candles had been replaced by fake electric ones. Fowler saw Pross looking at it.

"Not bad, is it? Even allowing for the bulbs."

"It's very attractive," Pross said.

Fowler went over to the french window, pulled its heavy

68

curtains shut. Daylight was snuffed from the study. "Real candles are interchangeable, of course. I keep them in case of strikes."

Despite Fowler's brief smile, Pross was not sure whether he was joking.

Fowler moved to the desk, where he switched on a powerful lamp. He then reached into a drawer, took out a thick roll of several large sheets of paper. He spread the roll flat on the desk, and placed a heavy book at each end to prevent it from snapping back.

"Come and look at these, Pross."

Pross obeyed. He stared at the top drawing. It was of a helicopter. All the captions were in Russian.

Fowler did not look up. "Recognise it?"

"Yes." It was of the fighter-helicopters he'd seen and fought in the mist over China.

"I take it you can't read Cyrillic?"

"I don't exactly have use for it." Pross said pointedly. He continued to stare at the drawing.

Fowler's lips moved in another fleeting smile. "I'll be your translator."

"Is this the real thing?" Pross asked.

"Of course," Fowler answered as if the question were an insult. "Direct from the OKB."

"OKB?"

"Experimental Design Bureau."

"You can get these things from them?"

"We don't exactly say please can we have one of your plans," Fowler said patiently, "but we do have our methods, Pross. Just as they steal from us, we steal from them. Call it a sort of trade exchange. Sometimes we even make it easy for them to take something of ours . . . with subtle modifications. I dare say there have been times when they've found that a particular gunsight never manages to stay on target, or a particular airframe tends to fall out of the sky; but there you are. It's the name of the game."

Pross pointed at the drawing. "So what makes you think this is real? We steal, they steal. We dupe, they dupe."

Fowler's eyes seemed to gleam behind his glasses. "Sounds almost like Latin declension. I can assure you we have got the real thing. They don't even know it's gone. Now, please give it your undivided attention. Your life may depend upon it."

Fowler then began to guide Pross through each of the drawings.

"The aircraft which you fought so successfully in China," Fowler commenced, "was, as I've said, the first of the only two flying prototypes. Searle gave it a good name, but he got the wrong design number. The Mil-28 is the *Havoc*. This is the Mil-30, which we shall continue to call *Hellhound*. The *Havoc* is smaller, but slower than the *Hind*, and is definitely not what we're after.

"*Hellhound* has a good turn of speed, much faster than the *Hind*, at 390 kilometres an hour. That's nearly 244mph."

"Jesus!" Pross said.

"As well you might," Fowler remarked drily. "However, don't let the speed worry you overmuch. We have been working on the Lynx, and have squeezed her up to 230. *Hellhound* has a fundamental problem. It's a totally new design. There is some commonality with the *Hind*, but in real terms, this is superficial. For example, it uses the same twin Izotovs, at a shaft horsepower of 2200 each. Such big engines in that small airframe are bound to cause some stability problems until they've ironed the bugs out of the set-up. That does not mean we're dealing with a crock.

"Anakov has been recruiting excellent pilots for his programme. If he manages to persuade his bosses that his project is a flyer, then Western battlefield choppers would be in for a rough time should the unthinkable ever happen. Not only that, they may be tempted to go against normal practice and sell such a valuable bird to their friends. God knows what kind of cat that would set amongst the pigeons. There are plenty of little wars around to give them all the testing they would need."

Fowler began leafing through the drawings. "Take good note of the stub wings. On the *Hind*, they give the main rotor an off-load of 20-25%. On *Hellhound*, it is 30; so watch out for its turns, even at speed. And look here . . . flaps. A new innovation. They will aid its quick stop in combat and cause it to drift nicely out of your sights, to come tightening onto your tail. Now look at these . . . the controls. The cyclic is now a sidestick, nicely positioned at the end of the

70

armrest, and all switches neatly to hand. Vast reduction of workload. The collective as usual to the left, balances the two hand controls. Add the pedals and you have a finely turned control system. With the reclined seating and extensive vision afforded by that canopy, you have a true pilot's machine. I've always felt that choppers should have sidesticks. Anakov knows what he's on about."

Fowler paused briefly.

Pross said nothing, eyes glued to the drawings.

"Now we come to armament," Fowler went on. "The four-cannon configuration you told us about has disappeared. The second *Hellhound* uses this monster . . . the rotary cannon. They were obviously trying both systems out to see which would be the more effective." Fowler gave one of his grim smiles. "Ironically, we had the same thought. We have given the Lynx a rotary in place of the twin cannon.

"*Hellhound* also carries four rocket pods, and a full complement of eight air-to-air missiles."

"Keep cheering me up, won't you?" Pross said. He didn't want to believe the specifications on the sheets before him. There was nothing to touch the bloody thing. The Lynx wouldn't last a second.

"Of course it will," Fowler said, unreasonably cheerfully, Pross thought.

Pross had not realised he had given voice to his fears. "Easy to say when you're not going to fly it."

"I have every faith in you."

"I'm glad somebody has. Perhaps you could mention it to my wife when you can find the time."

Fowler said, "I think you should realise, Pross, that unless you take this on, Anakov will come for you. He does not want the Lynx to succeed any more than we would like *Hellhound* to. It's his career, possibly his life, that's on the line. He's not going to sit still."

Pross said nothing. He was staring at the rotary cannon. Thirty bloody millimetres. Rounds the size of milk-bottles slamming into the breech, massive charges detonating to send a whopping great lump of explosive metal hurtling your way at God knew what speed and rate.

Pross said, "What's the performance of that gun?"

"Not dissimilar to the Fairchild A-10. The A-10 was once

71

the most powerful flying gun-platform, but not anymore if this thing succeeds."

Four thousand rounds a minute. Good God. It ought to fall out of the sky after firing something of such heavy calibre.

"But that's a tank-busting gun."

"Anakov's not taking chances. He knows he has to show that even though the *Hellhound* may have been designed as a dedicated fighter-chopper, it needs to show other capabilities. He's heading them off at the pass, so to speak. Hit the critics before they hit you, seems to be his philosophy." More shuffling of paper. "Next, avionics and assorted equipment. It's got the lot. How effective, and how reliable is still open to question, but its equipment fit is superior to that of the *Hind;* so you can expect low-light TV, thermal imaging, HUD, target acquisition, ECM, and so on. In addition to the ECM, there may even be ECCM . . . counter-counter-measures." Fowler traced a finger over a drawing. "Here, here, and here, are those I've just mentioned. The ECCM is not included, but we've heard rumours. We take them seriously. You should. If he sends a radar homer at you and your own ECM makes no difference, you'll know he's countering it."

"That really makes me feel good. What then?"

"I'm sure you'll think of something."

"I don't know why I bothered to ask."

"Come on, Pross. We've done pretty well by you with the Lynx. You'll be quite pleasantly surprised, I assure you."

Fowler had pulled a large colour photograph of the *Hellhound* from another drawer. He laid it on the desk. It showed an all-black chopper, fully armed, in flight, against a rugged mountain background.

Pross stared at it. "Nasty-looking thing." Even as he continued to stare, he felt a subtle shift within him. The taste of combat was almost a palpable sensation on his tongue.

He looked up suddenly, straight into Fowler's shrewd eyes.

Fowler said, "Think you can take him on?"

Pross said, accusingly, "You were hoping for that, weren't you? You were hoping that I'd get the taste for it."

"I was not hoping for anything," Fowler said evenly.

"Of course you weren't."

Fowler said, "Look. I'll leave you here with these drawings and the photograph. Study them. There's one upon which I've scribbled the relevant information in English, under the Russian captions. I'll pop in a little later to see how you're doing. When you feel you've learned sufficient for your uses, we'll call it a day and you can return to Cardiff. We'll be in touch after that."

"How? Logan?"

Fowler shook his head. "You won't be seeing her. She's got other duties."

Pross felt acutely disappointed. "I see."

Fowler's gaze seemed again to acquire more strength than his supposedly weak eyes warranted. "Like her, do you?"

"We seem to get on."

Fowler smiled. "We all like her. She's very valuable." He turned to go. "When you're through, you'll be flown back by chopper. Study well." Another brief smile, and Fowler walked quickly out of the room.

Pross stared at the closed door for some moments before returning his attention to the stolen Russian drawings. He focused his scrutiny on the photograph. Could he take that on and win?

"I'd better," was what he said to himself.

He tried not to think of Dee and the children.

Chapter Five

The little Citroën 2CV, in its appalling shade of green, tottered up the hill on its spindly wheels. Across the back window were stuck five circular, identical badges: red centre on a yellow background, a smiling sun superimposed upon it. The message was the same, in different languages. NUCLEAR POWER? NO THANKS. In English, German, French Italian . . . and Japanese.

Logan drove past the main gate to the airfield, continued until she came to the turning she was looking for. She turned right, off the main road.

She looked totally different. Gone were the smart, if nondescript clothes of the day she had come in the XR. They had been replaced by solid boots, the decrepit jeans, the baggy sweater, and padded nylon jacket. Her hair had somehow lost its sheen, and her fake glasses gave her an air of studious earnestness. She pulled up next to a group of women near the outer fence. They were staring in her direction. Some of them were smiling, and seemed genuinely pleased to see her.

She turned off the engine, and climbed out.

"Hello, Minty," one of the women said as she joined them. "How did it go?"

Logan shrugged. "As usual."

There were noises of sympathy.

The Department had given her a rock-solid cover, somehow managing to persuade a peer of the realm to pretend to be her father. The peer in question had a real daughter who was safely away in America trying to be an actress, and conveniently using a stage name. As Araminta, Lady Dilke-Weston, she lived the part to the hilt, taking care not to attend any social functions that would blow her cover.

A tall skinny woman, with enraged eyes and dark crescents beneath them, came to stand close in front of Logan. She had severely cropped hair, and was dressed in dungarees and a railway worker's donkey jacket. There was a long, dirty scarf about her throat, and on her feet were heavy workmen's boots. She stared at Logan with open distaste.

"Oh dear. Our frail Minty is back, is she? What's it like at Daddy's palatial home, then? You should have stayed there."

"Clara!" another woman began sharply. "That's not fair. Minty's done her bit. She's been hassled by the police just like everybody else. She's gone over the fence, she's been out here in freezing weather; and when Jean got knocked over in January and was bleeding all over the place, I didn't see you rushing up to help. It was Minty who tended to her. You nearly fainted, as I remember it."

The one called Clara sneered. "It's easy to play Florence Nightingale when you're sitting on the kind of money and power her family has."

"I don't understand you at all, Clara," an older woman with sad eyes said. She had come up unnoticed. Her voice carried authority. "You insist on making this a class war. We come from all walks of life. We're not here to fight about stupid class divisions. We're here to fight for our survival. Minty can do as she pleases. She cannot be held responsible for the family she was born into, any more than you can." She smiled at Logan. "It's good to see you, Minty. From what I heard when you arrived, you've had another session with your father."

Logan smiled sheepishly. "A week's lecture on defence and the need for a deterrent. I'll never convince him, Jean."

"Some people need a war before they can be convinced. By then it's usually too late to matter. I must say I'm surprised by your father's stance. He spent part of the last war in a Japanese prison camp, didn't he?"

"That's just it. He says nobody's going to put him in another. And if it's going to take a cruise missile to stop them, then he's all for doing that."

Clara said coldly, "Spoken like a Lord's daughter. Ten to one he was an officer, which meant he probably got privileges. Not like the shit the poor working-class soldiers had to put up with. Cannon-fodder, just like those idiots walking the perimeter today. Those soldiers should be out here with us. They'll be the first to die, when the officers finally lose their marbles and press the button."

"For God's sake, Clara!" someone else said in exasperation. "Stop speaking in bloody slogans. Give it a rest."

"Aah!" Clara said disgustedly. "Sometimes, you lot make me sick, you're so wet. This is not a nice day by the seaside. This is open warfare on your rights, and you're letting it happen."

"You mean that's why we're here in the cold?" Jean asked mildly. Her sad eyes settled on Clara, without hostility. "You call these past months doing nothing?"

Clara turned her eyes to heaven, looked at each in turn, then walked away towards another group of women further along the perimeter, shaking her head in despair.

Jean said, "Not much of a welcome from Clara, Minty, but we're all happy to see you. You know what she's like. Oversensitive about her background." Jean laughed softly. "My own father was a coalminer from Yorkshire, so God knows she doesn't have a premium on being working-class."

"But you don't talk like one, Jean," the woman who had rebuked Clara said with some amusement. "She can't forgive you for betraying your roots. You're socially mobile. That's a crime."

Jean sighed. "Sometimes I can't believe the rubbish she spouts . . . even for her."

"She's good in a fight though," another said. "I'll never forget the way she clobbered that policeman with those boots of hers. He was whacking at Mary for all he was worth. If Clara hadn't waded in, I don't think Mary would have escaped without serious injury. You've got to hand it to her. She's got guts."

"But we're not here to *fight* them," Jean said. "We get enough of a bad press as it is. The great unwashed attacking policemen! Only to be expected of Soviet dupes."

"Don't be bitter," Logan said to her. "Rome wasn't built in a day." She looked her most earnest.

Jean said, "Some people would like to see it burnt down before it's built."

"What do you mean?"

"Oh, last night a couple of the tents were set on fire."

"Anyone hurt?"

"No, thank God."

"Any ideas?"

Jean shrugged. "Who can tell? There are plenty of nutters around who would do it." She smiled tiredly. "Come up to my hovel. Are you staying for the night?"

"For a few days."

"Oh good."

The small group dispersed, leaving Jean and Logan.

Logan said, "I've got to lock the car. Got to get my bag too." Even as she had been in conversation, she had never let her eyes stray from the 2CV. The magnum was in there. She got her bag, locked the car, and walked over to Jean's small tent. They crawled in.

"Well," Jean began, "has your father found out about the money?"

Logan shook her head. "It's my account. I can do what I want with it." Inwardly, she smiled at the thought of the squeal that had come from Winterbourne. Waste of public funds! As if he really cared. Fowler had shut him up. The operation justified it.

She still didn't fully know what the operation was.

Jean was saying, "Every bit helps. You were very generous. Thank you."

Logan shrugged shyly, as if embarrassed by the gratitude. "It's my planet too. I don't want to see it destroyed. Jean," she went on, "you're looking tired. Why don't you go home for a while? I'll stay with the tent. How long has it been this time?"

"Oh, I don't know. A month, I think?"

"You need a break," Logan said firmly. "I don't think you've fully recovered from what happened to you in January. No, no arguments. I insist."

Jean smiled wearily, giving in. "Perhaps in a day or two."

"Tomorrow."

"Alright. Tomorrow. Tell me, Minty. Am I crazy? I have a husband, and three teenage children. What am I doing here?"

"Worrying about their future," Logan answered. She had spoken as Araminta Dilke-Weston; but, as Logan, she also meant what she had said.

She wondered what Fowler would have thought of that.

About two days after Logan had returned to the peace camp, Anakov was shown into an office in Tashkent, headquarters of the Turkestan Military District.

His face showed pleasure as he entered respectfully. "Comrade General, it is kind of you to come all the way down here. I fully expected to be ordered to Moscow."

They greeted each other like old friends.

"I needed the journey," Sogovyi said mysteriously.

He was as tall as Anakov, but a much larger man. In fact, he fitted exactly the popular Western conception of what a Russian should look like: a big, heavy-set figure with the rough features of a hardy peasant, small eyes hidden in folds of skin, thick, jet-black, swept-back hair and thick eyebrows, straight, receding hairline on high forehead. If he'd had a moustache, he would have looked like a larger version of Stalin.

Anakov removed his cap, tucked it beneath his left arm. "Trouble?"

Sogovyi glanced at the cap. "You remind me of an American when you do that." They laughed at the joke. "But," Sogovyi went on, "don't do it in front of Semachev. He's a bit funny sometimes."

"Who is Semachev?"

Sogovyi's face had lost its brief cheerfulness. Instead of answering, he waved Anakov to a chair. "Sit down, Alex."

The office was small, functional, military. There was an uncluttered desk with a telephone on it, and two hard chairs, one of which was behind the desk. The walls were bare. It was as if Sogovyi were about to move in. Two small windows let in the noon daylight from one side.

Sogovyi went behind the desk, sat down. The chair seemed too small for him. Anakov took the remaining chair.

Sogovyi said, as he was about to sit down, "Bring it closer."

Anakov obeyed, settled himself expectantly. He watched the general carefully. What, he wondered, was the old peasant preparing him for?

Sogovyi reached down, pulled a drawer open, and came up with a leather-bound flask and something that looked like a small binocular case. He put the flask down and opened the case, which came apart in two halves. In its yellow-lined interior were two exquisite tumblers of cut glass. He took the glasses out of their holder and proceeded to fill them from the flask.

Anakov was familiar with the ritual. Sogovyi always carried his own supply of very special vodka with him, complete with glasses. To be admitted to the ritual was to be very favoured indeed.

Anakov felt himself relax.

Sogovyi pushed a glass towards him. Anakov took it. Sogovyi raised his own glass in a silent toast. Anakov copied him. They drank the lot in one go, put the empty glasses down at almost the same time. Neither had so much as blinked.

Sogovyi said, "You can still take it." A hint of a smile. "Always have."

Sogovyi nodded. "Yes. Yes. And now Alex, to business."

Anakov felt himself priming, waiting.

"You asked about trouble," Sogovyi began, "and who is Semachev. Trouble and Semachev go together. You'll be seeing a lot of him. The success of your operations in the Hindu Kush have put you in a good light for the time being. The loss of the first prototype is not being used against us . . . until the next time. I have managed to convince them of the need for you to go to England to take charge of the search for the aircraft responsible — and of course, the pilot. They were impressed by your performance with the new ship, and with your recent success." Sogovyi paused. "Yes? You were about to say something?"

Anakov said, "Any demonstration can look impressive against targets that can't shoot back. The ship-on-ship combat may have looked good, but I was still fighting a radio-controlled target. There were no surprises. The man who shot down the first prototype is a specialist. I want him."

Sogovyi said, "We know what the aircraft was. A special type of Lynx. We don't know *where* it is. There have been searches throughout Germany, and England. No one has yet pinpointed it."

79

"And the pilot?"

Sogovyi shook his head slowly.

"I want him," Anakov said quietly. "I want him!"

Sogovyi stared at his subordinate. "There is a condition to your going to England."

Anakov waited.

"The KGB," Sogovyi said. "They want to be involved."

"Why? Do they think I intend to defect?" Anakov felt himself grow angry. "Is that why they want to look over my shoulder?"

Sogovyi was soothing. "Don't take it quite like that, Alex. You will be getting six highly trained people, all experienced in clandestine operations. You'll be in charge—"

"And what will this Semachev be doing?"

"Major Semachev is the team leader."

"That's another way of saying he is in command of the operation."

"He is to take his orders from you."

"When he feels like it?" Anakov was under no illusions about how the KGB worked. Semachev's loyalty would last only as long as it suited. "I asked for GRU," he went on, referring to the army's own intelligence service. Their loyalty at least, would have been more assured. "I asked specifically."

"A price we had to pay," Sogovyi said. "I am not happy about it either. Watch out for Semachev. He does not like what he calls . . . elite groups. He already thinks you're too privileged."

"Privileged? I've worked for this."

"No one knows more than I, Alex. You do not have to convince me."

"Then why should I have to put up with this KGB ape?"

"Alex," Sogovyi warned, "I wish you would keep such feelings, pointed descriptions, to yourself. Even generals are not immune. You should know. Your own father, a highly decorated hero and a general himself, was purged when you were a boy. Be careful what you say, when you say it, and where you say it. I did not hear what you just called Semachev. One other . . . call it a piece of advice. Try, if you can, to keep away from the women. It has not been forgotten that you had an affair with an American woman

80

when you were in Washington."

Anakov remembered that episode with some bitterness. The woman concerned had been totally harmless, but she'd been shadowed by both the KGB and the Americans. Her political standing in America was now highly suspect and she was no doubt on a file somewhere in each country, as a potential threat to both the USA and the Soviet Union. The irony of it was that she was blissfully unaware of the attention she had attracted. Another innocent on the files. He wondered what she would say if she knew, if she were told that the charming Austrian with whom she had spent a brief but exciting time was in reality a colonel in the Soviet Air Forces.

"Semachev will be watching you," Sogovyi was saying. "Always remember that. No. Don't tell me. I can see it in your face. Yes, you are loyal to the Motherland. Yes, what you have embarked upon will greatly benefit our forces, especially in effectiveness against the West and yes, you have an impressive service record. I could say the same of your father. Remember it."

Anakov tightened his lips, nodded slowly. "When do I leave?" he finally asked.

"Very soon. Semachev's team is being fed in. They have been sent, in pairs or singly, since last December."

Anakov stared at his superior. "I knew nothing of this, Comrade General."

"Do not become formal with me before I sanction it, just because you are angry, Alex." A cutting edge had come into Sogovyi's voice. "I dictate the level at which this conversation takes place. Do I make myself clear?"

Again, Anakov nodded. "Yes. Yes."

Sogovyi grunted. "You know what happens when the KGB gets its hands on an army operation. I now expect you to make the best of it. You know exactly what is at stake. You will have to apply the same ruthlessness that you do in combat. I would rather see you become a general than spend the rest of your days on an island in the East Siberian sea. Now let us have another vodka before we end this meeting, and you can tell me in your own words about your little adventure in the Hindu Kush while we drink." Sogovyi laughed suddenly. "Let us drink to the confusion of our enemies."

Anakov knew the KGB were included in that toast, even though Sogovyi did not say so aloud.

He also knew that if he failed, Sogovyi would do nothing to prevent his being sent to a prison camp, or to save him from any other fate he might suffer because of that failure. Sogovyi had his own neck to think of.

Anakov drank the vodka and accepted that, in reality, he was on his own.

Later that day, at their special base near Sherabad — inside Turkestan, but close enough to the Afghan border — Anakov told Kachuk he would be in charge of the unit.

"For how long?" Kachuk now asked.

"Till I return. Keep the crews on their toes."

"You can count on it."

Anakov had no doubt of that: Kachuk would work them hard.

Kachuk looked across the landing field to where six of the special *Hinds* squatted. A little distance from them, in solitary splendour, was the sleek black shape of the *Hellhound*. It seemed perched for lift-off, even though it was silent and empty. The configuration of its landing gear gave it a slightly nose-down look, adding to its air of belligerence and making it appear ready to do battle, just standing still.

Kachuk said, "What about the bird?"

"You fly it . . . but no one else."

"Any trips across the border?"

"Absolutely not, and doubly so for the bird."

That particular *Hellhound* was not to be flown in combat. Anakov had no intention of putting the last prototype to such risk. Unauthorised combat had destroyed the first and had cost him one of his better pilots. He was quite confident Kachuk would not be so stupid as to disobey his direct order.

Kachuk said, "Your little Georgian gunner wants to be a proper pilot. I think he doesn't want to be left out when we go on to single-seaters. Shall I give him instruction?"

"He panicked when that vulture hit us last week," Anakov began thoughtfully, "but he's very cool under fire."

"I know. I've seen that picture he took of one of the pigs aiming a SAM right at you."

"Try him out," Anakov said, almost absently. "Let me know what you think. Be harsh in your assessment. I want only the best for the new ships."

"You can depend on me."

Anakov knew he could. Kachuk might be the roughest of diamonds, but he was the right man for the job. That was all that mattered. Kachuk's contempt for the Afghans did not alter the fact that he was a superb pilot and a highly competent officer. In combat, those were the qualities that would count.

Kachuk was saying, "If you find the time, bring back a pair of those tight jeans for my daughter."

"I'll try."

They both laughed.

02.00, three days later, in England.

Logan came awake slowly, listening to the shuffling noises outside the small tent. Her hand had already found its way into her bag which never left her side. Her fingers closed about the magnum. She cocked it, the sound barely audible from within the bag. She brought the gun slowly out of the bag, held it across her chest; waited.

The shuffling outside the tent had halted, but now there was whispered conversation. Logan lay there, primed.

Jean was still away, so she'd had the shelter to herself. It was pitched a short distance from the others, a fact that had pleased her.

The shuffling outside the tent had begun once more. Someone was trying to get in. She did not move. Her body was alert, the gun ready. Her eyes had attuned themselves to the dark.

The intruder was crawling in. Logan waited until whoever it was had reached her head before she moved. The whispers had betrayed the prowlers as men. She moved with a sudden swiftness that took her uninvited guests completely by surprise. The magnum poked at an ear, remaining seemingly fixed to it.

"One move," she hissed, "and the last thing you hear will be the bullet from this gun taking your brain with it."

"Logan, for God's sake!" came an answering hiss, shaky

with apprehension. "Put your bloody artillery away!"

She was astonished, but did not move. *"Sanders?* What the hell are you doing here?"

Sanders was a field man who sometimes masqueraded as a Squadron Leader. He was senior to Logan.

"If you stopped trying to drill your wretched cannon through my ear, I might be able to tell you. And show some respect for a senior officer."

"Balls." Logan still did not move. "You broke into my tent. You didn't expect a welcome, did you?"

"Are you going to move that thing?"

"Why are you here, Sanders?" Coldly.

"Fowler wants you brought in. We're going to make it look like an arrest. There's a raid on . . . all part of making life uncomfortable for the peaceniks . . . and that will give us good cover."

"A raid with real policemen?"

The gun moved up and down as Sanders nodded. "There. That's them."

The night was suddenly filled with racing engines, the squeal of brakes, doors slamming, heavy footfalls, grunts and screams. A battle began to rage.

"Take that thing away, for God's sake, Logan! We've got to get a move on."

She moved the gun fractionally. "Out!"

The tent shuddered as someone fell against it.

"You bloody pig!" someone screamed. Clara. *"You bastard!"*

"Logan —"

"Out!"

Sanders backed reluctantly out of the tent. He grunted as someone heavy tripped over him. A policeman. Immediately, more bodies fell upon him.

"Let go, you idiots!" Sanders roared into the night. "I'm your senior officer!"

In the tent, which was rapidly becoming a battle casualty, Logan smiled, and put the Ruger safely away. Taking her bag, she began to leave.

Someone grabbed at her immediately. "Here! Give me a hand with this one!" Sanders.

Someone else had taken hold of her. She fought realistically, felt a blow on her cheek. It hurt. She lashed out, heard a satisfying wheeze of pain.

"You don't have to be so bloody realistic, Logan!" Sanders admonished in a sharp, low whisper. "You might have damaged Tingey."

Logan was unrepentant. "Tell him to be more careful and he won't get hurt."

All around them, police and the women were locked in battle. As usual, the women were losing. Some of them, offering passive resistance, had simply lain on the cold ground and were being dragged unceremoniously away. In the lights of the vehicles, the struggling figures took on a nightmarish quality, a scene straight from an imagined hell.

As she was taken none too gently towards a waiting car, Logan saw Clara looking at her.

"Spit in their faces, Minty!" Clara yelled in a rare moment of solidarity, before she was bundled roughly into a police van.

Logan thought she'd seen blood on Clara's face.

The car began to move. All along the road, police vehicles were revving their engines and moving.

The car, a white Rover with police sidestripes, began to pull swiftly away from them. Logan sat between Sanders and Tingey, in the back.

"What about the Citroën?" she asked.

Sanders, still miffed about his reception, said, "The police will take it in. It will be delivered to you later."

After a while she said, "They didn't have to be so rough on the women."

Sanders said, coldly, "If these people are prepared to sabotage the defence of this country, they deserve all they get."

Logan thought about his words for a few moments.

"You know, Sanders," she then said in a mild voice, "if I were American, I'd say you were an asshole."

The driver tried not to titter. In the back, Sanders and Logan travelled in hostile silence.

About an hour later, the Rover arrived in London, and drew to a halt in a quiet mews in Chelsea. It had stopped outside the address that Logan used as Lady Araminta.

Sanders got out, stood back for her. "Fowler's waiting inside."

Logan climbed out slowly, keeping her bag close. Sanders re-entered the car.

"Aren't you coming?" she queried.

He looked up at her. His face was in shadow, expression unreadable. "Fowler apparently thinks I am not to be included on this. Now he had something else to be miffed about.

Logan said, "Oh dear. Not having much of a night, are you?"

Sanders withdrew his head, barked something at the driver. The Rover's engine had been idling, its exhaust wisping plumes of condensation into the chilly air. Now its noise increased softly as it began to reverse out of the mews, headlamps glaring balefully at Logan. It swung into the street, paused as the driver shifted into first, then accelerated away with a brief squeal of tyres.

Logan remained where she was for a full minute, hand inside her bag, firmly on the magnum. She listened to every sound that came on the night. Satisfied, she went up to the door of the little mews house, and with her free hand took some keys from her jeans. They were attached to a heavy chain that was clipped to a loop on her waistband. She turned first one key, then a second. The magnum was cocked and ready.

She was conscious of her exposed back, but this did not make her hurry. Someone coming up behind her would have a nasty shock. She would still be able to move swiftly enough to counter that threat. Taking one from the magnum at close range would not be a pleasant experience for a would-be attacker.

No one came at her. She withdrew the keys slowly and with deliberation, fed them back into her jeans. She entered.

The building was three-storeyed. The ground floor was taken up by a garage, and a narrow internal staircase that led up from the heavy, wooden door. There was an entryphone complete with video. Logan wondered whether Fowler had been watching her.

She did not switch on the lighting for the stairs. Instead, she shut the door quietly, removed her boots, and began to make her way up on stockinged feet. The Ruger was out of

86

the bag now.

There was a crack of light that spilled from beneath a closed door on the right of the small landing at the top of the stairs. This led to the reception room. She ignored it and began systematically to check out every other room in the house, including the toilet. She did so efficiently, quietly, without putting on a single light. It took fifteen careful minutes. There was no one in any other part of the house.

She made her way back down to the landing, stood for another half-minute outside the lighted room; then she reached forward, turned the knob in one swift motion, flung the door open almost simultaneously. She did not go in, but waited pressed against the wall, magnum at the ready.

"Eighteen minutes from the time I hear the car arrive." Fowler's leisurely voice came out at her with its usual calm. "Good to see you have not lost your usual sense of caution, Logan."

She relaxed, but did not put the weapon on safety until she had entered — still moving cautiously — and had seen that Fowler was indeed on his own.

He nodded his approval at her. "Good. Good. Despite my apparent calm, I might well have been held prisoner. What would you have done had that been the case?"

"You would have had to trust my marksmanship."

"Hm. Yes." He looked at her critically from the sofa upon which he had installed himself. His eyes went to her stockinged feet.

"Er . . ." she began, "I'll go and get my things. I left them at the bottom of the stairs."

She went out, collected her boots and the bag into which she put the magnum.

As she re-entered, she glanced at the empty cup on the low table before him. "I see you've made coffee. Would you like another? I need one . . . and a bath. At least Sanders had the grace not to sniff."

"That sounds as if you didn't like the way he handled things tonight."

Logan began to remove her jacket. "He brought a bloody regiment of coppers with him. They knocked a few of the women about; then he was crass enough to call them saboteurs." She dumped the jacket on a chair, went through to the kitchen which was reached via a short narrow passage, and down three steps. She had left her boots but had taken the bag, with the magnum in it, with her. "Do you want that coffee?" she called.

"Yes," Fowler answered. "I think I will join you." He picked up his empty cup, followed her into the kitchen.

Logan moved around, busying herself with making filter coffee. She spoke on the move. "Did you hear me prowling around?"

Fowler placed the cup down on the worktop with exaggerated care. He shook his head. "I knew you had come in. That was all. You're getting to be quite good."

She smiled to herself, but said nothing.

Fowler watched her as she moved, noting the lightness with which she did so.

"What's wrong with Sanders?" he asked.

"He's an idiot." Rank did not worry Logan. "The others are bound to wonder why I was taken away in a police Rover—Clara especially, when she gets her wits about her."

"The thin, cropped woman you've mentioned before."

"Yes."

The coffee machine began to burble.

Fowler said, "We thought about that, so a few more have been given the same treatment. Some have been taken to Reading. No one will wonder about it when you return in a few days time. I'll ensure Clara arrives later than you do. That ought to allay suspicions."

The coffee was ready. Logan poured out two fresh cups.

"Milk? Cream? Sugar?"

"One teaspoon of brown," Fowler said. "No milk, no cream."

"Just as well. I think the milk's gone off, and so has the cream." She put in the sugar, stirred it once.

Fowler said drily, "I have already found that out."

Logan gave a brief smile, rubbed an eye tiredly, had a drink of her coffee. She took it without sugar.

"Right," she said. "Now that the niceties are over, why did you pull me out, and at this time of night?"

"It made the raid more believable doing it this way. As for pulling you out . . . there is a good reason for it. The

88

Russians are bringing in a new 'cultural attaché.' " The quotes could almost be heard in Fowler's voice. "I want him tagged. He'll naturally expect to be, but he'll be looking for a man. I do not want him to recognise you after you've been at it for a while, so keep well away. That should not be too difficult. He's not one of their pros, but he's important. He's got minders, so watch out for them. They are the dangerous ones."

"And then?"

"And then what?"

"Isn't there more to it?"

"For the moment . . . no."

The green eyes stared at Fowler. "You're still not telling me everything."

"In due course, Logan. In due course."

The eyes did not turn away. "Is Pross involved?"

"That depends."

"On what?" The eyes still bored into Fowler.

Fowler knew how to handle Logan. He said, "On many things."

She turned away then.

"Trust me," he said, "as I trust you."

"A good thing for both of us."

"The target's name is Priakin. Watch only. No hit."

She said nothing, and did not turn around.

Fowler said, "You'll find the relevant details in the folder I've left on the sofa. I shall be back later to collect it." He drained his cup, then walked out of the kitchen.

Logan still did not move, even when she heard the front door being shut. She finished her coffee slowly, then at last went out of the kitchen and down the stairs to secure the deadlock. She took a hot bath, luxuriating in it for a full hour. Once, she inspected her legs critically, raising them out of the water to do so. They glistened as the bubbles streamed off them and she smiled to herself as she remembered how, on the last job, she had asked Pross not to look at them because she had thought them fat. He had told her they were alright, clearly liking them himself.

Her smile widened at the memory. That time, she had just come out of the bath too, in a little mountain-top palace in Italy. The water sent warm sensations through her

89

as she remembered. Nothing had happened, but still . . .

She sighed, climbed reluctantly out, wrapped a large towel about her. She pulled the plug and only then, with the water gurgling behind her, did she return to the reception room to pick up the folder Fowler had left for her scrutiny. She took it to the bedroom, climbed naked into bed and began to read.

It was six o'clock by the time she decided she knew enough of the subject for her purposes. Sunrise was still some forty minutes away. She yawned, switched off the bedside lamp.

She fell asleep almost immediately. The magnum lay on the floor between the bedside cabinet and the top right-hand corner of the bed. As she went deeper into slumber, her right hand crept over the edge of the mattress. It was a low bed and presently the hand was resting on the floor, a few millimetres from the butt of the weapon.

And Logan slept on, face smooth and unlined, freckles prominent. She looked her most vulnerable, like a child in untroubled sleep. Yet the slightest of untoward noises would have had that relaxed hand swiftly wrapping itself about the magnum.

Chapter Six

Logan awoke slowly at eleven o'clock. She picked up the magnum, got out of bed and put it back into the bag; then she stretched pleasurably. She had dropped the towel on the floor when she'd come to bed. Now, she picked it up, wrapped it about her and went into the kitchen to prepare breakfast.

She concocted a meal that would have made any diet freak reel: two fried eggs, four slices of grilled bacon, mushrooms, four pieces of fried bread. She stared at a can of baked beans, decided enough was enough and left it alone. She succumbed, however, to ketchup. It was a habit she had been initiated into at boarding school where it had been banned from the tables, and where getting hold of it clandestinely had been a supreme test of initiative. She'd never let on to anybody that she liked the stuff; not since her schooldays.

She stared at her laden plate. "So what?" she said to herself. "I'm a growing girl." And proceeded to eat with relish.

An hour later, she was ready for the day ahead. She looked stylishly elegant, like something out of Harrods, as Terry Webb would have said. Gone were the studious glasses, and so was the rich, reddish hair. She had put on a black wig that was so well made it was totally indistinguishable from the real thing. It had cost a fortune in Department funds, and she had no doubt that Winterbourne would give another squeal when he eventually found out. But there it was.

"One less bottle of fine old vintage port for you, my lad," she said to the full-length mirror in the bedroom. She was quite unrepentant. Whatever Fowler decided the mission was worth did not concern her. He was quite capable of handling Winterbourne.

She stared at herself for a few more moments. The effect of the green eyes and the black hair was quite startling.

She smiled at herself. "You'll do."

The magnum went into a bag that matched her outfit for the day, then she was ready to leave. At that moment the door buzzer went.

Fowler, and right on time.

She checked the door video. It was Fowler. She went down the stairs with the folder and handed it to him as she opened the door. The cobbled mews was quiet. All the other occupants were away at work; a fact that Fowler had allowed for when choosing the location.

The 2CV was parked close in, but clear of the garage.

Fowler said, "All set?" It was a cold but dry day, and the breath steamed out of him.

She nodded. There was no need for him to ask whether she had acquainted herself sufficiently with the subject. He would know that she had.

"Fine," he said. "Good luck."

Again, she nodded. Fowler turned away without another word, and walked towards where a white Rover was waiting broadside-on at the entrance to the mews. By the time Logan had shut and locked the door, the Rover had pulled away. She had not turned to note its departure.

She went to the garage, unlocked and opened it, raising the up-and-over door. The XR gleamed like blued steel at her. She drove it out, shut the garage, making sure it was locked. She then re-entered the car and drove slowly out of the mews.

Priakin. The folder had said he was a middle-ranking diplomat who would take every opportunity to use his status of "cultural attaché", and pay visits to as many places of entertainment and department stores as he could. Her job was to trail him to those places and to note the instant he deviated from that route.

She had not been told why this was necessary. She felt certain she would be given the full facts in due course, as the mission progressed. She hoped.

The photographs in the folder had shown a tall, elegant

man, much more elegant than she would have expected of a Russian. Quite handsome too. There håd been a brief but detailed history of Priakin, beginning with his birth thirty-nine years before in Kaliningrad (formerly Königsberg) in the Baltic, through to his part in the invasion of Czechoslovakia as a twenty-three-year-old tank commander, to his involvement in the tank industry as an innovator before finally achieving diplomatic status.

It was obvious, Logan decided, that the Department suspected Priakin of being in the country to check up on, and possibly siphon off, information about latest developments on British tanks.

She smiled to herself. "Cultural attaché" could mean many things, few of which would have to do with culture. She wondered how big a team Priakin had brought with him and what they would be doing while he did his ostensibly cultural rounds. No rank had been given for him. That didn't mean anything. All his photographs had been in civilian clothes, but he looked about as cultural as a barracuda. There was, she felt, something essentially dangerous about him, despite his incongruously elegant appearance. She wondered what Anatoly Priakin really was in his native Russia. What his real job was. An instinct told her there was more to him than the folder had intimated.

She drove the XR slowly along the King's Road, knowing why Fowler had picked her for the job. She was an unknown face. Priakin's minders would be unable to place her. It would not surprise her, however, if Fowler had also laid on one of the Department Rovers as a very visual tail. So far, she had not seen evidence of this.

She reached Sloane Square, went left and up Sloane Street towards Knightsbridge and Harrods. Priakin would be visiting the famed store, particularly its music department. How Fowler came by that information was not a source of wonder to her. Fowler sometimes seemed able to do the impossible; which was what made him so invaluable to the Department. Fowler ran the show. Winterbourne only thought he did.

Logan spent six minutes looking for a parking space. She had found it, but could not get in. An extra-long Rolls-Royce had managed to double-park, blocking the space completely. She decided she would give the thoughtless driver another five minutes. She did not have long to wait, however, for a smartly uniformed driver came marching towards the gleaming bronze car with its black coachline, with five covered Arab women in tow.

Logan watched amusedly as they trooped into the Rolls. London's biggest spenders.

The flagship of the motoring world whispered away haughtily and Logan reversed into the parking space swiftly, just in time to baulk a large BMW that had been trying to sneak in.

"Naughty," she said, and smiled at the driver, an angry-looking woman whose ears dripped with jewellery.

The woman gave her a killing look, drove away in a squeal of contemptuous rubber.

"Better luck next time," Logan said as she switched off.

She stepped out of the XR, slung her bag from her shoulder, and locked the car. She went up to the parking meter. As she was feeding it coins, a white Rover cruised past. She recognised it as belonging to the Department pool. Its occupants — two men — did not even glance in her direction. Priakin, this told her, was already inside.

She crossed the street and entered the building, looking for all the world like someone to whom the place was the local supermarket. She took her time going through the various parts of the store, until she eventually wandered into the music department.

It didn't take long to spot him. He was standing among the pianos, while his two minders were pretending to be absorbed by the record section.

Priakin seemed younger than his photographs and even more elegant in the flesh. His suit looked as if it had been bought expensively in America. His companions, on the other hand, looked exactly as expected: large, brutish men in indifferent suits. One of them, shorter but broader, had an exceptionally mean face. Logan decided he was the one in command. His whole manner shrieked it. Easy to detect if you knew what to look for.

She did not linger but passed through, as if totally unaware of the existence of anyone else in the world. She wandered through the store, not following, but making it appear as if *she* were being trailed by Priakin's party, should they for any reason choose to pay more than a passing interest in her. She bought herself some perfume, and a pair of earrings during her travels, drifted into "Way In", the department where the trendier fashions were sold.

A minute or so later, Priakin came in, followed by his heavies. Logan had to admit they did it well. To the uninitiated, the trio looked like businessmen reluctant to return to the office. She watched by the pop records section as Priakin made a surprising purchase.

He had bought a pair of designer jeans, to fit a young girl.

Logan sat in the XR, and waited. She had left the store while the sale assistant had still been attending to Priakin, and had noted the distinct expression of disapproval upon the face of the meaner-looking of the two minders. The folder had not given any names for Priakin's team. She would have to ask Fowler about that.

The white Rover cruised past. The man in the passenger seat gave her the briefest of glances. Priakin was on the move.

She followed the Rover into Knightsbridge, heading for Piccadilly. The traffic-light complex by the Underground station baulked them for a couple of minutes, and Logan was able to identify Priakin's car. It was first in the queue, ahead of a soft-top Mercedes. The Rover was behind that, with Logan almost on its bumper.

The lights changed, and she let Priakin's car draw away. The Rover sat practically on its tail as they threaded into the underpass. Logan continued to hang back, though never losing sight of her quarry.

The radio cassette in the XR had an additional function. One of the medium-wave push-buttons was a facility that plugged straight into one of the Department's special frequencies. She chose not to use it. You never knew who could be eavesdropping.

The little cavalcade towed its way through the heavy traffic around Piccadilly, and headed for the South Bank.

Semachev glanced through the rear window, to look expressionlessly at the white Rover.

Anakov said, "Still with us?"

Semachev settled back in his seat, replied drily, "Yes, Comrade Priakin."

"Aren't they being obvious?"

"Oh yes, Comrade. They are. Which is exactly what we would wish. They are determined that you should go nowhere without their knowledge. We shall establish a pattern that even they can follow, over the next few days. When they have become happy, we shall keep them occupied with your activities while my men get on with the real business, undisturbed."

Anakov looked at his companion. "You are not in command of this mission, Comrade. Remember that."

Semachev's eyes were hard as pebbles, and as lifeless. "I am in command of my men. *You* remember that, Comrade."

Anakov gave a quick smile. "It's the jeans, isn't it, Major? You are annoyed because I bought a pair of jeans."

"There are equally good jeans in Moscow."

"A present, Major. A present for a friend. Besides, as you are so obsessed by that white car, I would have thought it obvious that the occupants — or at least one of them — would have been following us in that store . . ."

"One was. I saw him pretending he wanted to buy something."

"Then I behaved quite naturally. I am after all, a tourist of sorts." Anakov smiled at Semachev.

The KGB man looked back at him, stony-faced. "It is easy to laugh at my expense, Comrade Colonel . . . for now. One day, you will make an error, and then even your privileged position will not save you."

Anakov closed his eyes briefly, sighed with some weariness. "Major Semachev . . . we are here for a specific purpose which is of great importance to our country. Can we at least try to bear that in mind and not bring interdepartmental rivalry into it? I was assured that you are the best operative for the task in hand. I would hate to think that both your superiors and mine could possibly have been wrong. Your job is to get the information we need. How you do it is entirely up to you. But do remember that only I can assess its value."

Semachev remained silent for a few minutes. He appeared deep in thought.

Eventually he said, as they were crossing Waterloo Bridge, "We shall do better than that, Comrade. We shall get the aircraft for you . . . and eliminate the pilot."

"I hope, for your sake, that is not an idle boast," Anakov said after a stunned silence.

"I never boast, Comrade."

Logan returned to the mews house by eight o'clock that evening. She put the XR away, went in to wait for Fowler. He turned up ten minutes later.

"Well?" Fowler said to her almost as soon as she had let him in.

"Drink?" she suggested by way of reply.

"Thank you, no. This won't take long. There are some things I have to attend to."

Fowler took an armchair while Logan, who had changed into a battered green tracksuit, sprawled on the sofa.

"I followed him everywhere," she began. "From Harrods, he went to the South Bank to do all the touristy things, National Theatre, Festival Hall and so on. Then we took off for Greenwich. He spent nearly two hours there before returning, taking his time. I left him to the Rover in Kensington and came back here. A very fruitless day."

Fowler said, "Not as fruitless as you might think. Are you quite certain they were not aware of you?"

"Quite certain. They were too busy watching the Rover."

"As I'd hoped. But they made no effort to lose it."

"None at all . . . which was very strange."

"Yes." Fowler was quite calm about it. "Sanders was baffled too. I asked him to join one of the relay cars."

"The blue one," Logan said. "It picked us up after Greenwich, but even with the change of colour, Priakin must have known."

"Oh, I'm certain he did. Any comments?"

"Priakin bought a pair of jeans in Harrods; a young girl's

97

size. The information you gave me said nothing about children."

"He has none. Perhaps it was for a niece. Anything else?"

"I saw Nelson. He was a bit obvious."

"He was under orders to be."

"I see. Oh . . . there was something I thought we might be able to make use of. One of the minders, brutish man, nasty . . . he didn't seem too pleased by the purchase."

Fowler said, "Ah yes. Semachev. Patronising a capitalist store would be, to him, a mortal sin, if he believed in religion. He must have found being in Harrods a singularly unpleasant experience. An ideologue, and fanatically so. Nasty is too gentle a word with which to describe him. A killer through and through. He steals things, too," Fowler added thoughtfully.

"You can't be thinking he's going to try for a *tank*, "Logan said sarcastically.

"Anything is possible." Fowler seemed to be talking to himself. Then he appeared to return from wherever his thinking had taken him. "But watch out for Semachev. We did not know he would be on the team until today. Take especial care. Don't get hurt." Fowler's eyes, behind his glasses, were quite serious.

Logan was equally serious. "I won't."

"Good. I'm afraid," Fowler went on, "you're stuck with following Priakin for a few more days yet. You'll also have to put in an appearance at the peace camp at weekends. You'll be officially released by the police in time for this weekend. Your friend Clara will be released on Monday." He reached into a breast pocket, pulled out a long envelope which he handed to her. "Tomorrow's itinerary."

Logan opened the envelope, took out a single sheet of paper with a list of place names upon it.

She looked up. "These are all in Cambridgeshire."

"Enjoy the country." Fowler gave one of his tight smiles. "There'll be a Rover along to play tag and keep their attention riveted. Semachev is planning something. I don't want that car lost when he decides to make his move. Right," he continued, rising, "time to go. Good luck tomorrow."

Logan got off the sofa to see him out. When she returned, she switched on the television. A film was on; about helicopter pilots in Vietnam.

She thought of Pross, and wondered what Fowler had in mind for him.

In Craig Penllyn, Pross was watching the same film, his mind on Fowler, who had not been in touch since the visit to the Cotswold mansion. No news, as far as he was concerned, was bad news.

Dee came in from the kitchen with cups of coffee. The Dawn Patrol had finally made it to bed after determined resistance.

"How can you watch these things?" Dee asked as she handed him one of the mugs.

"God knows," he said; but he did not change the channel.

She sat down on the settee next to him. "Have you heard anything from them?"

He knew she was thinking of Fowler. He shook his head slowly, then took a sip of the coffee.

"I don't suppose it could mean nothing's on."

"We both know better than that."

"Yes," she said quietly. "We do."

She put down her coffee, put her arms about his waist and her cheek on his shoulder. He reached out with an arm to hold her close.

On the television, helicopters began to fall out of the sky.

Logan started early the next day and caught up with Priakin and his inevitable Rover escort near Mildenhall. According to the list, it appeared that Priakin was making a tour of the Cambridgeshire air bases. She wondered why a tank expert was so interested in what went on there.

She resigned herself to a long day of it, and decided to enjoy the Fens.

Semachev was looking pleased with himself. It was now well past two o'clock and the white Rover was still with them.

"What I like about the British," he said, "is that they are so predictable. No wonder it is easy to penetrate them."

Priakin was not so sure. "I would have thought that they would not have fallen for anything so blatant. We are quite openly taking routes that bring us close to some of their sensitive bases. If *they* were doing this on our side of the fence, we would have pulled them in by now."

"Your own words, Comrade," Semachev said, "explain why I am KGB, and you are not. Our very openness sows suspicion. The kind of suspicion I want. Let them follow us. A few more days of this, and we can seriously think about getting you your helicopter."

"And the pilot?"

"He is as good as dead."

"But have you located him?"

Annoyance showed on Semachev's face. He did not like having his ability questioned, even by colonels with powerful backing. The KGB was subordinate to none.

Semachev said, "We shall locate him, and kill him. You can be assured of that, Comrade Colonel." His pebble eyes fastened upon Anakov. "You can be assured." It sounded as if he was pronouncing the sentence of death upon Anakov as well.

Anakov's own eyes carried a chill of their own. "For your sake, Major, I hope you are right. Now let us take our friends to the next point on our guided tour."

Semachev maintained a hostile silence as the Rover followed them along the A10 towards Waterbeach, and Cambridge.

Far behind, slotted into the traffic, the XR tagged along.

That evening, Logan said to Fowler drily, "Well, I saw a lot of Cambridgeshire."

"Didn't you enjoy the countryside? The beautiful Fenlands? The sense of history?"

"Hereward the Wake being clobbered by William of Normandy was the last thing on my mind."

"So you didn't enjoy the countryside."

"A bit difficult when you're trying to keep tabs on a target."

"Just a little longer," Fowler said soothingly.

"Where is it tomorrow? Cornwall?"

"We *are* tetchy tonight."

"I don't like going in blind. I hate it." The green eyes stared at Fowler. "Something doesn't feel right. You're not being straight with me. That's what doesn't feel right."

"This is not like you, Logan," Fowler said calmly. But his eyes had become distant.

"This is not like you, either."

Fowler continued to look at her, saying nothing for a few moments.

"Good luck for tomorrow," he eventually said. Then he left her to it.

The next day, it was the turn of the tank training grounds of Salisbury Plain. That, at least, Logan thought, was in keeping with Priakin's background. She decided to wear a blonde wig.

Semachev glanced out of the rear window, before settling back in his seat with a thoughtful expression.

Anakov said, "Still worried about our faithful friends?" The Rover was about 200 metres behind.

"About them? No."

"Then whom?"

"I think I have seen another car."

Anakov glanced round.

"It isn't there now," Semachev said. "I believe I saw it about two hours ago."

"You are not certain?"

"It's a feeling, Comrade."

Anakov said, "More Intelligence subtleties, Comrade Semachev? There is a whole string of cars behind that white car. How can you be certain it is not one of them? How can you be certain there *are* any others?"

"As I have said, Comrade," Semachev began stiffly, "it is a feeling. The car I am thinking of is no longer behind us."

"You sound puzzled, Major . . . as if you're not even certain that you have seen it. You sound unsure of your own feelings."

"I am certain," Semachev insisted stonily.

"Ah yes, of course. I forgot. Only members of the KGB can be certain of uncertainties."

"Tomorrow," Semachev said coldly, "we shall visit Greenham Common."

Anakov glanced once more out of the rear window, resisted the temptation to wave at the white Rover which was now only a few yards away.

"They should enjoy that," he remarked lightly.

Semachev looked rigidly ahead, and said nothing.

"Greenham," Logan remarked at the end of the day to Fowler. She sounded concerned. "I can't follow them there."

Fowler was unworried. "Enjoyed Salisbury? I don't suppose they took in the cathedral . . ."

"Mr. Fowler," Logan said patiently.

Fowler gave her his fleeting smile. "All going according to expectations. No, Logan. You won't have to follow them there. In any case, Minty is due to return to the camp this weekend. You are to remain there till Monday. I want your friend Clara—"

"She's not my friend."

"Of course. But as the most hostile person you have encountered there, it will strengthen your position if she now feels you have something . . . er . . . an experience shared."

"We've both been arrested before."

"Yes, but not kept in custody for so long. She'll appreciate that."

"You can be cynical when you want to be."

"Not cynical, my dear. Realistic. When you return from Greenham," Fowler went on, "we shall move on to the next stage." He raised his glasses to rub the bridge of his nose, tiredly.

Logan, once more in her battered tracksuit and lounging on the sofa, watched him warily. Something was coming.

Fowler said, "Priakin, as you know, frequents the Royal Festival Hall. He attends concerts regularly. It could mean that he's getting as many in as he can because his time here is short, or simply because he likes the current programme. As Lady Araminta, suitably attired for the occasion and in keeping with the lady's character, you're about to discover similar joys." Fowler's eyes gleamed behind the glasses. "Priakin has a reputation for a taste in Western women. I want him to notice you."

The green eyes had become fathomless. "Do you want me to kill him, or to sleep with him?"

"I want neither. I simply want you to get close."

The eyes showed a sense of betrayal. "You were not shocked by my question. You expect me to sleep with him, don't you? You'd do that to *me?*" Logan had sat up now, back straight, and was staring at Fowler.

"Logan, I've just said: I want neither. I know you're quite capable of looking after yourself, whether in combat or fending off unwanted attentions. You are famed for demolishing the egos of several of the male staff. Some of those men have notorious reputations to defend. The ice queen, I've heard one or two call you. You're capable of handling one randy Russian, surely?"

"Lie back and think of England," she said with quiet bitterness. She stood up, went over to a window to look out.

She could see down the mews. The night was cold, and a layer of frost lay upon the cobbles. She could not see the Rover that had brought Fowler. Perhaps he had not come by a Department car, but had taken a taxi instead.

Fowler's voice came from behind her. "It's nothing of the sort. I would not ask that of you."

Logan chose not to speak. She continued to look down the mews. The house was situated mid-way along it, giving her a perfect view of its entire length, from the house at which it terminated, to the open end which emptied itself through a high sculpted arch and into the street.

There were just two cars parked there: Logan's 2CV, and a red Volvo which she knew belonged to someone who lived three doors up, on the opposite side. No movement caught her eye.

She turned, walked away from the window. "At least, they don't appear to have found me out. Do I keep my gun?" She perched on an arm of the sofa.

"Yes."

"That's something, I suppose."

Fowler stood up to go, shifted his glasses, a rare sign of

discomfort. "Look . . . Logan . . ."

"It's alright, Mr. Fowler. I shan't let you down." There was no warmth in her voice.

She stood up, went with him down the stairs.

"Goodnight, Logan."

"Goodnight, sir."

Fowler gave her a quick, sudden look as if the reserve, the formality in her voice was somehow shocking, before going silently out of the door. A car had entered the mews. One of the Department Rovers, she was sure. Fowler had timed the delivery of his news perfectly.

She locked up, went slowly back up the stairs.

Chapter Seven

Logan arrived at the peace camp the next morning in the 2CV. The XR had been safely locked away in the mews garage and the elegant young woman had again given way to the apparently shy, bespectacled campaigner. The day was cold, with frost still on the ground.

Jean was there to greet her.

"Minty!"

They embraced, pleased to see each other.

"Where did they take you?" Jean asked as they walked towards her small tent. There was a brazier near it, warming the immediate vicinity. "We tried to find out, but got nowhere."

"Up to London," Logan replied. A few people waved to her, calling cheerfully in welcome. She waved back at them.

"It was the same with Clara."

"Is she back?"

Jean shook her head as they stopped to enter the tent. It was reasonably warm inside. "At least we know where she is."

"Oh? Where?"

"Reading."

"Why would they take her there?" Logan asked as they made themselves comfortable.

Jean shrugged. "God knows. I think she hit a policeman."

"That's not good news."

Jean's sad eyes were troubled. "I wish she wouldn't keep doing that. It only gives them an excuse to get even worse. She likes to fight too much." She paused, then said in a low voice: "We are trying to arrange a peace meeting with the Russians."

Logan stared at her. "Another one? Last year's wasn't

exactly auspicious.

"We're not going to Russia. We're hoping for neutral ground, so to speak."

"Neutral ground? You can't mean Switzerland."

"Oh no. Afghanistan."

"What? You call Afghanistan *neutral* ground? And who will they be sending? Their 'official' peace movement — generals in civilian clothes — or the people who would really like to talk to us?"

Jean looked anxious. "The details are not yet finalised. We have tentatively agreed to Kabul —"

"Kabul! My God, Jean . . ."

"We've got to try, Minty. We've got to try everything and anything. These people are going to blow us up!"

"Alright," Logan said gently, soothingly. "It's alright.

Whenever Jean returned from a home visit, her fears tended to become heightened for a few days.

Jean sighed. "This always happens every time I see them. I think . . . these are my kids. I should be with them, looking after them. God knows James has enough on his plate without having the extra problem of keeping a check on two pre-O-level tyros. Then I say to myself that's what I doing here. I *am* looking after them. I've got to make sure they're going to be around to make use of those O-levels. Minty, do you think I've got my priorities right?" Jean looked about her, at the cramped quarters of the little tent. "Sometimes I wonder."

Logan said, quietly, "I think you've got them right."

Jean smiled in gratitude. "You're very good to me, and for me . . ."

Logan felt awkward. "Nonsense, Jean. I —"

"Oh yes you are. I know some of the others think you're just slumming it . . . Clara especially . . . and that you'd really like to be somewhere else. No, no, let me finish. I think they're wrong. I think you're probably more honest than they are. I think you believe more than they do."

Jesus, Logan thought. *I can just see Fowler loving this.*

"That's why I'd like you to come with us to Kabul," Jean went on, to Logan's astonishment.

"Me?" This was a development she had not foreseen.

"As I've said, it isn't settled, but I hope you'll say yes. I'd very much like you to accompany me." Jean gave a half-apologetic smile. "Sort of moral support. Perhaps that's what I'm really saying."

"Well . . . isn't . . . isn't anyone else going?"

Christ, Logan was thinking, how am I going to get out of a thing like this?

"Oh yes. But I'd like to have you in my group. There'll be four of us. It's not common knowledge as yet."

"Who are the others?"

"Tina Myerson . . . and Clara."

"Clara? Oh great."

Jean said, "That's just it, you see. I want you with us because I know Clara will go over the top. We couldn't leave her out. You know how she sees herself as the great revolutionary. It will be less trouble to take her than to leave her. We could do with a sane voice. God knows the world's insane enough as it is."

Logan was silent for some moments. "I . . . I don't know what to say, Jean. I'm so surprised." *And I'm not joking either,* she thought drily. "I've always thought that most people around here see me as a sort of overgrown schoolgirl. I mean . . ."

"But you're not," Jean said. "I've had plenty of time to study you since you joined us. You keep your own counsel when everybody else is spouting off. You listen; and when you speak, you usually make sense."

"I wouldn't put it quite like—"

"And you're far too modest," Jean interrupted firmly. "I want you to come. What do you say?"

Logan played the hesitant Minty to the hilt; but it was not all play-acting. She had lived the role too well. Now look where it had got her. Fowler would have to think of a fast way out of this one.

She said, "Can I . . . think about it?"

"Oh of course you can." Jean sounded relieved, as if Logan had already given acceptance. "There's still quite a lot to arrange." She seemed to think it was a foregone conclusion. "We had some interesting visitors yesterday," she added as an afterthought.

"Oh?"

"Reporters. There were the two Japanese who were here

last month; but a little later, these Hungarians turned up. We're making more news abroad than we're doing here." Jean gave a deprecating shrug. "We're old hat these days. People are becoming bored with us because we haven't really stopped anything. But the Hungarians said that everywhere abroad our fight is being followed with great interest. Clara would have loved to hear what one of them said. He was very nice. He said that we gave people in Hungary inspiration. We could use our rights to protest. Over there, they can only think about protest, not act upon it. I have a feeling he was not carrying the official line. He spoke like that to me only when his colleague was well out of earshot and chatting to someone else. I invited him back."

"Think he'll come?"

"Who knows? A really nice man," Jean went on thoughtfully. "Quite good looking." She gave a little laugh. "George Black."

Logan stared at her. "He has an *English* name?"

"Oh no. He translated it for me. Even spelt it. Geörgy Nagy." She spelt it for Logan. "But they pronounce it 'Nadge'."

"You seem to have had quite a cosy chat. Watch out. Handsome, you said?"

"Oh I can just see the headline: 'Married Peace Woman Falls for Communist Reporter'."

They laughed.

"Well," Jean went on, chuckling. "They've got to find new headlines, after all." She paused, reflective now. "Anyone who listens is worth talking to. Who knows? He might talk to some of his own people, or even write about it in his paper. Not the official line, but what he really thinks."

"And earn himself a one-way ticket to wherever they send people in Hungary?"

"Anything can happen," Jean said philosophically. "Come on. Let's have a little walk." As they left the tent, she said: "I've been chatting about all sorts of things and I haven't asked how they treated you."

"They weren't too bad. They just asked the usual lot of stupid questions, mainly about my non-existent Russian connections."

"The usual rubbish. Were you fined?"

"No. Although one of them said he couldn't understand how a titled lady could get mixed up in this."

"They ought to look to their bloody moles," Jean said with unusual vehemence. "Plenty of bloody titles there." There was another pause as each became occupied with her own thoughts. Then, "Clara will get a fine. She'll probably rant about privilege and say you didn't get one because your father's a lord."

"She probably will," Logan said.

They smiled resignedly at each other.

When Clara arrived on the following Monday afternoon, driven in a friend's car, she behaved exactly as expected. The brief moment of solidarity had vanished like smoke before wind.

"No fine," she said accusingly to Logan. "Aren't we lucky to have a daddy who's a lord," she added in a mock child-like voice.

Logan opted for friendliness, despite the provocation. "I saw you bleeding," she said, "when they took you away."

Clara smirked. "It wasn't my blood. Pig's blood."

Logan stared at her, remembering the mess she had seen on Clara's face. "You hit a policeman?"

"Yeah. Nutted him, didn't I."

For an instant, Logan held in her mind's eye an imagined vision of that cropped skull smashing into the unsuspecting officer's face.

"My God," she said, in the perfect tones of a shocked Lady Araminta.

Clara was unrepentant. "The bastard had nearly wrenched my arm off. He was lucky I didn't get his balls." She gave Logan a disgusted look. "You're a bloody softie. That's what's wrong with you. Must be all that posh up-bringing. When are you going to wake up, Minty? All these men who come down here to stomp all over us, or all those behind that wire protecting their weapons of doom, do you think they really care that they're going to blow the world up with their men's weapons? It's left to us to stop them. Bloody warmongers!"

Logan refrained from pointing out that women leaders were not averse to a little warring themselves.

She said, "That's too simplistic, Clara."

Clara looked as if someone had just held a stink-bomb beneath her nose. "Simplistic?" She sighed loudly. "There's no bloody hope for you, is there, Minty? You think this is just another jolly hockeysticks game. Play straight and up the school, ho ho ho. Fuck a bloody duck!" She stalked off, her contempt etched upon her thin face.

Logan stared after her. Clara, she decided, had all sorts of problems. She wondered what had happened to the thin woman to have made her so bitter. It had to be something more than just her childhood experiences. Logan wondered whether Jean knew what it was and made a mental note to ask about it later.

She was about to walk over to a group of women when Jean, who had been to the main gate, called, "Minty! Look who's come back. Our Hungarian friend!"

Logan turned, and found herself staring at the man approaching with Jean.

It was Priakin.

As Anakov walked towards the scruffy woman in the glasses, he thought again of the conversation he'd had earlier with Semachev. It was not a recollection of pleasure.

"I am not taking over command, Comrade Colonel," Semachev had said with barely disguised glee, knowing he'd got Anakov where he wanted him. "It is obvious that the British are interested in your movements. What better way of securing their total concentration than your presence at the Greenham Common base? The whole affair of the peace camps is such an embarrassment to them, it would be beyond their ability to resist following you there. Indeed, they have shown that wherever you go, they will be there. It is exactly what we require. I am now able, while their attention remains diverted, to begin my search for the helicopter and its pilot." Semachev's eyes had become even more lifeless. "Those are the conditions under which you were allowed to come into the West. You are not required to go into the field. That is my job. Now . . . do we have agreement, Comrade?"

Anakov had looked into the pitiless eyes, masking his own intense dislike of Semachev. "We have an agreement, Major . . . but do not fail."

"I detect a threat in your voice, Comrade. Do not threaten me. It is never wise. Valentinov and Garshin will accompany you; for your protection."

Anakov felt his distaste for Semachev coat his tongue with the flavour of bile. He tried to think of something that would make him smile and remembered the paint-sprayed sign he had seen on the large roundabout that fed traffic into the town. Underneath the TOWN CENTRE sign, he had read the one word that said it all: HIROSHIMA.

He smiled now. The message was at once chilling and a barbed joke at the expense of the authorities. Kachuk would have seen the humour in it.

The white car had even followed faithfully, as Semachev had said.

It was Logan's training and her own highly developed instincts for survival that prevented her from betraying herself.

Jean was saying, "Geögy, I would like you to meet Minty, my colleague and very good friend."

The man Logan knew as Priakin smiled with great charm and said: "I am very pleased to meet you." He took her hand, gripped it briefly with the barest hint of a linger. "Minty. An unusual name."

"It's short for Araminta," Logan said.

"Ah! That is a beautiful name. I like it better, I think."

"You speak English very well."

"I try to speak it." Deprecatingly. "It is necessary for the job."

"It's much better than my Hungarian, which is non-existent."

They laughed.

Logan noted that two men, dressed casually, were standing apparently disinterestedly some distance away. She knew they were his minders, even though Semachev was not one of them. She recognised one from the day at

Harrods.

As she, Jean and "Geörgy Nagy" conversed, Logan's mind went into high gear, trying to make sense out of this new development. "Geörgy Nagy" asked journalistic questions, looked concerned and sympathetic. They went for a walk to the other groups of women, along a stretch of the perimeter. "Nagy" chatted to them all, always with sympathy.

Logan noted that the two men trailed behind. She wondered if the Department had any of its own men on the ground. Had the Rover followed Priakin here? She hoped so.

She was very conscious of the magnum nestling patiently in her bag which was slung crosswise from her shoulder. In her mind, she worked on how quickly she could get it out to take care of the two men before turning to Priakin, if anything went suddenly wrong. She stilled the tension within her as she continued walking and talking quite calmly.

But nothing happened.

Then it was time to retrace their steps. The two who had been drifting casually behind met up with them, passed without exchanging anything more than nods, wheeled round again when a sufficient distance had lengthened between them.

Clara, who had gone further along the perimeter and had not met "Nagy", came rushing up. Jean introduced her.

"Perhaps you'll write something about our arrest," she said to "Nagy" in her typically no-nonsense fashion. "The papers had nothing about it." She twitched her mouth in a down-turn. "We're not as important as bingo these days. Here's a nice line in irony for you, Geörgy. The people are being given cake to eat and they're enjoying it. Marie Antoinette knew what she was on about."

From then on, Clara dominated the conversation. Jean and Logan left her to it and walked on ahead. Logan remained in her state of high alert, prepared for anything that might transpire. She didn't think the Russians would be so clumsy as to start any hostile action so openly, even if they knew who she was; but you never knew with these things. It was always down to the individual in the field and

112

the way he or she would jump in a particular situation.

She saw another man coming casually up the road, and recognised him as Telford, a young Turk from the Department. Telford was always trying to get her to have dinner with him. For once, she was pleased to see him. If anything did happen, at least she'd have reasonable back-up. Telford knew how to shoot. The Rover had followed Priakin, after all. That was heartening to know. She wondered where the others with Telford were. Close enough, she hoped, if the shooting started. She'd have to ensure that Jean did not get caught in the resulting crossfire.

As they walked, she found herself surveying her immediate surroundings, looking for likely cover into which to push Jean if the need arose. She could hear Clara talking to "Nagy" at full speed. Clara would have to take her chances.

Telford came abreast, walked past without recognition: which was as it should be. But Logan knew he'd be ready if the whole thing suddenly came apart. There was a sudden silence as Clara stopped talking, and Logan braced herself, ready to give Jean what she hoped would be a life-saving push when the firing started.

Then one set of footsteps was coming up behind. She touched Jean gently, who paused to look at her.

Logan turned casually. "Nagy" was approaching. Clara had stopped to converse with a small knot of women. "Nagy" was smiling as he came up.

"A very angry woman," he said to them. "Sometimes, I think she wants to bite my head off."

Jean said, drily, "Clara has that effect on people."

"So. I must go now," he went on. "I would like to talk to others around the base. But perhaps I shall come again."

"Anytime," Jean told him.

He gave a little nod. "Thank you. That is very pleasing." He looked at Logan. "Araminta. Such a charming name. I will see you too if I return. Yes?"

"I'll be here with Jean."

He nodded once more. "Good. Good. Now, I must say goodbye. Thank you for your kindness."

"Thank you for listening," Jean said.

He shook hands with each in turn, and walked away. His shadows followed discreetly behind.

"A really nice man, that," Jean said as they watched the trio move on.

"Yes," Logan said neutrally. "Nice."

Jean looked at her. "What's up? Didn't you like him?"

"Oh he was pleasant enough. But did you see those two men who were hanging around?"

"Those?" Jean was dismissive. "They were the ones who were with him the last time. Well . . ." she went on uncertainly, "I'm not so sure about one of them."

"Didn't you say he wouldn't talk in their presence?"

Jean said quietly, "You don't think they're some sort of Hungarian secret police, do you?"

Logan shrugged. "Who knows what kind of people come here masquerading as journalists?"

"You don't mean our side as well?"

Logan said, "You'd be surprised at what governments can get up to, as my father is fond of saying during his moments of candour."

Jean stopped, looked through the wire and at the base beyond.

"No," she said in her sad, quiet voice. "No. I wouldn't be surprised."

"Hungarian journalist," Fowler remarked mildly that evening in the mews house. He smiled. "Not a bad ploy, and one that is of advantage to us."

"What about Semachey?" Logan asked.

Fowler did not seem particularly worried. "Up to no good, I'm quite certain. But we're prepared for him. He's not your concern. Tomorrow evening, you're off to the Festival Hall. There's a Bartók programme on at the Queen Elizabeth." He pulled out an envelope from his jacket, placed it on the low table before him. "Your ticket. I do hope you like Bartók. It's *Mikrokosmos*. Selections from its 150 piano pieces."

Logan said, unenthusiastically, "My God."

Fowler appeared to be smiling. "I appreciate it's not exactly a disco, but there it is." Logan, as he well knew, was quite able on the piano.

"Priakin had better be there," she said.

114

"He will be. Incidentally," Fowler went on, "I've organised a shoot for you at the range."

"Good," Logan said. "I could do with that."

"Thought you might. Telford said he knew you had primed yourself to shoot, by the way you were walking near that perimeter today."

"He ought to spend less time watching my legs. He always does that." She did not sound pleased. "If he's going to be anywhere near me, I want him to keep his wits about him."

"You can tell him yourself tomorrow. He's on range practice with you."

"Thanks a lot."

Fowler stood up. "Don't be too hard on him. He's just a bit keen. Good man, though."

"He can be keen on someone else," Logan retorted, unrepentant as she escorted Fowler out of the room and down the stairs.

"Hm. Well . . . I'll see you tomorrow night."

She nodded, and held the door open for him to leave.

The next morning she was at the range, deep beneath the building in the sleepy London square that the Department used for its innocuous offices, by nine o'clock. She wore a pale blue sweater and a denim skirt with press-studs down the front. There was a practical reason for this. Today, she wore the twin, bullet-loaded garters around her upper thighs.

The targets were set up and she pulled the magnum out of her shoulder bag, fired almost in the same motion, holding the weapon two-handed as it roared like a thing alive. The individual shots were so closely spaced she might have been using an automatic. When the gun was empty, she broke it open, pulled at the front of her dress. The studs snapped out with sharp, rapid pops; then she was reloading from the left-hand garter. In an incredibly short space of time, the Ruger was bellowing once more. Again it was empty, and again Logan swiftly reloaded, this time from the right-hand garter. For a third time, the magnum snarled at a target; then once more, it was empty.

"Excellent, Logan," an amplified voice said into the ensuing silence. The weapons officer, in the bullet-proof, glass-enclosed control room behind her. "Quite magnificent. A neat group in each target, covering the area between the eyes and above the nosebridge."

"Can I see one?" A mike in the ceiling relayed her voice to the room.

"Certainly."

There was a soft hum, and one of the targets came towards her from the butts. The hum subsided as the plywood square with a life-sized human head sketched upon it reached the stop. There was a jagged hole where the heavy bullets had torn through it, in the area that the weapons officer had mentioned. The remaining part of the sketch was completely untouched.

"The others are exactly the same," came the voice on the speakers. "You've still got the touch." There was pride in the voice.

"I had a good teacher."

"I only worked on an instinct that was already there."

"Such modesty!"

A short laugh came at her, then the voice once more became authoritative. "Your weapon is now cool. Reload."

Logan commenced reloading, taking ammunition from the small cardboard box on the rough table next to her. She also put fresh rounds into her garters and fastened the skirt.

"Ready!" she said.

She held her right arm along her side, gun pointing downwards in her hand. A new target popped up on the butts. The arm came up swiftly, left hand sweeping in to brace, body crouching. The Ruger barked twice.

Another target. Aim switching, lining up. Two more shots, rapid, running into each other it seemed.

Third target. Find it, hit it. Twice.

Silence.

"You don't need practice." The voice dry, from the control room. "Two killing shots in each target. No reload necessary. Very economical, Logan."

"It helps when they're not firing back." Ever since she'd been shot, she had not used the magnum in anger. She was not sure how she would perform under pressure when the occasion next arose.

The weapons officer had no such anxieties. "I don't think

you have anything to worry about. Would you like to see a target?"

"No. I'll take your word for it."

Logan reloaded. When she had done so, she returned the Ruger to her bag, then picked up the box with the remaining ammo, and the spent cartridges. She would hand those in as she signed out. She would be keeping the live ammunition.

Telford entered the range just as she was leaving. He grinned at her. He was very good-looking, and knew it.

"That was fantastic shooting," he said. "I came in a little late, so I missed your act with the skirt." His eyes looked her up and down. "Pity."

Logan's green eyes surveyed him for long seconds. The freckles seemed to stand out on her face.

"Piss off, Telford," she said at last, and walked out.

The weapons officer, who had heard the exchange, smiled to himself. They'd never learn to leave her be, and would continue to be slapped down until they did.

He smiled again, this time with fondness.

"Look after yourself," he said to her as she signed out.

"Don't I always?"

The green eyes smiled back at him.

The Head of Department's office would do justice to the inner sanctum of a highly exclusive private club; which, Fowler decided drily was perhaps the only way to describe it properly. The Department *was* a highly exclusive club.

Rear-Admiral Sir John Winterbourne sat behind the large inlaid desk in the red-carpeted, oak-panelled room and read the report on Logan's prowess at the range. Fowler stood to one side, well away from the wide windows, and watched him read.

The tension between them was not helped by the fact that Winterbourne was Navy, when most of the executive staff were either air force or ex-air-force personnel. Kingston-Wyatt had been air force, and once Pross's CO. It did not help that Fowler also considered Winterbourne incompetent. Winterbourne could not fill the dead Kingston-Wyatt's shoes. Kingston-Wyatt had blown himself away, and it rankled that Winterbourne had been appointed without consultation. There were those who disliked the Department's independence, Fowler knew. Jealousy, he thought unworriedly.

The petulant cherub's face that was Winterbourne's looked up from the report. He was well aware of what Fowler thought of him. Their days were spent in constant subtle skirmishing.

Winterbourne said, "Exceptional shot, that young woman. I'm impressed." He frowned worriedly. "Won't go berserk, will she? You know the mood these days about issuing guns. It's bad enough with the police. Think what would happen if one of our people took out a few passersby."

Fowler stifled a sigh, said patiently, "Weapons cleared her, Sir John. Handling that magnum is second nature to her."

"She was quite heavily wounded on that mission to China, and has not faced a firefight since. Will she cope?"

"If you mean will she go out of control, the answer is no. Logan is psychologically sound enough to handle weapons. There are some people I know walking around with official guns whom I would ground without hesitation. Unfortunately, they are not within my jurisdiction. I would trust Logan above any of them."

"I hope you are sound in your judgment, Fowler. You have given her an extremely delicate operation to handle."

"She is up to the job," Fowler said in his customary, calm voice, his neutral expression belying the contempt he felt for the man before him.

"And what's to be done about Pross?"

"We'll be moving him soon."

"We can't afford mistakes, Fowler."

Fowler knew Winterbourne was thinking of his own head. One of Winterbourne's most sought-after goals was a peerage. He wanted nothing to blot his copybook.

"I must be kept informed of every stage," Winterbourne was saying. "*Every* stage, Fowler. I may not as yet know all the ropes, but *I* am in command here."

"Yes, Sir John," Fowler said dutifully.

Idiot, was what he thought.

The stages were too far advanced to be of any value to

118

Winterbourne, who would have gone straight into shock had he known the half of it. He would also have interfered.

When Winterbourne interfered, disaster invariably followed. Fowler intended to make quite sure that did not happen.

Logan sat in the foyer of the Queen Elizabeth Hall studying the evening's programme. She had timed her arrival so that only a minute or two was left before the first of the warning gongs for the commencement of the performance. If Priakin did turn up, she did not want to have a long conversation with him at this early stage.

She had dressed demurely in a simple, calf-length dress of pale blue. She wore her glasses, and had done her hair in such a way that while it seemed neat, still managed to appear dowdy. She sat primly, as would be expected of someone as uninspiring as she looked, who tended to go to such functions on her own. In the bag at her side, however, was the magnum.

About her, the other concert-goers milled and chatted, some talking loudly and pretentiously about the merits and demerits of the work. Others listened with the patience of saints. Logan's senses were not focused upon them.

The electronic gong sounded its first warning. People began to drift away. Logan remained where she was, apparently absorbed by the programme in her hands.

Then she was aware of someone approaching her. She did not look up.

"Hello! This is a charming surprise."

She judged her moment nicely, looked up with the sort of startled diffidence that would go well with the character of Lady Araminta.

"Gosh!" she said. "It's you!" She stood up, looking embarrassed.

The man she knew as Priakin smiled. He appeared genuinely pleased to see her.

"I wish I had known you liked Bartók," he said. "Then I would have asked you to accompany me tonight when I spoke to you at the camp."

"There was no reason for me to have told you."

"No. You are right. There was no reason. However, it would have been very nice to have known."

An awkward silence fell between them as they stood irresolutely while the people continued to file into the auditorium. Logan did not look for Priakin's minders, but she knew they'd be there among the crowd.

"Well," they began together, laughed sheepishly.

Then Logan, "I'd better be going."

"Yes. Yes. Where are you sitting?"

"My ticket's for the rear stalls, centre, first row. I . . . I like to sit there. More leg room." Logan sounded as if she were apologising for making her own decision.

"Such a pity. I am in the front part. Many seats in front."

Logan gave a quick, awkward smile. "Oh well. Can't be helped."

"A drink, perhaps?" he said as she turned to go. "During the interval."

"Oh. Well. I . . . I don't know. I . . ." She appeared uncertain, reluctant.

"Please say you will."

"Oh. Ah . . . Alright. The interval." She hurried away as if eager to get into the concert hall.

At the interval, Logan spent most of the time in the Ladies, coming out to meet Priakin when there was just enough time for one quick drink. She noted his minders, strategically positioned at each end of the foyer, pretending to be uninterested in him.

He grinned at her. "We have perhaps only a little time, I think, but enough for a drink. Yes?"

"Oh I'm so sorry . . ."

"Please. A lady must be allowed her time to beautify herself. What shall I get you?"

"Oh . . . er . . . a glass of white wine, thanks."

Anakov bought two glasses of wine. The gong began to sound just as they began to drink.

"And there goes our time," he said regretfully. "Perhaps later after the performance . . ."

"Er . . . no. Thank you. That is most kind, but I must be getting home."

"Ah. I see."

"No. You don't. I'm not trying to be rude, but you

120

see . . ." Logan made herself appear confused. "Oh dear, this is so awkward. What I'm trying to say . . ."

Anakov gave an understanding nod. "I think I begin to understand. You think I am too . . . mm . . . forward. Yes?"

"Yes. No, no, no. It's not quite like that. Look, Mr. Nagy—"

"Geörgy, please. We have already met."

"Look, Geörgy. It's very nice having this drink with you. You're a charming man, and I'm flattered. Really. But I'm afraid . . . Oh dear. This is really so awful. I . . ."

Anakov took it with good grace. He smiled at her. "I think now I do begin to understand. I have been unkind . . ."

"No . . ."

"Please. I am very sorry. But do not blame me if you come to another concert and I am here, and I ask for another drink." He smiled charmingly at her.

"You are being very considerate. Thank you." She smiled at him now.

"Incredible," he said softly. "You are very beautiful when you smile."

Logan wiped the smile off quickly.

Anakov looked dismayed. "And now I have done something else wrong."

"No no no. It's alright. Now I really must rush off. The gong will be stopping any moment now. Goodbye. Thanks for the drink."

She put her glass down and hurried away.

"Logan," she muttered drily to herself as she entered the auditorium, "that wasn't bad going. Fowler ought to give you an Oscar."

At the end of the performance, she made sure she left without being seen. She drove a long roundabout route that took her through a large part of south London, before eventually making for the mews house in Chelsea.

Fowler was there, waiting.

"Have fun?" was the first thing he said.

"It was interesting," she said as she removed her useless glasses. "Bartók was a great composer, but tonight was not my night for him." She ruffled her hair with both hands, tossed her head as if to free the strands. The hair bobbed briefly about her face. "I'm starving. I'm going to make a snack and some coffee. Care to join me?"

"The coffee will do."

Fowler accompanied her to the kitchen where she told him about what had taken place at the concert hall. She worked on the snack as she spoke.

"Sounds quite the charmer," he commented drily when she had finished. "His visit to the camp makes your meeting totally natural. Good work, Logan. You've done well."

She handed him a cup of coffee.

He sniffed appreciatively at it. "Mmm. Thank you."

She began cutting into a loaf of bread. The pieces were more like chunks than slices.

"Good God," he exclaimed. "What do you call those?"

"Food." She slapped ham and lettuce between the thick slices, then cut them into squares. She bit into one. "Lovely." She had made eight pieces. She placed them on a plate, offered it to Fowler.

"I think I'll pass," he said, viewing the quartered chunks with suspicion.

"They're very good."

"I'll take your word for it."

She shrugged. "Suit yourself. When's my next cultural outing?" she went on.

"Friday. The programme is Borodin, *In the Steppes of Central Asia*. Priakin will not miss it for the world. We happen to know it is one of his favourite compositions. I've brought your ticket."

Logan bit into a second square. "Of course." She smiled at him suddenly, green eyes impish. "I don't suppose you arranged the programming."

"My dear Logan, would the Department interfere with the running of the Festival Hall concerts?"

"Of course it would."

"Well, believe it or not, we had absolutely nothing to do with it."

Logan's look was most skeptical. "I'm still not going to bed with him."

"No one expects you to."

Her eyes said she didn't believe him.

Anakov and Semachev were not having a good time of it.

"I am perfectly aware that your men report to you even when I sneeze, Major," Anakov was saying coldly, "but do remember it was you who suggested we visit the peace camp. And it was you who insisted . . . note that I say *insisted* . . . I remain in plain view while you carry out the search for the helicopter which, I must add, you have not yet found."

"I shall find it," Semachev retorted. "I have taken action that will ensure success. Just because it is necessary for you to be seen, Comrade, it does not mean that you should consort with the local women."

Anakov stared at the KGB man wearily. " 'Consort', 'local women'. Must you always speak like that, Major? And what is wrong with a mild diversion? She is an idealistic young woman who has as much idea of the real world as you have of helicopters, otherwise she would not spend time on that waste ground for her ridiculous crusade. Still, it helps us." He smiled reflectively. "She has an atrocious taste in clothes, but beneath all that, I feel she is an exciting woman. I have an instinct about these things."

Semachev said, "I do not have the Comrade Colonel's taste for Western females, nor am I a glamorous pilot of the helicopter regiments. But I work for the Motherland in my own way, and I let nothing divert me." His eyes stared coldly back at Anakov.

Anakov looked at Semachev as he would at a subordinate, KGB or no KGB. "Find me that helicopter, Major, *and* its pilot, and I will take care of my diversions. Do not make the error of thinking that my interest in her is anything but a superficial desire for her body. She is shy, unsure of herself, easily confused. That attracts me. But like you, Comrade Major, I know where my duty lies. Do not, in future, ever accuse me of not being aware of it. I hope I have made myself clear."

The twin pebbles of Semachev's eyes stared at Anakov for long moments, then Semachev went out without another word.

Anakov sighed, went over to a window. From his high

123

vantage point, the darkened expanse of Hampstead Heath stretched before him. He shook his head slowly in exasperation. An excess of zeal and narrow-minded puritanism tended to go together. He had found that in the West as well as in the East.

But none of this was important to him; not the zealous Semachev, not Araminta, not the peace camp and its forlorn hopes. All that mattered was the success of his project and the eventual creation of several regiments of his fighter-helicopter gunships.

He stared at the darkened Heath, but did not see it. In his thoughts were another helicopter, and another pilot; the obstacles to his dream.

Chapter Eight

Pross was discussing the local area weather with Pete Dent on the flight line. The information from Met gave them a radius cover of forty nautical miles. An anticyclone over the north of the country brought a strong easterly blast this far south, giving a surface wind that sometimes gusted to 35 knots.

Pross said, "You don't have to go up, Pete. You can feel what it's like down here, and there's severe turbulence up to 8000. That's slap bang within today's operating envelope. I'm prepared to postpone. It's gusting up to 50 at 5000 feet. They can pick another day for their survey."

Dent looked briefly up at the sky. "I've been in much worse. It's a good, bright day. Visibility up to 20 kilometres. No weather to speak of." He smiled at Pross like a son telling a father to stop worrying.

Pross had not dug too far into Dent's previous Army career; but he had seen from the latter's capabilities with the Jetrangers that flying helicopters was second nature to him. Thinking of Dent's Army flying made Pross think reluctantly of Fowler, and thoughts of Fowler made him wish almost wistfully that Fowler had picked on Dent instead. Dent was certainly well-skilled, and had the dashing flair that should have been more suitable for Fowler's clandestine games.

But things never worked like that in real life. Sod's law was all.

Dent was saying, "I'll be alright."

"Well don't bend yourself."

Dent grinned. "Bet you say that to all the boys."

"Be off with you, pongo," Pross said with a smile.

125

"Yes, boss."

Pross shook his head in mock despair and left Dent to it. He returned to the office to find he had a visitor.

"Hullo, Pross."

Fowler.

The expression on Pross's face said it all. "I was just thinking about you."

"Good thoughts, I hope."

"I knew it would be too good to be true," Pross went on, as if Fowler had not spoken.

Cheryl Glyn, confused by the exchange, said, "Mr. Pross, this gentleman . . ." Her voice faded, uncertainty clouding her features. She always became formal in front of strangers.

"Time for your tea break," Pross said to her.

"But Mr. Pross, I don't usually . . ."

"Tea break, Cheryl. There's a love."

She stared at him for a moment or two, then said as she left her desk, "Right. Tea break it is."

She edged her way past Fowler, her eyes looking at him with all the nervousness of a woodland animal listening to the tread of a hunter.

Pross said, after she'd gone, "She probably thinks you're some kind of gangster who's come to offer us protection, or else. Come to think of it, that's almost why you're here, isn't it?"

"What's this, Pross? Second thoughts?"

"I never even had first thoughts."

"That was not the impression I got when I saw you studying the *Hellhound* drawings."

"I woke up when I got back. I had returned to my family and my firm. My kind of reality."

The sound of G-JADE passing overhead came to them. Pross gave a nod towards the ceiling. "Now there's the person you really could use. I'd be happy to spare him. I'm sure you know all about Pete Dent. Bags of time on Lynxes, Scouts, and Gazelles. A nifty chopper jockey, with no personal responsibilities. Full of flair, and he would go for it like a Trojan."

"You've just given me the perfect description of the kind

126

of person I most certainly do not want," Fowler said in his calm way. "Dent is a good pilot, maybe even a very good one; but he's not stable . . . at least, not by my terms of reference. Now you, Pross, are stable in my sense of the word. You have plenty to lose. You have responsibilities. You want to survive. To do that, the *Hellhound* has to die, and I believe you're quite capable of taking it on . . . and winning.

"Dent would go at it like a magnificent man in his flying machine, and Anakov or one of his pilots would chew him up. You can't *afford* to get chewed. That's what I'm banking on. I want that chopper turned into a burning heap of junk; and I want it done in such a way that it drives home to them that their precious gunship is a combat lemon. Besides," Fowler gave one of his briefest of smiles, "Anakov is after you, not Dent."

"I feel so relieved to know you're looking after my interests. My wife will thank you forever."

"Instead of dousing me in sarcasm, how about offering me some coffee?"

Pross sighed, shook his head slowly in resignation. "No wonder they've given you this job, Fowler. I used to think that perhaps you were not as hard a bastard as Kingston-Wyatt used to be, even when he was squadron CO; but I'm not so sure now. Nothing seems to touch you."

"You'd be surprised," was all Fowler said.

"Berlin!" Pross said loudly. "That's in bloody *East* Germany."

Pross had made coffee. Fowler was leaning against a wall, warming his hands on the mug which he held as if in prayer. Pross was perched on his desk. He had not made any for himself.

Fowler said, "Thank you for the geography lesson." He began to drink two-handedly. He stared briefly at the mug. "Do you know," he continued conversationally, "I picked this habit up from childhood. I saw a gardener my father employed drinking his tea like that. I copied him. At times, the habit makes a return. Funny how some things stay with you all your life."

Pross said, "I thought we were supposed to be keeping away from the Russians, not running towards them."

"A man who won't be diverted from the subject," Fowler observed. "I like that."

"Why Berlin?"

"Why not Berlin? You can get to Switzerland from there."

"You can get to Switzerland from a lot of other places."

"Ah. But in your case, Pross, you will fly to Berlin from here. You will then be put on a plane to Munich. From Munich, you'll fly on to Zurich-Klöten, Switzerland. A helicopter will take you to Betten, in the southern canton of Valais. Your Lynx will be waiting. The Swiss have been most co-operative."

"Then what?"

"You'll see when you get there." Fowler smiled fleetingly. "I promise you won't be bored."

"Will Logan be accompanying me on the flights?"

"I'm afraid not, Pross. You'll be minded by someone else. You may not see him till you land, but he'll be around."

"I see." Pross was acutely disappointed, but it had been worth a try.

"Sorry, but we need Logan for other things. No cause to look so crestfallen, Pross." Fowler two-handed the mug and drank more of his coffee. "Your coffee's not too bad."

Pross barely heard what was a virtual accolade from Fowler.

"I feel safe with Logan around." He turned from Fowler to stare out at the check-in desks and the reception area beyond.

"Sorry," Fowler repeated. "But there it is."

"When do I have to leave?"

"Tomorrow's flight from here leaves at 16.00. I've brought all the necessary tickets, and an appropriate passport."

"Appropriate?" Pross queried, somewhat dazedly. He was thinking about how he was going to explain it all to Dee.

"Your passport is in the name of George Milner," Fowler said. "Can't let them know of your movements, can we?"

Pross looked alarmed. "You're saying they already know my real name?"

"Good heavens no. But this way, we take no chances. Don't worry about anyone here noticing the discrepancy. You'll be boarding the aircraft from the flight line. No boring formalities for you."

"Thanks very much," Pross said with his old sarcasm. "You think of everything, don't you?"

Fowler said, serious, "No, Pross. I don't. No one ever can. If I had, you would not be going to Berlin, and Logan . . ." He allowed his words to die.

Pross did not believe Fowler's piety for one second, but he could not restrain himself from saying, "Logan? What's happened to her? I knew it. I knew she was involved in this somewhere. Come on, Fowler. What mess did you throw her into? Is she hurt?"

Fowler gave a world-weary smile that lived no longer than his previous ones. "It's quite touching the way the two of you worry about each other."

"Don't read too much into it."

"I wouldn't dare." The smile came on again. "She might shoot me with that cannon of hers."

"So she's alright."

"Yes, Pross." Patiently. "She is quite alright."

"But you've given her something dangerous to do."

"Pross, you worry about yourself, and let me worry about Logan. Everything will work much better that way. Don't you agree?"

Fowler put down his mug, at last empty, and picked up the flat leather briefcase he had brought with him. He placed the black case on the desk, handle upwards. He opened it by running a lightpen that looked like an ordinary ballpoint over the locks. The catches sprang free softly within. There were no keyholes in the metal squares. He put the pen away, reached into the case to pull out a large brown envelope which he handed to Pross. He snapped the case shut.

"Everything's in there," he said. "Documents, and money. You may not need to use any of the cash, but it's nice to know you've got it."

Pross stared at him silently.

"Fine," Fowler said drily. He lifted the case off the desk. "I must be going. Have fun in Switzerland. Lovely country, if you like snow-capped mountains."

"Who's going to be with me in Switzerland?"

"Wait and see, Pross. Wait and see."

"My wife's going to love this," Pross said gloomily. "I come home on a Thursday night and tell her I'm off to Berlin the next day. Just like that."

Fowler's eyes gleamed with a sudden cold fire behind his glasses. "You say nothing, Pross. As far as she is concerned, you are not even leaving the country. Tell her you're off to Scotland, or North Wales . . . anywhere except abroad."

"You don't seriously expect her to fall for that, do you?"

"What she doesn't know about, she can't tell."

Pross's eyes widened. "What the hell is that supposed to mean? I've told you before. My family are *not* going to be put in danger again. If there's the slightest hint of that, you can stuff your documents. Find another pilot to do your dirty work."

Fowler was most calm. "Don't be naïve, Pross. You'll be putting them in greater danger by remaining here. You do not seriously believe that Anakov and his friends are going to give up, do you? The stakes are far too high. It is literally their survival against yours. You've got to take that gunship on, Pross. There's no other way."

Fowler went out, leaving Pross staring after him.

"Scotland?" Dee said later with mighty skepticism. "I'm not stupid, David. Is that the best you can do?"

Pross, thankful that the children were safely out of the way in bed, felt miserable. The last thing he wanted was a row. It would not be a good note upon which to take his leave tomorrow. He knew he would be worried all the way to Berlin and wherever else Fowler might decide to send him.

"I don't have to be a genius to know that those people have been to see you," Dee was saying into his misery, "so spare me the tales. I was a service wife once. Remember?"

Pross sighed. "Dee, I can't tell you." Now she was throwing sarcasm at him.

"Why not, for God's sake?"

There was a tightness in her voice that warned him she was trying not to shout and was barely succeeding in maintaining control.

"I think it best that you don't know," he said.

"You think? Or *they* think?"

"Dee," he began patiently, "this is hard enough for me as it is. Let's not have a row about it. I don't want to leave you like that. I mean . . ."

She paled suddenly, eyes searching his. "It's worse than the last time, isn't it?"

"Nothing and no one could be as bad as Ling. No. It's not as bad as the last time."

"Don't lie to me, David. You're not some screen hero going off to bomb the enemy with a stiff upper lip and every hair in place. I can take the truth."

He stifled another sigh. This was not what he wanted. He said, "For your sake, for the children's sake, I'd rather not say any more about it."

"Fine," she said. She had been sitting next to him on the sofa in the lounge. She stood up abruptly, and walked out of the room without another word.

Watching as she left, Pross cursed Fowler richly in his mind.

In the early hours of the morning, they made love gently, taking their time about it.

"I'm sorry," Dee said softly afterwards. "I'm sorry I was so hard on you earlier." She kissed him with gently searching lips. "Don't get yourself killed, will you."

"I'm not—"

"Shhh." The lips stopped his words in the dark of the bedroom. "Don't say anything. Don't make up a story for me. Just take care, and come back in one piece. Alright?"

"Alright," he said.

Pross settled back in his seat as the aircraft heaved itself off the Cardiff runway. He was next to a window and he had a fine view of a port wing. He wished he hadn't. He was one of those pilots who hated being flown by others. The one exception had been Gallagher.

But Gallagher was not on his mind. He was thinking of Fowler and, as usual, his thoughts on that subject were not charitable. Earlier in the day, he had finally persuaded himself to look at the documents and money Fowler had brought him. Everything had been perfectly done, as was to be expected, he thought drily, of a clandestine unit like Fowler's. The passport in George Milner's name looked even more authentic than the Passport Office's original for David Pross. Something else, however, had brought on the new wave of hostility towards Fowler. It had been in the pile of currency Fowler had left.

Among the banknotes of German marks and Swiss francs had been Nepalese and Afghan currency. Pross had felt his bowels lurch.

Afghanistan? Nepal?

Now, as the aircraft gained height and south Wales disappeared beneath cloud, he indulged in another mental round of swearing. It did not make him feel better. He wondered if the way he felt was similar to that of animals being led to the slaughterhouse.

He decided there was little point in getting worked up about the situation he had been dumped in. All he had to do was get out alive. He smiled grimly. Easier said than done. Come back in one piece. Dee. He would have liked to have had Logan with him, but Fowler had already scotched that idea. There was nothing for it but to make do with what he had: himself, and the barest of trust in Fowler.

He closed his eyes, and found himself listening to every nuance of the plane's sounds and vibrations.

It was going to be a rotten flight to Berlin.

At about the time that Pross was reluctantly accepting what Fowler had dished out to him, Anakov was looking forward to the coming evening's concert. He hoped Araminta would be there. He had actually visited the camp on the off-chance of seeing her. His disappointment at finding her absent now served to fuel his anticipation.

Her absence from the camp did not necessarily mean she would be attending the concert, but there was a good probability. The woman called Jean had said that Araminta had spoken vaguely of going to a concert, but had not said which. Anakov hoped it would be tonight's.

He needed a diversion. Semachev had still not come up with anything. Time was running out. The helicopter had not yet been found, and neither had its pilot. He was becoming tired of playing decoy.

Anakov stared out at the Heath. Semachev was not as forth-coming as he should be. That was certain. Semachev, despite all sorts of protestations, was carrying out the mission in his own way and reporting only what he thought fit. The full details, Anakov was sure, would be going to the KGB. He was almost hoping Semachev would fail. That would wipe the smug expression off the face of the self-important little toad. He would have to talk to Sogovyi about Semachev when they got back to Russia.

Anakov grimaced as if he had taken a bite of something bitter. Semachev seemed to think that the enjoyment of the company of a woman somehow made one less loyal to the Motherland.

"A bureaucratic moron," Anakov said to the Heath as if sharing a confidence.

But Sogovyi had said that the KGB man knew his job.

Anakov twisted his lips briefly in contempt. From what he had so far observed, Semachev was only good for stealing ballpoint pens. Frequently, on their diversion-creating visits to stores, he had seen Semachev pocket the pens from various temptingly laid out displays. Tempting, if you had a penchant for ballpoints.

133

Anakov found himself smiling without humour. Kachuk and his designer jeans, Semachev and his ballpoints.

"And I," he said, speaking his thoughts, "and my Araminta."

All products of the West. The irony of the situation amused him. He began to laugh, this time with a real feeling of humour.

Logan decided to be daring; daring in the sense that Minty would be. She wore a red dress that fitted her closely and which set off her nylon-clad legs attractively. She also wore her fake glasses, and her hair looked as if she'd taken some trouble with it. Her apparent manner was of someone who was not quite at ease with the bold way in which she had chosen to attire herself for the evening.

She stared critically at herself in a bedroom mirror, decided the masquerade would have the required effect on the man she knew as Priakin. She picked up her bag, the loaded magnum safely within it, and went out.

In the mews, she climbed into the little green Citroën, and drove cautiously out into the street. There were no darkened cars lurking.

The 2CV stuttered its way towards the Festival Hall where Anakov was already waiting.

He scanned the gathering crowd eagerly, hoping for a glimpse of her; but as the time passed he began to feel a creeping sense of disappointment. She was not going to come.

Valentinov, Semachev's duty watchdog for the evening, hovered a short distance away, now and then favouring him with a stony look. They would not be sitting together, for which Anakov was grateful. He strongly doubted whether Valentinov would be appreciative of the evening's performance. Semachev's minion was there to guard, and to report; not necessarily in that order.

Then Anakov felt a sudden lifting of his spirits. The

gloomy thought of having to sit through the concert with Valentinov's baleful stare upon his back vanished like early mist in the morning sun.

She had come.

Logan saw him coming towards her as she entered from the wide, high-level terrace that overlooked the Thames. There was no disguising the eager gleam in his eyes, and she felt somewhat taken aback by this. He appeared to be truly pleased to see her. She warned herself that this little game could present more problems than she had at first considered.

She kept her hand firmly on her bag as she went to meet him, a look of feigned surprise upon his face.

"Geörgy!"

"Araminta!"

They had spoken simultaneously. Now they stopped a few feet from each other, awkwardly, like children meeting for the first time. Logan allowed a hesitant smile to come upon her lips.

"I didn't expect—" she began.

"I am so happy to see you—"

They had again spoken together. They paused, laughed a little selfconsciously.

Then the man she knew as Priakin said, "You must speak first." He smiled at her. "I shall tell you about myself later. Shall I get you a drink? A coffee, perhaps?"

She shook her head, smiled back at him nervously. The perfect Araminta. "No. No . . . thanks. I . . . don't want anything for . . . for the moment." She gave him another nervous smile. "Well. This is a surprise." As soon as she had seen her target coming towards her, she had expected to see a shadow. Now she spotted him, lurking among a group of people near a pillar. Her expression gave no indication of this; but she had pinpointed him, her instincts tracking him so that she could place him precisely should anything go wrong.

She did not expect even the KGB to start a shooting-match among the concert-goers, neither did she expect her target to be armed; but his shadow certainly would be. No harm in knowing where your first shot would have to go. Just in case.

He was saying, "For me, this is the fulfillment of a hope. I went to the camp to look for you. The woman . . . er, Jean, said you would be going to a concert. She did not say which. I am glad it is this one. You are very beautiful tonight, Araminta."

Logan gave him a shy look. "You don't have to be kind, Geörgy," she said deprecatingly. "I know what I look like. But thank you." Her smile told him she was pleased.

"You know," he said, "I believe you are truly unaware of how attractive you are. Your glasses, I think, give you the wrong impression of yourself."

"I've always worn them. From childhood."

"They do not do you justice."

His eyes had strayed, she noted, to the teasing swell of her breasts that peeped tantalisingly out of her dress. The cut was not daring by her standards as Logan, but as Araminta it certainly was. She twitched her lips nervously, a butterfly unsure of herself, in her new bold colours. The effect she was having was far better than she had hoped.

If only you could see me now, Fowler, she thought drily.

She gazed dreamily away, eyes scanning the crowd, apparently aimlessly. The shadow had moved, pretending to study the books on display outside the music bookshop.

Then the first warning gong sounded.

"Ah!" she said brightly, and with relief. It would be an expected reaction. "Time to go."

"But we have some minutes yet."

"I like to sit and wait. I prefer to be well settled before a performance. There's nothing more embarrassing than trying to reach your seat while the orchestra is about to come on."

"Where is your seat?"

She told him.

He sighed. "Again we are far from each other. There is one way to resolve this."

"Oh?"

"You must allow me to take you to a concert."

136

"Oh," Logan said again, as if unsure of how to take this offer. "Well. I . . . don't know. Well . . . perhaps . . ."

"Say yes. It is so simple."

"Well . . . yes. Alright." She had spoken uncertainly, as if the decision were momentous in the extreme.

His smile was triumphant. "Now I am prepared to let you go in. Shall we meet in the interval?"

"Er . . . alright."

"And afterwards?"

"Afterwards?" Quickly, almost startled.

"But yes. Can we not have a longer drink? There is somewhere we can go after the performance, perhaps?"

"I . . . I . . . don't know. I'll have to think about it. I'll let you know." She hurried away, climbing up the wide stairs to the auditorium.

Anakov watched her go, a pleased smile upon his lips. His eyes lingered upon her legs in admiration. They were strong, well-shaped legs, he noted. Behind that hesitant exterior was the kind of body he liked to enjoy, and he intended to do so at the earliest opportunity. Araminta Dilke-Weston needed awakening and he was the man who could do it. It would be the perfect diversion; the very thing he needed to take away the unpleasantness of having to work with Semachev.

He grimaced briefly. He was not working *with* Semachev. The KGB man was calling the tune.

Anakov permitted himself a tiny smile. Semachev was only temporarily in the command seat.

Valentinov had come up. "Are you going after the woman, Comrade?" he asked softly, in Russian.

Anakov looked at him coldly. "Do you have objections?"

"No, Comrade . . . but I must make a report to Comrade Semachev."

"Of course you must," Anakov said acidly. "Then tell him this. I shall be seeing her during the interval and, after the performance, I shall take her somewhere for a few drinks. *After* that, we may go back to her place. Who knows? Anything is possible. It is possible that I may spend the night with her. Make your report, *Comrade.*"

Anakov turned away, went across to the other side of the huge lounge where stairs led up to his part of the auditorium.

Valentinov stared balefully after him.

The twin turbo-prop HS748 had deposited Pross at Amsterdam's Schipol airport, and the stewardess had announced transit passengers would be changing aircraft for Berlin.

Pross had remained irresolutely in his seat when everyone else had stood up and had begun to busy themselves with getting at their cabin baggage before leaving the aircraft. No one had approached him during the flight.

Then someone had leaned over from behind his seat. "This includes you, Mr. Milner." A London accent.

Pross had looked up into a hard face, the military-style haircut making the man seem even more forbidding. They had left the aircraft together, Pross disliking the fact that he would have to completely trust total strangers all the way. He could only hope they would all be Fowler's people.

The hard man had directed him to the transit lounge. "I won't be going with you. You'll be looked after on the flight to Berlin, and you'll be met."

"Are you with Fowler?" Pross had asked. The man had seemed so unlike the languid Fowler's style. Probably outside units were brought in to do such routine work.

"We should know better than to ask such questions, shouldn't we?" the man had said.

Thereafter, barely a word had passed between them until it was time to board the new aircraft.

"Have a good flight," was all the hard-faced man had said in parting.

Now, Pross relaxed in his seat as much as he could, as the BAC One-Eleven winged its way towards Berlin. The man, he decided, must have been Army, or from a special police unit. He had definitely not been one of Fowler's own smoothies.

Pross closed his eyes, although sleep was far from his mind. He had not seen anyone on board who had looked like a replacement for the hard-faced man. But that meant nothing. It could be any of the passengers, just as his non-talkative former companion had been.

He wondered what was waiting for him in Berlin.

The aircraft landed at Berlin-Tegel at precisely 21.45 local time. No one was waiting, and no one had approached him on board. Pross now found himself in the baggage-claim area wondering what the hell to do next. All about him, people were talking in a constant stream of rapid German. He felt completely isolated.

As he stood by the revolving conveyor, he saw two men sitting carelessly by a wall, on two plastic chairs. They were talking to each other animatedly. One, youngish, was dressed indifferently in tattered jeans, a thick shirt, and sleeveless denim jacket. He conversed with a crumpled cigarette fixed to his lips. The older man was even more unprepossessing, and seemed ready for a drink to follow one of the many he'd already had. Pross wondered whether they were passengers still waiting for their baggage. He had not noticed them on the plane.

He looked away, returning his attention to the conveyor. His slim suitcase was curving towards him. He picked it up, and began to follow the other passengers out, trying not to look worried.

What the hell was he going to do? He had no idea about where he was supposed to go. Where was he to catch the next plane to Munich? Where the bloody hell was Fowler's man?

"Excuse me, sir?" A German speaking English with an American accent. The young man from the chair was standing before him, showing him an ID. "Customs. Would you please come with me?"

Christ, Pross thought wearily. *That's all I bloody need. An undercover Customs man.*

The man before him had bloodshot eyes, and a constellation of three spots growing from a stubbled chin. The spots were in urgent need of attention.

Pross said, not caring if he were tempting fate, "Do I

139

look as if I'm smuggling drugs?"

The customs man didn't seem to mind. "Just routine, sir. Please come with me." He led Pross through to a cubicle where he paused just long enough to say in a low voice, "I am sorry if I gave you a surprise, Mr. Milner, but I was told to take you through here." He opened a door, stood aside for Pross to enter, before following.

They were in a large office. In it were two men. One was a uniformed, armed policeman. Pross stared at them. From outside, the muted sounds of aircraft came to him.

The civilian said: "Mr. Milner, we are your escorts to your hotel. Tomorrow morning, we shall return you to catch your plan to München. Shall we go?"

"Er . . . yes. Yes."

"Good." To the scruffy young man, the civilian went on, *"Danke,* Max."

Max waved a hand, turned to go. *"Chuss."*

"Chuss. So, Mr. Milner," the civilian said, turning back to Pross as Max left, "we go now."

Pross nodded, allowed himself to be taken through a series of corridors until at last they were outside in the cold air. They were in some sort of compound. The policeman, who had now taken the lead, directed them to a police car.

The civilian said, "If anyone was watching for arrivals, they will not know you have come here. A police car is a police car. We are secure. Please get in, Mr. Milner. I will put your valise away."

Pross climbed in, after surrendering his suitcase to the unknown civilian. As he settled into the back, the car bounced slightly as the boot was opened, the case put in, and the boot shut once more. There was a brief, soft conversation in German between the two men.

Pross wished acutely for Logan. *I could disappear tonight,* he thought with some apprehension, *and Fowler wouldn't know until too late.*

He wondered how reliable these people were. He tried not to worry about it; a task easier said than done.

The men entered the car, both taking the front seats. They clipped on their seat belts.

The civilian turned his head in the gloom of the car as the policeman started the engine. The BMW motor burst smoothly into life.

"Are you alright, Mr. Milner?"

"Yes."

There was a brief chuckle. "Do not sound so worried. You are safe with us." The civilian turned to the front once more.

I bloody well hope so, Pross managed not to say.

The policeman drove out of the compound, threaded his way skillfully through the airport traffic and headed towards the city at high speed.

About ten minutes later, the civilian said, without turning round, "Mr. Milner, have you ever been to Berlin?"

"No," Pross answered, looking out at the rushing lights from the depths of the back of the car.

"Ah. A pity you are not staying with us for longer. This is an exciting city."

Pross did not doubt it, but the last things on his mind were the sights and urgent excitements of Berlin. When you're living so close to nemesis, there was no choice but to be exciting . . . and neurotic.

Pross closed his eyes, shutting out the neon enticements of the city. The car hurtled through the traffic, took corners on what felt like two wheels until, at last, it drew to an almost subdued halt.

"We are here, Mr. Milner."

They had arrived at a quiet street and had stopped before what looked like someone's home.

"My hotel?" Pross queried, disbelievingly. What was this? Had he been kidnapped? Were these people not real police after all?

Pross felt a mounting anger that was directed at the absent Fowler. Had Fowler's people screwed up?

As if he knew what Pross was thinking, the civilian said, "You are safe with us, Mr. Milner. Believe me."

"That's what you said before."

Pross climbed gingerly out of the car, stared at the house, then up and down the street. It seemed like a neighbourhood of some quality.

He said, "This looks like someone's home."

"It used to be." The civilian had taken the suitcase out of the boot.

"Used to be what?"

"Someone's home. For tonight, it is your hotel. Shall we go in, Mr. Milner?"

Pross again glanced up and down the well-lit street. There was not a single person in sight. Silent cars were parked along one side. There were lights in windows, but no one was looking out, and no voices could be heard.

Pross said, "After you."

The civilian smiled, led the way up a short flight of steps. The policeman stayed with the car.

At the door, the civilian pressed a bell-push. Pross heard no answering chime or ring but in seconds, it seemed, the thick wooden door was opening. An attractive blonde woman of about thirty stood there. She smiled at Pross.

"Ah, Mr. Milner. It is nice to see you are safe. Please come in."

Pross entered, followed by the civilian who shut the door.

"I am Lene. My colleague and I will look after you for the night. Everything has been prepared. You are hungry? I can make you dinner. Also, if you wish for a bath, there is plenty of hot water. There is a bath in your bedroom." She seemed anxious to please.

Pross decided he could probably relax. If these people had been out to harm him, they would probably have done so by now.

The civilian said, "Mr. Milner is a little worried about us. He is not sure that we are his friends." A tall, well-set man with thinning blond hair and a friendly face, he was still wearing the fawn-coloured military-style coat he'd had on when Pross had first seen him at the airport.

He showed no inclination to remove it. Pross wondered whether he'd be going back to the waiting police car. Was someone else now to take over? Were there others in the house with the woman who called herself Lene?

The woman smiled. "It is to be expected. After all, Mr.

Milner feels very much alone."

They're talking about me as if I were a piece of furniture, Pross thought with some annoyance. He kept his thoughts to himself.

Lene continued, "Please do not worry, Mr. Milner. You are in good hands. Now if you would like a bath before dinner, my colleague will show you to your room. You would like to eat, yes?"

Pross nodded. He did feel hungry, and a bath would certainly be welcome. "Thank you," he said. "I'd like that."

She smiled once more. "Good. If you will go up to your room, I will attend to the dinner." She gave the civilian a little nod, and left them.

"Come, Mr. Milner," the man said. "I will take you to your room." Still carrying Pross's suitcase, he began to climb a wide staircase of dark marble which began on the right side of the entrance hall.

Pross had no option but to follow.

The house was warm, and much larger than its outward appearance indicated. It seemed original, and Pross marvelled that it had withstood the pounding that the city had taken during the last war. No doubt repairs had been done on it, but they had been so well carried out that nothing of this showed. Its vaulted ceilings and carved walls with niches for family busts seemed to belong to an age two centuries ago.

He followed the unnamed man up two flights of the marble staircase until they came to a landing that ended in a long corridor which stretched from both sides. Here the floor was of highly polished parquetry, with a heavy-duty red carpet running full length along the middle. The carved walls were covered with paintings that would be worth a fortune, Pross decided. Some hotel.

But no other guests, it seemed.

They turned left, walked along the carpet for a few yards until the man stopped before a carved door.

"Your room, Mr. Milner." He handed Pross the suitcase. "It is open, so you may go in. The key is on the inside, should you wish to lock it when you go to sleep. This house is a very secret place, and you will be quite safe."

"I wish everybody would stop saying that."

The man smiled briefly. "We wish to reassure you. Lene will come to find you for dinner. You will not be seeing me again until the morning. *Auf wiedersehen*, Mr. Milner. *Schlaf gut*." He gave Pross a vague salute, turned, went back along the corridor and down the stairs.

Pross stared along the now empty corridor for some moments before pushing the door open. He entered uncertainly. The lights were already on.

He was in a large, cream bedroom; cream carpet, cream-painted walls. There was a huge bed and, to one side, a three-piece suite with a low glass-topped table. There was a large-screen TV set with remote control. There was no window.

Wise precaution, he thought drily.

He put down his suitcase, shut the door, then went through to a bathroom. It was one fit for a Roman emperor, decorated in cream and gold mosaic, with the substantial bath itself placed like an altar in the middle. There was no window here either, but a powerful extractor was set into the ceiling.

If this were what Fowler would call a safe house, Pross mused, it was a wonder any of its guests wanted to leave.

How many defecting Russians had passed through here? Was this display of opulence intended to blitz senses more used to spartan conditions? Pross did not doubt that this house had all sorts of methods with which to seduce those coming in from the other side. Well, such things did not concern him.

He got undressed, and began to run the bath. Everything had been prepared for him. He thought with grudging respect, of Fowler's organisational capabilities. He thought of something else too. When the time came for him to meet the *Hellhound* in the air, no one would be able to help him; not Logan, not Fowler's legions. Fowler was going to get him to that destination, hopefully in one piece. After that, coming back again was going to be in his own hands. At the moment, he could not see how he was going to defeat a man who'd be flying a remarkably advanced aircraft, and who'd had several months of actual combat experience under his belt. Only one of them would come out of the encounter alive, and Pross was not certain he would be the one.

With that sobering thought, he lowered himself into the hot bath.

Chapter Nine

"Mr. Milner! Your dinner is ready. Will you come please?" A discreet knock had preceded the call from outside the door.

Pross had been amusing himself with the TV. He had switched it on, to be greeted by the vision of an appalling British pop group performing for a bemused German studio audience. The Dawn Patrol were usually well up on groups and these had not been mentioned. Pross was not surprised. They were probably in hiding. In England, they would have been mercilessly booed: the German audience was politely patient.

He had then used the remote to switch channels. A familiar American import had come on-screen. Set in Hawaii, and featuring a red Ferrari and a red Hawaiian shirt, it had amused him by being dubbed. The Ferrari sounded the same, the shirt was having a rough time of it.

After a while, he had grown tired of the game and had discovered that the cupboard upon which the TV set stood was full of video cassettes, all of major films, in English. A further search had shown that the TV and video was a combined unit. He had been just about to insert an amusing comedy Western — he needed something to take his mind off what was to come — when Lene's call had interrupted him.

"Coming!" he called back at her.

She had obviously misunderstood, for the door opened and she came in.

"Ah," she said, "you have found the video."

"Yes."

"Did you have a good bath?" Her eyes inspected the

room swiftly.

"Yes," Pross repeated. "Thank you."

"Do you like the films?"

"There are many that I like, yes."

"All in English."

Pross had no doubt that had he been Russian, there would have been Russian films. "Fowler thinks of everything, does he?"

Her eyes seemed to cloud over. "Ah yes. Mr. Fowler. We have been in touch to tell him you are safe. You like your room?"

"Quite a gilded cage," he said.

"Gilded cage?"

I may be green in your line of business, Pross thought sceptically, *but not that green.* He was certain she knew precisely what he meant.

"It's not important," he told her.

"We should go now."

"Of course."

He followed her out and she led him back along the corridor, and down the marble stairs. Her movements were full of grace. She walked like a ballet dancer, seeming to float; nothing like Logan's purposeful, sexy walk.

Wish you were here, Logan, he thought drily. He felt strangely vulnerable without her.

Lene took him to a room where a long table with eight chairs was laid for one. The entire length of the table was covered with spotless linen, and the place setting was at the head. There were several dishes, much more than Pross felt he could cope with.

Lene said, "I hope you do not mind eating alone. There is much that I have to do about the arrangements for your flight in the morning. Also, the food is a cold buffet, but there is plenty of it. Help yourself to whatever you wish." She gave him a quick smile. *"Bon appetit."* Then she was gone.

Pross stared at the table for long seconds before checking out each of the dishes. She had certainly prepared a varied repast. Everything looked appetising. He took his seat slowly, and began to eat. There was even some fine Rhineland wine.

Pross had his meal, feeling like a highly prized captive and for a brief, terrible moment, the frightening thought came to him that he had actually been taken by the Russians.

He paused. All this could be an elaborate screen to make him believe he was still in friendly hands. Perhaps Fowler had not been so clever after all, and the Russians were well ahead of him? Fowler had said that they wanted both the Lynx and the pilot who had flown it. Suppose they had already succeeded in one of their objectives? Everybody knew Berlin reeked with undercover operations of all kinds. You didn't have to be in Fowler's world to realise that. With the wall dividing the city and its armed guards peering coldly westwards, it would be a miracle if the undergrowth were not crawling with all sorts of maggoty enterprise.

Pross looked about him. A gilded cage, he'd said to Lene. Facetiously, he now thought. Suppose this cage belonged to the Russians? There was nothing to tell him otherwise. This was simply an alien house in an alien city within which he was tightly sealed up.

He felt a stab of panic. He fought back at it, forcing himself to continue eating.

"Logan, Logan," he muttered. "Where are you when I need you?"

At 22.30 London time, Logan walked slowly out of the auditorium at the end of the performance. Her plan of action was firmly fixed in her mind. As she walked down the stairs, she saw the man she knew as Priakin waiting for her. People were milling about, some getting their coats from the green-uniformed attendants, others standing around discussing the evening's concert.

"Did you bring a coat?" he asked.

She shook her head. "My car's just round the back. Besides, this dress is quite warm."

148

"It was kind of you to agree to have a drink with me. Where shall we go?"

"Not far. In fact, it's very close to where I've parked the car. We've just got to go behind this building. There's a wine bar under the railway arches. Lots of people go there after the concerts. There's just about enough time for a short drink, if you'd like."

He smiled at her. "I would perhaps prefer somewhere a little more . . . intimate and quiet, but as you have been so kind to allow me to spend a little more time with you, I am happy to go to the wine bar."

Logan smiled a nervous Minty smile. "Er . . . fine. Alright. Let's go, then."

They went out onto the terrace, turned left then turned left again when they had come to the end of the building. They walked on until the walkway took them over Belvedere Road. They descended to street level, and crossed over to the wine bar. It was crowded and noisy, but they were able to find a table which, though for four, had only two chairs. The others had been taken for use by a large group of people clustered at two tables a short distance away.

Logan was pleased by this. She had not been looking forward to an enforced sharing.

A pianist and a vibraphone player were smoothing their way through old standards.

He said, "This is an interesting place."

"Do you have these in Hungary?"

"We have our cafés, of course, and yes, places perhaps a little similar." He smiled. "But of course the music is different and sometimes, very exciting."

She nodded. "I can imagine."

"So. Are we served here, or must we go up to the . . . er . . . counter?" He looked to her for confirmation.

"Counter will do," she said. "Yes. On this level we've got to buy at the counter."

"Fine." He stood up. "I will get it. What will you have?"

"I think I'll stick to wine. White. Thank you, Geörgy."

He nodded. "I will get it."

149

The piano and vibraphone were on *Stormy Weather* when he returned with a bottle and two glasses. Logan was humming to the tune.

"You know this music?" he asked as he sat down and began to pour.

"Yes," she answered, then held up her hand briefly to stop him from putting too much into her glass. "Whoops. That's it, thanks."

He looked at her. "It is all you want?"

"I've got to drive home."

"Oh yes. Of course."

She gave him a sideways look. "You sound disappointed."

"I had hoped . . ."

"You had hoped what, Geörgy?" Judging her moment nicely, Logan went on, "We're having a drink, Geörgy. That's all. When we're finished, I go home and you to your hotel or wherever you're staying."

"And now, I have offended you."

"Oh you haven't, Geörgy. I'm just making sure there are no misunderstandings."

"Yes . . . yes. I understand."

Logan sighed. "Oh dear. You have misunderstood."

"Perhaps I may see you tomorrow?"

She sighed again, smiled at him uncertainly. "You don't give up, do you?"

He shrugged engagingly, smiled at her.

"Oh alright," she said at last, as if she had reached the decision after a great mental debate with herself. "Tomorrow."

He grinned at her, raised his glass. "To tomorrow."

She smiled back at him, shyly.

Semachev and Valentinov were sitting in a darkened car beneath an arch which straddled the road.

Semachev said, "He is in there with the woman?"

"Yes. He is hoping to sleep with her tonight."

Semachev made a sound of disgust. "He believes that

150

because some people think him a hero of the Afghan war he can come here and try to get between the legs of any Western woman he lusts after, with complete disregard to—"

"Comrade Major, if I may—"

"Do not ever interrupt me again, Valentinov," Semachev cut in dangerously.

"No, Comrade." Valentinov's survival instincts were finely tuned.

"Anakov will push his limits too far eventually," Semachev went on, "and then I shall have him."

Valentinov waited until he was quite certain his superior had stopped speaking, before saying, "Comrade Semachev, have you heard from the contact?"

Semachev nodded, annoyance with his colleague now gone as swiftly as it had come. "They have moved the pilot."

"Out of the country?"

"Yes." Semachev did not seem particularly disturbed by the news.

"And the helicopter?"

"I would expect them to move it too."

Valentinov remained silent.

"You are wondering why I am not disappointed by this," Semachev remarked. "You can voice your thoughts, Comrade."

"I did believe," Valentinov began cautiously, "that our mission was to kill the pilot, and destroy the aircraft."

"That will eventually happen. Be patient. And in the end, I shall get Anakov too, *after* his precious gunship has gone into full-scale production."

"And the woman?"

"The contact says she is what she appears to be, but I shall have to prove that to my own satisfaction."

"If I may suggest, Comrade Major, we shall have to be careful about what we do to the woman. The Comrade Colonel has the good offices of many powerful people."

Semachev's voice was as cold as a chill Arctic wind: "I shall do the worrying about Comrade Anakov's powerful friends and *you* will carry out my orders. Do I make myself understood, Comrade?"

"Yes, Comrade."

"Thank you. Now return to your car and wait for him."

Without another word, Valentinov climbed out into the cold of the night.

Fowler was at the mews house when Logan eventually returned.

"Had a nice time?" he said in greeting.

"So-so. I think you would have been pleased with my acting. Priakin came on very strong and I played the shy, retiring virgin, but not so shy that I would not be prepared to do a little cautious dabbling. He wanted to spend the night with me. I'm sure of it."

"And?"

"I said no. He gave me the disappointment act and I relented. I said I would see him tomorrow. I'm sure he thinks he manipulated me into that decision."

Fowler gave one of his brief smiles. "Excellent. By the way, I think you may be due for some attention from friend Semachev," he went on mildly. "He followed you this evening."

"I know. I saw the car."

"We put a Rover openly on his tail so he gave up . . . for now. I think he's about to pull something. Be careful."

The green eyes were luminous. "I'll be careful."

"Try not to kill him here if he gets too close. Talking of which," Fowler went on, "are you bringing Priakin back here tomorrow night?"

"I don't know what I might do. It depends on the situation. Why? Are we going to videotape?"

Fowler looked at her reprovingly. "My dear Logan. Who do you think we are? The KGB? Besides, as he's going to die anyway, what need have we of such things?"

Logan stared at Fowler levelly. "So he is my target."

"Did I say that?"

"No. But you haven't said he isn't."

Fowler's own eyes gleamed behind his glasses. "Don't worry, Logan. It will all come out in the wash."

"And that's my answer?"

"For now, yes." Fowler stood up from the sofa where Logan had found him when she'd returned. "I must be going. I'm sure you'd like some sleep. Don't bother to see me out."

Logan had not been sitting, but had been pacing around from time to time as she had conversed with Fowler, something wild on a leash. Now, she stopped before him, eyes fixed upon his.

"Where's Pross?"

Fowler's fleeting smile sped across his features. "Really, Logan. You are getting somewhat fond of that young man. Worry not. He's in safe hands. Now I really must leave you. Have fun tomorrow." He glanced at his watch. "Silly me. It's already today."

Logan watched him leave. When she heard the door click shut at the bottom of the stairs, she kicked her shoes off savagely. Both sailed into the air. One landed harmlessly in a corner: the other crashed into an ornamental lamp, shattering it.

She stared at the pieces indifferently. She had not paid for it anyway.

"Mr. Milner! Are you awake?" The knocking and the voice had come almost together.

Pross's eyes sprang open, as if surprised to find himself still alive. Years of the Dawn Patrol's morning raids had conditioned him. His faculties were almost instantly on stream.

"Yes," he called in answer.

"Good," Lene said. "Please get ready if you wish for some breakfast. Your flight is in a little more than an hour."

"Right."

He glanced at his watch on the bedside table. 05.50. He yawned, climbed out of bed. He'd had a very comfortable night. So these were Fowler's people, after all. He felt immensely relieved, and tried not to think of his family.

He thought of Logan instead, and wondered where she was.

At six o'clock, Lene was back outside the door. "Mr. Milner, are you ready?"

"Yes."

"Good." She came in. "Ah. You are very quick."

Pross smiled at her. She looked as fresh as the night before. "Ready when you are," he said.

"Okay." She smiled back at him. "Your breakfast is prepared. There is just enough time. There will be no formalities at the airport so you do not have to be there until fifteen minutes before. My colleague will make sure you are on time."

"Glad to hear it," Pross said, and followed her out. He gave the room a final glance and wondered who the next occupant would be.

A very special hotel.

The excellent breakfast took fifteen minutes, then it was time to leave. The civilian arrived, wearing the same coat. It was as if he'd worn it all night, standing stiffly somewhere in a dark corner waiting to be switched on again with the coming of day. Lene came to the door.

She held out her hand. "Goodbye Mr. Milner. Have a safe journey."

Pross shook the hand. "Thank you for looking after me so well."

Her eyes twinkled briefly. "I am pleased you think so." A quick smile, and she was gone.

The civilian took his suitcase and said, "Please get in, Mr. Milner."

It was the same police car, but not the same driver. Pross got into the back while the man in the fawn coat put his case into the boot. Then the man was coming round to the front to get in next to the policeman. The driver started the engine as the man clipped on his belt. The BMW shot off with a startled squawk of tyres, hurtled down the quiet, damp street. It had rained during the night and the road still glistened darkly with its passing.

The car turned right, and Pross saw flashes of blue dancing off the wet buildings. The policeman had turned on his roof beacon, but had kept his siren quiet. He did not need it. What traffic there was at that time of the day gave the BMW a wide berth.

Buildings on either side streamed past in a blur. Pross tried not to think of Grazziella dell'Orobianchi. Why, he wondered, was he always being driven by maniacs?

"Mr. Milner. Mr. Milner!"

Pross opened his eyes. The civilian had twisted round to look at him.

"Why were your eyes closed, Mr. Milner?" The man was staring at him unblinkingly.

"I was just thinking," Pross said, trying to sound casual.

"Ah. I see. I have your ticket for München." He handed it over. "The boarding pass is inside. We shall be going straight to the plane."

"Thank you," Pross said.

The man nodded once. *"Bitte."*

The car hurled itself round a corner. See Berlin and die, Pross thought grimly. See Berlin? All he could see were blurs.

The man was saying, "Please listen carefully, Mr. Milner." He spoke calmly, completely ignoring the fact that the driver was treating the streets of the city like his own personal race-track. Every now and then bursts of German came over the police radio. No one spoke to it. "When you get to München, go through customs normally and wait for your valise. When you have picked it up, go to the check-in area, walk right to the end towards the domestic flights exit. There is a waiting area with seats and a bookshop. Wait there until exactly fifteen minutes past nine by the clock near the departure board. By the time you have got there, I do not think you will be waiting for more than perhaps five or six minutes.

"At fifteen past nine, you will go through to the toilets. There is a passage at the other end of the waiting area, between two shops. Go down to the toilets. Someone will meet you with your ticket for Zurich."

"And if he's not there?"

"Someone will be there."

"You're sure of that?"

The man's eyes were neutral. "I am sure," he said in his calm voice.

The BMW cornered on two wheels.

The man said, "He is a very good driver. Better, I think, than his colleague last night. You think so, yes?"

Was the man laughing at him? The lips showed nothing. Pross said, "He's brilliant."

"Brilliant." The man seemed to test the word. "Brilliant. Yes. So, Mr. Milner. You have understood?"

"Perfectly."

"Good. You will have to wait until 13.45 for your next flight. You will be taken care of until then. It has all been arranged."

Pross nodded, not trusting himself to speak as the BMW briefly sped through traffic, going the wrong way. Cars pulled over to the side to make way for it.

The man had turned to the front again. "Soon we shall be at Tegel," came his voice over the roar of the racing engine.

Had he been inclined to, Pross would have appreciated the crisp, neat manner in which the specially rigged automatic transmission went through the gears, but his mind was on other things: his continuing survival. Much to his surprise, they arrived in one piece.

At the airport, the car was driven into the same compound as on the previous night. All three climbed out. The civilian retrieved Pross's case from the boot and led the way into the building. The policeman brought up the rear. Once inside, the policeman remained in an office while the man in the fawn coat delivered Pross to the waiting aircraft. The suitcase had been sent to the hold.

"Have a safe flight, Mr. Milner." The eyes were neutral, but the hint of a smile appeared at the corners of his mouth.

"Thank you," Pross said, and held out his hand. "And thanks for the hotel."

The man shook the hand briefly. "A pleasure," he said, and turned away.

Pross started after him briefly, before entering the aircraft. They had made it with fifteen minutes to spare.

Pross smiled wryly to himself as he went towards his seat. There was still nothing to prove conclusively that he had been looked after by Fowler's people. No reason at all why — just supposing Lene and Co. were Russians — they would not let him go in order to find out more about Fowler's operation, while still keeping tabs on him. No reason at all why any one of his fellow passengers should not be a shadower or a tail or whatever nomenclature Fowler gave such people.

He found the seat number that corresponded with the one on his boarding card. 23A. A non-smoker, and right next to a left-hand window. The outer seats of the row of three were already taken, and he had to disturb the occupants in order to get in. The aisle seat had been given to a pretty, slim young woman in business attire, and the centre to a tough-looking youngish man with a mass of dark hair. He seemed well over six feet. Pross worried a little about that.

Pross sat down, fastened his seatbelt. He looked out of the window. He had a fine view of the whole of the port wing and beyond. He wasn't sure whether that was a good thing. He told himself he was not going to fly the aircraft mentally. The pilots were quite capable.

He glanced to his right, and saw the big man next to him begin to fidget as the engines began to spool up. He glanced down. The skin at the base of the man's thumbnails seemed blistered. He soon realised why. They were not blisters. Each thumb was alternately digging nervously at its neighbour. Take-off jitters.

Pross felt better.

The aircraft, a Boeing 727, had been substituted for the smaller 737 normal for that route, and was therefore not particularly full. Pross tried to see if he could spot anyone who looked like a shadow, but gave up after a while. Craning his neck round would only alert such an individual. He settled in his seat as the aircraft surged forward on its take-off run, and once more felt vulnerable. As it tilted its nose into the sky at the beginning of a steep climb, he found himself wishing yet again for Logan's presence.

The 727 climbed through cloud cover and broke into brilliant sunshine. Pross watched the upward tilt of the wing as the plane continued to gain height. The square shape of the in-board high-speed aileron lifted briefly as the aircraft banked into a gentle left turn before settling onto the new course. Then it levelled out.

The cloud cover had now become a petrified white dunefield far below and stretching to the horizon. Here and there in the distance, great protuberances pockmarked the seemingly endless carpet like mountain peaks in an alpine landscape. Pross wondered if that was how it would seem in Nepal.

He knew precious little about that country—or Afghanistan, except that Gurkhas came from one and the other was crawling with Russians. The Gurkhas at least, were friendly. He tried not to think of being blown out of the sky among the inhospitable ranges of the Himalayas.

A movement across the cloudscape caught his eye.

Just ahead of the wing tip and far below, almost skimming the white dunefield, a speck was travelling on a parallel course. Behind it streamed its perpetually spiralling contrail, even whiter than the background against which it moved. The visibility was so good Pross could clearly see the moving helix of the condensed vapour stretching far behind the distant aircraft.

As he watched, he felt a sudden quickening of his pulse. The speck had now become a target upon which he was about to swoop. Unconsciously, he had begun to see the cloud carpet and the sky above it as a battleground. His eyes roamed the distance, picking out tufts of nimbus below and streaks of cirrostratus above, like an infantryman seeking out cover. His eyes followed the swiftly moving shape of the other aircraft, imagining it to be his quarry. He felt himself move outside the 727 to plunge in a curving attack upon his prey.

Then he felt eyes upon him. He turned, saw the big man looking at him concernedly.

"You are alright?" the man asked. He had a soft voice that belied his tough exterior.

"What? Oh, yes. Yes." Pross felt sheepish, and hoped it didn't show. "Why do you ask?"

"Your eyes. They look at nothing, so I think you are ill." Pross smiled at him. "Day-dreaming."

"Day . . . dream? Ah." The man nodded, smiled. "*Tagestraum*. Yes. I understand."

No you don't, Pross thought as he looked out of the window again.

But the target had gone. The emptiness of the sky and the striated cloudfield greeted his eyes once more. It was a friendly sky; but one day, if Fowler could be believed, it could become inimical to Western helicopters operating beneath that cloudbase, easy prey for Anakov's *Hellhounds*.

He reclined the back of his seat slightly, settled himself more comfortably, and closed his eyes.

Friendly sky. Not if the 727 was still in East German airspace, it wasn't. Perhaps the contrail had belonged to an Ilyushin bomber on a training flight. Its crew were expendable, just as he was.

He smiled tightly at his grim joke as the 727 continued to wing him smoothly south towards Munich.

They landed on time and Pross stared out of his window as the plane taxied back towards the red sprawl of the terminal building. No one had approached him throughout the flight.

When he left the aircraft, he followed the instructions he had received in Berlin. He went through customs unhindered, picked up his suitcase from baggage reclaim, and went to the check-in area. It was as he had been told.

He walked towards the domestic waiting lounge. Ahead of him, two policemen in olive-green trousers and avocado-green shirts were patrolling. One of them, in addition to the holstered pistol attached to his hip, carried an automatic rifle slung across his back. Pross found it unnerving to see policemen so nakedly armed.

He walked on past the policemen, who looked ridiculously friendly, and into the lounge. Everything was as the man in the fawn coat had said. Seating was a series of chrome frames arranged in rows, and upholstered in black to give six individual chairs abreast. Pross took one, and was surprised to find it very comfortable. He sat facing the clock. He amused himself by watching the departure board go through its digital choreography. Within the chorus of German, he heard American voices. He didn't feel any less isolated.

At exactly nine-fifteen, he stood up, turned and walked through the passage between the delicatessen and the camera shop, to the toilets. There was a wooden barrier across the entrance.

"GESCHLOSSEN," it said.

Even Pross could work that one out. The man in Berlin had said nothing about a barrier and the place being closed. Pross remained irresolutely where he was for brief moments. A flight of steps began just beyond the barrier, going down and turning out of sight.

The man had said someone would be waiting. Perhaps the barrier didn't matter. Perhaps there were workmen down there. The man in Berlin could not possibly know when the airport authorities would decide to work on their toilets. There were all sorts of reasons for the barrier.

Pross decided he might as well go past it. It was either that or be stuck in this place like a lemon.

He inched his way past, made his way down the steps and stopped aghast as he entered the lavatory proper.

A man was dragging a limp body of another man by the armpits. The man's head jerked towards Pross, eyes cold and dangerous. They were the palest green Pross had ever seen. Pross sensed his mouth was hanging open.

Christ, he was thinking. *Christ!*

The man snapped, "Milner?"

"Er . . . yes."

"You were told nine-fifteen." Not an English voice, but

very good English.

"It *is* nine-fifteen. Past that now."

"Shit! Give me a few moments to dispose of this."

The man continued his interrupted work and hauled the body into a cubicle. He propped it onto the seat, then shut the door while still inside. The lock clicked home; then the man was climbing out over the top. He dropped to the floor, came towards Pross who unconsciously backed away.

The man noted the reaction, seemed amused, but the eyes remained cold. His breath came quickly.

"Is . . . is he dead?" Pross asked, thinking of the policemen upstairs, particularly of the one with the rifle. Imagine being shot in an airport loo by a German policeman.

The green-eyed man said, "What do you think?" Then as if feeling further explanation was necessary, went on, "He was waiting for me. He knew I would be here. We fought." He shrugged. "He lost. Now let us get out of here. I have a car outside. We shall keep away from this place until it is time for your flight to Zurich. I have your ticket. Come." Without waiting to see if Pross would follow, he hurried up the steps.

Even as he obeyed, Pross questioned the wisdom of it. The dead man in the cubicle could well have been his real contact, but he had no choice but to follow. Had he wanted to, the green-eyed man could have killed him just as easily. Just as in Berlin, he was once again at the mercy of individuals whose allegiance was a complete mystery to him.

At the top, the man moved the barrier out of the way. "Open for business again," he said emotionlessly.

"What about the policemen?" Pross queried urgently in a low voice. He could only hope he was talking to the right contact.

"They are not your worry. Come."

There was a way out without the necessity of going back through the lounge. The man hurried, Pross followed.

"We must get to the car quickly," the man said. "There may be a partner watching."

"Who was he?"

"Someone who didn't want you to get to Zurich." The pale green eyes raked Pross before turning away.

The man smoothed his clothes down with quick hands just before they left the building. They walked out, seeming for all the world like a couple of businessmen. Pross hoped the expression of calm he had forced upon his own features did not appear too strained. The man had no such problems. He was entirely relaxed.

Logan, Pross thought ruefully, would have known exactly how to cope with the situation.

"This is my car," the man said. "Give me your case. I shall put it in the boot."

The car, parked on the terminal access road, was a big grey BMW saloon. Pross handed his suitcase over and the man put it away.

"Get in," he said to Pross.

Pross got into the front with him, put on his belt, and steeled himself for another rubber-scorching drive. He was not disappointed. He decided it was his fate to be subjected to such experiences. At last the man parked the car in a sidestreet in the Schwabing district, just off Leopoldstrasse. Throughout the journey, there had been silence in the car.

"We get out here," the man said. "We'll leave your case. We're only going in there."

"There" was a café outside which the car had stopped. The man chose a table away from the plateglass window, but with a full view of the parked BMW. The only other customer was a middle-aged woman sitting well away from them.

"We can see if anyone comes near," the man explained.

Pross nodded as he sat down.

"Are you hungry?" the man went on. "A strong coffee, perhaps? You do not look well."

"What do you expect?"

"Ah. You are thinking of the man at the airport." The pale green eyes were quite undisturbed. "It was necessary. There were people like him waiting at many airports in

Germany, and outside. In Berlin, Hamburg, Köln . . . even at Westerland on the island of Sylt, and at Schipol. There were others in France and, I am certain, in Switzerland."

Pross couldn't believe it. A whole network of people on the lookout for him? Fowler had not warned him about this. But would it have helped him to know? Or would it have frightened him even more? He believed the latter.

He said, "What do you mean—"

"One moment, please," the man interrupted. A waitress had come to their table. "Would you like something?"

"Just coffee," Pross said, trying not to think of the man at the airport. He had seen dead people before. On his previous mission for Fowler, a man had been shot dead in the face next to him in a car. He himself had killed too; but that had been in the Lynx. He had not really seen those he had fired his rockets and guns at. He would never come accustomed to it, as this pale-eyed man facing him obviously had.

The man nodded, spoke to the waitress in rapid German that, to Pross's untutored ear, sounded faultless. She went away to prepare their order.

Pross said, "What do you mean they *were* at those airports?"

"They were expected, and neutralised."

"Neutralised? You mean like the man in the toilet?" Neutralised, Pross thought. Some euphemism.

His companion shrugged. "It is a risk we all take."

"Not me, mate. I don't take risks. This is your little game. Play it for all you're worth if that's what turns you on. I'm strictly temporary. I have a family to go back to."

The pale eyes seemed to smile. "Many of us have families too. Ah. Here's your coffee, and my breakfast."

Pross stared out thoughtfully as the McDonnell Douglas MD80 taxied to its take-off point. He had again been given a left-hand window seat, except that now he was sitting a little ahead of the leading edge of the wing. He had a practically uninterrupted view.

The aircraft taxied past the executive jet park. Pross saw several Lears and Cessnas. Lots of rich jet-setters, he thought idly. The MD80 reached its point, turned and began its take-off run almost immediately. Within moments, it seemed, in the grip of its powerful acceleration, it had launched itself into the air.

Pross watched the earth below tilt as the plane went into its steep climbing turn. Soon, it was climbing through tufts of cloud that raced past, while the landscape played hide and seek. Then it was again bright sky above a blanket of cumulus.

A rustle to his right distracted him. He looked. The seat next to him was occupied by a man who looked like a rising young executive. He had opened up the *Zücher Zeitung* and was deeply engrossed in it. Next to the man sat a young woman who looked like his secretary. They were certainly traveling together for they had boarded just ahead of Pross. The man had been carrying both boarding passes. The young woman was quite pretty. Lucky for some.

Pross allowed himself the wry thought before returning his attention to the unpressurised sky outside. In his mind, the pale-eyed man's words still echoed.

Almost right up to the moment of his return to the airport, he had not fully trusted his companion. He still did not know who the man was. No absolute proof that he was one of Fowler's.

During the drive back, the man had said, "I don't know what your part is in this operation, Milner, and I don't want to. My job is to look after you in Munich. Once you're on that plane, that will be my part done. I've seen you looking at me with a mixture of distaste and wariness. I can understand the wariness. I'd be the same in your place. The distaste, I know, is because of the man I've had to kill. Well let me tell you, Milner. My job is to keep you alive for this section. When the time comes for you to keep yourself alive, you'll kill too." The pale green eyes had given Pross a raking sweep. "Won't you, Milner?"

Pross had said nothing. There had been no evidence at the airport, when they'd arrived, to show that the dead man had been discovered.

Pross wondered now whether he was still sitting there, silently occupying the cubicle.

Chapter Ten

London, 12.45. Semachev was not at peace with the world.

"All of them!" he said savagely. "Every one in position, and every one taken. Some of them got wet."

Valentinov, understanding the euphemism for a killing, chose his words cautiously. "How many dead, Comrade?"

Semachev took a long time replying as he fumed. He felt little sorrow for those who had been killed. He was angry because he had been outmanoeuvred. Months of preparation had seemingly gone to waste. He needed something to take the bitter taste from his mouth.

Semachev and Valentinov were in the big house Semachev had rented under an assumed name and nationality. It was close to the one where Anakov was quartered.

At last, Semachev made reply to Valentinov's question. "Five went down."

Valentinov was shocked. *"Five?* And the others?"

"They might as well be dead for all the use they are to me. The West now has bargaining counters for future exchanges."

Semachev spoke with a tight anger. Valentinov knew his superior well enough to say nothing that would bring on explosion directed his way. Semachev would have very strongly upon his mind the fact that such a disaster would not go unnoticed by those whose decisions could send a man literally out into the cold for life. Semachev would have to make good soon, and in this quest it would be fatal for anyone who got in his way or who incurred his displeasure.

Valentinov, in an attempt to say something constructive,

asked, "Is the contact reliable?"

It was the wrong thing to say. The contact was Semachev's own recruit. Questioning the contact's reliability was like questioning Semachev's own decision-making capabilities; a reckless undertaking. Valentinov wished he could have crammed the offending words back into his mouth.

Semachev's pebble eyes bored into him. "Are you questioning my judgment?"

"No, Comrade," Valentinov said quickly, "I think highly of the Comrade's judgment."

"The contact," Semachev went on coldly as if Valentinov had not spoken, "has been screened, and is of prime quality; well placed for this operation. I do not expect to hear you voice further doubts. Do you understand, Comrade Valentinov?"

"Perfectly, Comrade Major." Valentinov was not suicidal, whatever the nature of his defects in Semachev's eyes. "Perfectly," he repeated, just to make sure.

"We shall pull in the woman."

Valentinov did not think that a good idea, but wisely kept his council for the time being.

"Have you no comment?" Semachev demanded bitingly, spoiling for a fight.

"No, Comrade Major."

"You are not a village idiot, Valentinov! Don't answer me like one. I know you want to say something. Spit it out!"

Valentinov knew that Semachev was now at his most dangerous. Smarting from what had happened, he could become vicious and unpredictable. There were those who would say that Semachev worked best when angry. Valentinov knew better. What Semachev did best when angry was to kill people; friends and enemies alike. Valentinov could remember a job in Sweden that had begun to go wrong. Semachev had decided that the operation's second-in-command, a senior Captain, had been responsible. Semachev had shot the unfortunate man on the western shore of Stora Le, near the Norwegian border. As far as Valentinov knew, the body was still in the lake. Semachev

167

in a bad mood was poison.

Despite his own trepidation, Valentinov felt he would have to make some kind of comment, if only to defuse his superior a little. Besides, pulling in Anakov's woman was fraught with all sorts of dangers. Despite the way Semachev was treating him, Anakov was still a highly favoured Colonel and not a man to let such things pass unheeded. If Semachev got it wrong, it would be prudent to have registered an objection. The trick was to do so without alerting Semachev to the reasons for it.

Valentinov said, "Perhaps the Comrade Major should consult with the Comrade Colonel before . . ."

Semachev had a highly developed instinct for survival too, and could see a caveat while it was still beyond the horizon.

"Worried about your neck?" he said with contempt. The pebble eyes were lifeless. "Worry about me, Comrade. I am a greater danger to you. I am not happy about that woman, and when I am not happy, I must find the reason. For the moment she is the reason."

Valentinov showed some courage, and risked his neck. "And if we are wrong?" the "we" was a sort of apology for daring to make the suggestion.

"I am not wrong," Semachev remarked with cold finality.

Logan spotted them early, and did nothing about it. The green 2CV stuttered its way through the patience-defeating traffic system of Soho as she looked for somewhere to park. At last, she found a space in a cul-de-sac just off the faded glory of Carnaby Street market. She parked the little car half on the pavement, locked it, and set off through the pedestrian way that led into the market itself. She knew her shadowers would see the car and believe that was where she had gone. They could spend a good half hour entertaining themselves trying to find her in the crowd of milling tourists.

She smiled to herself as she walked quickly away from the market. She knew they were going to pick her up.

After what Fowler had told her about the clean sweep in Europe, it was only to be expected. Fowler had not gone into detail about what had happened, only that it was linked to Priakin. No mention had been made of Pross.

Logan was in her Minty persona, except that she was carrying the magnum in her bag. She was now about to do something she was most reluctant to do; but there was little choice. She was going to get rid of the gun. Lady Araminta Dilke-Weston would have had a very tough time indeed explaining away such artillery.

She entered a large department store in Regent Street, took the escalators up several floors. She knew just where she would hide the weapon.

On the top floor, Logan went into the ladies' toilets, found an empty cubicle. On a peg were brown paper bags for the disposal of sanitary towels. She took one, put the magnum in it. In another, she put her spare ammunition. She then lifted the top of the disposal bin, placed the gun and bullets in it, put the lid back on. She tried not to think of what it would be like in there when she came back to retrieve the gun. She also hoped it would still be there. Perhaps the lavatory attendant would not empty the bin for some time, otherwise the store would be in for a shock.

Logan smiled wryly. There would be some panic among the management as they came to the understandable but wrong conclusion that they had stumbled upon a terrorist plot; but that could not be helped. She did not think the Russians would hold her for long, so she expected to be back before the store closed. She hoped.

As though taking leave of a valued friend, she reluctantly left the cloakroom with the gun safely hidden, and made her way down to street level. The attendant had been nowhere to be seen.

She returned to Carnaby Street and began to saunter, stopping now and then to scrutinise the wares on a stall, or a clothes-rack. Within minutes, her shadows had picked her up again. She towed them behind her for another fifteen slow minutes; then when she had judged they were becoming impatient, she went back to the car.

169

They were on her just as she was unlocking the door. "Leave it!" Semachev commanded in a low voice. "Do not scream. I have a gun on you. It is silenced. You will be dead before anyone is aware of it." He let her briefly see the automatic pistol. It was indeed silenced.

Logan allowed her eyes to open wide with fear behind her fake glasses. Her anxiety was not totally false. She had not expected them to behave so drastically. A gun kidnap was pushing it a bit. On the other hand, she reasoned with some chagrin, it was very neat.

She went into a great act of opening and closing her mouth in a terrified manner, with no words coming out.

"Good," Semachev said with satisfaction. "We understand each other. Come with us, please."

Logan went meekly with them, and they pushed her into their car, a dark blue Mercedes that had been parked round the corner from the 2CV.

"Who . . . who are you?" she whispered at them in a frightened voice. "What do you want with me? This . . . this is London. You . . . you can't just take people off . . . off the streets and . . ."

"Shut up! Of course we can. I want to hear no more from you until I ask you to answer my questions. And you will answer. I should tell you that I hate the privileged classes . . . of any country."

As the Mercedes sped away, taking chances with traffic, Logan wondered if she made the wrong decision in leaving the magnum. Then she reversed her thoughts.

Semachev was searching minutely through her bag.

Anakov was looking forward to the evening. He was certain things would go better with Araminta. This feeling of anticipation helped ease the exasperation he felt, because of Semachev's continuing failure to come up with anything that looked remotely like some measure of success on the mission. Time was ticking away.

Anakov felt a brief chill of anxiety, shrugged it off. No need to start feeling despondent, but something had to show soon. Even Sogovyi might not be able to keep the wolves at bay. Sogovyi, to safeguard his own neck, would probably join the pack. It was the way things were.

A noise made Anakov look round. He had been standing near a window, looking down into the street three floors below. From his vantage point, the house were Semachev and his KGB colleagues lived was easily observed.

Garshin had entered the room. Semachev had left him as a guard dog. Anakov saw him more as a jailer.

Anakov said, "What is it, Garshin? Do you think I am about to jump out of this window?"

Garshin looked uncomfortable, retreated. Anakov smiled to himself. He could hear soft conversation going on in another part of the house; Russian conversation. Members of the house staff.

He looked out of the window once more, stared incuriously at Semachev's house. He had no doubt that many KGB activities to which he was not privy went on in there. There were many things, he thought with a sense of helplessness, that Semachev kept from him. No matter. It would all be resolved on their return home.

Not for the first time, he felt part of him wishing for the KGB Major's failure. It was unfortunate that Semachev's failure was also linked to his own.

He sighed. They should have given him a GRU unit, as he'd wished.

Anakov knew nothing about what had occurred on the continent; for the simple reason that Semachev had chosen not to tell him. Anakov did not even know that those operatives had been placed in position.

The oblivious Anakov continued his casual study of the street. Parked across the way was a line of four cars, pointing in the direction of traffic. At the moment, the street was quiet. Anakov watched with mounting interest as a bareheaded man wearing an army-type camouflaged field jacket approached the cars. There was something furtive about him that made Anakov continue to watch.

The man was obviously a thief, for he went up each car in turn and surreptitiously tried the door. He was lucky the third time. Not only was the door of the car, a white Fiat, open, so was the front window on the passenger side.

Anakov was like a scientist studying bacteria under a microscope. Western petty crime in the act of taking place. His amused attention was totally captured. He felt no sympathy for the owner of the car. The door and window should not have been left open.

The man leaned in swiftly after a quick glance around, picked up what looked like a soft briefcase and ran.

Anakov shook his head. Not only had the car been left open, leaving something valuable in such plain sight was bordering on criminal negligence. He smiled at what he thought Semachev would have said had he witnessed what had just taken place. Semachev would have commented that back home a car could have been left open, with briefcase in full view; because there was no crime . . . unless what had been left happened to be a set of ballpoint pens, Anakov thought drily.

Anakov's smile widened as the thought continued to amuse him. He remained at the window, waiting to see whether the owner of the car would realise that he had suffered a loss; and it was because of that casual car thief that Anakov remained where he was long enough to witness something far more serious taking place.

The sudden appearance of the familiar dark blue Mercedes pulling swiftly to a halt outside the house where Semachev was staying now drew his attention like a magnet. Disbelievingly, he watched as Semachev climbed out of the back, firmly holding on to someone who followed him out, to take her into the house with him.

Anakov left the room at a run.

Logan was shown none too gently into a small bare room with a single straight-backed chair in it; and no windows.

"You will wait here," the brutish Semachev snapped at her.

The door was shut firmly as he went out. She thought she heard the lock turn.

She looked about her, as a bewildered innocent would. Mindful of hidden video cameras. From the ceiling hung a solitary bright light and in one corner was the sort of powerful lamp that could be found in a photographic studio. The room had a bare wooden floor. It was also cold.

Logan hugged herself for warmth. It was what Minty would do. Semachev had taken her coat away. She kept a look of terrified bewilderment upon her face.

Minutes after she had been brought in, there was a commotion in the house. Voices were raised in loud argument. Soon she recognised the voices of Semachev and Priakin, yelling at each other in Russian.

Logan could speak three foreign languages, two very well, the third reasonably so. Neither of those was Russian, but she could recognise the language easily and could understand snatches of it. Assuming that what was going on outside was an act for her benefit, she maintained the frightened expression upon her face.

"Where have you got her, Semachev?" the man she knew as Priakin was shouting. "I saw you bring her in. How dare you take such an action without first consulting me?"

"If the Comrade Colonel would allow me to tell him, I was about to inform him of developments."

"Don't give me any of your nonsense, Major! You had no intention of telling me anything! Are your efforts to find that helicopter and its pilot such dismal failures that you resort to dragging harmless citizens of a foreign country off its streets, in a desperate attempt to find clues? Do you seriously intend to find that helicopter in the peace camp?"

Through the door, Logan could hear the derision in Priakin's voice. Much of the fine detail of what had been said had been lost to her, but the salient points had been picked up. She now knew Priakin was a Colonel. KGB? The comments about a helicopter and its pilot could only mean the Lynx, and Pross.

She felt several emotions go through her and fought to keep the outward expressions of fear upon her face, for the benefit of anyone secretly observing her. Deep down, however, it was another matter altogether. For if Priakin and Semachev were in a real argument, it meant that not only had Fowler lied to her, he had also deliberately sent Pross into danger, without having her as a back-up. She had been used to keep Priakin happy while Pross was sent off God knew where.

She kept her anger off her face as she tried to pick up more snatches of the conversation. She decided she would have to find out the truth about Priakin, when she got out of here. She was certain she would. Unless Semachev really knew who she was, he would be forced to let her go.

If the row going on outside was a piece of theatre, it meant that Semachev was clutching at straws. If not, he was still in trouble, and had upset his Colonel to boot.

But Logan did not feel complacent. Semachev was a pro. Something about her was worrying him. She would have to be extremely careful.

"Comrade Anakov," Semachev was saying harshly. "I shall make a full report about this, with my own recommendations!"

"And I shall make a report, Major. I can assure you that *my* recommendations will be considered by a suitably appropriate authority. Now release Lady Dilke-Weston immediately! And that, Comrade, is a direct order."

"The Comrade Colonel will regret this."

"We shall see, Major. We shall see."

No, Logan thought, stunned. *It's not an act. His real name is Anakov! You owe me a bloody explanation, Fowler.*

The key was turning in the lock, the door was flung open, and Anakov strode in, followed by ferocious-looking Semachev.

Logan went into her own act. "Geörgy!" she cried, almost on the brink of tears. "What . . . what's going on? Who *are* those men who brought me to this place?" She shrunk from Semachev.

Anakov, maintaining his Hungarian façade, came towards her with an embarrassed smile upon his face. He opened his arms.

"Araminta. I am so, so sorry for what has happened. These men are my colleagues as well as my . . . how

174

would you say it . . . bodyguards, and perhaps a little over-zealous." His arms dropped slowly to his sides as she shrunk away from him too.

Logan hugged herself tightly, inching along a wall, towards the door. Her eyes looked trapped behind her glasses.

"Over-zealous?" she screamed suddenly. Both Semachev and Anakov jumped with the unexpectedness of it. *"Over-zealous?* Is that what you call kidnapping? It's an offence over here. Do you . . . do you know that? My father is a lord and he can make a lot of trouble for you!"

Logan did not miss the venomous look Anakov gave Semachev.

"Araminta," he began pacifyingly.

"Don't! Don't come near me!" Logan felt perhaps she shouldn't push it too far. She was not out of the woods yet. Semachev did not look as if the threat of a peer of the Realm's wrath would make him lose a fraction of a second's sleep. "Just . . . just let me out of here," she went on in a more subdued voice. "Okay? Just let me out."

"Yes, yes," Anakov said. "Araminta, I knew nothing of this. I am so . . . ashamed? Yes, ashamed. I am ashamed of this. Please allow me to take you home."

"No thank you! I'll make my own way. I don't want to go into another of your cars. I'll find a taxi."

Anakov gave Semachev another searing look. "Of course. Please come with me."

She pointed at Semachev. "He took my bag and my coat. Tell him to give them back."

Anakov said coldly to Semachev, "The lady's coat and her bag. Immediately!"

Semachev glared, but he went out to do as he was told.

Anakov led Logan to the front door where Semachev met them with the bag and the coat. He handed them over silently.

Anakov said, as they left the house, "You must allow me to make amends." He helped her with her coat.

Logan let him, with the right amount of reluctance.

"You must," he said again.

She'd been making a great play of looking up and down

the street for a taxi, knowing she would have to get to the main road to stand a chance of getting one.

Now, she stared at him. "You expect me to continue seeing you after *this?*" She turned briefly to look back at the house. Semachev's pebble eyes were balefully upon her.

For a fleeting moment, something in each pair of eyes challenged the other. Logan saw a brief confusion flit across the brutish features, and knew then that the next time they met, they would be in combat. Semachev was still trying to work it out when she turned to Anakov once more. She hoped the magnum was still safe in its hiding place and felt an urgent need to get back to it.

She jerked a contemptuous thumb briefly over her shoulder. "He's not going to try that again, is he?:

Anakov was still looking embarrassed. "No. I shall see to it that he does not."

"Fine. Well . . . I'm off."

"Please. Will you not let me explain?"

"Why do you need bodyguards anyway?" It was the kind of sudden, tangential question that would be expected of Minty.

"May I explain later?"

Hesitation. A woman unsure of herself. "I ought to be really angry with you, Geörgy. I ought to go to the police."

Anakov smiled charmingly, with the right amount of uncertainty. A man who feels he has won. "Shall we meet later?"

"I . . . I don't really feel I should, after what's happened." Logan began moving away from him.

He kept pace with her. "I shall be at the place under the railway arches. I shall be there at seven, and I shall wait until you come."

"I don't know, Geörgy. I don't know." She quickened her pace.

He hung back. "Say you will come."

"We'll have to see." She hurried with urgent steps, as if wanting to put distance between herself and the place of her abduction as quickly as possible.

She knew that, behind her, Anakov was watching with a satisfied smile upon his lips. It was what she wanted. As for Semachev, she knew he would not give up. Next time, she'd be waiting.

Semachev watched her walk down the street, with no expression upon his face. Anakov came up the steps, walked past him.

"Inside, Major."

Semachev took his time, but he re-entered the house and closed the door behind him. He faced the enraged Anakov unflinchingly.

Anakov said, "I have just saved us from a very awkward situation. By your precipitate action, you very nearly destroyed the mission. How I behave towards Western women is none of your affair. Only when I jeopardise the mission, or my actions appear to do so, will you have any justification for interfering. For the moment, the only one of the two of us who seems to endanger what we have come here to do is yourself, *Comrade*. I have managed to persuade her to take no action . . ."

"And do you not find that strange, Comrade?" Semachev took the liberty of interrupting.

"Don't be a bigger fool than you have already shown yourself to be, Major. She is a rather awkward person who is flattered by the attention she receives from me. This is not a unique phenomenon, Semachev. It happens all the time, all over the world, between men and women. A shy man is flattered when he receives attention from an unexpected quarter. The same is true of a woman. At the moment, Araminta is a mass of confusions. Her sense of outrage is in conflict with her desire for male company. By tonight, she will have chosen the latter. I am doing precisely what you want of me, Major. I am keeping very visible in order that you may do your digging. You have so far shown me that you have done little to justify my confidence."

Anakov turned, opened the door, and walked out.

Valentinov, who had been in another room throughout,

177

chose that moment to put in an appearance.

Semachev stared through him. "He is wrong. Something about that woman disturbs me. I intend to find out. And close your mouth, Valentinov. When I need your advice, I'll ask for it."

Valentinov had been about to counsel against antagonising the colonel further. He decided that, in Semachev's frame of mind, discretion was the wiser course.

The taxi dropped Logan off outside the store. She hurried in, bought herself a scarf, got a plastic carrier bag with it, and made her way back up to the lavatory.

The cubicle was occupied.

Curbing her impatience, she entered the one next to it, shut the door, and waited. It seemed ages before she heard flushing, and the cubicle was vacated. She waited until she heard the click of heels leaving. She waited some more. Then she hurried out, entered the one she wanted.

She lifted the lid off the bin. It had received more bags since she'd been in. She would have to feel for the gun and the ammunition. Suppressing a feeling of distaste, she plunged her hand in and began to search.

Ugh, she thought. *The things I do for this bloody country.*

Then her hand felt something firmer than the soft bags about it. The magnum was still there. She pulled out the now-soiled bag which held it, fished once more for the ammunition. For some reason, it had gone deeper and she had to do some rummaging before that too was brought up. She discarded the bags, and wiped both gun and ammunition carefully with lavatory paper. She would give them a proper clean when she got home.

She wrapped the gun and the ammo in the scarf, put them into the plastic bag, then replaced the lid on the bin. She flushed the toilet then went out to give her hands a thorough wash. She left the lavatory just as the attendant was coming in. Even as the door was closing behind her, she heard the first bin being emptied.

She left the store, went back to where she'd left the 2CV. She didn't think Semachev would make his move

178

very soon after the recent one, but she still felt uneasy with the uncleaned magnum lying wrapped up in the plastic bag.

No dramas occurred when she got into the little Citroën and drove home. Only an hour and a half had passed from the time Semachev had kidnapped her.

As soon as she got in, she stripped the gun, cleaned it with great care, and put it together again. She tested the action. It was as beautiful and as smooth as ever. She reloaded. She felt complete once more.

Logan now felt she could turn her mind to what she had inadvertently discovered. She decided she would not ask Fowler about it. He would only throw up a smoke-screen. She'd find out for herself.

She went to the phone, punched in a number. It rang at the other end. The person who answered was the last one she wanted.

"This is Logan."

"Aha. My favourite lady."

Logan shut her eyes briefly. Just her luck that Telford was duty officer. It couldn't be helped. She'd just have to make use of him.

"I'm coming in," she said, and hung up.

She changed out of her Minty guise and became Logan again. Deliberately, she put on a skirt that showed off her legs. For once, she was going to capitalise on the effect they appeared to have on Telford. The thought that Pross liked them too teased at her. She smiled wistfully. It was different with Pross.

She left the news house, and took a taxi to the sleepy square where the Department had its outwardly nondescript offices.

The MD80 came to the end of its fifty-minute flight and landed in cold sunshine at Zurich-Klöten. Pross saw who was waiting for him and groaned inwardly.

"Well, Mr. Milner," Sanders began cheerfully. "Had a good flight?"

Pross waited until they were out of casual earshot

before saying, "Apart from finding dead bodies in airport loos . . . yes, you could say I had a nice flight."

Sanders' manner changed immediately. "Look, Pross—" he began once more, this time in a hard voice.

But Pross interrupted him. *"You* look, Sanders. Nobody told me there would be people at every airport out to stop me, and—"

"Keep your voice down, Pross!" Sanders was looking nervously around, eyes checking out the people about them as they walked through the airport lounge towards the exit. "Would telling you have helped in any way? It would only have served to frighten you."

"I was already bloody frightened."

"You were covered, Pross. All the way."

"Oh yes?"

"Everyone who sat next to you," Sanders said tightly, "was a minder."

This surprised Pross. "On every aircraft?"

"On every one. We're not as inefficient as you would like to think." Sanders could not resist a touch of smugness.

Pross remembered the big man with the nervous thumbs. He described the man to Sanders.

Sanders said, "He was one."

"He was bloody scared of flying."

"It would not have prevented him from doing his job, and that's all that matters." They had now come out of the building. Sanders went on, pointing to a white Jaguar. "That's our car. Get in. Put your suitcase in the front. We're not leaving the airport."

Pross said drily as he complied, "I can tell the good times are over. No one's carried my luggage for me. Lovely weather, isn't it?" he added to the driver who looked stonily back at him.

Pross got into the back next to Sanders. The Jaguar glided away across the tarmac, towards the private aircraft section. The journey was made in silence.

The Jaguar eventually came to a stop next to an Aéorspatiale *Dauphin* helicopter with Swiss civil markings.

"This is where we get out," Sanders said. He was

already opening his door.

Pross climbed out, picked up his suitcase from the front of the car. As soon as he'd shut the door, the Jaguar spurted away, retracing its route.

He turned to Sanders, "Talkative, wasn't he, your driver?"

"Get in, Pross."

"Oh we are in a mood."

Pross climbed into the nine-seater aircraft. Sanders, following behind, did not help him with the case. There were two pilots inside, strapped in and be-headphoned at their stations. They glanced incuriously at Pross, and started up as soon as he and Sanders had settled in.

The helicopter lifted off and began its journey to Betten, in the southern Swiss canton of Valais.

The first thing Logan noted was that Telford's eyes were making a meal of her legs and decided, resignedly, that she would have to put up with it. He would not be enjoying his treat for long.

She chose the friendly approach. "Wake up, Nigel." She smiled at him.

Telford shifted his gaze away from the view with obvious reluctance, and caught the full power of Logan's green eyes.

He cleared his throat. "Well, Logan. It's not often a poor duty officer has the pleasure of seeing you here on a Saturday."

"Unless I happen to be duty officer myself."

"So what's this all about?"

"I've got to check something in the files."

"Whose office?"

"Mr. Fowler's."

"You know he hardly keeps any in there. Mrs. Arundel handles those."

"This is a particular one we're working on and I need the information right away."

They were walking towards Delphine Arundel's office. Telford paused. "Why not get in touch with Mr. Fowler?

181

He should be at his town flat." Telford went on, drily. "He's usually either here, or over there, or travelling from one to the other. You'd think he had no home to go to."

"We'll be meeting later on today," Logan said; then she added the lie: "I don't want to trouble him."

Telford appeared to hesitate. "I'll have to make a report about it, of course."

"For God's sake, Nigel, do you want me to pull rank on you?"

Telford looked at her, and was again caught in the silent blast of her eyes. "Well no . . . but . . . Look. I wish you'd stop treating me like a schoolboy . . ."

"Then stop behaving like one. Open the key safe, then leave me. I'll call you when I'm through. I'll take all responsibility."

They entered the office. Logan stood back while Telford went behind Delphine Arundel's desk. On the wall was a group of push-buttons arranged in order similar to that of a calculator, within an area the size of a cigarette packet. Telford entered a sequence of several numbers. The wrong sequence would trigger off an alarm, bringing armed security officers running. The sequence was changed every day.

The safe clicked open. When closed, the outline of its door was very difficult to detect.

Telford still looked worried as Logan came up. "I'm not sure . . ."

Logan smiled patiently, "You know I'm working closely with Mr. Fowler on this. You've been down to the camp a few times yourself, to keep an eye on things. The other day, you were my back-up. Well this concerns the whole operation, sections of which do not concern you. I'll take the keys I need, you close the safe, and I'll call you when I'm finished. Alright?"

Telford nodded.

Logan reached into the safe, selected three keys. "These will do." One was for a filing cabinet in the office, the others were spare keys for Fowler's desk, and for his office. "Alright, Nigel. Shut the safe, and leave me."

Telford, still in thrall to Logan's friendly manner, did

so. At the door, he said, "I'll be in the duty office."

"Thanks, Nigel. Perhaps when this is all over, I might be able to persuade Mr. Fowler to let us work together. I'm not promising anything. It's just an idea."

Telford smiled at her. "You're on." There was a speculative glint in his eye, however, that served to destroy the feelings of guilt she'd been having because of the deliberate way in which she'd used him.

"You've got a hope," she muttered to herself after he'd gone.

She began with the filing cabinet, looking under Priakin. What she subsequently found merely confirmed the story Fowler had told her. She put the file back, shut and locked the cabinet. Nothing much there. It would have to be Fowler's office.

She went out, walked along a lino-floored corridor until she came to Fowler's small office. She opened it, went in, turned on a light. She shut the door, locked it after her. She went to the desk, inserted the key into the only drawer with a lock. It was a deep one. She pulled the drawer open, and began searching.

At last, she found something. The file had no security markings, but its purple colour gave it all the classification it needed. Only Winterbourne and Fowler, of all Department personnel, would have seen it. Given the stage of things between Fowler and Winterbourne, Logan doubted whether even Winterbourne knew what was in it.

She sat down in Fowler's chair, and began to study the sensitive document.

The file gave Anakov his full, true name, and his rank. It also gave his service history in detail. There were photographs. Some were of Anakov in dress uniform, others of him in his combat flying suit. He looked handsome, she found herself admitting in a detached manner, as she studied the face in the photographs. Another photograph sent a chill through her. It was of the *Hellhound*. She immediately thought of Pross and what, she was now quite positive, Fowler intended him to do.

She read the file thoroughly. Fowler's plan was there to see, even though not set down in fine detail. She was sufficiently familiar with the workings of his mind to know what he was concocting. She also now knew Pross would be going. There was something else.

Fowler had penned a note indicating that he suspected someone in the Department of leakage. No. The note did not say *in*. *Attached* was the word he had used. Attached? She knew of no one from another service who was attached to the Department. Who then did he mean?

Was even her own cover secure? Had the unknown suspect been feeding information to the Russians . . . information that had prompted Semachev's hasty kidnap attempt?

She shook her head slowly. Semachev had not been sure. She was positive he had not received information about her. At least, not yet.

Her knowledge of the technical workings of helicopters was scant, but the apparent performance figures for the *Hellhound* did not require a genius to appreciate what they really meant in terms of actual combat; especially if it meant Pross was going up against such a monster. Anakov's own combat record was frightening.

"Oh Pross," Logan said softly. "You need me."

She tightened her lips in anger as she closed the file, thinking of Fowler's scheming. She replaced the document as she had found it, pushed the drawer home and locked it.

She stood up, turned off all lights, left and locked Fowler's office. She returned to Delphine Arundel's office, called Telford on the phone. Within a couple of minutes, he had joined her.

"All finished?"

She nodded. "Yes. Thank you."

As he went to reopen the safe, he glanced at her curiously. "Are you alright?" He punched at the buttons.

"Yes. Yes. I'm fine."

The safe clicked open.

"Your eyes look different," he said as he pulled at its door.

"They're still green."

He smiled. "Are they ever. But they're different all the

184

same."

She shrugged, put the keys back. Telford shut the safe. "I'm glad that's done," he said with relief.

"Don't worry. I'll tell Mr. Fowler myself. Thanks again, Nigel." Logan began walking out.

Telford followed. "You won't forget to ask him, will you? About working together, I mean."

"I won't."

"I suppose you'll be busy tonight?" he queried hopefully.

"Yes. I will."

"Ah well . . . another time."

"Yes."

There was a brief silence, then Telford said, as if to make conversation, "Do you really believe the Russians use the peace women?"

"Everybody uses them."

Logan was not really listening to Telford. She was thinking about what she had to do.

Chapter Eleven

Pross looked out at the breathtaking Alpine landscape as the big *Dauphin* cruised at 2000 feet. It flew through deep valleys, and the steep, snowclad sides of the hills and mountains seemed to rise from every quarter. On some hillsides, great dark patches showed where the snow had not settled, and there were valleys that showed up a deep rich green where snow had not even fallen. Clusters of tall pines looked like toy cones thrown in a gesture of abandon by a child.

Snow-topped houses looked like icing-coated sweets stuck into a huge bowl of frosted cream that had been whipped so frenziedly, it had flung itself to the edge of the bowl, rising from there in great jagged peaks that hung petrified in the sky.

Sanders noted Pross's scrutiny of the mottled landscape.

"This is like the kind of terrain you'll be seeing, only much more so," Sanders began. "There's someone waiting for us who'll tell you all about it. He's been there."

Pross glanced round. "Where?"

"Nepal."

"Wonderful."

"I'd pay attention to him if I were you."

"You're not me, Sanders."

Another silence followed. Pross continued to stare out of the aircraft, thinking about how he could best use the Lynx against the *Hellhound*. The more he thought about it, the less he liked the options.

The helicopter's roomy passenger cabin had six comfortably upholstered seats arranged in rows of three abreast, opposite each other. Further to the rear, the remaining seats had been removed. Pross assumed that was to make room for load-carrying. He was sitting in the left-hand seat, facing rearwards. It reminded him a little of travelling in RAF transport aircraft.

Sanders was sitting directly opposite, trying not to look at him. The silence continued.

Suddenly, the *Dauphin* banked sharply to the right, losing height. Pross heard the sudden loud scream of a piston engine. Something black and gleaming flashed across his line of sight. His suitcase bounced across the cabin. There was cursing from up front. Pross stared at Sanders as the helicopter swung back on course and returned to its cruising altitude.

Sanders was not looking worried.

Sanders said, "We're nearly there. That was a welcome from one of the people you'll be practising against. We were just bounced by a Pilatus PC-9. Judging by the racket up in the office, it was not appreciated." He gave a smirking smile.

Pross said, "You can hardly blame them. If I'm going to get smashed against a slab of rock, I'd rather do it myself, thank you, without help from some nut in a trainer."

The Pilatus was a new-generation turbo-prop trainer, built in Switzerland. It was very nimble.

"No one told me I'd be going up against fixed-wing aircraft as well," Pross went on, alarm rising in his mind. He had unpleasant visions of being cornered by MiGs, in the cold Himalayan mountains.

"We don't expect you to, but it won't do any harm to get a little practice in against fixed wings. You never can tell what might turn up."

"Oh I can. I can."

"Let's get one thing straight, Pross." Sanders said tightly. "You don't like me, and I don't like you. Left to me, I would not involve you at all. I don't like amateurs."

"Hear, hear. Give me a ticket home and see how fast I'll move."

"But I haven't the choice," Sanders carried on, ignoring Pross's interruption. "*You* haven't the choice. So let's make the best of it, shall we, Flight-Lieutenant Pross?'

"The last time you called me by my old rank, I told you I didn't carry it out of the service with me. I'm not one of your 'Captain', or 'Major' retired, types. I don't care what rank they've thrown away on you now, but you don't outrank me. Get *that* straight."

Jesus, Pross thought in exasperation. Why did Fowler have to lumber him with Sanders? There was more than enough already on his plate.

The bright sun gleaming off the snow made him feel cold. He tried not to think of Dee and the children. He tried not to think that every beat of the rotors was taking him further way from them.

Now that he was irreversibly committed, he needed something to totally occupy his mind; to take him over completely.

He needed action.

The *Dauphin* did not land at Betten. Instead, it settled onto hard-packed snow three kilometres away and 6500 feet up, near an isolated cluster of three buildings a kilometre or so from the holiday village of Bettmeralp. The buildings were near a small lake, about 200 metres across, that was covered by a thin layer of ice.

Pross and Sanders climbed out. As soon as they were clear, the helicopter lifted off, tilted away, and seemed to hurl itself down a steep slope.

"They're returning to Zurich," Sanders explained. "They'll be back for you when we're finished here. For the next few days, this is your home. Enjoy the view. People pay vast sums just to see this once a year."

"I'm not exactly on holiday, am I?"

Sanders said nothing. They began walking towards the nearest of the buildings, a two-storeyed alpine chalet; the snow crunched beneath their shoes.

Behind the chalet and to one side was another, slightly

smaller, standing at the edge of a large colony of pines. Set among the pines was the third building. This was long and low, and looked like either a large barn or very spacious stables. After the noise of the helicopter, the place seemed unnaturally quiet. Pross felt the warmth of the sun beating down from a cloudless sky and bouncing off the snow, despite the fact that the temperature was only three degrees Centigrade.

He squinted against the brightness as a man came out of the main chalet towards them.

He said to Sanders, "Took his time, didn't he?"

"He had to check. He had to be sure."

"Of *us?* I would have thought the chopper would have radioed ahead to expect us, especially after the ace of the skies tried to send us into a mountain."

"He was nowhere near, Pross. You exaggerate. As for this place," Sanders went on, "we don't take chances. A radio message does not show you who's in the aircraft. We have been in the sights of at least six people since we came out of the helicopter. After all, someone could have taken me out and forced you to come here, thereby compromising the entire operation."

The thought of someone taking Sanders out had a seductive attractiveness for Pross. He enjoyed it privately.

"Are you telling me," he said, "that rifles are pointing at me from those buildings?"

"Of course."

"And what would have happened if you had been . . . 'taken out' as you put it and I'd been brought here by force?" Pross thought he knew the answer to that one, but still wanted to be proved wrong.

"Both of you would have been shot dead within seconds."

"Thanks a lot." Grimly. "What nice people you are."

The man who came up to them was small, bantam-like, and his features reminded Pross of old newsreel pictures of Neville Chamberlain. Even the haircut, and the moustache, were the same. Pross wondered whether the man would also speak in the same, historically famous high tones.

"Mr. Pross, Mr. Sanders . . . welcome to a little corner of England in Switzerland, or wherever." He grinned.

The voice astonished Pross. It was exceedingly deep, seeming totally wrong for the body to which it belonged.

Sanders said, "Pross, this is John Rushman. Served as an officer with the Gurkhas and knows Nepal like the back of his hand."

"I wouldn't put it quite like that—" Rushman began.

"He's also a damned good chopper jockey," Sanders drove in, "and will be your mentor during your stay at this little resort." Sanders smiled as if he'd made a joke.

Pross had noted a brief clouding of Rushman's lively brown eyes at Sanders' rude interruption; but Rushman was smiling again. They shook hands, and all three resumed walking towards the chalet.

Rushman, who was wearing a padded green zipped jacket over an olive-green tracksuit, took a small two-way radio out of a pocket.

"Okay," he said into it, before putting it back.

Pross said, "Does that mean the rifles are now pointing somewhere else?"

Rushman glanced at him quickly.

Sanders said, "I told him."

Rushman gave Pross a quick grin. "Indeed it does."

"That makes me so happy."

Rushman was not quite sure how to take that.

Sanders said, "It's a bad habit of his. He picked it up from someone he used to fly with in the RAF."

Rushman chose not to pursue it further. "Here we are," he said as they reached the chalet. "Home from home."

"It doesn't look like Wales," was what Pross said.

Pross had been given a room that presented him with a view down the long slope to Bettmeralp, across the Rhône Valley, and the starkly white and streaked panorama of the Simplon range 12 kilometres away. The chalet was well heated to efficient Swiss standards, and he had changed into his own grey tracksuit which had been used for everything except running.

He went downstairs to the dining-room where a prepared meal was waiting. Rushman was there too, but a place had not been set for him.

"I seem to spend a lot of time eating on my own," Pross said as he joined Rushman at the table.

Rushman said, "I've already eaten. Sorry."

"No need to be," Pross said. "I'm getting accustomed to it. Where's Sanders?"

"He went out to the shed."

"The shed? Oh, I see. You mean the building in the pines. I take it that's where the ship is." It was certainly big enough to hold a chopper or two. Pross began to load his plate.

Rushman nodded. "The Lynx, and the aggressor ship." He gave one of his grins. "I'll be flying the aggressor."

"Will you now," Pross said. "Well, well." He began to eat, slowly. "What is it?" he asked after a while.

"The *Mangusta*."

Pross knew of the *Mangusta*. It was easy to see why Fowler had picked it. Made by Agusta in Italy and designated the A129, it was narrow and slab-sided, and was as near as was possible to the kind of target he'd hopefully be shooting at when the time came for him to meet the *Hellhound*. He could understand Fowler's reasons.

"We first considered the AH64," Rushman went on, "the Hughes Apache, but Mr. Fowler thought it was too big for his requirements. Between you and me, I think he's trying to keep American involvement as low as possible."

"Are they involved?" This was news to Pross.

"They lent us something. You'll see when you check the Lynx out. I'm not sure whether they know how we're going to use it. They'd probably have a fit. Anyway, Fowler swung it. It's a great piece of kit. I think you'll be pleased."

"I'll be pleased to come back in one piece."

"We'll all be pleased."

"Keep saying that, and I'll begin to believe it."

They fell silent as Pross concentrated on his food. Rushman stood up, walked away from the table to look out of one of the two windows in the room. It had the same view as Pross's bedroom. From time to time, Rushman would also glance in Pross's direction. Pross knew the other man was assessing him.

He finished his·meal. "That was excellent. Thank whoever prepared it for me."

"You can thank her yourself later. She's one of the avionics boffins working on the Lynx."

"*She?*"

Rushman smiled. "About fifty, bosses us about, and considers pilots to be just about the lowest form of life. Pilots bend aircraft. Not done."

"I knew someone like that once. *He* was an RAF airman. Talking of which, do you know a bloke by the name of Rees? Army sergeant with a nice line in downbeat insolence, particularly with people like Sanders. Great chopper jockey. We've worked together once before. I was hoping he'd be on this."

"You don't like Sanders, do you?"

"I could think of better ways to passing the day."

Rushman gave a tight smile. "If it's any consolation, I think he's a pompous prick."

Pross grinned suddenly. "And *I* think I may like working with you, even though you're harbouring the quite mistaken idea that you may be able to take me in that A129." He was beginning to feel the first tinglings of anticipation.

"We shall see. As for Rees . . . yes, I know him. I've had a taste of his insolence too. But he's got his punishment now. Who says there's no justice?"

"What do you mean, punishment? What's he done?"

"It's not what he has done. It's what's been done to him. He's gone before a commissioning board. The Army seems to think the safest thing to do is make him an officer."

They laughed at the idea.

"Poor old Cado," Pross said with some amusement.

"Well and truly hoisted."

"I'm here," Rushman said, "partly because he couldn't make it, and partly because of my knowledge of Nepal which, incidentally, is not as encyclopaedic as Sanders tried to make out. You need to spend years in Nepal before you can begin to have a slight knowledge of it. There are people here in Switzerland whose knowledge is much closer to what Sanders has in mind."

"But whom, of course, we can't involve."

"Absolutely not. However," Rushman went on lightly, "I believe I know sufficient to be of help to you. After all, you're not going on a holiday." He came back to the table. "Rees told me there was not much you can be taught about how to handle yourself in a chopper. I'll take his word for it. He's a better pilot than I am; but during the next few days, I'll find out about you myself.

"My primary function is to let you know what you're in for in that terrain. Here, we're at 6500 feet. Looking across to Simplon, that seems pretty high. We're up a mountain, almost. Over there, there are *valleys* 14,000 feet up. In one latitude, you can find a whole range of climatic conditions; vertical climatic zones from humid and tropical to biting arctic as you climb higher into thin air and breathing becomes painful, unless you take it easy and are climatised. Sudden winds that can slice through you; sudden storms and sudden mists. Peaks that make those things out there look like struggling molehills. In this area, we've got the Aletschhorn at 4,195 metres—that's about 13,700 feet, still lower than that valley—and Jungfrau, a mere pigmy at 13,500. Even the Finsteraarhorn, to the north of here, is still 24 feet lower than the valley.

"I'll be taking you all around these places to give you an idea of what to expect. But your mind will need to take a leap of imagination. Imagine peaks more than twice as high as those you will see, and only then will you begin to understand. But I'll tell you one thing—they're frightening, but they're bloody magnificent."

"You sound like someone who wants to go back."

"Not your way, I don't." Rushman was looking away from Pross and at the view outside, but seeing a different landscape. "But yes, I like going back. I've been a few times since I left the Regiment. I like the people too. So many visitors go trekking without really getting among the people. Shame, really." He came back from his mountains, turned to Pross once more. "Well? Are you fit? Would you like to have a look around?"

"No time like the present."

"I'll get you a jacket," Rushman said as they stood up. "Be right back." He went out and soon returned with his own jacket on, and a similar, larger one for Pross. "This was got for you. I think you'll find the size is just about right."

Fowler had prepared everything as usual, Pross thought drily. It was embarrassingly obvious that Fowler had never doubted that he would eventually get Pross exactly where he wanted him, programmed every step of the way.

Pross felt a sharp stab of resentment, but knew he had been hooked the moment Logan had come for him. Seeing the drawings and the photograph of the *Hellhound* had simply added . . .

What was he thinking about? He'd been hooked from the time he'd gone on that first job in China. Fowler, the master puppeteer.

He zipped up the jacket, went out with Rushman. It was still warm outside. He tucked his hands into the jacket pockets nonetheless.

Rushman said, as they began to walk, "The smaller chalet is the boffins' quarters. In our own place, we'll have Sanders, I'm afraid, and two bods with rifles and other associated equipment. There will be two in each building."

" 'Associated equipment'? Sounds like code for an armoury." Pross said.

Rushman stroked his thin moustache briefly. "Let's put it this way . . . if we were attacked, we could hold off a small army for some considerable time; long enough for the Swiss to bring in their alpine troops. For a citizen army, those laddies are tough."

"You seem to have got a lot of co-operation."

"From the Swiss? Oh yes. For example, for the duration of our stay, the whole area within a kilometre-and-a-half radius of this place has been made out of bounds to the good burghers."

"And they'll obey it?"

"Oh they will. Very individualistic people, the Swiss, but very jealous of their united patriotism. If the authorities say they want a piece of a mountain for a few days for defence purposes, it's done. After all, who are the authorities? The good burghers themselves. Neat."

"And who was the Sunday driver in the black Pilatus? Another co-operative burgher?"

Rushman laughed briefly. "That was H-E."

"H-E? Who's that? Some faded continental noble? His Excellency Whatever-Whatever with a nice line in buzzing choppers as a sort of diversion before lunch?"

"Sanders is right about you," Rushman said mildly. "You do have a touch of vitriol in your veins."

"I wonder why. So who's the ace of the alpine kingdom?"

"Hans-Ruedi Bitsch," Rushman answered with a straight face. "Don't laugh. That's his name. There's even a place of that name just down the road, near Brig. Nice little spot too. Leutnant Bitsch, when he's not attacking choppers, is a banker in his spare time; or the other way round."

"He would be, wouldn't he?" Pross said drily. "This being Switzerland."

Rushman went on with a smile, "It was thought a good idea to give you a one-to-one experience with a fixed-wing, as well as the A129, just in case."

"Of what? MiGs?" Pross liked the thought even less than when it had first come to him in the *Dauphin*.

Rushman glanced at him. "We weren't thinking of MiGs. The 21 or the 23 would be too fast for the terrain. Not enough manoeuvring room for their speed, if they're chasing something like a chopper. More than likely fly into a mountain. We're thinking of *Frogfoot*, the Su-25.

195

They've been using it like the A10 Thunderbolt, in Afghanistan. It's got enough wing area to allow it slow manoeuvring through twisting valleys to enable it to achieve a good shoot-down solution; possibly."

"Am I glad you added that."

"It may not happen, of course," Rushman's unnaturally deep voice went on. Pross thought he was trying not to sound too ominous, and failing. "But it's always nice to be prepared."

"Once a scout, and all that."

"This is serious, Mr. Pross. It's your neck."

"Don't you think I know that?" Pross said with sudden heat.

"Well. Well, yes. I suppose you do."

"Right. Go on."

But Rushman had stopped. Pross halted, looked at him. Rushman was staring into the pines. Nothing was moving out there.

"See anything?" he asked Pross.

"Snow, and pines . . . and the shed."

"Look again."

Pross squinted. The sun was still bright upon the snow.

Rushman noted the squint. "Your helmet's polarising visor will combat that. You'll be wearing it down, throughout all flights. There are sunglasses in the chalet if you need them."

Pross shook his head. "No . . . no. I'm fine. I still haven't seen anything. What am I looking for?"

Instead of answering, Rushman was walking on. Pross followed.

Rushman said, "I'm responsible for three things here: on-site security, a flying target for your dubious pleasure . . . "a brief chuckle" . . . and to give you a rough idea of what Nepal's like. I could never tell you nearly enough about that in the time we have; but I'll try to give you a few pointers. What you're supposed to be looking for," he went on, "are my men. They're dotted about the place, on constant watch."

"Don't they sleep."

"They get their sleep." Rushman took the radio out of his pocket. "Look to your right, Mr. Pross." And when Pross had done so, Rushman said to the radio, "Wave an arm, Simpson."

Something white moved briefly among the pines. Pross nearly missed it, even though he'd been looking.

"Bloody good camouflage," he said. "Fantastic."

"They're all out there, making sure no one gets close. But," Rushman carried on, returning the radio to his pocket. "I did not ask Simpson to wave in a fit of bravado. He'll have moved to a new position by now, incidentally. Think of how difficult it was for you to spot him. It will be ten times worse when you're trying to find a chopper against the background of the peaks and valleys of the Himalayas. Not seeing it in time could be fatal. Relying on the avionics won't be enough."

"Point taken," Pross said.

"But don't worry. We've given you some help too, as you'll soon see." Rushman gave a quick grin. His moustache actually twitched.

They had entered the pines now, and were a few metres from the shed. Pross could hear the soft murmur of voices, and soft metallic sounds. There was also a subdued hum of machinery.

Pross said, "How much do you know of what I'm supposed to be doing out there?"

"Only what my brief is; which is to prepare you, then turn you loose. I don't know the reasons and, frankly, I don't wish to. What I can make of it from the little I do know, tells me it's a very dodgy game indeed; and I can already get a faint whiff of the diplomatic pong that would result should things go wrong and the shit hits the fan. If that does happen, I don't suppose you'll know much about it anyway."

"For that kind thought, thank you," Pross said sarcastically.

"Any time. Now let's hear what Mabel has to say."

"Mabel?"

"Wait and see," Rushman said mysteriously.

197

They had reached one end of the shed, in which were set huge double doors. In one of them, was a smaller door.

"What is this place normally used for?" Pross asked.

Rushman shrugged and said, "Who knows?" He pushed the smaller door open. "After you."

Pross went in, followed by Rushman who shut the door after him. The shed was nicely warm and the sounds he'd heard from outside increased sharply. Voices had paused at their entry. Pross unzipped his jacket; and stared.

"Oh my God," he said slowly, softly. He was conscious of Rushman standing a little to one side, a tiny smile upon his lips.

There were several outward changes to the Lynx since Pross had last seen it. It looked slightly narrower, and much meaner. It crouched, as if ready to spring, on its wide-spread tricycle landing gear that was now retractable. Faired housings had been added to accommodate them. It seemed a trifle shorter, but was sleeker, and the rear, horizontal stabilizer set low on the tail had grown a small stabilising fin at each tip. He wondered if its twin Gem engines had been uprated as much as Fowler had said. Just looking at it seemed to give the impression of immense power waiting to be unleashed.

The rakish lines of the nose, once broken by the sensor units for target acquisition and night vision, had now been neatly smoothed by a transparent nose cone through which the units could be seen. And of course, there was the weaponry.

Outboard pylons on each side of the fuselage carried, at each tip, four missiles on launcher rails, and beneath each of these was hung a fat multiple-rocket pod. In-board, on each pylon, were dispensers which Pross recognised as being for chaff to confuse radar, and flares with which to decoy missiles. He recognised the Lynx's own missiles as a mix of his favourite *Stinger* air-to-air and *Hellfire* air-to-surface. The *Hellfire* was an anti-tank job.

Tanks? went Pross's mind in bewilderment, but the Lynx continued to enthrall him.

He found himself staring at the massive new rotary cannon that had replaced the twin 25mms, beneath the chin. The new gun was off-set to the left to clear the nosewheel. 30 bloody mm. Christ.

I'll have to watch that, he thought. *When it goes off, it might pull the Lynx round, and lead off the target in a right turn.*

In a left turn, however, it might lead *into* the target. He'd have to compensate. Deflection was all. He shrugged mentally. Perhaps they'd got the stabilisation so perfectly the off-set weapon would be no problem.

He squatted briefly, better to see the line of the gun. It appeared to have a very slight inward diagonal that moved upwards into the Lynx's underbelly. A fairing hid the cannon completely, save for a short length of perforated muzzle for escaping gases.

Pross was aware that he now had an audience of three more people. They were on the periphery of his vision and he ignored them as he continued his scrutiny of the Lynx. It was the paint job that finally completed his total entrapment. Finished in a mottled white and dark olive, with a greater quantity of white, it personified its namesake of the upper Indus Valley, the four-legged predator that hunted at 11,000 feet.

To Pross, the helicopter seemed alive, wild and dangerous. There were no insignia, no national markings. Mounted atop the four-bladed rotor was a stubby mast sight with a 360-degree capability.

"Hooked, line and sinker," he heard Rushman say behind him drily.

Behind the Lynx was the aggressor A129 with its humped back, narrow flat-sided body and twin tandem cockpits, looking like an angry warthog. It too was tooled up with a mixed weapon fit, one of which was a gun pod on the left outer pylon. The A129 was painted in a wavy pattern of different shades of green and olive.

The shed had been turned into a field hangar, and of the three people Pross had noticed, one was Sanders who was unsuccessfully trying to keep a self-satisfied smirk off his face. Another was a short man with thinning wispy hair and thick glasses; and the third was something else.

The third was a tall stringy woman with streaked grey-ing hair. She wore enormous glasses perched upon the tip of her sharp nose. They seemed in perpetual danger of falling off, but would probably never have dared. About her neck was a double string of pearls that Pross reckoned would have paid the salary of a high-powered executive for at least two years. She wore a white smudged coat in whose pockets various small tools nested. On her feet were strong boots, into which were tucked what Pross assumed were ski trousers. She had, he noted, large strong-looking hands.

What next, he thought. A helicopter engineer with pearls.

Sanders was coming forward. "Impressed?"

"Impressed," Pross said. He went up to the Lynx, stroked it gently. For one crazy moment, he thought he heard it purr.

Sanders was saying, "This is Professor—"

"Don't be so pompous, Sanders," the woman interrupted in a voice that reminded Pross of Lady Bracknell. She came up to Pross. "I'm Mabel." She took his hand in what felt like a deathlike grip. "Bend this beauty, and I'll bend you."

Pross believed she would too.

Then she was smiling at him, completely transforming her forbidding countenance. She had tucked her head down, and was peering at him from above the rims of her spectacles. Her eyes seemed to twinkle.

"I've heard a lot about you," she went on. "Are you as good in these things as they say? Should I entrust you with it, do you think?"

It was almost like the first day at school. For a few moments, Pross was so taken aback by her, he did not know what to say.

"Well . . ." he began.

"I tend to have that effect on people," she said into his intended words with the voice of experience. "Well? Should I?"

200

She seemed determined to have an answer from him. Pross saw that one of the "tools" in a coat pocket was a fat, unsmoked cigar.

"Yes," Pross said. "You should."

She gave him another smile. "Wondering about my cigar? I gave up smoking them a year ago, after fifteen years of it. I keep it around to remind me. Never know when I might feel I need one. You're not going to drive me back to the habit, are you?"

Thoroughly bewildered, Pross said, "Er . . . no. I won't bend the Lynx. I promise." Strange woman.

"A word of advice. It bites."

"I'll remember."

"Do you like my cooking?"

How many questions were rattling about in her head at any one time? Pross said: "I do. Very much. Thank you for preparing a meal for me."

Mabel changed tack once more. "This retiring gentleman," she said, inclining her head in the direction of the man with the wispy hair, "is Jack Parmitter. What he does not know about this particular machine would be covered by a postage stamp. He has lavished care and affection upon it. He also has a weak heart. Don't break it."

The more he listened to her, Pross thought, the more she sounded like Lady Bracknell come to life. He shook Parmitter's hand.

"Mr. Parmitter."

"Jack," the little man said. He had a soft voice.

Pross nodded. "I'm David." He'd been hearing sounds coming from the direction of the A129. Now two men in overalls appeared from behind it and began doing something to its tailwheel. He said, "When do we start?"

It was Sanders who answered. "Tomorrow."

Mabel was looking at Pross. "Would you like to climb in to see how it feels?"

"Yes. I would."

The look on Sanders' face said he hated being overridden, but he made no objection.

"In you get," Mabel ordered. She appeared to be smil-

201

ing, but Pross wasn't sure.

It wasn't Sanders' day.

Pross opened the pilot's door and climbed up into the right-hand seat. He sat there, feeling the aircraft settle itself about him. It was as if his presence in the cockpit had displaced part of it, the way water is displaced by the weight of a ship upon its surface; and as the water alters itself to accommodate the ship, so did Pross feel the Lynx shift and alter to incorporate him. He was being welcomed.

He slowly put his right hand onto the cyclic, the left onto the collective down by the seat pan. Both controls felt solid and, even with the engines dead, powerful. The Lynx was only sleeping.

He looked out across the sleek, rounded nose and saw Rushman staring back at him. Rushman's expression was neutral.

The left-hand door opened. Mabel was looking at him. "Would you like to take it up? I'll have the avionics on-line and we can have a roll-out in fifteen minutes. Your flying kit's waiting in your room."

Pross said, "Judging by the preparation, everyone knew I was coming . . . except me."

Mabel's twinkling eyes peered at him from above her glasses. "But now that you are here, you look at home."

"You would say that, wouldn't you?"

Mabel's eyes stopped twinkling suddenly. "Never make the mistake, David Pross, of equating me with some of the morons you've been dealing with." He knew she was talking about Sanders. "When I say something to you, I mean it. Now out you get. I've got work to do. Your ship will be ready in within fifteen minutes."

"Yes, ma'am," Pross said.

She smiled. "If you cause me to start smoking again I'll never forgive you."

"I'll try not to." He smiled back at her, climbed out of the Lynx and walked over to Rushman.

Rushman said, "Whatever your feelings when they first came to you, they've got you now."

"Don't you start."

They began walking towards the small door. Pross zipped up his jacket.

"As I've said," Rushman began as they went out. "Hooked."

Pross said nothing to that. He wondered what Dee's reaction would have been had she been there to hear. Thinking of Dee made him think of the Dawn Patrol; which in turn made him think of Anakov . . . who would be waiting. Suddenly, he wanted to see his family again.

He shivered in the warm sun.

Rushman glanced curiously at him as they walked back towards the chalet, but made no comment.

Pross said, "Where in God's name did they find Mabel?"

"I don't really know, except that as far as choppers are concerned, she's their resident genius."

"I thought that was Parmitter."

"Parmitter's good, but she's brilliant; the true leading light."

"I've never heard of her . . . and I operate choppers as a business."

"That means you and much of the rest of the world. She's hot stuff. Couldn't afford to lose her to the other side."

"Meaning?"

"She'll be going with you to Nepal."

"*With* me?" Pross was astounded. "What for?"

"To look after the Lynx. She won't be going with you, so to speak, but she'll be there when you arrive, as will the chopper. They'll be doing a LAPES job at the site. She's going to make sure all the sensitive bits are still working after that."

Pross knew what LAPES was: low-altitude parachute extraction system. A transport aircraft would come in low on the deck with everything hanging out, rear doors open. A drogue chute would stream out, followed by the main chute which would drag the equipment out a few feet above the ground as the plane made its pass. Great for jeeps, APCs and tanks; but the Lynx?

"Can it take it?" Pross now asked. "Even at a very low speed, it's still going to be a bump."

"Don't worry. It will be alright. It's all been worked out, so Sanders insists."

"Which of course, he would."

"Trust Mabel."

"Talking of Mabel . . . will she be able to take the climate?"

"I wouldn't let her hear you say that. By the way, did I tell you about the leeches?"

"Leeches?" Pross queried weakly. He hated the things with a vengeance. He had once done a jungle survival course in Malaysia. Great four-inch horrors had got into his clothes and had latched themselves greedily onto his skin. He had tried pulling them off until he'd been shown how with a lighted cigarette. "I hate the bastards," he added with feeling.

"Done a jungle course, have you?" Rushman said with sympathetic insight. "Nepalese leeches are special," he went on with what Pross thought was undue relish. "Hordes of them during the monsoon season, in the *terai*. That's the tropical lowlands. Jungle, if you prefer. Little brown things they are. They hang out on leaves, bushes, grass and actually reach out for you, or plop onto you from above. They can get in through the smallest opening in your clothes; then the little blighters drink themselves silly."

"Thank you, Mr. John Rushman. Got any more cheerful stories like that one?"

Rushman laughed as they reached the chalet. "Still, you won't have to worry. The monsoon season does not begin till April. You're not likely to be there then, unless something goes very wrong."

"As a court jester, you're a failure."

Rushman laughed again. "Come on. Let's get suited up. I'm coming up with you."

Chapter Twelve

Pross walked towards the Lynx with Rushman, helmet in hand. The Lynx had been towed outside by a snow tractor modified for the job. Even as he looked at it, it seemed to appear and disappear, so well did its camouflage work against the background of the surrounding landscape.

You'll have a job finding me, Anakov, he thought with lifting spirits.

Rushman glanced at him. "You're looking pleased with yourself."

Pross gave a quick smile, but said nothing.

In the chalet, he had found his gear all neatly laid out. He had given up trying to work out just how much manpower Fowler could call upon. Among the gear had been the familiar white undergarment with its spread-fan pressure system. He had not seen one since his air force days. There had also been a full oxygen-mask intercom unit with the integral helmet.

"A *G-suit?*" he had said to Rushman later. "In a chopper?"

"You'll be needing it, and the oxygen, for where you're going," was what Rushman had replied without explaining further.

The snow tractor was moving back into the shed when they reached the Lynx. Both cockpit doors were open. Mabel was in the left-hand seat.

"Everything's ready," she said as he climbed in behind the cyclic and strapped himself in. She watched him as he looked about the wide cockpit. All the avionics he remembered were still there: tactical air nav, Doppler, IFF, IR jamming, the acquisition and night vision monitors, and the rest; but there was more and, in particular, something very special that had been added to the head-up display.

"What the hell is that?" Pross asked as he plugged himself into the aircraft's life-support system. All sorts of new information had appeared on the HUD.

Mabel said, "IFFC. Integrated Flight and Fire Control, modified a little by my good self—if you will allow the uncharacteristic expression of pride . . ." she peered at him from the tops of her rims ". . . and mated to the central computer."

"Very nice, but you haven't told me what it does."

"What it does, young man, is make shooting the other bugger down much more a matter of scientific inevitability."

Pross tried not to smile at the incongruity of the descriptive word coming through in such accents.

"The IFFC," Mabel went on smoothly, still peering at him like a stern headmistress, "is part of a system for the F-15 Eagle. We . . . er . . . managed to persuade them to let us try one out, with our own mods, of course."

"What you mean is they wanted to know if it would work in real life. It's all well and good shooting at drones. It's a bit more dodgy when the target is being driven by a shit-hot jockey. You don't mind my saying shit-hot, do you?"

The eyes did not blink. "Of course not, young man. I could make *you* blush, not the other way round. Shall I continue, or do you want to sit here till the sun goes down behind those mountains?"

"Pray continue, Mabel."

"Thank you." The eyes were twinkling. "The Americans don't know what we're going to do with it."

"You hope."

"You're interrupting me, young man." Another censorius stare above the rims. "They would obviously have a fit if they thought there was the slightest risk of its falling

206

into the . . . er . . . wrong hands. If you were shot down, for example. But you're not going to be, are you?"

"I'll try very hard, Mabel."

"Jolly good. Now . . . pay attention. This graduated vertical scale, on the left, is your airspeed at a given moment. As the airspeed climbs, the indicator will move downwards. Note that the speed is marked out in increments of 50. Directly beneath and offset to the right, is this figure which gives you the number of rounds remaining. Silly if you haven't any and he's still in the air, wouldn't you say?"

"Oh I would. I would."

"Jolly good. We're getting somewhere. Further down, again with a right offset, would have been the Mach number. I've removed it. No rubbish about choppers travelling at Mach speeds. It will come, of course, but not for some time yet. The next figure, therefore, is your load factor, the amount of G you'll be pulling; an important factor with this particular Lynx, as I shall explain later.

"I don't have to tell you about the central reticle and gunrange. Beneath the reticle is your pitch ladder, plus target designator. The right hand vertical scale is altitude, reading *up* as height increases. When simulating, as you will be with John Rushman, the IFFC will give you a shooting cue, as well as a breakaway cue if you're getting too excited and going in too close for sanity. The gun camera will of course record everything."

"It doesn't fly this as well, does it?" Pross queried.

She peered admonishingly at him. "I've modified the IFFC so that you can fly a simulated shoot against an actual target. When you've scored, the sights will pulse as normal."

"I do hope you're right, Mabel. I don't think Rushman would be pleased if simulation turned too real, and I blew him out of the sky."

"Think you're that good?"

"I'll find out tomorrow. What if there's a glitch in the system?"

"While not admitting to the possibility of glitches in any system I've worked upon, should the impossible indeed happen, you can uncouple and return to unaided shoot. And as you seem to think you're good enough without it, that should not be a liability."

"Ouch," Pross said.

"David," Mabel spoke his name with such seriousness, he found himself staring at her. "Anakov is very, very good. The IFFC might be just what you need to give you the edge, particularly if he decides to bring some of his friends to the party. He has a good team, the nucleus of what he hopes to build. Incidentally, the system will predict the number of hits on target. The required figure will appear just beneath the altitude readout. The system will also automatically compensate for lead and ballistics requirements. Child's play, wouldn't you say?"

"Oh yeah. Child's play. How much warning will I have if your infallible IFFC does decide to run out on me?"

"The entire HUD will glow a bright red," Mabel answered, ignoring the aspersion. "You won't be able to miss it. You can find out for yourself. Uncoupling produces the same effect. You'll be on standard HUD from then on. Now to controls. Everything you should need in combat is hands-on-stick; on both the cyclic and the collective. For weapons selection, your air-to-air is on the right, and air-to-surface on the left pylon. The air-to-air rockets are armed with flechette heads. Being unguided, you won't need a direct hit with these. A proximity burst will do a lot of damage if you're close enough.

"Don't worry about the gun. Stabilisation has been sorted out. There won't be any pull. Recoil will be straight along the centreline. You will have noticed the narrowing of the fuselage, and the loss of some cabin space. This has been taken up by ammunition storage and extra fuel; but the weight has been reduced. The side doors are also narrower, but there is still sufficient room for two or three extra people, with no additional weight penalty.

"Finally, additional manoeuvring. There are six fixed

208

nozzles to give you rapid displacement in two directions horizontally, vertically, and laterally, controlled by two groups of three push-buttons: the yellow ones here on the cyclic, and the collective. Those on the cyclic will give forward, upward, and lateral displacement to the right. Those on the collective will give rearward, downward, and lateral displacement to the left. These will be sudden, to throw your opponent off his gun or missile solution. Treat them sparingly if you don't want to run out of fuel. They're like mini-afterburners." Mabel drew a deep breath, let it out slowly. "And so, here endeth my lesson." She glanced to where Rushman was standing a little distance away, talking to Sanders. "We'd better call John in, don't you think? He might think he's been planted in the snow, and must be dying to get away from Sanders."

Pross said, "I'd like to ask who you really are, but I don't suppose you'd answer me."

"What a suspicious mind you've got, David. I'm exactly what you see . . . a helicopter engineer."

"Of course." A helicopter engineer who seemed to know a lot about Anakov; more than Rushman, certainly, and possibly even more than Sanders. What scale was she in Fowler's Department? Pross wondered. She seemed able to bawl Sanders out as she wished. Some chopper engineer.

"Don't try and work it out, David," Mabel said. The eyes seemed kindly as they twinkled at him from above the rims. "Just do the job, and come back in one piece. We'll all be very happy with such a result."

"Including me," he said, and he put on his helmet and began his start-up sequence.

She smiled at him briefly, climbed out just as the first Gem lit up, followed swiftly by the second. Rushman had turned to look at the first sound of the Lynx coming to life. Now he came forward, crouching as the blades began to turn. He climbed in, shut the door and strapped himself in. He put on his helmet.

"Well?" came his voice on the intercom. "How was the

dragon lady? Stimulating?"

"Bloodthirsty," Pross said.

Rushman grinned in his mask. "Alright, Mr. Pross. Let's see what you've got under your belt."

Pross held the Lynx on the ground, feeling the power of the new engines flow through him. Outside, a tornado of powdery snow was churned into a frenzy by the whirling blades. He saw Sanders duck and move further out of the way. Mabel stood her ground, watching him, he was sure, a tall thin and seemingly immovable figure. He could almost imagine her contemptuous thoughts as Sanders ducked away. Other people had come out of the shed to watch.

Pross continued to hold the Lynx down, keeping it steady with sensitive feel of pedals, collective and cyclic. Then he raised the reassuring solid arm of the collective slightly, keeping cyclic and pedals central. The Lynx eased itself off the ground smoothly. Pross held it at the hover at about two feet, for two minutes while he waited for warnings of any skittishness. He needed to make a very few minor corrective movements with the controls to hold it in place.

It was beautiful. The cat was on the prowl.

"Wonderful," he said softly. "Wonderful." Then he took the Lynx into a sudden, heart-stopping climb.

It shot upwards, its speckled form launching itself into the cold blue of the sky.

"Jesus!" Rushman said. "Give a bloke some warning."

Pross smiled in his mask. "I hope you had a light breakfast."

The Lynx was still climbing, still hurtling for the heavens.

Rushman scanned the air about them. "We're alright in this area. We've got three operational windows a day. 05.00 to 08.00, 15.30 to 17.30, and 22.00 to 00.30. We had to fight for the last one. They didn't like the idea of our keeping the good burghers awake. Fowler managed to swing it, somehow."

"Fowler always manages to swing things . . . somehow.

210

He's got a way of calling in favours."

"That sounds like the voice of experience."

Pross said nothing.

Rushman said, "But you like the toy."

Again, Pross did not comment. Instead, he asked, "Do these windows mean we've got the area to ourselves? No other traffic?"

"Not unless there's an emergency . . . alpine rescue and such. In the event, we'd be warned."

Pross nodded.

Rushman said, calmly. "Mind if I bring in the gear?"

"What? Oh Christ. I'd forgotten all about that."

Rushman punched a button on the console. There was a whirring as the wheels began to come up, then solid thunks as the doors closed behind them. The monitor lights went out.

"Now you're cleaned up," Rushman said, adding sympathetically: "I got caught out too. It's only to be expected after you've been on fixed-gear choppers for a while."

Pross said, ruefully, "As long as I don't forget to have them down when I land. How could I face Mabel?" So much for a fancy lift-off.

"How indeed," Rushman said, and they both laughed. "Visors," he added.

They pulled their dark visors down, becoming progeny of the machine.

Pross spent a few more minutes getting to know the Lynx and getting the feel of it. He made gentle turns, watching the panorama of Valais pivot beneath him. The machine fairly hummed with power.

Rushman acted as aerial guide, pointing out landmarks.

"The great ribbon over there, to the right, is the Aletsch glacier. And those peaks are Grosser Aletschhorn, Jungfrau, Mönch and of course, the world-famous Eiger." Rushman sounded as if he were grinning.

Pross said, "They look beautiful, but nasty."

"They are . . . on both counts; but they're babies."

The Lynx was at 10,000 feet now, and Rushman continued to point out landmarks.

After a while, Pross said, "Is the glacier within our window?"

"Yes. Why?"

For answer, Pross took the Lynx down in a sudden spiral. He continued until the helicopter was only a few feet off the glacier.

"Heyyy!" he heard Rushman cry involuntarily. It sounded like one of alarm. "Christ. I thought we'd had it. I never expected this thing to stop. You're crazy."

Pross kept the Lynx low, following the meander of the 3-kilometre-wide sheet of ice. Glistening walls of ice and rock flashed menacingly past as he hugged the left bank of the glacier. He rounded Aletschhorn, moved down into the Aletschfirn towards the smaller ice-sea of the Langgletscher. Six kilometres away to his right, Jungfrau reared skywards.

The Lynx handled beautifully. Pross felt its power taking hold of him. He was beginning to feel more confident that he could use it like the weapon it was designed to be.

The mottled shape skimmed the glacier, its camouflage appearing continually to change definition as it fled against the equally mottled background of snow, ice, and rock. A fine mist hovered at the end of the glacier. Pross hauled the Lynx up into a tight climbing turn above it and headed for home. They had covered the thirty miles in under ten minutes.

Rushman had been silent throughout. Now, he said, "There's one other thing the Swiss wouldn't like us to do."

"Oh? What's that?"

"Avalanches. They wouldn't like us to start them."

"Are you trying to say I was too close to the mountain?" Pross's voice had the sound of levity within it.

"Flashing blades and all that," was what Rushman said.

Pross smiled to himself as he brought the Lynx round in a tight circle over the site. He remembered to lower the gear. He took the Lynx straight down, alighted with the feather touch of a man who knew his machine. He began to shut-down.

Rushman said drily, "Cado Rees was right. Not much I can teach you."

"You never know. Tomorrow is another day."

"Ah yes. Tomorrow."

As the engines died, they freed themselves of the clutches of the various systems in the Lynx, removed their helmets, and climbed out. The tractor came up to the aircraft to tow it back into the shed. Mabel and Sanders were waiting. Mabel had her cigar in her hand.

"Well, Pross," Sanders began, "you do not appear to have lost your touch."

"That's something."

Sanders wasn't sure what to make of it, decided to stare blankly at Pross before going off to talk to Rushman. Mabel waited until they had walked some distance away before speaking.

"How did it handle?" she asked. She watched like a mother hen with a new brood as the tractor was coupled to the nose-wheel assembly. There was a slight bang. "Good Lord, *watch it!*" she yelled suddenly.

One of the two men involved with carrying out the task said contritely, "Sorry, Mabel." He didn't seem to mind being yelled at.

She peered ferociously at him. "Do that again and I'll have your balls."

"You probably would too," he retorted.

"As long as you know."

The Lynx began to move off. Pross shook his head wonderingly.

Mabel turned to him again. "Well? Where's my answer?"

"I was waiting to get a word in edgeways."

She barked a short laugh at him. "No wonder you're too much for Sanders. Doesn't think you're sufficiently respectful."

"My heart bleeds. To answer your question . . . a dream."

"Makes you feel you could take on the world, eh?"

"A little."

"Don't become over-confident, David. I don't have to tell you it's one way of getting killed; one of the surest ways, in fact. She had become reflective.

Pross stared at the cigar. "Why the cigar, Mabel? I thought you'd given up. Have I driven you back to it already?" He smiled at her.

"I was only sniffing it," she said, almost guiltily. She put the cigar quickly into a pocket. "Walk a little with me," she went on. They began slowly towards the chalet where Pross was quartered. "You care for Logan, don't you?"

Pross felt an immediate stab of alarm. "What's happened to her?"

"You've just answered me," Mabel said drily. "Nothing has happened to her . . . for the time being."

"What do you mean 'for the time being'?"

"Please let me go on," Mabel said with unusual mildness. She glanced towards were Sanders and Rushman were, clearly not wanting Sanders to hear what was being said. "Let's walk on for a bit." When the distance was to her satisfaction, she continued, "I want to be certain that Logan can depend upon you. Wait. Before you rush your fences and say of course she can, I want you to understand what I'm saying. Whatever happens, whatever you hear from whichever quarter, believe in Logan . . . *even* . . ." Mabel stopped, gave Pross the benefit of her most piercing look. The eyes above the glasses seemed to nail him to the spot. ". . . *even* against the evidence of your own eyes."

"So I will be seeing her." He felt pleased about that. They were a team.

"I said no such thing."

"But . . ."

"I said against the evidence of your own eyes. I did not say you would be seeing her. I could easily have meant *written* evidence, or pictorial evidence. Now . . . can she count on you?"

"Of course," Pross said without hesitation, at the same time trying to imagine what kind of trouble Logan could have possibly got herself into.

"I hope you mean it," Mabel said. "I'm now going back to the shed. I'll see you later."

A bemused Pross watched her make her way back. He carried on towards the chalet, completely unaware that both Sanders and Rushman were staring interestedly at him.

London, 20.00.

Logan dressed as Araminta, parked the little Citroën, got out, and began walking towards the wine bar where she knew Anakov would be waiting. She had timed it, she felt, just right.

Anakov had taken the same table. The place was again crowded, and this time the music was supplied by a lone pianist who was playing *The Nearness of You* with commendable skill.

Logan watched with inner detachment as Anakov's face lit up at her entry. He stood as she reached the table, pulled a chair for her.

"I hoped you would come," he said. "I have been here from seven."

"I'm still not sure why I've come," she said with the right amount of uncertainty and lingering sense of outrage. "I must be out of my mind. I really should be having an early night. I'm off to the camp tomorrow. And I'm not sure I've forgiven you, Geörgy."

"Please, Araminta. I truly had nothing to do with it. If only I could convince you."

"You could try by offering me a drink."

"Of course, of course." Anakov paused, looked at her concernedly. "You are different tonight. Araminta."

"Am I?" Logan said in a brittle voice. "Not surprised, are you?"

Anakov thought he understood. "Ah yes. I think I know. You are nervous because you believe my colleagues

215

might misbehave . . ."

"Misbehave? Is that what you call it? I have a stronger word."

"Araminta, I promise you it will not happen again. I promise."

Logan decided it was time to appear conciliatory. "Alright, Geörgy," she said after a long pause. "Alright."

She watched dispassionately as he walked away to get the wine and by the time he had returned with a bottle and two glasses, she had once more become Araminta.

They spent nearly two hours there, talking and apparently making up after the morning's disaster. Logan allowed Anakov to place his hand on hers.

Anakov said, "Can we leave this place and go somewhere else? A little place more private, perhaps. It has become very noisy."

Logan said, blinking a little at him, "Are you trying to get me into bed, Geörgy?"

He seemed taken aback by her frankness. "I did not mean —"

"Perhaps not immediately, not this minute. But later? Isn't that what you're hoping for?"

He was still floundering. "Well I . . ."

"Alright." She stood up. "I'd better stop drinking anyway, or I won't be able to drive home. It doesn't take much to make me drunk." Logan was coldly sober.

Anakov stood up, unsure of how to handle the situation. Control had neatly shifted. He saw before him a shy woman who had been emboldened by drink, but not too drunk to prevent her from going to bed with him.

He said, "Perhaps we should talk outside."

Logan wanted to smile. Anakov was actually embarrassed! A streak of puritanism?

They left the wine bar, walked towards Logan's car.

"Where's your car?" she asked.

"I came by taxi."

"Then you'd better come with me, hadn't you? You'll find it a bit cramped after your limousine."

Anakov took that to be an oblique reference to what

had occurred earlier in the day.

"Araminta, how many times do you wish to hear me apologise?"

"No more." They had reached the car. "Let's go home."

He stared at her. "Home?"

"My home. It's what you want, isn't it? Besides, I need some coffee, and I don't want to sit in another bar, or café."

He was staring at her uncertainly. "You are angry with me?"

She said, with the exaggerated care of someone trying not to sound drunk, "No, Geörgy, I am not angry with you." She unlocked the car. "Now please get in before I lose my nerve and run home alone."

Anakov got into the little car. Logan climbed in behind the wheel and in a few moments the 2CV was tottering its way towards the Waterloo roundabout.

The Mercedes was parked beneath the railway arch.

Garshin said to Semachev, "The Comrade Colonel appears to have persuaded the woman to say nothing."

"Yes," Semachev muttered thoughtfully. "He appears to have."

"Valentinov will be following them?"

"He will need a very good explanation if he does not." Semachev's voice made it quite clear that no explanation would be acceptable. "Is the Rover that has been following us still there?"

Garshin looked briefly in his mirror. "Parked in the same place, Comrade."

"Start up. Let us give them a tour."

Semachev's desire for a counter-blow after what had happened on the Continent was as strong as ever. He was not finished yet. Far from it.

The Mercedes pulled away from the kerb. At a discreet distance, the white Rover followed.

Logan had seen the shadow almost immediately. Now, as she turned into the mews, the car drove past. She knew it would be stopping a little further on; to wait.

She parked as usual in front of the garage which housed the XR.

"A very nice, quiet little street," Anakov said as she stood waiting for her to open the door of the house. He followed her up the stairs, looked about him as she led him into the reception room. "Very, very nice. You have a fine home."

"My father's, actually," Logan said in a shameless lie. "He sort of gave it to me."

"You are very lucky to have such a father."

"I suppose so." She blinked at him, seemingly ill at ease now that he was in the house with her. "Would you . . . would like some coffee? I'm . . . I'm making some for myself."

He looked at her, a smile forming slowly on his lips; a man who knew he had scored. "I would like coffee, yes, Araminta."

"Please . . . please sit down. I won't be a minute."

She left hurriedly, aware that his smile had become more sure of itself. She busied herself in the kitchen, making a lot of noise, as if she found co-ordination difficult because of her drinking. She dropped a cup. It shattered loudly.

"Araminta!" came his voice. "You are alright?"

"I'm . . . I'm fine," she called back. "Just a bit clumsy." She gave a little laugh that was slightly hysterical. "What's a cup between friends?"

"Nothing, my dear Araminta. Nothing."

She could hear the smile in his voice. *You smug bastard,* she thought coldly. Her bag, with the magnum in it, was with her. If the car she had seen contained Semachev and the rest of them, and if they tried to come at her, they'd all be dead. She would not be taken a second time.

"You have very fine paintings," Anakov called.

She heard him moving around, obviously studying

218

them.

"My father's," she called back. "They're alright, I suppose."

She smiled grimly. The paintings belonged to Fowler, and were all originals. She was amused by what she thought he would say to hear them described thus. Then the smile went.

Fowler was playing a deep game, leaving her blind. She did not like that. And who was the person he suspected of leaking? She could not even begin to guess, and felt annoyed with herself. Of all the operatives she knew of, not one seemed a likely candidate. She did not doubt there were some whose identities were totally unknown to her. She understood that. The Department she worked for could not function in any other way, for the sake of its own security; but even so, she felt there were things that Fowler could entrust her with.

Unless he didn't trust her.

The thought was so shocking to Logan that she felt herself involuntarily lean against the worktop for support. Fowler not trusting her? No. No. She could not accept that. It would be against everything she believed. There were those in the Department, despite their known dependability, whom she would not personally trust against all the odds. Winterbourne was one for a start. Sanders was another; and Telford. She did not consider either of those as leakers, but she would not trust them to back her totally in a tight spot. She would trust Fowler.

Perhaps, she added now in her mind, uncertainly.

She would trust Pross.

She smiled ruefully. The one totally rank amateur. She would trust Pross with her life. After all, he had saved it once.

The coffee was ready. She put everything on a tray, hung her bag from an arm and returned to the room. She put the tray down.

Anakov was sitting on the sofa. "This looks excellent," he said. "It smells very good."

"I'm sorry I was so long." She began to fill a cup for

219

him.

"You were not very long."

She was aware that he was staring at her legs. Now it begins, she thought.

"Would you like milk?" she asked. "Cream? Sugar?"

"I shall have it as it is."

"Alright."

She handed him his cup, began to fill her own, taking sugar and cream. She sat down in an armchair opposite, ensured her bag was with her, before leaning forward to pick up her coffee; then she leaned back in the chair, closing her legs primly together. She was aware that he had watched her every move.

A tense silence had descended.

"Araminta," he said.

She appeared to jump at the sound of her name. "What . . . ? Oh . . ."

"Araminta, there is no need to be so nervous."

"Why not? I've . . . I've got a strange man in my home, at night . . ."

"I am not a strange man. We have known each other for some days. People can sometimes become very close after a few minutes. It happens all the time, all over the world. Release yourself. Allow yourself to do what you truly wish." He took a drink of his coffee, watched her steadily.

She blinked at him from behind her fake glasses. "I . . . I don't know what you mean."

"Of course you do . . . but you hesitate. You go so far, then become afraid. There is no need to be." He spoke caressingly to her, like someone trying to calm a skittish colt. "Look at you. You are a fine woman, yet you dress to hide yourself. You have magnificent legs . . ."

"My . . . my legs are fat. You can see that."

He shook his head, smiling. "They are not fat. How can you say such things about yourself? They are beautiful, and strong. They are as a woman's legs should be."

"I've . . . I've always been fat," she insisted.

220

He laughed. "You are remarkable. In Hungary, you would be a thin woman. I think even here in England, you are not considered fat. You have the shape of a sensuous woman. You should allow yourself to be aware of it."

"Men have never thought me so," Logan lied, remembering the reactions of some of the Department's male personnel, particularly Telford.

Anakov rose from his seat, came across to lean over her, hands bracing him on the arms of the chair.

She watched him, warily.

"I will show you how wrong they have been," he said softly. He reached towards her with his mouth.

She allowed him to kiss her, but she kept her own mouth still.

"You must release yourself, Araminta. Try. You will be very pleased if you do."

He kissed her again.

Logan pushed him gently away. "Alright," she said. She stood up as he watched her expectantly. "Give me a minute." She picked up her bag. "My room's at the top." She went out, leaving him staring after her with a slight smile on his lips.

She did not miss the triumph in his eyes.

She lay on top of the bed. The bag with the magnum was close enough to hand on the floor, by the bedside chest. There were no lights on, but the room was itself not totally dark. Lighting from the mews threw a faint glow into it. There was just enough paleness in the gloom for shapes to be distinguishable.

Logan watched as Anakov removed his clothes. He threw them on the floor in his eagerness to get to her. Then the bed was sinking gently with his weight and he was reaching for her.

His hands began to caress her body. They filled themselves with her breasts.

"Oh Araminta!" he whispered in a shuddery voice.

"You have such beautiful breasts. So, so beautiful . . ." He kissed them over and over. His hands ran over her thighs. "So, so beautiful . . ." he kept repeating.

He began to inch himself over her and she felt him harden against her body. His movements began to grow in urgency. His legs began to push hers open.

Logan had closed her eyes, forcing herself to go along with it; but now, just as Anakov was preparing to enter her, her mind was filled with a sudden, startling image.

A helicopter was bursting into an orange ball of flame, and in that flame . . . was Pross.

Her entire body went rigid.

"No!" she screamed. *"No!"* It was not all play-acting. She gave a sudden push that threw Anakov off her. "No!" she said again. She raised herself, sat on the edge of the bed with her head resting in her hands. "No, no, no," she repeated softly. She sounded as if she wanted to cry.

Anakov didn't know what to make of it. "What are you doing?" He sounded at once annoyed and worried. "Araminta? What it is? What is wrong?"

Logan had regained control of herself after the shock of what she had seen in her imagination.

"I'm . . . I'm sorry, Geörgy," she said. "I . . . I suppose I'm just not like other women. I . . . need more time. I'm sorry." She did not turn to look at him.

She heard him mutter in another language to himself. She knew it was Russian. He sounded frustrated, angry. He took a deep breath, and when he spoke again, he had managed to suppress whatever he was really feeling about the situation.

He sighed. "Very well, Araminta. You may have it as you wish. I shall get dressed, and go home."

She continued to keep her back to him as he began to put his clothes back on.

After a while, he said, "I am finished with my dressing. I will say goodnight, Araminta."

"Goodnight, Geörgy. I am so sorry."

He stared at her in the gloom. "Do not come to the door. I shall find my way down."

222

She still did not turn round when he left the room. She heard him stomp angrily down, heard him struggle with the locks on the door, heard the door bang shut as he went out.

Only then did she straighten up before getting off the bed. She felt herself shiver. She stayed where she was, wrapped her arms about her, and stared at the street glow from the windows.

She had planned to stop Anakov before he'd got too far. Her intention had been to get him hooked on her without giving him everything, to allow Fowler to control the mission successfully . . . whatever the bloody mission was. She paused, listening to all kinds of alarm bells in her mind.

Whatever the mission was.

She knew it involved Pross and Anakov; knew that Anakov and Pross would eventually meet in combat, and that Anakov would kill him.

Unless she got Anakov first.

But how to do it without ruining Fowler's grand design and in consequence running afoul of him?

A germ of an idea began to form in her mind; but it was full of risk. It could cost her own life.

She thought again of the way in which Anakov's intended love-making had come to its unceremonious halt. Pross, in a fireball, coming so strongly to her.

"Oh Pross," she said so softly, and hugged herself in the darkened room.

Anakov saw the car as he came out of the mews.

"Do not say a word, Valentinov," he said harshly as he got into the back.

Valentinov wisely remained silent and put the Mercedes in gear.

As the car moved off, Anakov pondered upon what had happened in the bedroom. He was surprised at his reaction. He should have taken her, despite her protestations. She was a sensuous woman, with a quite wonder-

223

ful body. He had felt it, tasted it.

He felt a stirring in his loins as he remembered.

So why hadn't he continued? All that suppressed sexuality had been his for the taking. He could have unleashed a perfect torrent. Yet he had done nothing. He had meekly acquiesced. Why? Pride? Was he going soft?

Or was it something else?

The thought of Araminta Dilke-Weston could possibly be more than a brief sexual adventure disturbed him. He could not afford to become entangled with a Western woman, however much Semachev laboured beneath the thought of such a ludicrous thing happening. Anakov was well aware of his own responsibilities. Araminta was of no importance. There were other things far more important than she could ever be.

Why therefore had he left her alone in that house when he could simply have spread her legs and taken her anyway? When he could have overcome her uncertainties and enjoyed her all night?

He remembered how angry he had been when Semachev had exceeded his limits by bringing her in. Had that been simply because he had considered Semachev insubordinate?

No answers came to him. But he knew he wanted to see her again. He had touched her, felt her, pressed himself against her naked body. He would not forget that. He required fulfillment.

The stirring in his loins demanded it.

Semachev watched the Mercedes leave.

"Do we search the place now, Comrade?" Garshin asked him.

"No," Semachev replied. "We shall choose another time. I am quite certain," he added drily, "that the British are watching. Let us take them home. They have done enough for tonight."

"The Comrade Colonel did not seem very pleased," Garshin said as they walked back to their car.

Semachev laughed shortly. There was real humour in it. "The English virgin must have given him a difficult time."

Garshin laughed with his superior. "Then you do not think she could have been planted?"

Semachev stared balefully at Garshin.

"But you said, Comrade," Garshin began uncertainly, "that she was a virgin. Would the British use a virgin . . ."

Semachev sighed. "A figure of speech, Garshin. A figure of speech."

Telford watched the white Rover trail after Semachev's car. He had seen the man who had come out of the house, and had felt a twinge of jealousy. Who had the man been? And what had Logan been doing with him?

Telford preferred not to dwell upon that part. So that was what she had meant by being busy. He felt his lips tighten.

Despite the jealousy eating at him, Telford still knew what he had to do. The two men had obviously been trailing the car that had picked up the man who had been with Logan. And the Department Rover had trailed *them*. Someone, therefore, had to watch Logan.

Telford settled himself down for a long, cold night in his blue VW Golf.

Chapter Thirteen

05.54, Bettmeralp.

The new day's sun sent a golden glow from across the Simplon range that was absorbed by the non-reflective paintwork of the two waiting helicopters. The speckled Lynx looked dangerous, crouching it seemed, prior to launching itself at its prey. A short distance from it, the Agusta 129 looked brutish and full of malevolence.

As Pross walked towards the Lynx, the peaks, which seemed in the clear air to be far closer than they were, appeared to be on fire as the sun rose. In their long talk about Nepal the night before, Rushman had mentioned the effect. In Nepal, Rushman had said, the crystal-clear atmosphere of the higher valleys sometimes gave the unnerving impression that a peak was only a mile or so away, when in reality you could count on at least twenty miles.

Rushman had tried to give him as much information as possible, that would be of some help. A Department-supplied map had shown Pross some of the most mountainous terrain he'd thought he would ever see. Rushman had not known where the site in Nepal was going to be, but had said it would be reasonably close to the Arniko Highway; reasonably close, Rushman had added, meaning at least 25 miles. Not far if you were flying, but a hell of a long way if you had to walk it.

Pross did not like the way the Arniko seemed to make a beeline for Tibet.

How far from Tibet, he now wondered, was the site going to be? Why close to Tibet, anyway? Rushman would be holding another session with him after the flight; but he doubted whether Rushman would know.

Sanders and Mabel were near the Lynx. Rushman had already installed himself in the rear cockpit of the A129. The front cockpit, normally the co-pilot/gunner position, would be remaining empty.

Mabel said, "This is where you find out, David." She peered at him.

"Shouldn't you still be in bed?" he said to her.

"I shall ignore that remark." She was fiddling with the cigar.

He smiled at her. "Of course you will. And leave that poor cigar alone."

"Giving the orders now, are you?"

"I'm not brave enough."

The peering eyes softened. "And that's all the insolence I'm going to take from you, young man."

He grinned at her as he did a walk-round about the aircraft, making final checks. The A129's own Gems started with a challenging shriek as Rushman prepared for lift-off. He would be going on ahead of Pross, to mount various ambushes. The Lynx's Gems were much more powerful and the aircraft was itself of greater performance than the Agusta; but that didn't mean Pross could be complacent. Rushman was supposed to be very good. Pross did not intend to take chances.

As Pross watched, Rushman lifted the A129 in a nose-up climb and went thrumming high over the Aletsch glacier.

Pross smiled. He was not going to fall for *that*.

He completed his walk-round, turned to Mabel and said, "I hope these weapons are safe. I don't want to shoot poor old John down by mistake, the way some bods in a Phantom totalled a Jaguar last year."

Sanders spoke his first words to Pross. "They are absolutely safe, Pross. No matter how you tried, you could not fire them. The same goes for the Agusta."

"That's reassuring."

"You don't have to doubt everything I say."

"Blame it on my childhood. I have a natural mistrust, the legacy of a deprived childhood."

"I happen to know that's far from the truth, Pross."

"Then it must have been my father. He threw bowls of cornflakes at me when I was a baby. I thought people ate cornflakes, you see."

Sanders' face went still. "For the life of me, I'll never understand why Fowler insists on involving you and that other reprobate Gallagher in Department affairs."

"Reprobates. My God. The last time I heard someone use that word was at school. He was a permanently constipated housemaster- -"

Mabel, who had been enjoying the exchange, cut in before Sanders burst a blood vessel. "In you get, David. John Rushman's waiting somewhere in the mountains. And it is true the weapons won't fire. We've doctored them all. They are there to give you familiarisation with a full load. They'll be fully live in Nepal."

"And besides," Sanders put in nastily, "the Swiss wouldn't like it if you started shooting up their countryside."

"Especially on a Sunday," Pross said as he climbed in. "Back for breakfast, Mabel!"

He shut the door, strapped and plugged himself in quickly, put on his helmet and was lighting up within seconds, it seemed. The blades began to turn, gained flying speed. He lifted off swiftly, pulled hard over in a steep climbing turn, heading down towards Betten. He had the satisfaction of seeing Sanders lying flat in the snow where he had thrown himself in panic as the whirling blades churned a maelstrom of white about him.

Mabel had not moved. Pross fancied there was a look of quiet amusement on her face; but that could have been his imagination. His glimpse of her had been of the briefest, behind the thin curtain of dancing white powder.

Pross took the Lynx at 1500 feet above the Rhône Valley towards Fiesch. To his right, the edge of the ridge that housed Bettmeralp and Kühboden towered a further 2000 feet above him. Guns sited all along that ridge, he thought idly, would play hell with helicopters flying through the valley. No wonder no one fancied the idea of invading somewhere like Switzerland, or Nepal, or Afghanistan . . . unless they were head-cases.

"But I'm going to Nepal," he said to himself, "to take on another head-case."

He swept his monitors with a practised eye. Nothing as yet. Where are you hiding, Rushman?

He lost some height. Mustn't go too low. Can't disturb the good citizens on their Sunday. He was over Fiesch. The snow-topped houses looked good enough to eat.

Fiesch gave way to Fieschertal. He went lower as he passed the last of the scattered groups of chalets, curved left and continued towards the small Fieschergletscher which roughly parallelled the Aletsch on the other side of the range.

Still nothing on the radar. Where are you, Rushman?

The Gems, spooling powerfully as Pross once more gained height to clear the rising ground, had been modified for operation in the high thin air of the Himalayas. They sounded smooth and healthy. There was little vibration. The Lynx felt at home.

He would, he decided, perhaps tomorrow, carry out some engine-out exercises. It was all well and good having wonderful things like fighter radar and IFFC; but they were of little use to you if the things that kept you up chose to go on strike. That would kill you just as easily as the bloke who wanted to put great holes into you. If you knew how to use a dead engine, or even both, it could save your life . . . and even get the other bloke into the bargain.

He remembered when, during his days as Gallagher's navigator, Gallagher had deliberately killed an engine to go suddenly unstable in a practice fight. The Phantom had simply fallen out of the attacker's sights. It always helped, of course, if when the time came, the engine re-lit on cue. Bad news if it didn't.

Never go by the book, had been one of Gallagher's motifs. The book can kill.

True enough, in some cases.

Everyone studied combat tactics, scanned other people's theories for new ideas. Not much good if the jockey behind knew exactly what you were about to do at any given moment. The thing was to go outside his envelope. When it came down to it, the solution depended upon the soft bit in the cockpit; the part that could get hurt and therefore wanted to survive.

Pross brought the Lynx higher, turned west, climbed steeply. He was now heading towards the 9500-foot peak of Eggishorn. He did not intend to get too close. A strongish wind was coming off it, not quite buffeting the Lynx, but giving perceptible tugs. Pross did a 100-degree flat turn to the left, pointing his nose towards Kühboden.

The radar's look-down mode was searching as far out as 24 nautical miles when there were no peaks in the way. It was still quiet. Rushman was hiding, probably . . .

The radar suddenly shrieked.

Pross pivoted the Lynx round, dropped like a stone. The shrieking stopped. He slowed his descent, came to the hover. He was close to the Fiescheralp cable-car system, but his blades were safe. Just beneath the wires, a jagged formation of rock sprouted angrily upwards, the streaks of snow making it look as if monstrous jaws were forcing themselves out of the earth.

He gave the cyclic a gentle shift towards him. The Lynx eased smoothly backwards, stopped at the hover. He manoeuvred carefully until he had placed the Lynx behind the rock formation. He waited.

One minute. Two.

Had Rushman seen him on radar? Had he moved fast enough?

Three minutes. Four.

Pross held the Lynx steady, feet and hands teasing at

the controls. The Lynx remained at its station, barely shifting, seeming to hang motionless in the clear alpine air. Its mast sensor peeped between the rocks.

Five minutes.

Then he saw it; an image had appeared on one of the cathoderay tubes. It was coming towards him. The A129.

It was coming up the Rhône Valley from the direction of Brig, and was about ten kilometres away.

Pross smiled. Rushman had made a great show of going towards the glacier, obviously hoping Pross would have followed, leaving himself open to a nice bounce. Meanwhile, Rushman had gone across then and turned left down the open swathe of the glacier to curve round in a wide arc before coming up the valley.

"Nice try, John," Pross said, "but forget it."

He stayed where he was, surer by the second that Rushman did not know where he was. He watched the Agusta come closer. He was also certain that even when Rushman got close enough, he would not spot the mast sensor between the rocks. It would have blended nicely into the background.

The HUD was on and glowing, coupled to the IFFC. It was almost embarrassingly simple. Pross brought the Lynx up suddenly when the A129 was less than a kilometre away and closing on a track that would take it right across his nose. Rushman flew right into the sights.

Pross had selected the gun, and he squeezed the trigger even as the A129 started to take evasive action; but Rushman had not given himself sufficient room. In his efforts to stay low, he had come too close to the rising ground for violent evasion. He was therefore severely restricted in his choice of manoeuvre.

"Bang!" Pross said.

The IFFC registered ten simulated killing hits.

The Agusta pulled up steeply, climbing to 1000 feet above the Lynx.

"Luck," came Rushman's voice. He sounded disgusted with himself. He had been taken like a novice. "Let's see what you can do in a straight fight."

"You're on," Pross said, and climbed after him. "Lesson number one," he went on to himself. "Never get caught too close to the deck."

They went high over the glacier. Fifteen minutes later, Rushman was even more disgusted with himself. Throughout, he had come nowhere near achieving a gun solution. Pross had "shot" him down a further three times.

"Break," Rushman called. "Let's go home."

They flew back in formation. There was no banter over the air. They landed in the continuing silence.

Rushman came over to Pross as he climbed out of the Lynx. "You were either very lucky," he said, "or you're very good."

"I'd prefer to think I was lucky."

Rushman smiled. He didn't seem to mind. "Modesty, modesty. Your next session is with Gunga Din himself. Hans-Ruedi. Let's see how you do against a fixed-wing."

"My luck may hold," Pross said.

It was all well and good scoring against Rushman; but Anakov would not be play-acting, and would be using real cannon shells and missiles.

Winning in a practice shoot was nothing to write home about.

07.00, London.

Telford had been kept awake by his flask of hot black coffee. It was two hours now since the two men he had seen earlier had returned to keep a watch on the house. He was beginning to wonder whether he'd have to remain for the whole day, too, when Logan appeared. She was dressed for a visit to the camp.

The streets were white with a light frost, and there was no wind. He wondered what it was like at the camp. Bloody cold without a doubt. Crazy women.

Logan got into the light green car. It started at the first go, puffed whitely from its thin exhaust. She began to reverse out of the mews.

"Naughty Logan," he said reprovingly. "Didn't your driving instructor tell you never reverse into the street? Women drivers!" He smiled at his weak joke.

The 2CV pulled into the kerb, then rolled forward and away, puffing frantically in the cold air like someone with a first cigarette.

Should he follow her? Telford was not sure of what to do. He was intrigued by the two men, who did not start their car. He decided to wait to see what they intended to do. He knew where Logan was going.

Half an hour passed before the men made their move. Telford watched with mounting interest as they left their car and entered the mews. They stopped by the garage where the Citroën had been parked. They conversed briefly, then one of them took something out of his coat pocket, and began working at the lock. The other acted as a look-out.

In about a minute, Telford judged, the garage door was unlocked. It was an up-and-over door and the man lifted it open. So much for garage locks.

The men were now staring at the XR. The one who had forced the lock pointed repeatedly at the car while he talked animatedly to his companion; then together they pulled the door back down and left for their car at a run.

Telford reasoned they'd be going after Logan. He waited until the Mercedes had shot away with a squeal of tyres before taking up pursuit. He kept his distance, intending to keep them unaware of his presence; but after twenty minutes of careful shadowing, they still spotted him. At the very next traffic lights, they lost him by jumping a red.

He swore. There was no choice now but to head for Greenham Common. His Golf was a GTi. It was fast enough to get him to the camp in time.

Logan saw the Mercedes almost as soon as it had appeared in the distance behind her, on the A34 out of

Newbury, heading towards the airfield. It was coming up fast. Her instincts told her what that meant, and she took a hand off the wheel to reach for her floppy bag which lay on the seat next to her. She opened it. The magnum, fully loaded as always, was within easy reach. Leaving the bag open, she returned her hand to the steering wheel. A glance in the mirror showed her that the Mercedes was still closing. On this early Sunday morning, there was no traffic to baulk it. It would soon catch up.

At the A34 roundabout, still keeping an eye on the mirror, she turned left onto the A339 which would take her along the sweeping curve towards the main gate, not her usual route. The frost on the roads was thicker here than in London, and the little 2CV twitched now and then. Another glance in the mirror showed that the Mercedes had negotiated the roundabout and was coming her way. No doubts now. She decided she was going to have to take them. They would leave her no choice.

About 200 yards from the gates, she saw a couple of women on the grass verge, stamping their feet to keep the cold of the ground at bay. They recognised her car, waved. One of them was Clara. She gave them a brief wave in return, but did not slow down. She had a fleeting impression of seeing their heads turn to follow her passage.

She gave the mirror a brief scrutiny. There seemed to be another car, some distance behind the Mercedes. It too was apparently being driven fast. It was not a white Rover.

A turning to the right onto a narrow road came up. She turned into it at speed. The 2CV lurched but stayed on the frosty road, which led to Ecchinswell. Ahead, the road presented her with an unblemished coat of white, and was slippery. Behind her, she left an easy trail marked' upon it by her tyres. The world about her seemed still, as if frozen in place; waiting.

The Mercedes did not appear to have made the turning. Perhaps it had been baulked by some traffic coming out of the airfield; then on a curve through Brock's Green, she saw it coming up again. She had just about sufficient lead to put into action what she had planned.

Half a mile or so before Ecchinswell, she turned sharply left onto an even narrower road. There was no room within which to turn a big car quickly, if at all. They wouldn't know that.

Just under a mile from the turning, she came upon a sharp bend. She took it at a lower speed, slewed the car across the road, blocking it. She could only hope no one would turn up before the Mercedes got to the bend. It seemed most unlikely on such a back road; but there was always someone somewhere who would turn up at the worst moment to screw things up. Like the hump-backed bridge in the middle of nowhere with not a single other car for miles around . . . except for the one you'll find hitting the hump at exactly the same time, bang in the centre of the road.

"Whoever you are, Mr. Sod," Logan muttered as she grabbed the Ruger and spare ammo from her bag, and left the car quickly, "stay at home today . . . at least until I've finished."

She hurried off the road, and found herself an ambush position. Cover near that part of the road was sparse, opening as it did onto exposed ground; but she found a low, frosted hedge on the left side of the road, in the direction in which she'd been travelling. There was just about enough cover for her purposes. She intended to get the driver first. The Mercedes was left-hand drive.

She'd barely had the time to settle herself down on the cold, hard ground, when she heard the racing motor, revs mounting every so often in a shrill scream as the driver skidded his way along the narrow road. She thought she could hear another engine as well. It hardly mattered now. She was committed.

She could not see beyond the bend now that she lay flat to make most of the cover; but that would not affect her arc of fire. The Mercedes would slow right down when the men in it saw the Citroën, if they were quick.

235

It would give her all the time she needed.

"Comrade!" Valentinov shouted to Semachev as he saw the car and immediately began to slew the big Mercedes round.

"Don't stop!" Semachev roared. *"Ram that car!"*

But it was too late. Valentinov was an excellent driver and both his skill and his instinct for survival let him down. Instead of following Semachev's orders, he brought the Mercedes to a safe stop, broadside, a few feet from the Citroën; and jammed into the bank on both sides of the road.

Semachev did not waste valuable time remonstrating with him, although that was what he would dearly love to have done.

"Out!" he bawled, already opening his door.

He was still too late, and knew it with a sense of chagrin mixed with rage. He had miscalculated, and that idiot Valentinov had compounded everything by stopping when he should have ploughed that stupid little car out of the way. The British had planted the woman, just as he'd always thought. He had recognised the blue car in the garage. He had seen it following them.

Semachev hit the ground, rolling.

Logan was very fast. She did not waste priceless ammunition with a snap shot at Semachev. The magnum roared twice at Valentinov, just as he was getting out of the car.

He was hit twice in the chest. They were killing shots. He slammed backwards against the car, collapsed into it, his feet protruding from beneath the bottom of the opened door which then crashed back against the dead shins.

Logan was already swiftly seeking out Semachev, who for some unaccountable reason had raised himself to a crouch and was pointing his pistol back along the road.

236

Telford brought his Golf to a skidding halt when he saw the Mercedes blocking his path. He had barely enough time to see the gun pointing at him as he tried desperately to get out.

Logan heard the bark of Semachev's weapon simultaneously with the screeching of the brakes and the roaring of the engine of the second car. She raised her head slightly, felt despair when she saw who it was. She knew she would be far too late to save him.

Even as Semachev fired at Telford, the Ruger bellowed at the brutish man in the thick coat. It roared four times, so rapidly, the shots sounded like a continuous blast. All four bullets hit Semachev. They were head shots.

Even as he fell, a fleeting thought had briefly lived in Semachev's mind, accompanied by a terrible sense of failure.

I should have killed her that day.

Logan ran across the road, reloading as she went. She'd have to be quick. The noise would bring the curious, even on a Sunday, particularly because the airfield was not far away.

There was little need to check on Valentinov and Semachev. She knew they were dead. When she shot to kill, she killed.

She rushed to Telford, not really expecting him to have survived. Why had he been there? She could find no reason, unless the Department had set him to watch her. She didn't like the feeling of that at all.

Telford appeared to be still breathing. The whole of his chest was a mass of blood. He was not going to make it.

There was nothing she could do. She'd have to leave him and get as quickly away as possible. It would not do for her to be found near the scene.

She stopped, took his hand. "Nigel . . ." she began, "I'm sorry." Her eyes darted from him, scanned the immediate area for people or cars, turned to him once more.

His own eyes were closed. Now, they fluttered open. "Saw . . ." he began in painfully low whisper, " . . . saw . . ."

"Don't speak, Nigel. Save your strength." Her eyes darted round again.

"What . . . what for?" There was irony in the weak voice. "Saw . . . saw them . . . in your garage . . . looking at . . . car. Came . . . to . . . help . . . Partners . . ." The weak voice faded for good.

Logan squeezed her eyes shut briefly, and squeezed the dead hand. "Nigel," she said softly, and her voice shook.

Then she was running away from the Golf and back to her own car. She had to climb up a bank to get past the Mercedes. Semachev's body had fallen against a skeletal hedge, and was grotesquely propped up by it. She did not look at the ruined head.

She climbed into the 2CV. It was totally unscathed.

She put the magnum and her remaining ammo back into the bag, and turned the key. The little engine started at first go. She heaved a sigh of relief, turned the car and drove away from the Mercedes as quickly as she could on the frosty road.

It took her back to the A339 where she turned left. Five hundred yards later, she turned right onto the road that would eventually take her round the airfield.

"Thank you, Mr. Sod," she said, "for staying away."

Jean greeted her with a warm smile. "Minty! Great news!" Then Jean frowned. "Are you alright? You look a bit wan."

"Oh I'm fine. Feeling the cold perhaps. Tell me about

238

your news."

"Come into the tent. I've got some tea, just made. That should put the warmth where it's needed."

Logan followed, carrying her bag. In the tent, with a hot mug of tea warming her hands, she said, "What's the news?"

Jean's eyes lit up like a child's who had been given an unexpected present. "We've got it!" She smacked Logan's knee in her excitement. "We've got the trip. They've *agreed*. I can hardly believe that at last we're getting somewhere. The Russians have agreed to meet us in Kabul. Oh Minty! Isn't that fantastic?"

Logan said, "You're sure they're not just sending generals in civvies?"

Jean was too overwhelmed by events to let this deflate her. "What does it really matter? If there really are generals, at least we can speak to them. We can ask them why they want to blow up the world and everything on it. It's a start, Minty. It's better than generals talking to generals; the deaf talking to the deaf."

"I'm pleased for you, Jean. You've put in a lot of hard work. You deserve to succeed."

"I'm not going alone," Jean said. "You're coming too. I hope you've been thinking about it. I'm counting on you."

Logan had already been thinking about it for her own reasons, but she pretended to be uncertain, hating the role of deceit she was forced to play with Jean.

"I . . . I don't know, Jean. I mean . . ."

"Oh nonsense, Minty. No excuses. You know I want you there with me not only to keep Clara from going over the top, but as a friend I know I can depend on. Say yes."

Logan thought about it, judged her moment nicely. "Alright, Jean. I'll come with you."

Jean hugged her. "I knew you wouldn't let me down. I knew it!"

"When do we go?"

"Next Wednesday. I hope your inoculations are all up

to date." Jean suddenly looked dismayed. "Oh dear. I forgot to ask you about that. I've been waiting for this for so long, I prepared myself some time ago."

Logan said, "Wednesday! That's a bit soon."

"We have no choice. We've got to take it when it comes, I'm afraid. But what about your inoculations?"

"I'm alright there. I mean, I travel with my father on occasion, so I'm always jabbed up." Logan's lie neatly covered the fact that it was Department policy to keep all personnel's inoculations up to date.

Jean sighed with relief. "Thank God for that. Well there's nothing to stop us now. Visas will be ready by Tuesday, as will the tickets."

"Who's paying for them?"

"They've already been paid for. That's not your worry. Just pack what you think you'll need for a three-day stay, and leave the rest to me. Alright?"

Logan nodded. "Alright, Jean."

"Good. By the way, Clara said she saw you earlier on."

"Yes. I thought I'd take a little drive around before I came here, just to clear my thoughts."

"Trouble?"

"Not really. Just something silly."

"Can I help?"

Logan shook her head.

"It's not . . . it's not that Hungarian, is it?" Jean asked with sudden insight. "He has been coming around asking about you."

Logan said nothing, allowing Jean to come to the obvious, but totally wrong conclusion.

"Trouble with *him?*"

Logan shrugged. "He's too . . . oh I don't know," she said eventually, giving the impression of great uncertainty. "I don't think I really need personal complications at the moment, Jean."

"It's just as well the trip's come up then. Do you good to get away."

"I suppose so."

"Oh . . . I almost forgot in the excitement. There's

240

something else happening; tonight. They're going to try and move a missile on a practice run. We're going to block the road. Some people have said there was a lot of banging going on a little earlier and thought it might have something to do with tonight's exercise. You don't think they're practising to shoot at us, do you? I mean, this isn't some banana republic."

Logan shook her head, thinking of Telford's body out there in the cold country lane, keeping Semachev and Valentinov company in death. They were on the same side now.

"No, Jean," she said quietly. "We're not a banana republic. Not yet, anyway."

15.30. Bettmeralp.

Rushman walked with Pross towards the Lynx. Only Pross was suited up.

Rushman said, "Hans-Ruedi will be coming at you from any quarter. It's all up to you how you counter him." Rushman gave a quick grin. "After this morning, I don't suppose you'll be short of ideas."

Pross said, "I'll just have to see what I can pull out of the magic hat."

"I can hardly wait to hear Hans-Ruedi's comments. He hates to lose, I've been told. By the way, did they get your jabs sorted out? Nepal's got all sorts of lovely ailments with which to lay the unwary low: cholera, typhoid, smallpox, dysentery—"

"Are you always so cheerful?"

"Only at three-thirty in the afternoon, in the Swiss Alps. Nepal is beautiful, but it hates people."

"Thank you, John Rushman."

"Any time." Rushman grinned. The Chamberlain moustache twitched.

They had reached the Lynx. Pross opened the cockpit door, and climbed in. He looked at Rushman.

"Sorry to disappoint you, but I am fully inoculated. I was done some months ago when I came back from the last job."

"At least you won't get loose bowels at 16,000 feet. Just imagine, you're about to shoot and . . . whoops!"

"Rushman, you've got a low mind."

"So my mother always said."

Pross shook his head in mock despair as he connected himself to the aircraft. "Where's Sanders, anyway?"

"Getting an earful from Mabel, I should think."

There was a compact communications system in the shed. Sanders had wanted to monitor the flight by listening-in and giving instructions. Mabel had said that as Pross would not be getting instructions from anyone once he was in the air in Nepal, it was hardly worth it.

Sanders had objected. They were still arguing about it.

"Close me up, will you, please?" Pross said as he put on his helmet. He flexed his fingers in the thin and nicely sensitive kid gloves, and gave the thumbs-up as Rushman shut the door.

He started up the Lynx, waited for the avionics to come on line, then lifted it high and fast in a swirl of snow. It was only when he was cruising at 1000 feet above the valley and again heading towards Fiesch that he realised what he had said to Rushman.

True, he had been given a full range of inoculations on his return from the Far East. Fowler had said then it had been to combat any possible infection he might have been exposed to, during his brief stay. With a business to run, the last thing he had wanted was to fall ill to some unknown bug. He had readily agreed.

But that had not been Fowler's reason at all. Even as far back as that time, Fowler had been preparing him for this.

"Scheming bastard," Pross said to himself.

No point railing about it now. The thing to do was to look out for Gunga Din, otherwise known as Leutnant Bitsch, banker and part-time combat pilot.

Pross kept close to rock faces and slopes. A fixed-wing attacking a chopper would not like being close to the ground. The fixed-wing needed manoeuvring space.

They didn't like the ground, with good reason. Pross intended to make Bitsch commit himself to attacks that would frighten the life out of him. There were lots of lovely peaks, slopes and valleys to give a fixed-wing pilot a few grey hairs.

The mottled Lynx hummed over Fiesch. The warning radar stayed obstinately silent. Pross thought about the Pilatus. He had not been given any performance figures for it, and wondered whether this had been a deliberate omission. Rushman, however, had told him that the PC-9 was fast enough, and had HUD. They were obviously trying to make it as hard as possible for him. He'd make it bloody hard for dear old Hans-Ruedi.

He took the Lynx low between the snow-clad mountains. A fixed-wing trying to spot him from above was going to have a tough job finding him. He flew slowly, to make his displacement across the terrain as undetectable as possible. Fast movement catches the eye.

He took the same route he had earlier flown against Rushman. The radar was still silent. Not surprisingly, given the walls of rock about him. He lifted the Lynx slowly, still keeping it fairly close to the ground as he followed the incline. The terrain levelled out. Three lakes passed beneath him: the Marjelensee. Then he was moving out towards the glacier. His eyes searched.

The warning came at about the same time that something flashed high in the sky from the northeast. Leutnant Bitsch had arrived.

The black Pilatus plunged downwards, catching up fast. Pross waited until he had judged that Bitsch was lining up for his shoot, then went into a tight pivoting turn that took him head-on, but leading off a few degrees. The manoeuvre completely destroyed Bitsch's line and the Pilatus had to commence a turn in the opposite direction to try and keep the Lynx in its sights.

Pross again reversed his turn. The Pilatus had to obey the laws of physics and curve past, completely off target. Pross wheeled the Lynx round, and got a fleeting image of the PC-9's tail in his sights; too fleeting to try for a shot. But it had been close.

"A clever move!" came a voice in his headphones. It sounded surprised. "But next time, I shall have you." Bitsch had a lilting accent.

Pross knew nothing about the various Swiss accents; but Rushman had told him that the pilot of the PC-9 came from canton of St. Gallen. He didn't know what a St. Gallen accent was like, but assumed this must be it.

He did not make reply to the banter, but watched as the Pilatus again began curving towards him, wings vertical. He dropped out of the bottom, going straight down. The Pilatus passed frustratedly above him. He kept descending until he was about 500 feet above the surface of the glacier. He turned 180 degrees, saw the Pilatus winging over back down towards him. Frustration must be settling in on Bitsch by now, he reasoned. In real combat, time was vital. A quick kill and get the hell out; if you could a sense of frustration was therefore bad news for the concentration.

A gentle push on the collective, and the Lynx sank further. Bitsch would have to take note of his own clearance above the ground. More load into the calculations. He'd be worrying about hitting now, and would be more cautious.

Pross watched him, did a fast lateral shift to the left, out into the middle of the glacier. Bitsch almost lost it. He had begun to reverse bank in a desperate attempt to keep on target when the nose seemed to drop. The wings came level quickly and the PC-9 pulled into a climb.

"*Gottfür . . . !*" came the startled exclamation. There was the sound of shallow breathing, then: "You are dangerous, my friend."

Again, Pross said nothing. The continuing silence would give the Lynx a palpable air of menace; more points on the psychological board. It all helped.

Pross smiled grimly. Anakov would not be talking to him; just shooting. This little game above the glacier was a million miles from the real thing. He would not be playing will-o'-the-wisp with an increasingly frustrated part-time pilot. He'd be up against a deadly professional, in an equally deadly machine, and who would be throwing live stuff at him. But he was getting to know the Lynx, and that was what mattered.

The Pilatus had disappeared. Pross gained height to tempt it; definitely not a stunt he'd consider pulling in a real situation . . . not unless he'd become suicidal. But he wanted to know how the Lynx would handle in the manoeuvre he next intended to carry out. You never knew. His life might depend on it one day.

Bitsch fell for it and came howling down, lining up on the Lynx's tail. Pross went into a gradual straight-line descent, pulling the Pilatus after him. Altitude fell off as the gun range closed. Pross hoped Hans-Ruedi would be so eager to get his sights lined up, he'd miss the fact that he was losing height fast, despite his earlier scare.

In combat manoeuvring, it was as fatal to telegraph your move, as to leave it too late. Too soon, and the man behind would have plenty of time to correct, especially if he was good at anticipating. Too late and . . . well, you were too late.

Pross judged the moment nicely, just when Bitsch was nearly within gun range. He shifted the Lynx suddenly in a flat dart to the right, jabbed at the right pedal. As the tail swung out, he caught a glimpse of the Pilatus going into an anticipatory reverse bank, hoping for the corresponding shift to the left.

Pross smiled, pivoted the Lynx round to complete his 360 degree sudden turn, shifted laterally to the left, each manoeuvre flowing smoothly into the next. He had also dropped altitude while carrying out the moves.

The Pilatus found itself with empty sky in its sights, was caught in a tight curving left turn, and was losing height. Pross was waiting as it flew straight into the sights. They held, pulsed. Shoot cue came on. Pross squeezed the trigger.

"Bang!" he said. The IFFC showed him 26 hits before the Pilatus, with the pines of Reideralp perilously close, pulled up sharply like a startled horse baulking at a fence.

There was no exclamation this time from Bitsch, but Pross heard rapid shallow breathing in his helmet. Bitsch had really frightened himself this time.

At last, the voice came. "I am glad we are not really fighting each other. I think I would be dead. You agree?"

"I agree."

There was brief laughter. "A man with no doubts."

If only you knew, mate! Pross thought. "I wouldn't quite say that."

Another laugh, quite rueful. "One day, you must show me."

"One day."

"And now we call a break. Yes?"

"Yes."

A dark shape slid into view to Pross's right. The Pilatus, sleek to its black paint, was keeping station with him. Only the front seat of its tandem cockpit was occupied. Grey-clad shoulders, topped by a white helmet with visor down and oxygen tubing hanging umbilically down from the mask, was visible above the cockpit rail. The be-helmeted head was turned towards him. A hand was raised in a brief, casual salute.

Pross nodded twice, exaggeratedly, in return.

"Tomorrow," came the voice, "I shall have a surprise." Then the Pilatus tilted its nose, accelerated upwards in a sudden burst of speed. It performed two beautifully executed climbing rolls before disappearing in the direction of Sierre.

"See you tomorrow, Hans-Ruedi," Pross said to himself, and turned the mottled Lynx for home.

He felt satisfied. The Lynx was handling perfectly.

Chapter Fourteen

00.45, Monday morning, Greenham Common.

Logan sat with Jean on the cold ground before the main gate. She held her bag tightly to her, as if to keep warm. Around her other women also sat, closely packed across the entrance, completely blocking it. The human barrier was six deep. There were many placards, some in day-glo, glaringly etched out in the blaze of the powerful security lights about the gate.

"DO NOT MURDER OUR CHILDREN!" they shouted silently.

Like their placards, the women too were silent. The airfield police stared back at them impassively from behind the gate. As yet, there were no overt expression of hostility between the two groups. The policemen stood there like people who had seen it all before, and already knew the outcome.

Then a light snow began to fall, the flakes drifting downwards, performing impossible aerobatics in the light breeze that took them darting in all directions, moths that expired against faces, uniforms, and the hot lenses of the lights. They sizzled as they died there.

Everyone was waiting in the silence of the night, disturbed only by the distant, continuous hum of the heartbeat of the airfield. A policeman stamped his foot, perhaps to relieve a cramped toe. The noise he made sounded inordinately loud. A snowflake alighted upon the shiny peak of his cap. It remained there like a white badge.

Logan felt someone move against her. She looked around curiously. Clara, who had been sitting away to the left, had made her way to her side.

Clara said, in a low voice, "Didn't get a chance to talk to you earlier. Were you alright this morning?"

"Yes. Why?"

The thin face looked mysterious. "Thought perhaps you were in trouble with the pigs. Two cars turned down the road you took."

Logan kept the look of bewildered curiosity upon her face. "I don't understand. People must use that road all the time."

"They had to stop to let a transporter out. I had a good look at them. Those in the first car were ugly bastards. Real pigs. They were carrying D-plates, so perhaps they were fucking Yank secret pigs. I'm certain they've got plenty of those in there." She glared at the gate.

Logan shrugged as if all this were totally beyond her comprehension. "I went for a little drive to clear my head before I went to meet Jean. That's all."

Jean heard, and leaned across to say softly to Clara, "Minty's had a difficult time with someone. It's personal. Leave her alone, Clara."

Clara's hot eyes stared at Logan, smirked. "Our Minty's got man trouble? Well. There's hope for us all."

Jean said, "Clara! Don't be so unkind."

Others had heard Clara's last remark, and were giving her dirty looks.

"God," she said disgustedly. "Protection for Lady Silverspoon." Then she brought her face close to both Jean's and Logan's. "By the way, there's a rumour going round that there was a shooting today, out near Ecchinswell. Three dead."

Jean's eyes seemed to pop. Logan made sure looked equally shocked.

"What?" Jean whispered. She glanced around nervously, to see if anyone else had heard. No one appeared to

have.

Clara was nodding. "The noise we all heard this morning."

"But who . . ."

Clara said, "Who knows, and who cares? As long as they're shooting each other, I don't give a fuck."

"My God," Jean said in a shaky voice. She paused, looked around once more. No one seemed to be taking notice. "They're not going to use guns tonight, are they?"

Clara said, "I'd put nothing past those fascists." Logan said, "How do you know all this, Clara? How can you be sure anyone was shot today?" She continued to keep her voice low, but apologetic, just the way Clara would expect of her.

"Marion told me. She said . . ."

"Honestly, Clara," Jean interrupted. "Sometimes you'll accept anything if it coincides with your belief."

"Isn't that what everybody else does?" Clara countered in a sharp whisper. "People like the image of us as smelly viragos, so they believe it."

"Well . . ."

But further conversation was interrupted by a new sound upon the night. It was the sound of a laden transporter, approaching the gate from within the airfield. A loud sigh, almost of relief now that it was really coming to the gate, came from the assembled women. As if in concert, the snow began to fall more heavily, coating bare heads, dampening shawls, sliding off anoraks.

Clara's short hair was soon soaked.

The women remained seated, despite the discomfort. Suddenly, from behind the gate, reinforcements appeared for the men at the entrance, their number swelling alarmingly.

"They've got hundreds!" someone said.

Then the main road was full of lights and racing vehicles. Cries of surprise and anxiety now came from the crowd.

Clara was saying bitterly as the vehicles screeched to a halt, and there was the sound of running feet, "The bastards. I felt they would pull something like this." She began to jump and yell, *"Pigs!* Bastards! Fascists!"

"Clara!" Jean objected. "You'll only provoke them."

Clara rounded upon her, eyes wild. "What do you mean *I'll* provoke them? They're already provoked just because we're here!" She turned from Jean and moved through the women, some of whom were now getting up in anticipation of a massed charge from behind. Others remained where they were.

The transporter had now come into sight, its lights flooding the gate area, adding to what was beginning to look like an increasingly nightmarish tableau. The transporter, with its lethal cargo, was almost at the gate now. Logan thought it looked monstrous.

Even as the thought went through her mind, things began to happen in several areas at once. The gate came open, and out poured the men to drive a wedge through the protesters. From behind, the expected charge came. There were screams and curses as the women were picked up one by one and dragged away. The transporter moved inexorably forward.

Logan stared at it all. The glare of the lights, the shouts of the men and the screams of the women; the roar of the transporter's engine, the fall of the snowflakes, the struggling bodies, all looked like a scene from hell. The terrible blaze of the lights was its fire.

She found herself in a mêlée, fought to stay upright and to keep hold of her bag. Then suddenly she was seized from behind.

An arm wrapped itself about her neck. Her right arm was pulled behind her back and up. The bag was snatched from her free hand.

She went limp, prior to countering.

"Don't try it, Logan!" came a fierce whisper. "I know that one. The way I've got you, I can break your pretty neck before you can do anything. You're coming with us. The gun comes too."

She was hauled away into the darkness.

Logan sat in a hard chair. A powerful lamp was shining into her eyes. She blinked several times, aware of other people in the room, though she could not see them. Someone was smoking, and it irritated her. She had not been bound.

She knew where she was.

"Where is Mr Fowler?" she asked abruptly.

All movement stopped. There was soft breathing. The cigarette smoker inhaled deeply before exhaling. She heard him.

At last, someone said, "So you know who we are."

"Of course."

She had been bundled into a Mercedes, driven back to London in total silence. Her captors were strangers to her, but their type was unmistakable.

"There's a smell about your kind," she went on. "You used the Mercedes to make me believe you were Russians. You're Security or, as someone I know would say, secret pigs."

There was more silence from beyond the light.

Then, "Made nice friends out there, did you? Began to think perhaps they are right? Perhaps you even gave them a few bits of information . . . from Lady Dilke-Weston, of course." The voice sounded amused.

An approving snicker came from behind the light.

Logan refused to be intimidated. "Don't be more stupid than you already are."

"And *you* don't get fancy with me, Logan," the voice said harshly. "You're in deep trouble."

"I don't know what you're talking about."

"Of course." Sarcastically.

"Why did you kill Telford?" A new voice had thrown the sudden question at her.

Her mouth hung open in shock. *What?*

"Oh look at that," the first voice began with fake concern. "She's so surprised. Poor Telford. She doesn't even know she shot him. He would really appreciate that. Pity he's not around."

251

Logan felt a chill in her stomach. What were they trying to do? Where in God's name was Fowler?

She hid her increasing anxiety from them. "Which is the less stupid of the two?" she asked coldly. Were there only two? "I'd like to talk to him. I might get something through to what passes for a brain."

Angry steps approached. *"Now watch it!"*

Whoever had been angered was stopped before he could cross into the light.

"I would not upset them, Logan." A third voice, calmer, but also unrecognisable. How many from Security were attached to the Department? "They won't take any notice of the fact that you're a woman; an attractive one at that . . . as your Russian boyfriend no doubt thinks. Shame he's no longer in the country. We would have liked to have had him in for a few questions."

Anakov gone!

My God, she thought. *Pross.* She saw again the fireball from her dream.

Had Anakov gone back because of Semachev and Valentinov? Or was it because of a much deeper game that she had not even begun to see? And why were these people trying to frame her for Telford's death?

She maintained her cold exterior. "What boyfriend? It's really true about Security, isn't it? You need an especially low IQ to take the job."

"Oh she is tough." Derisively. "I'm getting worried."

"I've warned you, Logan," the calm voice said. "We all know you by reputation. We are not awed. Don't make it any harder on yourself. I'd strongly advise discretion."

Don't needle them, her own caution warned her. Wait for Fowler. He'll sort it out.

"I want to see Mr. Fowler," she said. "He's my superior. I'll talk to him."

"Sir John Winterbourne is also your superior, Logan . . . *and* Mr. Fowler's. He is Head of Department. You answer, ultimately, to him."

Winterbourne. She might have known. Trust Winterbourne to put both feet in it.

"Did Sir John order you to bring me in?"

"I don't see why we should not tell you. Yes. The order was his."

"Why?"

"Do not ask tiresome questions, Logan. You know why."

"You're being absurd. All of you. I did not shoot Telford. I shot the man who shot him. I saw it happen."

Silence. All she could hear was the sound of breathing, and the intermittent inhalation of the compulsive smoker. She tried to peer beyond the rim of light without success. She decided to stand.

"I'd sit down if I were you, Logan," the calm voice said. There was an underlying hostility to it that made her lower herself once more even before she had fully stood up. She did so slowly.

She could not believe it. They were treating her worse than the Russians had; but then, Anakov had interrupted that little session. It appeared that no one was going to come to her aid now. Where was Fowler?

"I did not kill Telford," she repeated, the steadiness of her voice belying the apprehension she felt. "If you've already seen the three bodies, you'll find my bullets only in two of them; neither of which was Telford."

"Oh we found your bullets in those two alright," the harsher voice admitted. "Well . . . not exactly *in* them. That piece of artillery you carry tends to leave great holes in people. The bullets also tend, on occasion, to go somewhere else; but we found them. We also found one more . . . in Telford."

"But that's ludicrous! You could not possibly have found one of my bullets in him. Not unless someone put it there."

"And who would that be, Logan?" the calm voice asked. "You are the only member of the Department with a Ruger magnum."

"I'm not the only person on earth with one," Logan said scathingly. "Why don't you pick everybody else up?"

"Ah. I see. Someone followed you, waited till you had

gone, then put a bullet from your gun, into Telford. Does that sound alright to you? Is it sufficiently ludicrous — to use your own word — to gain favour with you? Perhaps you can tell us who that person is. Are we to believe that an operative as highly trained as you are would have been unaware of someone hiding in the bushes? The cover there is so sparse, there was no suitable place close enough."

"There has to be an answer. Someone else was responsible."

"Oh, there is an answer. Unless you would like us to believe that a third car followed you all the way from London, knowing exactly what was going to happen, waiting only to put one of your bullets into Telford. As the bullet in question was spent, it would have meant searching for one to use, and to insert it by hand. Who, I wonder, is the enterprising candidate?"

Even to Logan, it sounded crazy. Yet if they were telling the truth . . .

"You're lying," she accused. "You found no bullet, except those of the man who really shot him."

"Ah. Did you all hear that? We're lying."

Silence descended once more. There was the creaking of shoe-leather, the soft breathing, and the maddening inhalations. The tobacco smoke was beginning to annoy now, but Logan forced herself to ignore it.

"See how calm she is. A credit to the Department. Pity she took a wrong turning. Why did you do it, Logan? For your boyfriend? To stop Telford because he knew too much? You'd better tell us, or I promise you, we'll keep you here till you rot."

"I want to see Mr. Fowler."

"I'll tell you what," the calm voice went on as if she had not spoken. "I'll let you know what we know, which is quite a lot; then perhaps you'll see reason and be more co-operative. We would hate to resort to more physical methods. I came certain you would hate it too.

"For example, we know you were picked up by the Russians and in a remarkably short space of time . . .

254

presto, you're released with not a single hair out of place. Next, you con Telford into allowing you to inspect files without authorisation. We are very interested in knowing what you found in Mr. Fowler's office. I know you'll tell us. I have every confidence in you. Let's see . . . where was I? Ah. Yes. Then, you later go to a wine bar to meet the man whom you were ordered to keep under close surveillance, but with whom you decided instead to become involved.

"Of course, I do not blame you. He is a very attractive man, and you will not be the first Intelligence operative to become . . . let us put it delicately . . . attached to a subject. You will certainly not be the last. History is full of such casualties. After the wine bar, you took him home—the *Department's* house, I should say—where he spent some little time with you. Don't look so outraged, Logan. We did not videotape. Mr. Fowler would not have it. Pity, really. We might have had something with which to bargain with our friends across the Curtain.

"Finally, you leave for Greenham Common where poor Telford, no doubt following you conscientiously, gets shot for his pains. You killed the others to cover your own tracks, to make it look as if you were only doing what the Department expects of you. Meanwhile, the boyfriend has scarpered. Am I doing alright so far?"

Logan had been listening to the incredible fabrication with mounting disbelief. She let it show. She decided attack was the best form of defence. To hell with them.

"Are you in charge of this team of morons?" she asked in a chill voice. She heard intakes of breath that had nothing to do with smoking. "If so," she went on before anyone could say anything, "you are well suited. *I have never heard so much bullshit!* How . . ."

A door opened, and the lights came on. Fowler was standing near the light switch. The three Security men looked sheepishly at him, looked at Logan who was in the act of rising, looked at Fowler again. He moved forward to turn off the bright light.

He said calmly, "What is the meaning of this?"

The man who had been speaking in the patiently calm voice to Logan, said, "Sir John asked us to . . ."

"Please leave us, Martins," Fowler said, still calmly, cutting into the man's words. "And take your men with you."

Martins was a small man with a pinched, mean face. His colleagues were totally the opposite. They were big men, built like rugby players.

Logan looked at them coldly.

Martins was reluctant. "Mr. Fowler—"

"No one," Fowler began with a hard edge to his voice now, "pulls my personnel from the field without my say-so. Am I clear, Martins?" The eyes behind the glasses seemed to pierce the smaller man. *"No one."*

Logan found it ironic that twice in just under forty-eight hours, she had been hauled in by both the Russians and her own side, and had been released because of intervention by someone with more authority than her captors, and in almost the same manner. She did not smile.

She was now feeling angry, and relieved. She was also afraid; for Pross, who was being pitched into great danger now that Anakov was gone. She felt angry once more because Fowler had not been totally honest with her; and though she was relieved at his intervention, it did not serve to dissipate her anger. She needed a target.

Martins and his men were reluctantly leaving the bare room.

"Wait!"

They halted, looking at her expectantly, neutrally. She went up to them.

"I'll remember you, Martins." The green eyes, full of anger, blazed a cold fire at him. She looked at the other men in turn. "And you, and you. For the record, if you can get it into the sawdust you use for brains, I didn't kill Telford. But if you come near me again, I'll shoot you, you bastards." She held out a hand.

They stared at her.

"My gun," she said contemptuously.

Martins said, almost with glee, "It's in the armoury, being checked."

The eyes bored into him. *What for?*

Martins flinched, but stood his ground. "Proof," he said, and walked out, followed by his men.

One of them paused at the door to wink at Logan. The smoker.

Logan said to Fowler, "I didn't kill him."

"Of course you didn't kill him."

"Then why —"

"Because they've made a report and it has to be seen through."

"Including this interrogation?"

"That was Sir John's doing. I'll take it up with him."

She eyed him suspiciously. "Where were you while the three wise men were having a go at me?"

"Coming here to do what I have just done. When I heard about Telford and the other two, I sent someone down to keep an eye on you. I didn't know that Sir John had decided to step in with his own ideas. When I found out what had happened, I came as soon as I could." Fowler paused. "But it doesn't end there, Logan." His eyes were hard as they looked at her. "What gave you the idea that you could break into my desk to search any files I might have there? You are aware of the breach you have committed? A very serious breach? People can be sent to prison for less these days."

Logan was unrepentant. "You were less than honest with me, *sir.*"

"You are my subordinate, Logan. I expect and will receive, a certain amount of trust from you. You are told, at any given time, all that you *need* to know. This is how the Department works. If you do not trust me, how can I in turn trust you?"

"You know better than that."

"Do I? Is it a fiction that you burgled my desk? Well? Have you nothing to say for yourself? I thought not. Alright. Let's get out of here."

257

They left the room, and took a long flight of concrete steps that would take them up to ground level.

On the way, Logan said, "What about my gun?"

"What about it?'

"When do I get it back?"

"As soon as Arms are finished with it."

Logan stopped as they reached the ground floor. Fowler paused, looked at her inquiringly.

She said, "*You* don't really believe them, do you?"

"I have already told you what I believe. However, Martins did not lie. A .357 magnum round was found in Telford's body. I want to know who put it there, and why. Meanwhile, you go back to the house and wait until you hear from me."

Logan's green eyes looked steadily into Fowler's for long moments. Fowler gazed back at her almost benignly.

"You have seen the Anakov file," he said, "yet you have said nothing about Pross."

She said evenly, "There's not much I can do for him now, is there?"

"No, I suppose not." Fowler continued to look at her, as if searching for something.

"You suspect someone of leaking," she said. "You don't think it's me, do you?"

Fowler's eyes gleamed behind his glasses. "Had I thought so, Logan, I would have left you with Martins and his boys." He glanced at his watch. "It's six o'clock. Go home and get some sleep. I'm going on up to the office. I'll be in touch."

He turned away and left her to her devices.

She stared after him for some moments. She had already decided what she was going to do.

07.00, Bettmeralp.

Pross lifted the Lynx smoothly, headed out towards the glacier. Today, he was going to practise his engine-out exercises, and autorotation.

Not everybody thought autorotation was a good thing

to practise, and some manufacturers specifically forbade it except in dire emergency. Pross himself would never carry it out on his Jetrangers; but this was a different game altogether. He had to know how the Lynx would cope. He might need it.

Most people believed if a helicopter suffered a loss of power, it would glide like a stone. Not so. In the hands of a good pilot, a helicopter could have better gliding properties than a fixed-wing aircraft. Since falling through the air will create an airstream through the blades, setting them at a low angle of attack will cause them to turn, thereby generating sufficient lift to support the weight of the aircraft. A controlled descent is thus possible. Nearer the ground, the descent can be slowed by increasing the angle of attack until the helicopter has settled smoothly. Lift would end only when it was on the ground.

So much for theory, Pross thought. All he had to do was find out.

He took the Lynx to 3000 feet above the glacier, and looked down. It seemed a long way to go without engines. The petrified stream of ice looked suddenly menacing.

He decided to try the engine-out first, and took power off the port engine. The Lynx began to sink and the remaining engine automatically increased power to compensate. He steadied the aircraft, carried out a few manoeuvres to make sure he had absolute control. Despite the loss of performance, the Lynx was still comparatively agile. At a push, he could still fight.

He carried out a re-light. The engine came on smoothly. The Lynx seemed to leap for joy. He'd have to watch that. Perhaps he could use it to achieve displacement in a fight. He repeated the procedure with the second engine, got the same response. This time he was more prepared, and found he could use the sudden changes of handling and attitude to advantage.

Again, he took the Lynx up, this time to 4000 feet above the glacier.

Then he took power off both engines.

The sudden loss of engine noise was heart-numbing; and even as he took the collective down to lower the angle of attack and avoid stalling the blades — a sure way to sudden death, without engines-on — he wondered if he'd done the right thing.

The Lynx sank. Pross checked his rate of descent, saw it would take just a little under two minutes to reach the glacier surface. Insulated as he was within the confines of his helmet, the lack of the background noise of the engines made the world about him seem abnormally silent.

The Lynx continued to sink under perfect control. At 1000 feet to touch down, he remembered the gear. He had 27 seconds. Would the wheels come down in time? They did. He was pulling gently on the collective to slow descent even as the gear locked. The Lynx settled with a slight jar, but surprisingly gently, all things considered.

Pross heaved a sigh of relief. He patted the cyclic as if to tell the aircraft well done.

He was about to re-light when great shards of ice suddenly leapt into the air about 50 feet from the Lynx, to his right. His eyes opened wide in consternation. A sudden scream came from overhead.

"What the hell . . . !" he exclaimed, startled; but did not waste time trying to work it out and put the power on immediately. The twin Gems shrieked lustily.

He lifted the Lynx off the glacier, heart beating. He knew the scream of a jet fighter when he heard one. He also knew all about cannon shells. Someone was trying to kill him, right here on the bloody glacier. He suddenly realised that the only reason his unknown attacker had missed was because of the autorotation. The mysterious pilot had expected to see the Lynx climb and had misjudged.

But who would want to kill him in an airfight here in deepest Switzerland? And why had the tail radar not warned him?

He looked and saw why. It was not on. He had not

turned the damn thing on. Not expecting a practice fight, he had not put his combat avionics on line. He had forgotten one of the basics of his own training. Always be tooled up and ready to go.

Christ, Christ, he thought as he turned everything on. How long to ready state? How long?

And where was that bastard?

Pross searched the sky. Nothing. He took the Lynx into a 360-degree jinking turn. Still nothing.

The avionics were warming up nicely. Come on, come on!

Tooled up. He wasn't tooled up. With its armaments nobbled, the Lynx was about as fearsome as a day-old kitten.

Sweet Jesus!

Pross kept jinking the Lynx across the glacier. Don't remain still for a second. Don't give the bastard another chance.

But who was he?

Pross frowned. *Leutnant Bitsch.*

Bitsch had said the day before he'd be springing a surprise. Was this it? Was the surprise an unexpected bounce in a jet fighter, and had the cannon shells not really been aimed at the Lynx after all? Was this Hans-Ruedi's idea of a joke revenge for yesterday's defeat?

Pross selected the frequency designated for the practice flights and called Bitsch on it.

"Leutnant Bitsch! What the hell are you playing at?"

Silence.

Pross tried the shed. "Feline to Base. Feline to Base."

"This is Base." Mabel.

"You're not going to believe this. I've just been attacked by a bloody jet fighter!"

"Any damage?"

Good old Mabel. Straight to the point. No time-wasting exclamations. Pross glanced at the avionics. Nicely on-line, thank God. At least he would know what was going to happen, even if he couldn't defend himself.

"Any damage?" Mabel repeated.

Bloody hell. He'd forgotten to answer her. Get hold of yourself, Pross!

"No damage. Yet."

"Keep away from him. Don't return to base."

Keep away. Did she think he was going to say come and get me, here I am? And what was this about not returning?

"Why not base?"

"Hold him off till he runs out of fuel."

Oh great. Just like that.

"What if I can't?"

"Then you can't."

"Thank you for the kind words, Base. Can I use my weapons?"

"No. They are quite inoperative and even if they weren't, you would not be authorised."

Better and better.

"What about flares and chaff?"

"Inoperative."

"That's very cheering. I just hope he hasn't any bloody missiles."

"Sorry."

"Out," Pross said, and ended the transmission. Now it was see Switzerland and get it in the neck. Nepal was very far away.

Then the tail radar was shrieking at him.

He swung the Lynx round, saw the jet falling out of the sky, heading in his direction. He couldn't believe it. The twin booms were unmistakable, as was the shape. A De Havilland Vampire FB.6, used for advanced training in the Swiss air force. An old aircraft, but more than fast and dangerous enough if it meant business. If he could keep out of its way, he could probably use its speed against it. It would not be able to turn as tightly as the Pilatus for a start. And maybe, just maybe . . .

The Vampire was now curving towards him, lining itself up.

He made a second attempt to call the other pilot. "Leutnant Bitsch! What are you playing at?"

Silence.

Now it was Bitsch's turn to play the psychological game. Pross decided he wasn't going to take any chances. Just as he gauged the Vampire was ready for its shoot, he took the Lynx skidding to the right, then turning and dropping quickly.

The Vampire actually fired. Pross saw the tracers passing harmlessly by. The other aircraft had reversed bank swiftly, trying to bring its fire to bear. But the manoeuvre had proved useless. The speed differential had been far too great.

Pross watched now as the jet shot into a steep climb, winged over and came plunging down again. He took the Lynx to the deck where the battleground would be more in his favour. Manoeuvring a jet at fifty or so feet in combat with a helicopter was not something Bitsch was going to relish.

The move worked, for the Vampire broke off its attack and pulled up again; but it had not finished. It circled above, a hawk waiting to pounce.

"*Bitsch,* you mad bastard!" Pross shouted into his mask. "Cut it out!"

Silence.

Alright, Pross decided. Have it your own way.

He was going to kill Bitsch.

Keeping the Lynx low, he headed along the glacier towards the steep slopes of Reiderhorn and its frosted pines. He wondered if Bitsch would remember, or whether he would fall for the same trick twice. The higher speed of the Vampire would be a deciding factor.

When he had judged the moment was right, Pross brought the Lynx up to 1000 feet above the glacier. He continued to head towards Reinderhorn. The Vampire took the bait and came hurtling down.

Bitsch would have to make this one count. Any moment now, the Swiss air force would be coming in to investigate. A pair of F5s to see him off perhaps.

"That's not going to be of much use to me if he gets me first," Pross said to himself. He had little faith in the

263

idea that the cavalry always appeared in the nick of time. That only happened in films.

The tail radar was shrieking. The CRT showed the Vampire's progress. Pross forced himself to wait as he gradually lost height, towing the jet lower.

Mesmerise the bastard. Mesmerise him with the approaching ground. Get him ground-happy.

Pross now had less than 500 feet beneath him as he approached the 7000-foot mountain. The time was . . .

Now!

He dropped the Lynx suddenly, losing 300 feet and displacing laterally to the right. The Vampire brought its nose down to try and stay with it, attempted to correct its mistake, but too late. Its wings waggled desperately. The nose went up. It slammed into the waiting ground, tearing through the frosted pines to do so. A sudden ball of orange marked its passing.

"He fell for it," Pross said to himself in wide-eyed relief as he took the Lynx high and headed home. He couldn't understand why it had happened. He couldn't believe that someone in the Swiss air force had been one of Anakov's people.

When he landed, he was going to have a go at Sanders, Rushman, and Mabel. One of them should have known; at least.

The big *Dauphin* squatted in the snow, rotors turning. Two men were hurrying towards it with a stretcher. There was a body on the stretcher.

Rushman's.

They secured the stretcher, and ran back from the aircraft. They were clothed in snow-camouflage combat kits, and carried automatic rifles which they had worn slung across their backs as they had dealt with the stretcher. They now slung the rifles as they ran, to take up concealed positions among the pines.

Sanders came out of the shed, hurried to the waiting helicopter. He climbed in. The aircraft lifted off as soon as all doors were secured. Keeping low, it headed down for the Rhône Valley.

Mabel had been watching them from a window in the smaller chalet. She turned to her companion.

"Well," she said. "That's that." She took out the cigar, sniffed it. She continued to watch until the helicopter had disappeared.

"Yes."

"He was taken completely by surprise."

"I am good at my job."

The man had arrived earlier in the *Dauphin*. Rushman had come out to greet the aircraft and was surprised to see the newcomer. That was all the time he'd had for a reaction before the two bullets, fired from close range, had slammed into him. He had been flung backwards to die in the snow, a look of astonishment upon his face. The guards, watching from their concealed positions, had done nothing.

The man who was now with Mabel and who had done the shooting, was the same one who had met Pross in Munich.

Mabel sniffed once more at the cigar before putting it away.

Pross brought the Lynx down lightly. He shut down slowly, reflectively; then he removed his helmet, held it against his chest. He remained strapped in his seat, staring out at the three buildings as the rotor spun down into stillness.

"Well," he said quietly, "I'm still alive."

Mabel had come out of the small chalet. He still did not move, but watched her as she approached. She came up to the pilot's door, and opened it.

Pross looked at her.

The eyes peered at him. "You're not staying there all day, are you?"

Pross continued to look at her. He still said nothing.

"You were good out there. We saw, and heard some of

265

it. That was clever flying. We watched you through binoculars."

"I'm glad someone was entertained."

"I understand your anger—"

"Wonderful."

"—but we didn't know about this until it was too late."

"That really increases my sense of security. Where are those two bright sparks, Sanders and Rushman?"

"They're gone."

Pross stared at her. "What the hell do you mean, *gone?*"

"New developments. That Vampire was one of them. We've got to move faster. Sanders and Rushman have gone to prepare things for Nepal. You'll be moving soon. No more flying practice. The next time you climb into the Lynx, it will be for the real thing."

"What do you think I just went through?"

"You know what I mean."

"And how about the ace of the skies, Leutnant Bitsch, *picked* by you lot?"

Mabel's eyes looked suddenly hard. "That was not Hans-Ruedi. I knew him well. He was killed yesterday. An imposter took his place."

Pross was unconvinced. "Just like that?"

"These things are possible. Sufficient motivation is all that is needed. For example, this aircraft you're sitting in is due to a certain amount of motivation. We're sending you half-way across the world on a mission that has been well thought-out. Stealing a Vampire is a picnic by comparison. I don't know what you're complaining about. You're alive, aren't you?" The eyes seemed to twinkle.

Pross hung on to his anger. "And the Swiss air force? They're going to be entertained by the thought of people shooting up their air space, are they?"

"London will see to it."

"Ah yes. London."

"Come on, David. Cheer up. Get out of there. There's an old friend of yours I want you to meet. He's going to look after you."

Pross had felt a momentary surge of excitement at the

mention of "an old friend", thinking it might have been Logan. The "he" soon brought back his gloom.

"That really cheers me up," he said, and began to free his harness.

He climbed out of the aircraft and walked back with Mabel towards the chalet. People had come out of the shed and had begun working on the Lynx.

Mabel said, "They're preparing for flight. Someone came in to fly it out to the ferrypoint. The next time you see it after today will be in Nepal." They had arrived at the chalet. "Here we are. In you go."

Pross entered, and came face to face with the man from Munich.

Chapter Fifteen

Logan arrived at the camp at one o'clock in the afternoon.

On her return home, she had found the 2CV parked in its usual place, and had left it strictly alone. She had also seen the Department car—not a Rover—parked discreetly away from the mews entrance. She had then gone quickly into the house, packed everything she'd thought she would need into a grey canvas travelbag, and had gone to a window that looked out on the mews; to wait.

Half an hour later, the couple she'd been looking out for had appeared at their door before leaving for work. Her neighbours with the Volvo.

She had gone quickly down the stairs and out of the house just as the man entered the car.

"Please," she had begun to them in seeming panic. "Something's wrong with my car and I've got to get to Victoria Station quickly. I'm sorry to trouble you like this, but would you mind giving me a lift to the King's Road? I can catch a No. 11 bus from there."

It was the woman who had answered. "It's no trouble. I work near Victoria, I'll take you to the station if that will help; as long as you don't mind if we go to Knightsbridge first. Jim's business is there."

"Oh that would be marvellous!"

The man had smiled at her. "Hop in then."

Logan had got into the back, and had contrived to be searching for something in her bag which she'd put on the floor of the car, just as they had driven out of the mews.

At Knightsbridge, the woman had taken over, and had driven Logan to Victoria Station. Logan had waited a good five minutes before taking a bus to Hyde Park Corner. From there, she had taken a taxi to Paddington Station, and had caught the train to Newbury. She had got out one stop before, at Thatcham, where a friendly delivery-van driver had given her a lift to the camp.

"Good on you," he said to her when she had climbed out. "I live near here, and I don't like it." He had nodded in the direction of the airfield, crunched his gears as he drove off.

Jean was pleased to see her. "Are you alright?" Her eyes were full of concern.

Logan sighed. "Yes."

"You look tired. Have you had any sleep?"

"Not much."

"Clara said she saw you being taken."

"Where is she?"

"They've got her too. She tried to help you. I was amazed. But you know Clara. Show her a policeman, and her feet get minds of their own. She kicked one, and that was that. Marion said she never got close enough to you after that. I hope they release her. We'll never hear the last of it if she doesn't make it to Kabul. What about you?"

"That's why I'm here."

Jean smiled. "That's good news! Have you got everything you need in there?" She pointed to the bag.

"Everything," Logan said. "Have you seen my car?" she added.

"I thought you'd taken it."

Logan shook her head. "No." It wasn't a lie. The Department had.

"My God. I hope it hasn't been stolen."

Logan rubbed a hand wearily across her face. "To tell you the truth, I don't want to think about it. What I need is some sleep." That wasn't a lie either.

"Look. Stay here in the tent. Have a snooze if you can. I'm leaving for home today. Come with me, stay till

Wednesday, and we can go to the airport together. What could be simpler?"

"But your family . . ."

"Oh don't worry about that. We won't be seeing them. We'll be staying at a little flat I've got in Barnes. I don't want the papers to know I'm going. They don't know about the flat."

"That's marvelous!" Logan said, pleased for more than one reason. "But what's going to happen about Clara?"

Jean shrugged. "She's been taken so often, we can only hope they'll let her off with a fine out of sheer frustration. It would be worse for them if they jailed her. She'd love that and make such a stink, it would give her all the publicity she'd like. They wouldn't want that. What about you? What happened?"

"They threw me out this morning when they managed to work out I wasn't a Russian spy." Logan hid the smile she felt coming. It was, after all, exactly what had happened.

Jean looked at her with mock reproach. "Minty! Really! That's the kind of thing Clara would say. Don't tell me you're getting to be like her."

Logan smiled tiredly. "That I very much doubt."

"Have your snooze," Jean said. "We'll leave for home in about two hours. You can have a good sleep then."

She went out of the tent and into the cold of the day.

Anakov relaxed in the seat of the military transport aircraft that was taking him to Tashkent, and closed his eyes. How tired he felt this Tuesday morning! It was hard to believe that only on Sunday, he had still been in London; and the night before that, he'd had a naked Araminta on a bed . . .

"I would put her out of your mind, Alex," Sogovyi said.

Anakov opened his eyes. Save for Sogovyi, there were no other passengers on the aircraft; not even a KGB guardian. That had surprised Anakov, especially after what had happened in England. He still could not understand how Semachev and Valentinov had managed to get themselves killed.

The tri-jet, 27-seat Yak-40 cruised smoothly towards its destination. At least, Anakov thought, Sogovyi was still in favour, otherwise he would not have had VIP use of the aircraft.

"It is difficult," Anakov said.

"Then I am glad, for your sake, that we were forced to close down the English side of the operation."

Anakov stared at him. "It is not a failure?"

Sogovyi gave a tight smile. "Semachev and Valentinov are gone." He shrugged. "Tragic." He did not sound at all sorry. "And many of those in Western Europe taken or killed. Again, tragic." He still did not sound as if it mattered to him. After all, the people who had been killed had been KGB, not GRU. Too bad. "But the operation is still running and you have still got your prototype. You are required to prove it . . . in combat."

"In *combat?* Where?"

"To begin with, Afghanistan."

"*Afghanistan!* Comrade General, with respect, this is the only remaining flying prototype. I cannot—"

"What you can and cannot do, Comrade Colonel, if I need to remind you, is entirely up to me." Sogovyi smiled suddenly. "Have faith, Alex. What you desire will come to you." The smile widened. "I have brought my vodka with me. Have some, then go to sleep. You need it."

08.00, Wednesday morning, east Nepal.

The Hercules C130 was coming to the destination of its long, air-refuelled flight; but it was not going to land. There was nowhere for it to do so. It would drop its load, then return the way it had come, its two crews, who had slept in turn, taking it back to its base in the UK. The skills learned in long flights across the South Atlantic had been put to efficient use.

271

The Hercules, painted white with a pale blue belly, carried no national markings, save for those of its civilian registration. At 16,000 feet, it flew a wide circle above the point of its drop.

The encampment seemed at the roof of the world, its position 14,000 feet above sea level giving it the appearance of the loneliest place in the universe. The area of reasonably flat ground upon which it was pitched appeared scarcely bigger than a football field; and all around its perimeter, the earth fell steeply away, into space it seemed. From the ground, it could be approached by a single precarious trail that began 10,000 feet below. The trail crossed the tiny plateau and exited down the opposite slope, equally precariously. Any other route taken would be to court disaster down virtually perpendicular inclines.

At the northern edge of the camp, the ground rose in a curving rampart that reached six feet at its highest point, and ran for about a quarter of the length of the perimeter. It tapered back to the ground at each end. The tents, a mottled white and fawn, were huddled within its shelter. There were six of those, of varying sizes. One was much bigger than the rest. Just outside its entry flaps was a collection of antennae and small dish aerials, mounted on tripod legs fixed deep into the ground. The dishes had a 360-degree scan. At the opposite end to the rampart, like guard dogs at a gate, were two *Blowpipe* missile air defence systems in quad launchers.

Thin sheets of ice, like bits of pastry, speckled the ground. Where there was no ice, grass stubble, tanned a light brown by the unfiltered sun, formed a brittle carpet. Beyond the encampment, the ice-sheathed flanks of the awesome peaks gleamed all around, sometimes changing colour, every second it seemed, in the rays of the morning sun; and like a moat protecting a castle, a bank of cloud encircled the camp, hiding completely all views of the valleys far below.

Small armed men, in outfits camouflaged to the same

272

pattern as the tents, stood watching the circling Hercules. They were Gurkhas. There were others with them too, also watching the aircraft; three men, taller Europeans, wearing similar combat outfits. Their field jackets had draw-string hoods which covered their heads.

The cadence of the aircraft's engines changed as the Hercules broke its circle and came in for a low east-west pass. Someone on the ground had obviously spoken to it.

The wheels came down, and flaps were extended to give added lift for the slow approach. Its rear doors were open. Though the winds coming off the mountains could be sudden and vicious, for the moment the air was still. The aircraft held a steady course as it came on. Everyone watched anxiously, knowing that the slightest of miscalculations would send the Lynx tumbling off the site to crash 10,000 feet below.

The drogue chute streamed, then came the main canopy which in turn drew the cocooned, rotorless Lynx out of the bowels of the C130. The drop had been beautifully judged. The helicopter, its main blades secured to its flanks, landed right in the middle of the drop zone. Men ran forward to release the chutes. The Hercules hauled everything up, closed its doors, made a saluting pass, and headed off across the peaks as men swarmed about the Lynx to free it from its wrappings.

The encampment was just four miles, in a straight line, from the nearest point of the Tibetan border.

At the time that the Hercules was making its delivery, it was 05.00 in the Turkestan Military District when Anakov arrived at his base. There were sealed orders waiting for him. He opened them. They were instructions from Sogovyi, telling him precisely what was to be done. He stared at the destination indicated.

Tibet.

What, he wondered, would the Chinese have to say about that?

Sogovyi was ordering him to take what was the equivalent of a small assault group — including the prototype gunship — to a location in south Tibet, and to wait. To wait for what? Was the military command under its own secret instructions to carry out another invasion?

Anakov thought that most unlikely. No one wanted trouble with the Chinese. What then, was behind those orders?

At least, he thought drily, Sogovyi was not still ordering him to take the prototype to Afghanistan. He had been given twenty-four hours within which to organise his team. He decided he would take among others Kachuk, Vanin, and Dznashvili. He would need a good team if things got hot.

But before he did anything, he would catch up on some sleep first. He went to bed regretting not having pressed home his advantage with Araminta. Her glorious body still haunted him.

At least I got Kachuk's jeans for his daughter, he thought as he fell asleep.

Wednesday morning, London Heathrow.

The Boeing 747 heaved itself into the air, climbing steeply, at the start of its long flight to Delhi. Logan sat with Jean and Clara, and the only man accompanying them, Danny Rawlins, in a central four-seat row. In a way, she was glad he had come. He was kind, and would look after Jean. She would not now feel so guilty when she slipped away from the party at Delhi, and it would not be as bad as leaving Jean to the tender mercies of Clara.

Logan was relieved, but mildly surprised, to find no one watching out for her at Heathrow. Perhaps Fowler had not yet worked it out; in which case when he eventually did, he'd be too late.

Jean had managed everything, sorting out the visas and having all the tickets ready. As for Clara, she had again been let off with a fine. The police had probably been relieved to see the back of her.

The aircraft settled on its course, and people began to

release their seatbelts. Logan watched as Jean commenced studying the agenda for the proposed meeting and felt even more ashamed of the role she had played. She wondered if Jean would ever forgive her. After this was all over, she would not be seeing the older woman again. Would Jean condemn her in her absence?

Jean was looking at her. "Minty? You look very thoughtful. You should be excited. It's a small start, but it's something. We've got to try, haven't we?"

Logan smiled at her, fondly. "We've always got to try, Jean."

They were thinking of different things.

Winterbourne was furious. Fowler was present in the spacious office, as were Sanders, and Martins.

"What have you to say about this, Fowler?" Winterbourne tried to say forcefully. It came out as an outraged squeak.

"What would you like me to say, Sir John?"

"None of your games with me, Fowler! I gave express orders that Logan be brought in. She had been consorting with Anakov, and those ragged women at the camp. I was not happy about this idea of yours from the beginning."

Consorting, Fowler thought wearily. *Good God.*

"Ever since I took charge of this Department," Winterbourne went on in full spate, "I have noted and disliked your evident addiction for rule-bending. You give your field people far too much autonomy. Logan is one such. I knew that one day you would live to regret it. We are now faced with a situation where we have an operative with valuable information on the run, probably to her Russian boyfriend." Winterbourne shook his head slowly, as if the weight of the entire world had been thrust upon his shoulders. "What, Fowler, do I say to the Minister?"

"That we'll keep him informed," Fowler answered calmly.

Winterbourne stared at him in disbelief. "Are you

quite mad?"

"Not to my knowledge, Sir John."

Sanders said, into Winterbourne's barely controlled anger, "I think we should put out an immediate search for her. She's dangerous. She could do us a lot of damage."

Martins said, "Her gun is still here. I thought the legend was that she never went anywhere without it."

"Logan is dangerous with or without a weapon. Her knowledge, in the wrong hands, is inimical to us."

"We don't know that," Fowler countered. "We don't know that she is hostile."

"She shot Telford, Mr. Fowler," Sanders said harshly. "Can you deny that?"

"Can you *prove* it, Sanders?" Fowler looked at each of them in turn. "I want it placed on record that I am no part of this kangaroo court. If you wish, Sir John, I shall ask Mrs. Arundel to type up a letter to that effect, to be put on file."

Fowler watched dispassionately as hesitation flitted across Winterbourne's features. Bawling each other out was one thing. A formal objection, witnessed and on file, was quite another. Fowler waited for the oblique climbdown.

"I do not like my orders being countermanded, even by you, Fowler," Winterbourne began as a preamble to his descent. "I'll rephrase that—*especially* by you."

Fowler said, coldly, "When I'm running an operation, Sir John, the lives of those in the field are my responsibility. I cannot afford to take chances with them. I would therefore expect consultation *before* changes to the accepted routine are undertaken. Martins was unnecessarily forceful and appeared to take delight in attempting to bully Logan. I say attempting because it was quite clear she was not impressed by his methods. Then, of course, he threatened physical violence. I am prepared to make all this into an official report and personally take it to the Minister." He gave Martins one of his coldest stares, then he turned again to Winterbourne. "Unless you intend to take the operation out of my hands, Sir John, I

276

suggest we let it run as before."

"And Logan?"

"She'll turn up. I'm sure of it."

"Yes, Fowler . . . but *where?*"

"Let us wait and see, Sir John."

"I think," Sanders began, refusing to let go, "someone should go after Logan, find her, and bring her back . . . by force if necessary."

Fowler looked at him steadily. "And if she resists?"

"Then extreme prejudice . . ."

"Extreme prejudice." Fowler repeated the words as if they tasted like a lemon he had just bitten into. He turned to Winterbourne. "Sir John? Do you agree?"

Winterbourne looked unhappy. "Well—"

Fowler again spoke to Sanders. "Bad luck, Squadron Leader. Perhaps next time. I shall remember to mention it to Logan when the two of you next meet in my presence. I have rather a lot to get through," he went on, "so if we are finished here, I shall be getting on. Sir John. Gentlemen."

He left then, enjoying the memory of Logan's ability to needle Sanders. She always called him Major, whenever the hawkish, but slightly pompous Sanders overreached himself. Sanders hated it.

Still, Sanders was a capable operative for all that.

Fowler walked along the corridor to his office. He had said nothing in there, but Logan's disappearance worried him too; for entirely different reasons.

Pross glanced at the man sitting next to him as the airliner winged high over the Alps, on its way to India. After Pross's initial shock on seeing him again, he had been introduced by Mabel as Michael Hansen. Pross strongly doubted that was his true name.

"I thought you were finished with me," Pross had said.

"Things change," Hansen had remarked emotionlessly.

The site had then become a hive of urgent activity as plans were brought forward. The Lynx and the Agusta were flown off — to what destinations, no one had thought to tell him. Instead, the *Dauphin* had arrived to take both Hansen and himself to Geneva where he had spent the whole of Tuesday in a hotel room, albeit a very comfortable one, claustrophobically guarded by Hansen.

Midday on Wednesday had found him high in the sky, on his way to the confrontation with Anakov. He felt a tiny flutter in his stomach, wondered if that meant he was truly beginning to feel afraid. Why not? There was nothing wrong in being frightened. It made you fight more strongly for survival; if it didn't paralyse you first.

He looked out of the aircraft window. They seemed to like giving him window seats, he thought reflectively.

He glanced once more at Hansen who had reclined his seat, and appeared to have gone to sleep. Hansen was now dressed in a lightweight pale suit. The international businessman.

We are both international businessmen, Pross thought, and smiled at his ironic joke with himself.

He wondered where Logan was, and whether she was alright.

16.00, Wednesday, the special *Hind* base near Sherabad.

Anakov and Kachuk were standing on the edge of the landing field, watching the activity around three *Hinds* and the sleek shape of the black *Hellhound*. Earlier, Kachuk had thanked him with touching pleasure for the jeans, and insisted that Anakov should visit the family to be there on the very first occasion that they were worn.

"My little Sonja would never forgive you otherwise," Kachuk had threatened.

Anakov had promised to visit.

"I've selected Voronov as pilot for the third 24," Kachuk now said.

Anakov nodded his approval. "Good."

Kachuk shook his head wonderingly. "Why an assault base in Tibet? Do we want the Chinese as well as the

Afghans?" He gave one of his loud laughs. "I don't want either of them."

Anakov smiled. "We'll be told when we get there."

"I smell KGB," Kachuk said sourly.

"Not GRU?"

"They've got more brains," Kachuk said, dismissing the entire KGB in four words. "They'd never pull something like that."

"Some of our assault troops belong to the GRU."

"Yes, but they're subordinate to you. This is not their operation. Still, if there's going to be a good fight . . . who knows? I might not mind. And now, Alex," Kachuk went on to his commander and friend, "leave the rest of this to me." He raised his chin briefly to indicate the activity around the aircraft. "You've only had two hours sleep and you've been on this all day. There is an adjutant, and people like me to do all the hard work while privileged commanders lie on their backs." he grinned. "The hard worker suggests that the commander continues with that occupation."

Anakov said, "For once, the commander will obey his subordinate and depart the scene."

As Anakov turned away, Kachuk said, "You did not say whether you met any nice English ladies. Is it true that they are cold? Or are they perhaps a little hot?" Kachuk's little eyes danced at the possibility.

Anakov gave a rueful smile. "Hot, and cold."

He went off, wishing Kachuk had not brought the subject up. It had stirred memories of Araminta.

He did not see Kachuk staring curiously after him.

At 04.00 on Thursday morning, Anakov was suited up and ready to go. He felt pleased with himself, with Kachuk, and with the rest of his assault force. They had managed to do it all within the 24-hour limit. The helicopter strike force, led by the prototype, consisted of three Mi-24s carrying six assault troops each, a full weapon load, and extra fuel. Two Mi-8s carried all the necessary equipment for setting up the base, ten additional assault troops, support troops to operate the base defensive equipment, and spare ammunition and weapons. The Mi-8s were piloted by crews recommended by Kachuk.

Air-refuelling rendezvous had been worked out for the long flight. All was ready. Sogovyi should be well pleased. The Mi-8s, because of their loads and lower performance, would dictate the length of time spent on the transit, but that had been taken into account.

Anakov had picked up his helmet and was about to go out to his aircraft when Kachuk entered, accompanied by an unknown colonel in full combat assault kit. The colonel was KGB.

What now? Anakov thought, and waited expressionlessly. Was this man about to take command of the mission. If that were the case, Ogovyi would have to authorise it. Nothing moved otherwise.

"I am Igor Chernskiy, Comrade," the newcomer began, "and as you can see, KGB. You are making a good effort not to show your true reactions to my presence," he went on without apparent hostility, "but you have no need to worry. I am not here to assume command. However, my presence is most essential to your mission."

"I do not quite understand, Comrade Colonel," Anakov said neutrally. "I was not warned of your arrival. You will have to enlighten me very quickly. My orders require that my force takes off within a few minutes. As you can hear, the engines are already being warmed up."

Chernskiy was short and round, and had a round eager face that appeared too ready to smile. He was also quite young, Anakov thought, to be a KGB colonel. A high-flyer then. Ambitious. Dangerous if crossed. Anakov intercepted a fleeting look from Kachuk. His second-in-command was also of the same opinion.

Chernskiy said, "I have no intention of delaying you, Comrade. I shall therefore be as brief as possible." His eager face smiled up at Anakov. "Your orders told you further information would be given to you on arrival at your destination. I have that information, and I shall give it to you on arrival. I shall travel in the Comrade Major's aircraft. Shall we go?" Chernskiy wheeled out without waiting for further comment.

Kachuk glanced at Anakov expressionlessly and followed. Anakov went out thoughtfully in their wake.

Five minutes later, the base was reverberating to the whupping thrum of six main rotors and the screaming roar of twelve engines as the assault force awaited Anakov's command.

In the *Hellhound,* he relaxed in his semi-reclining armoured seat and gave the collective a gentle pull. The *Hellhound* leapt into the still-dark sky like a ghostly beast unleashed. One by one, the other aircraft followed, climbing and keeping station on its navigation lights. They headed for the Afghan border.

Their route would take them across the northeastern province of Badakhshan, then east into the Wakhan corridor to avoid Pakistani airspace before crossing into Kashmir, for the long southeastern haul down towards the Tibetan frontier. Once into Tibet, they would continue on the same direct route to a point just three miles from Nepal, and eight from where the Lynx had been paradropped.

There would be three refuelling points on the way, with a tanker Mil-8 joining them for the last leg of the journey. This would be carrying extra fuel stores for the base. It would return to Afghanistan once loaded.

Anakov led his force east into the rising sun, and wondered what awaited him in Tibet.

While Anakov was in the air, the 747 carrying Logan and her companions landed at Delhi at 04.20 local time. Although it was still dark and the day not yet warm, the temperature was considerably higher than that which she'd left in London. She removed the lightweight cream jacket she had travelled with, hung it over her shoulder with a finger hooked into the neck loop.

The unique smell of India came to her almost as an assault upon her senses, but her mind was not upon the smells and mysteries of the great ancient subcontinent. It was occupied with the planning of her next moves.

Clara said, as they waited for their luggage, "This is almost like Southall."

Logan stared at her. "Is that the best you can do?"

"They live in Southall, don't they?"

Logan continued to look at her disbelievingly.

Clara said, "Oh dear. Minty's annoyed. Not done, dahling," she went on exaggeratedly. "So rude. It was a joke, for God's sake," she added in her normal voice.

"Is that what it was?"

Clara's hot eyes surveyed her with something approaching contempt. "Nobody heard me, for crying out loud. Stop trying to be so *good* all the time." She made it sound like a disease no one would want to catch.

Jean was about to intervene, when a man and woman approached them. The woman looked European, with a Slavic hint to her features. The man, in a Western suit, seemed Kashmiri, or Afghan.

The man spoke first. "You are Mrs. Jean Anscott's party?" His English was very good.

Jean said, "Yes. We are. I am Jean Anscott, and my associates . . . Araminta Dilke-Weston, Clara Saxby, and Danny Rawlins."

"I am Ahmad Mahmud, and this is Comrade Alya Malitskaya. We are here to take you on to Kabul."

Everyone smiled and shook hands as around them the many languages of India and of the world eddied and vied for supremacy. Mahmud was tall, with the pale complexion of a Nuristani. He had a handsome, aquiline face and even in his well-cut suit, Logan could imagine him in the robes of a hill tribesman. Malitskaya was small and compact, like all those gymnasts that could be seen on TV the world over. Logan would not have been surprised to find she was KGB. The surprise would be if she were not.

Mahmud was saying, "As you requested, there is no

press."

"Oh good," Jean said. "We managed to leave England without our own press being aware of it. We'd like to keep it that way for now."

"We understand," Alya Malitskaya said. She had a warm, rich voice that Logan thought would greatly appeal to men.

Logan found Malitskaya smiling at her. She smiled in return, the slightly hesitant smile of a well-intentioned person who felt she was rather out of her depth. She was more certain than ever now the small woman with the tight gymnastic body was KGB. It was all in the eyes.

Poor Jean, she thought. *We're all using you.*

Malitskaya said, "You must all be very tired." She personified that rolling Russian way of speaking English. On her, it was very attractive. She turned her smile on Danny Rawlins, who looked very pleased to have received it.

Enjoy yourself, Danny, Logan thought drily.

"When your luggage has come," Malitskaya continued, "we shall take you to your hotel for a short rest. Our flight to Kabul is at eleven o'clock. So perhaps you would like to sleep a little?" Her smile was again on Rawlins.

Jean said, "Yes. That would be fine."

"Something to eat before?"

"Well . . . I'm alright. I don't know about the others." Jean looked at her companions.

"I'm fine," Logan said.

"I'd just like some sleep," Clara said. "Any amount will do. Dozing on a plane is not my idea of a good night's rest."

"I think I could manage a quick coffee," Rawlins put in, his eyes on Malitskaya.

"That will be fine," she said. "We can have a little talk, perhaps?"

He nodded, looking pleased. "Yes. Nice. Nice."

"Good. We are settled."

"Oh very settled," Clara said drily, glancing at Rawlins, a tight knowing smile on her lips.

283

Malitskaya looked confused.

"Don't worry about it, tosh," Clara said to her.

She seemed even more confused, but the luggage arrived to distract everyone. Logan gave hers a swift, scrutinizing glance. It did not appear to have been interfered with.

The hotel was about a mile from the airport. They had been taken there in two cars, Mahmud sitting in front with the driver of the first, with Logan and Clara in the back. The other had carried Jean and Danny Rawlins, with Malitskaya accompanying them.

Logan looked at her watch. 06.50. It was time to leave. They should all be safely asleep in their rooms by now. Nearly two hours had passed since their arrival at the hotel. Time enough.

She smiled briefly, wondering whether Malitskaya's naked play for Danny Rawlins had had any success. All the better if the "coffee" had turned into something else. How fast was a KGB seduction? Malitskaya, occupied, could only be looked upon as a bonus.

Logan wondered where Mahmud was. Perhaps he fancied Clara. As Minty, she was quite safe. Too prim for Mahmud's taste, he hoped. It wouldn't do at all if he came sneaking into her room, to find her gone. She still felt guilty about Jean, but there was no choice.

Grateful for active libidos everywhere, she picked up her travelbag and let herself quietly out of the room.

It took her five minutes of careful avoidance to make her way out of the hotel unseen. It was coming alive with the new day but, as yet, staff and guests were still sparse upon the ground. She walked away from the building for a couple of hundred yards, before she hailed a taxi.

"The airport, please," she said in a rush.

The Sikh driver stared at her with liquid eyes as she climbed in. The look on his face had been eloquent. Another romantic who thought she could see all of

284

India in three days, and understand.

With the contempt of one who knew better, he shot off at a furious pace, almost flinging Logan back against the seat.

At the airport, she went into the Ladies and when she came out again, she looked quite different. Even the taxi driver would have thought hard before attempting to identify her. Yet she had done very little to alter her appearance.

She had removed the fake glasses and dropped them into a bin. She had passed a swift comb through her hair, altered her diffident walk, and recalled her own persona. Gone was the shy Minty. Logan, and the full power of her green eyes, was back.

The girl at the Royal Nepal Airlines desk was of Tibetan extraction with gleaming dark hair, and a smooth attractive face that smiled easily.

Logan said to her, "I am so sorry, but I must catch the 08.15 to Kathmandu. Are there any seats left?"

The young woman smiled. "I shall check." She looked at her manifest, looked up again at Logan. "There are some seats."

"Oh thank you!"

"Do you wish a return flight?"

"Er . . . I'll do that in Kathmandu, thanks."

As the hostess made out her ticket, she found herself hoping no one would think of checking her room until well after the flight had gone. She glanced at her watch casually. 07.15. Only an hour to wait. She could handle that.

She would be travelling on a diplomatic passport, under her own name.

Chapter Sixteen

07.20, local time.

Another Boeing 747 extended the giant sails of its flaps as it curved in on finals.

Hansen said to Pross, "Well, we're here." He looked as fresh as ever. "Our connection to Kathmandu will be less then one hour by the time we are in the terminal, and there will only be a very slight wait before we board. Time enough for a coffee, if you want. We won't be leaving the transit lounge."

Pross nodded. He felt wrecked. How could Hansen still look so unaffected by the long flight? Pross decided that, in his own case, flying as a passenger was far more energy-consuming than as a pilot.

"I think I will have the coffee."

Hansen smiled with seeming sympathy. "You'll be able to get some proper sleep in Kathmandu."

After the landing and when their baggage had been transferred, they went to the transit lounge. It was fairly crowded. A lot of people wanted to go to Kathmandu, it seemed. There were many Europeans, Germans, Swiss, and Brits among them, as well as Americans wanting to go to the magic Kingdom. Most were hardy-looking types — trekkers, Hansen had dismissively called them — others were plain old-fashioned tourists, eager for a sight of the Himalayas.

Pross would have felt the same kind of anticipation, had his reasons for being there not been more deadly. He looked at the oblivious people. If only they knew who was among them. He was not thinking of himself, but of

Hansen. Killer Hansen, smart-looking businessman.

Hansen found them a table in a secluded corner, and got the coffee. Hansen's eyes were seldom still, looking, looking, searching out possible adversaries.

I can't complain, Pross thought. *He got me this far.*

After the cold of Europe, the young day felt quite warm. Pross removed his jacket.

Hansen smiled, "I can't do that, of course."

Pross knew it was because of the gun Hansen carried. Arrangements had obviously been made for having it on board the aircraft.

"It will hit near 28 degrees Centigrade closer to mid-day," Hansen went on. "That's about 82 Fahrenheit."

"A good summer's day back home," Pross said.

Hansen said, "You want to be here in August. It hits the lower nineties then. It will be warm in Kathmandu," he continued, "but at your final destination it's going to be quite cold, and probably very windy. I expect they'll have prepared suitable clothing for you. In Kathmandu, you'll be met by a Gurkha officer, Lieutenant Lal. I won't give the rest of his name because you won't be able to pronounce it and in any case, you won't be around long enough for it to matter."

"I don't think I like the way you said that."

Hansen's pale eyes seemed amused. "I meant in Nepal. Lal is a Gurung. Do you know what a Gurung is?"

"No."

"One of the oldest of the Nepalese races. A Gurung is not a Gurkha. The soldiers in the Gurkha regiments are not all Gurkhas. They are *Nepalese:* Gurungs, Rais, Thamangs, and so on. Call Lal what you feel at ease with; Lieutenant, Mr. or just Lal. He won't mind."

Pross said, "You sound as if you really know Nepal."

"I know Nepal," Hansen said, and wouldn't expand.

"There was an ex-Gurkha officer at the site in Bettmeralp; a Brit, not Nepalese. Rushman. He knew Nepal. He took off with Sanders."

"Ah yes," Hansen said. "Rushman." He didn't say more.

Pross decided to leave it there.

They finished their coffees in a silence that lasted until it was time to board the 727 to Kathmandu.

Logan had felt a great wave of relief and pleasure when she had seen Pross enter the lounge; but had resisted the strong urge to go up to him. She had seen Hansen and had turned away, losing herself among the other Europeans.

She watched them now, as they went to the aircraft, keeping well behind.

Pross had the familiar window seat, decided either all the airlines had conspired to give him the same position, or Fowler had somehow managed to arrange it all. He suspected that the truth was far simpler: it had merely turned out that way, with no help from anyone.

The aircraft crossed over four of the seven natural zones that segment Nepal from west to east, on its journey to the Kathmandu valley; the southern terai strip, the hogs' backs of the Siwalik, the mountain barrier of the Mahabharat, until it reached the Midlands and began its run-in to Kathmandu. Pross had watched the unfolding landscape with an awe almost bordering on disbelief. Other first-timers throughout the aircraft were craning their necks to look. The regulars sat smugly quiet in their seats. Hansen, as usual, had his eyes closed.

"You've seen nothing yet," he said to Pross, his eyes still closed.

The 727 landed at 09.40 local time. A car was waiting for Pross and Hansen. On the drive from the airport, Pross stared out at the jagged white peaks that surrounded the valley like multi-rowed teeth from the circular jaw of some immense monster that had taken the valley into its mouth; but being unable to swallow it, was condemned to keep the jaw wide open for ever.

"Once," Hansen said, "this was beautiful."

Pross wondered what he was talking about. It was still beautiful. It was a fairytale land.

"What's wrong with it?"

"Civilisation has come. Tourists, and litter, and cars, and factories, and smog. Once, the air above the valley was always crystal-clear. Some days, it's almost like Los Angeles."

Pross said, "Don't tell me you're one of those people who feel that the people who live in such places should preserve it for your aesthetic pleasure while they live lives of misery. Rushman told me that beautiful Nepal kills its people."

"Ah yes. Rushman again. A true aesthete." Hansen did not make it sound like a compliment.

Another of their silences fell between them and for the rest of the journey to the hotel, no further word was spoken. Pross contented himself with staring at the waiting mountains.

Somewhere out there, among the peaks and high valleys, Anakov would be waiting. The legendary city passed almost unnoticed before his eyes, his mind beyond the mountains.

Logan had followed the car to the hotel. She asked the taxi to wait until Pross and Hansen had climbed out and had entered the building. She waited still longer, until she had judged they'd had sufficient time to book into their rooms; then she paid off the taxi and entered the same hotel.

It did not occur to her that she too, had been followed.

Pross stared out of his hotel window at the magnificent panorama. He had been surprised to find the fittings in his room as modern as any that could be found in any major city in the world. He smiled. He had expected something typically Nepalese. No doubt there were smaller establishments which were precisely that, but Fowler's Department was paying. He might as well enjoy it; while he still could.

Someone had entered the room. Pross turned. Hansen.

Hansen said, "All settled?"

Pross nodded. "Yes."

Hansen looked critically about the room. "Could be anywhere in the world, if it weren't for those mountains out there. This place is getting more like Los Angeles every day." He had spoken almost to himself. "Even the mountains are getting crowded." He looked at Pross. "You've got to book your climb these days, and pay for the privilege."

"Why should people use this country for nothing?"

The pale green eyes surveyed him. "You cannot understand."

A knock on the door interrupted further conversation.

"Come in," Pross said, while Hansen moved casually away to take up station against a wall. A small Nepalese in an open-necked white shirt and brown trousers entered. His black hair was neatly cut, military-style. He walked lightly, a man swift on his feet. He wore a neatly trimmed moustache. His dark eyes surveyed Pross and Hansen calmly, and even Hansen's alert stance did not seem to cause him concern.

"Mr. Milner," he said to Pross, "I am Lal." He turned to Hansen. "And you, of course, are Hansen. It does not matter whether these are your true names. I have no interest in the real ones." Lal spoke perfectly accented Sandhurst English. He smiled. "This is now my stage of the relay. We shall leave by helicopter tomorrow morning. Would you now like something to eat, Mr. Milner? Or would you prefer a little rest first? You seem tired."

Pross said, "I'm hungry, and I'd like to stare at that landscape for a little longer; but before all that, I think I would like a rest. I want to feel on top for tomorrow."

"A wise decision. Where we are going will not be as comfortable. Er . . . I'll leave you to it for now. We'll

290

talk later. I am totally at your service." Lal gave a little smile and went out of the room.

"He sounds very efficient," Pross said.

"He is." Hansen's pale eyes looked Pross over. "Sleep well. Lock your door." The briefest of smiles. "Watch out for yetis." Then he too, left the room.

The high Tibetan plateau, near the Nepalese border; 16.30.

Anakov looked critically about him. He did not like the spot that had been chosen for the operation. It was barren, windswept, with no cover for his helicopters and men who, with commendable speed, were putting up tents and all other necessary paraphernalia to turn the place into a fortified encampment.

Kachuk came up to him. "What do you think?"

Anakov glanced up at the empty sky, looked about him once more. What a desolate place, he thought. A region of barren hills, rising snow-capped from high flatlands nearly 5000 metres above sea level. Nothing else for over 1500 kilometres in any direction; hills, flatlands, lakes, and more hills. Rainless, it fed its lakes with melted snow from the peaks.

The base was in a shallow valley, a wide corridor formed by parallel lines of hills running north to south. To the north was more desolation; to the south, the bulwark of the Himalayas seemed to form a closed door, angry peaks soaring in the distance. For the time being, there was no wind.

"I'll tell you what I think, Grigoriy," Anakov replied at last. "I think we're exposed in this forsaken place. We're high, I know, even while we're on the ground. We're above the service ceiling of most helicopters, but not of combat jets. This valley is a funnel; for winds, and for an attack. And as for how the thin air will affect the men . . ."

"I don't like it any more than you do," Kachuk said, "but our KGB friend says it's all been fixed up diplomati-

291

cally. We'll not be bothered by the Chinese."

"I wasn't thinking of the Chinese. No . . . not the Chinese. I'll tell you something else; I'm not happy moving the prototype up here. But . . ."

"But," Kachuk went on for him, "we've got to obey our KGB comrade. I have a sudden urge to spit." Kachuk had glanced round.

Anakov heard footsteps on the morainic debris of some ancient glacier. It crunched amidst the noise of the camp being set up.

Chernskiy came up to them. "Well, Comrades," he began. "I congratulate you on your excellent flying and endurance, and also on the skill displayed by your men in setting up this base immediately on arrival. I would have thought they would have wanted a rest."

Anakov said, "They can rest when this place is combat-ready."

"An excellent attitude, Comrade Anakov. I have heard much about you, all very impressive, except perhaps for one or two lapses when it comes to Western women." Chernskiy gave a short laugh. "But we're all men of the world. Many Westerners find our female comrades attractive also. Interesting thing. A sexual exchange." Again, Chernskiy laughed.

Anakov and Kachuk did not. They watched him warily.

"You are of course anxious to know why you have been sent all this way," Chernskiy continued. A sly look had come into his eyes.

"It would help," Anakov said.

Chernskiy did not appear to resent the brusque manner in which he had been spoken to. The sly eyes looked at Anakov with palpable amusement within them.

"Comrade Anakov," he began with satisfaction "I have great pleasure in telling you that the KGB has conducted a most successful operation. That which you have been searching for is to be delivered to you, right here at this base."

Anakov stared at him. *"The British helicopter?"*

Chernskiy looked smug. "The helicopter, its pilot, and as a bonus, an agent we shall be very pleased to get our hands upon. The agent who outwitted Semachev." Chernskiy smiled. He had got all the cream. "We are in for an interesting time, Comrades. Are you not now glad we came here?"

He turned away from them, walked back to a tent that was now ready for occupation. His was the first.

Kathmandu, 17.00.

The soft, persistent knocking eventually woke Pross. He opened his eyes, remained where he was, lying on his back on top of the bed. His shoes were on the floor, his jacket on a chair near the bed, his tie removed and thrown upon it.

The knocking continued, urgently now.

"Alright, alright," he said groggily. "I'm coming." He rubbed his face with his hands, got up, and went to the door.

He paused, remembering Hansen's cautionary words. "Who is it?"

"Pross!" came a low voice. *"It's me!"*

He knew instantly. *Logan.*

Hardly daring to believe it, he opened the door eagerly. He stared. It really was Logan.

"Lo—"

She stopped him with a forceful, but brief kiss as she pushed him back into the room, entered, shut and locked the door behind her.

"Sorry I had to do that," she said. "But I had to stop you. You were going to shout my name all over the place." She did not look at all sorry. She smiled at him. "Well . . . fancy meeting you here."

"My God," Pross said. "Logan." He knew he was beaming, so pleased was he to see her. On impulse, he grabbed her, gave her a big hug.

"Hey," she said softly. "It's good to be appreciated, but I never realised how much." She was still carrying her travelbag which she now dropped on the floor.

He let go of her quickly. "Logan, I—"

"Don't be silly, Pross. It's a lovely welcome. I'd have been very upset if you'd gone all distant on me just because I wasn't around to look after you." She smiled once more, green eyes teasing him. "Well, I'm here."

Pross moved away to sit down on the bed. She joined him.

"I have to say it, Logan. I'm pleased you are. It feels good. I was getting fed up of going around with all sorts of strange people; including a killer with an ecological conscience."

"And who is *that* interesting person?"

"He says his name is Hansen. He minded me from Switzerland. I first met him in Munich; in the bog, of all places. I don't care if he works for Fowler. He gives me the horrors. He's in the hotel. Do you know him?"

Logan said, "Better tell me all about it. From the time I saw you last."

Pross gave her a comprehensive account of all that had happened to him, right up to the time when she'd knocked on his door.

"You've certainly been having a few adventures," she said when he had finished. "Most of the people you've mentioned are total strangers to me. I don't know Rushman, or Lal, or Hansen, or any of those you met in Germany." She became very thoughtful.

"What about Mabel? She seemed to know you."

"I know Mabel," she said, still thoughtful. She said no more about it.

"How about you? What have you been doing? Fowler said you weren't in on this at all."

"Fowler says a lot of things."

Pross looked at her questioningly. "What are you trying to tell me?"

"What I'm trying to tell you is that from now on, I stick with you."

Pross looked relieved. "That's the best thing I've heard for days."

"I've also got to tell you," she went on, "that I believe we've been infiltrated. Badly."

Pross sighed. "I knew it. Fowler has a knack for putting my neck on the line. It's the only bloody one I've got." A horrible thought struck him. "You're saying that all the people who passed me through during my little tour round Europe, right down to Mr Eco-conscience himself, are *not* Fowler's people? You're saying that all this time, I've been moved about like a pawn in a chess game by—"

"By our opponents. Yes. It's possible."

Jesus Christ. Pross felt a sudden spasm in his stomach. "So what do we do?" He asked her, hoping she had the answers.

"We continue as normal," she said calmly.

"What?"

"We've got to find out who these people are."

"Who's 'we'?"

"You and I, of course. The old team." She smiled impishly at him. "You've got to go on, Pross," she continued seriously. "You've come this far. Besides, it's the only way to stop Anakov coming after you. There's only one little problem."

"There's more?"

"I haven't got my gun."

"Oh great. I thought you never travelled without it."

"Ah. Well, you see . . . Fowler doesn't know I'm here. My gun's in England, at the Department." She smiled sweetly at him.

Pross stared at her, saying nothing for long moments. Then, "You are here, without your gun, without Fowler's backing . . . and you're telling me that we're going to take these people on, when we don't even know who they bloody *are?*"

"Would it help if we did know?"

"Of course it wouldn't, but that's not the point—"

"You're beginning to shout, Pross."

"I'm not . . ." He stopped, lowered his voice. "I'm not . . ." He stopped again, feeling helpless. "Oh Logan.

Why did you come, then?"

The green eyes looked at him steadily. "To look after you."

Pross found he could say nothing to her. The freckled pattern on her face seemed very prominent all of a sudden. He touched her very gently on the cheek.

"Oh Logan," he said quietly. "Sometimes, I really don't know what to do with you."

She smiled wistfully. "Don't ask. I might give you the answer."

A brisk knock sounded. A swift change came over her. She was off the bed and against the wall, close to the door. The speed and fluidity of her actions reminded Pross uncomfortably of the way in which Hansen had moved in similar circumstances. He had to jolt himself into remembering that soft, vulnerable Logan was extremely deadly in her own right.

"That must be Lal," he said as he went to the door. It was Lal. "Come in," he said to the little man.

Lal entered, stared at Logan. "Oh," he said, and paused, clearly taken off-guard. He seemed unsure of how to handle the situation.

Pross said, "Lieutenant Lal, this is . . ."

"Logan," Logan said, coming forward. She had something in her hand which she showed to Lal. "I'll be joining you tomorrow. I would think you've seen these before," she added as Lal studied what Pross assumed was a special ID.

Lal nodded. "Yes, ma'am," he said, answering Logan as he would a superior officer. He stepped back, almost standing to attention.

"Thank you, Lieutenant Lal," Logan said. "I'll take it from here. Warn the helicopter to expect an extra passenger tomorrow."

Lal nodded for a second time.

"Where's Hansen?" Pross asked.

"Mr. Hansen left the hotel some time ago, Mr. Milner."

Pross darted a glance at Logan whose eyes had become speculative.

"How long ago?" she asked Lal.

"Since before midday."

"Any idea where to?"

"No, ma'am. But I do know it's not to the site."

"I see. Thank you for your help, Lieutenant Lal. We'll see you in the morning."

Lal almost saluted. Instead, he gave a little nod. "Miss Logan. Mr. Milner." Then he went out of the room.

Pross said, as he shut the door, "So Hansen is gone. He didn't even bother to tell me he was leaving. Do you think he's one of the people we were talking about?"

"Difficult to tell at this stage. We'll just have to play it by ear." She picked up her bag, put it near the head of the bed. "If I remember correctly, you sleep on the right."

Pross said, "You're sleeping in this bed tonight?"

"We're not going to go through that again, are we? The last time we were on a job together I had to persuade you I didn't bite." She smiled at the memory. "It's practical. I've booked a room, but by spending the night in here, I can keep an eye on you, as well as keeping out of their way."

"They'll only look in here."

"Unlikely, I think. They won't expect me to be in bed with you." The hint of a mischievous smile. "And if they do try, we've got these." "These" were two small edges of wood she had taken out of her bag. "They go under the door. If they somehow manage to pick the lock, they'd have to break the door down in order to get in, and probably wake the entire hotel; not a very clever idea under the circumstances. But I have a feeling they won't try anything here. Whoever it is wants us at the site." She put the wedges back. "With everything closed up, it's going to be quite warm in here tonight. I hope you don't mind if I sleep naked." Suddenly, she giggled.

"What's so funny?"

"Oh Pross. If you could see your face! You're so sweet, at times like this. I think that's why I really like you. Now," she went on in a businesslike manner, "what we'll do is order some food, eat it in here, and spend a nice quite night together. Tomorrow, we'll be ready for what comes. And I promise I won't bite." The green eyes smiled at him. "Alright?"

"Alright," Pross said, and tried not to think of the size of the bed.

A double-bed it was not.

21.000, the high Tibetan plateau.

Anakov, Kachuk and Chernskiy were in the command tent. The field lamp, powered by small but potent batteries, glowed whitely, giving their faces a ghostly look. None of this light escaped into the pitch black of the Tibetan night. Outside, a vicious wind howled like a beast in torment. It was difficult not to imagine that all manner of monstrous creatures stalked beyond the confines of their shelter.

"It was a sensible idea, Comrade Anakov," Chernskiy was saying, "to put your guards inside the helicopters."

"It was the safest place for them on a night like this."

All things considered, Anakov felt, his troops had done a very good job of making the encampment as secure as possible. His combat engineer team had camouflaged the base area so well, spotting it from the air would be difficult for a high-flying jet. He was not worried about Western spy satellites. They were not going to be in this place long enough for it to be a factor.

Chernskiy said, fastening the wings of his fur hat beneath his chin, "I shall go to my tent now." He zipped up his parka. "We have covered everything. I am obliged to say again, Comrade, that your force has impressed me. I shall be putting in my report a high recommendation for the type of regiments you are planning. Goodnight, Comrades. Tomorrow will be an interesting day." He crawled his way out of the tent and into the wild night.

Kachuk said, "I suppose it's too much to hope that he'd get lost out there."

"Gregoriy," Anakov chided with mock reproof. "After

all, he has got us the British helicopter, and its pilot."

"Then perhaps he'll get lost *after* it is safe in our hands."

"That is no way to talk about a senior officer."

They smiled at each other, friends sharing a secret.

Then Anakov said, "I'm going out to make a final check, then it's sleep for me."

Kachuk sighed. "I suppose I'll have to come with you. I wonder," he went on conversationally as he put on his hat and secured it, "what the British agent looks like."

"We'll find out tomorrow."

Then they, too, went out into the night.

In Kathmandu, Pross lay sleeping quietly. By his side, Logan was wide awake. She was trying hard to persuade herself that the fireball she had imagined was in fact the Vampire that had crashed in Switzerland, and not Pross. The image would not leave her.

She wanted to put her arms about Pross, to hold him close.

Don't be ridiculous, Logan, she admonished herself mentally. *You're being unprofessional.*

But her hand reached in the darkness for his.

They were up at six-thirty, and when Lal knocked discreetly at seven, they were ready to go. If Lal thought anything about Logan's having slept in the same room, his face showed nothing of it. They had breakfast, and at seven-thirty a white MBB BK117 helicopter landed in the grounds.

Lal took them to it. They climbed in, Pross sitting in front with the pilot, a European in casual civilian clothes who smiled at Logan and nodded to Pross. When everyone was aboard, he lifted the aircraft swiftly, and headed northeast.

"Where's the site?" Pross asked him.

"Up ahead. The Lapchi Kang range."

It meant nothing to Pross. Soon, he found himself gaping at the landscape unfolding beneath, about, and above him. The helicopter flew low above stretches of land that would suddenly fall away for several thousands of feet. One moment you were a few feet above the deck; the next, solid ground had disappeared, and you were flying with a lot of space beneath you. Or there was an ice-wall staring you in the face. Or a peak rising thousands of feet *above* you, even though you were already thousands of feet in the air.

Pross stared through the curving screen of the helicopter. This was going to be his battleground; or something very much like it. He began to look now at the peaks, razor-sharp with distance, as possible enemies and allies. Range upon range stretched before him, looking like maddened layers of icing upon the biggest cake in the world.

How can you, he thought, *have all this space under your feet, and still have masses of rock going up into the sky?*

It was more than the mind could grasp without the time to fully appreciate it. Instead, he looked about him, seeing an environment at once magnificent and dangerous, which he hoped to use to his advantage.

Logan watched Pross from her seat, behind him. Lal was looking out with the indifference of one who had seen the scenery all before.

She could see Pross looking this way and that, and knew what was going on in his mind; knew he was working out how best to deal with Anakov. He had obviously not realised she had held his hand during the night, for he had said nothing about it. She was glad about that.

It would have been difficult trying to explain why.

The helicopter had begun to climb. It seemed to go on and on, and Pross began to think it would run out of breath. How high was its service ceiling? Still the climb continued, up a steep mountain, it seemed. An impossible path climbed the same slope beneath him. Then they were at the top. Pross found himself staring at a mini-fortress.

As the helicopter landed, the pilot said, "Anyone need oxygen? If not, you'll need to acclimatise. Go easy for the first few minutes. You may get a slight headache; after that, you should be alright. There are oxygen supplies in the medical tent if you feel the need."

No one needed to. They climbed out, Pross doing so gingerly, as if he had stepped onto quicksand. He felt nothing untoward. Someone familiar was approaching. Mabel in battledress, no rank showing.

Logan accompanied him as he moved away from the helicopter. Lal was walking towards a tent, and the BK117 lifted off, heading back the way it came. The fifty-mile flight had taken twenty minutes.

Mabel said, "So you've made it, Pross. And I see you've managed to bring Logan." She peered at Logan, gave her a quick smile.

"Hello, Mabel," Logan said.

"You're a resourceful young woman." Mabel turned to Pross. "Well? What do you think of our eyrie at the top of the world?"

Pross looked about him. "Expecting an attack?" He stared at the Gurkhas on perimeter defence duty, at the air defence *Blowpipes*.

"You never know," Mabel said.

Pross shivered a little. He had put on warm clothes on Logan's advice, but the early day was still cold this high up.

Mabel noticed, said, "You'd be surprised how warm it can get when there's no wind. But let's get you into your tent. Once you're suited up you'll feel better. How's the oxygen? Any headache?"

Pross shook his head. "No. Nothing so far." He looked at the Lynx. "How's the ship?" It seemed eager for action, silently waiting.

"Running sweetly," Mabel answered. "She's ready to take a bite of something." The eyes peered seriously at Pross. "You're man's over there." She looked to the northwest. "And not very far. Beyond that range is Tibet. That's where he's waiting."

Pross stopped, stared at the distant landscape, the curving range of peaks seemingly close enough to touch in the clear air. After the deep divide which separated the camp from the surrounding heights, the range marched almost straight ahead in serried rank, moving steadily westwards in an encircling curve. Now and then, plumes of cloud drifted to the peaks to be whirled upwards by windstreak past their flanks, turning them into centurions that guarded the land within. The sun played gloriously with them, painting delicate shades of colour that seemed to change second by second.

"It is beautiful, isn't it?" Mabel said from behind him.

It was beautiful. He suddenly felt lightheaded. Was it the altitude? Or was it the thought of having to fight to the death among these coldly beautiful citadels?

"Yes," he answered softly. "It is beautiful."

Chapter Seventeen

Pross pulled the diagonal zip of his flightsuit across his chest. He was now ready. Wearing the same full combat gear he'd worn in Switzerland, he was already feeling several degrees warmer. The tent he'd been given was generous and kitting up had not been too difficult.

Mabel had introduced him to a man called Planter—no rank was mentioned—who was in charge of the defence of the site. Pross had expected to see Rushman, but Mabel had given no reason for his absence. Hansen had been nowhere to be seen either.

Pross shrugged. It hardly mattered now. The reason for all that had occurred was approaching its climax. According to Mabel, Anakov was testing the *Hellhound* in the desolate wastes of the Tibetan Plateau, well away from prying eyes. Pross's job was to sneak up on him and blow him out of the sky. He had been given the coordinates of Anakov's testing areas.

He picked up his helmet thoughtfully. He would never cease to be amazed by Fowler's intelligence-gathering capabilities. The strong defence of the site was a precaution in case of an attempted pre-emptive attack by Anakov. Pross believed it was intended to be more of a rearguard action in case Anakov's enraged comrades came hunting, before the place was cleared.

Pross wondered where Logan had got to. She had disappeared into a tent with Mabel, but he had not seen her since. He frowned. It was unlike her not to be hovering around, especially as he was about to take the Lynx up for a test. He had been toying with the idea of

303

giving her a quick ride round the mountains, well away from the border.

He shrugged again, went out of the tent.

In an hour since he had arrived, conditions had changed. The air had become still, and where before he could see the dividing chasms that encircled the site, there was now a thick fleece of brilliant white cloud. The world below had vanished. The peaks had taken on a softer aspect now that much of their height was hidden. They looked somehow cosier. It was hard to believe anything existed beneath them.

Mabel had come up to him. "All ready," she said. "All weapons are live. We've swopped two of your *Hellfires* for a pair of anti-radars. They're light, brand new, and very fast."

"What are you saying Mabel?" Pross walked towards the Lynx.

"I'm saying," she began, walking with him, "that if Anakov is testing out there, he's going to have a support base, more substantial than ours. That means defensive radar. The two new toys kill defensive radars. You may never need them, but why take the chance?"

Pross looked at her. "You're sure you're not just looking for a convenient test-bed?"

"There is that element," she admitted with unashamed frankness.

"As long as I know," Pross said drily. "Where's Logan, anyway?"

Mabel pointed. "There."

Pross looked. Logan, fully kitted out, was looking back at him defiantly from the left-hand seat of the Lynx. She even had a bloody helmet on.

"Your idea, is it?" he said to Mabel.

"Hers."

"Where did she get the gear from? Oh never mind. If I know my Logan, she probably brought it on the plane with her."

"Not very likely, but yes, it did come on a plane. We brought it over. It was originally meant for Rushman.

304

Logan's about his size." She still didn't say why Rushman had not come.

"As long as she doesn't think she's coming out there with me," he said. "She's just coming for the test." He would never forget what had happened to her the last time. It was not going to be repeated.

Mabel appeared to smile. "You know Logan."

"Sometimes," he said, "I bloody wonder."

He went round the aircraft, giving it close scrutiny, patting it here and there, as if it were alive. Satisfied, he climbed into the cockpit. Logan, looking ridiculously child-like beneath the helmet, watched him warily.

"As long as you realise you're only here for the test," he told her as he connected himself to the aircraft.

"Of course," she said, too readily for his liking.

He looked at her. She seemed properly connected up, with only her oxygen mask hanging open.

"Are you fully secure?"

Her head bobbed. "Mabel helped."

"She would. Alright. Mask on. We're going up." He was about to start the engines, when he said, "What the hell?"

The BK117 had surfaced through the cloud like some creature from a primordial swamp, and was swinging in to settle.

"Better let him complete his landing," Pross said, aborting his starting sequence. He wasn't going to risk flying into the other helicopter. "I don't think he'd like it if we chewed him to pieces. Wonder why he came back?"

"He's got somebody with him," Logan said. She was staring intently, looking puzzled.

The helicopter was obviously not expected, for people were gazing at it curiously; Mabel included. It settled down a short distance from her. Someone got out. A woman.

Logan made a strange, startled noise. *"Clara?"* she said softly, disbelievingly. "What's she doing *here?*" Her voice faded as she tried to work out the meaning of this totally unexpected development. *"Clara?"* she said again in that

305

soft voice, more pensively now, as if pieces of some puzzle were being put together in her mind.

Pross looked on as the new woman seemed to be talking animatedly to Mabel. She showed Mabel something. An ID? Pross wondered. Then Mabel looked at the Lynx. Pross heard Logan give a sharp intake of breath as the woman followed Mabel's look.

"She's coming to the Lynx," Logan said, speaking more to herself.

"Do you know her?" Pross asked.

"I know her." Logan was still puzzled. "Clara Saxby should be in Afghanistan."

Pross stared at her. "Why Afghanistan? Is she another of Fowler's? And if she should be over there, why is she here?"

"That's what I'd like to know." Logan sounded very wary.

"Maybe she's got important news. Maybe the operation has to be scrapped. Anyway, we're going to find out."

Both Mabel and the newcomer were approaching the Lynx.

"I don't like it," Logan said abruptly.

Pross sensed a tenseness in her.

"I don't bloody like it," she repeated. A hard edge had now come into her voice. "What is she *doing* here?" She said it tightly, in a voice that was just above a whisper.

Pross could almost hear the questions churning in her mind as she tried to add what was happening to what she already knew, and to which Pross was not privy.

"Start up, Pross!" Logan said sharply, having obviously come to a decision.

"What?"

"Don't argue! *Start up!*"

Pross began to move, but it was already too late. The narrow side door was slid back and Clara Saxby jumped in. Logan, Pross noted, had released her straps, and was uncoupling the life support and communication systems of her suit. Mabel was standing outside, and further away, Planter was approaching. All this Pross saw with

306

the clarity of a freeze-frame.

Clara said, "Didn't recognise you in that outfit, Minty. Or should I say Logan?" Gone was the street-wise accent.

Logan had left her seat and had made her way into the cabin. Pross craned round to watch, trying to understand what was happening.

Logan said, "How did you get here, Clara?"

"You just saw."

"How did you get to Nepal," Logan said patiently, "and how did you know where to come?"

Clara leaned against the wall of the cabin and smiled. "You're not the only one with a diplomatic passport. I was sent by the Department to cover you. I've been doing that since the camp."

Logan's green eyes surveyed her with a fixed intensity. "Who at the Department authorised you? I've never heard of you."

"And I'd never heard of you. I didn't even know your real name until the day we left Heathrow. It was Fowler who put me in as back-up at the camp." Clara smiled.

"He never told me."

"That was the idea. You had to be natural. You wouldn't have reacted to me believably if you had known. It built your cover."

Pross was listening to all this in a sort of daze. He had not the faintest idea of what they were talking about. What had it to do with Anakov?

"Poor old Jean will be wondering what has happened to her peace conference," Clara went on. "Still, she's got Danny . . . If he can get away from the randy Alya. Clever piece of seduction she pulled." She glanced at Pross. "Shall we tell him? He's looking confused."

"Tell me what?" Pross queried, looking from one to the other.

"About Alya Malitskaya, KGB," Clara replied. "She seduced Danny to allow Logan time to run. Danny was watching Logan."

Pross stared at her in astonishment.

Logan said, "Have you suddenly gone off your head, Clara? No Departmental personnel would have fallen for such a blatant play."

"Tell him, Logan," Clara taunted as if Logan had not spoken. "Tell him how you slept with Anakov, and how you're going to deliver this Lynx and him, to your boyfriend over the border."

Pross felt sick, not wanting to believe a word of it. And what was that about Logan *sleeping* with Anakov? He refused to believe that of Logan. She wouldn't. Clara Saxby, or whoever she really was, was lying. Even so, he didn't feel good about it.

Logan was saying nothing.

"Go on, Logan," Clara was saying. "Let's hear you tell him it's not true that you went out with Anakov."

Logan still said nothing. She continued to watch Clara. Pross suddenly felt a deadness within him. He felt a sense of betrayal. His instincts told him that Clara was lying; but Logan had denied nothing. Yet . . .

Logan? No. Never. He refused to accept it. He would hold on to that.

Then he remembered something Mabel had said. *Whatever happens, trust Logan.*

But already, he was doubting her.

"You turned, Logan," Clara was saying into Logan's apparently guilty silence. "Anakov turned you. It's the name of the game. The bedroom is still one of the best places within which to operate."

Then Logan spoke. It was with a quiet, assured voice. "Start up, Pross."

There was a sudden light in Clara's eyes. "Do you see, Pross? She is so sure of you, she thinks she can make you do what she wants, just by asking."

Pross hesitated. He was conscious of Mabel still standing outside; of Planter next to her; of Logan doing nothing, saying nothing to counter the accusations.

"Do nothing, Pross," Clara snapped. "She's not going to deliver this. There are armed men outside, Logan. You've seen them. I've only got to call. This is one operation the KGB are going to lose."

"Bloody hell, Pross!" Logan shouted suddenly. *"Start up this shitting thing!"*

He was so shocked by her yell, and by the way in which she had spoken to him that, almost without thinking, his hands were swiftly going through the start-up sequence.

Then things began to happen quickly.

Clara was wearing jeans and a padded anorak. She reached into the anorak, and pulled out a gun just as the blades began to turn. Pross saw Mabel and Planter back away from the rotor downwash, and was only dimly aware of the gun.

"A magnum," he heard Logan say quietly, in a voice of someone to whom revelation had come. "Now I understand. It's *you*, Clara. You are the one we want. Take it up, Pross. Pross! Take the bloody Lynx up!"

Pross made his decision emotionally. Despite his doubts and confusion, he came down on Logan's side, refusing to believe what he'd heard about her. Ridiculously, what struck deeper into his mind was the part about Anakov. It was none of his business. What Logan did with her body was her own affair.

But it was no good. All the rationalising did not make him feel any better. Depressed by the thought, he yanked the Lynx off the deck. He would help her anyway.

As the Lynx shot up, Pross had a vivid impression of people getting hurriedly out of the way. It must have been a hairy lift-off. Evidence of his own inner turmoil.

At the moment of lifting off, there had been a sudden thump in the cabin that had nothing to do with the workings of the aircraft. He risked a quick glance round and felt his heart congeal. Logan and Clara were struggling.

And the side door was open.

He held the Lynx just off the site, about 500 feet up. The cabin would be cold, and the air just that much thinner. Breathing would be laboured for the two combatants, for Logan had no oxygen either.

309

He found himself glancing round frequently as the struggling continued. Once, both bodies came perilously close to the open door, and Pross looked on with a sense of total helplessness. He could not very well leave the controls; not with hungry mountain peaks jutting all around, out of the sea of cloud.

Logan and Clara were fighting in a peculiar way. They were not throwing blows at each other. Instead, they appeared to be wrestling. Clara was trying to get a good grip, while Logan was continuously fighting her off. Pross marvelled at the strength of the thin woman, who was aiming vicious kicks at Logan. Several times, Logan would slam her against the sides of the fuselage with a boom that resounded through the aircraft. Each time, Clara would hang on. Then Pross realised what Clara was trying to do.

She was trying to throw Logan out of the Lynx.

Pross decided it was time he did something. He took the Lynx into a sudden, tight climbing turn that threw them against the manoeuvre, deep into the cabin and away from the door. He held the turn, continuing to climb. As the aircraft climbed higher breathing would become more difficult. They'd be weakening soon. He hoped Logan would understand what was happening and take advantage of it. He didn't want to go so high as to starve her of oxygen completely. The Lynx, with its specially uprated engines and modified blades, had a ceiling of 26,000 feet, higher than any other known helicopter with the exception perhaps, of a record-breaker that had been stripped of everything to save weight. He was not sure about the *Hellhound,* but he doubted whether it would have such a ceiling.

The helicopter's true battleground was right on the deck where fast, tight manoeuvring was the order of the day. Up high, you were a sitting duck for everything; unless your battleground was a place like this where even at 26,000 there were still some places were ground level was thousands of feet above your anxious head.

He did not take the Lynx too high but brought it

down again in a spiralling turn that would keep Logan and Clara away from the door. He wondered what Mabel and the others were making of his antics. He had clipped on his mask, thankful for lungfuls of oxygen. He worried about how Logan was doing, and glanced round.

She was manoeuvring *Clara* towards the door!

Pross would never understand why he did it. At the moment of his glance, he had caught Logan's eyes. They seemed to be pleading with him. Instantly, he knew what she wanted and without thinking more about it, he did a sudden reversing diving turn. Logan released Clara with equal suddenness, and grabbed at fuselage support. She almost didn't make it as the counteracting force made her temporarily weightless, and she was flung towards the door. She hung on, her legs protruding over the lip to dangle over the terrifying drop. Her calves slammed painfully against the metal.

Clara was not so lucky. She went sailing out the door as if shot from a cannon, her appalling scream seeming to echo endlessly through the aircraft, fading swiftly as if someone had turned down a volume control with a sudden twist. He reversed the turn once more, hearing Logan thump safely back inside even as he saw the tiny thrashing figure of Clara curve downwards to plunge through the cloud surface. He tried not to think that she still had some 10,000 feet to go.

Christ oh Christ, he thought, sickened.

Had those on the site seen what had happened? He brought the Lynx level, heard Logan stumble over to the door to slide it shut. Then she was climbing through, making her way back to her seat.

Pross's mind was still in a state of mild shock. He had just helped kill one of Fowler's people. He still thought of Clara as such. But Clara had also wanted to kill Logan. He had been unable to bring himself to accept Clara's accusations; and so, he had acted accordingly.

Logan had strapped herself in, and had connected up. She was taking cautious gulps of oxygen. Pross could hear her slow breathing coming through on his helmet phones.

He looked at her anxiously as he circled the Lynx. "Are you alright?"

She nodded slowly, turned towards him. "I've collected a few bruises, but I'll be fine."

Pross thought her eyes were staring a little. He'd better get her back down quickly. The medical team could look after her.

Logan said, "We should be getting on."

"Getting on? Where to?" Was she crazy?

"To Tibet, of course."

"*Tibet* . . . !" Pross tried to curb the sinking feeling he was experiencing. No, he thought. It was the altitude, the fight with Clara, and the lack of oxygen. It had all got to her. She had to be taken down, and fast.

He broke circle, and began lowering the Lynx towards the site.

"We're going to Tibet, Pross."

"Don't be silly, Logan," he said, not looking at her and concentrating on his flying. "You're not feeling well, not surprisingly, after what has just happened. I've got to take you back so they can check to see that you're alright. The BK117 might have to take you to Kathmandu. Thank God it's still there."

Pross approached the site, preparing for landing. Everybody seemed to have gathered to watch his approach. After what they'd seen, he thought drily, it was small wonder.

"*Tibet,* Pross!"

Something in her voice made him look. She was pointing a gun at him. It looked like that cannon of hers.

For several unbelievable seconds, he stared at her, his flying instincts holding the Lynx at the hover. He could not find words to make comment on what was happening. Her eyes, above the oxygen mask, seemed strangely alien to him. He felt, and looked, deeply hurt.

At last, he said, inconsequentially, "I thought you'd left your artillery at home."

"This is the one Clara had. Not the same feel, but it

312

will do."

"So it's down to this, Logan. You're actually pointing a gun at me. I helped you to kill Clara because I believed in you; because I thought she was lying."

Logan said nothing.

"And if she wasn't lying, then it's true about you and Anakov."

"Yes. It's true."

"Fine," Pross said grimly. He hauled suddenly on the cyclic and the collective. The Lynx tilted its nose skywards, and climbed swiftly. "Let's take you to your boyfriend."

He would have to try something, he decided; but now was certainly not the time.

He did not see the sudden change in her eyes as she turned away to stare out of the windscreen.

Anakov stood with Kachuk and surveyed his camp. The night wind had died down, but he didn't like the place any better. It was still a desolate hellhole.

Nothing had been damaged during the night; a fact which pleased him. His men had done well. Even the insufferable Chernskiy had gone around beaming with satisfaction. Now, the camp was on full alert, with two of the three Mi-24s manned as well; just in case. The precautions were probably unnecessary, but he preferred unnecessary precautions to those that were necessary, and not taken.

He looked up at the two lines of parallel hills. A defensive radar, with accompanying missiles, had been put on each. His force was small, but it would give a good account of itself.

Kachuk said, "I think you've covered everything, Alex."

Anakov took his time replying. Then, "There always is something else, Grigoriy. Something you don't expect. That's the one that kills you."

A trooper with a manpack field communications unit had come up to them.

Anakov turned to him. "Any news from the radars?"

"No, Comrade Colonel. They have seen nothing."

"We won't get anything until it's past the mountains," Anakov said to Kachuk. "I think I'll put up a 24."

Kachuk said, "If he's being followed, the 24 might warn them. If he's alone, it might frighten him off and—"

"There is no need to put up a helicopter, Comrades," Chernskiy said from behind them. "Our agent will have him delivered at the point of a gun." He smiled as they looked at him.

Anakov said, "With respect, Comrade Colonel Chernskiy. I am the force commander, and I feel we should have some top cover."

Chernskiy's eyes were suddenly cold. "And I command the *operation*, Comrade; the prime objective of this exercise. I am not going to allow anything to cause it to fail. There is no need for you to feel you must do more at this stage. I am satisfied with your preparations." He smiled again. "The pilot has no options and, Comrade Anakov, there is a bonus."

Chernskiy walked away, looking pleased with himself. *Commissar,* Anakov thought with contempt.

Kachuk, looking at him, said, "Don't say it." He knew what Anakov was thinking.

"I won't, but I can think it."

Standing respectfully some distance from them, the trooper gave a surreptitious smirk. He knew what Anakov was thinking too, and approved.

Pross had kept the Lynx skimming the cloud surface at 13,000 feet, with the peaks rising some 1500 feet above him. He still had no idea what he was going to do about Logan. She was still holding on to the gun, and throughout, had not spoken to him; nor had she once looked in his direction. All that came from her was the regular sound of her breathing.

He didn't want to believe it was happening. He could

314

not accept that Logan was hijacking him to Tibet, to hand over the Lynx to Anakov, all because she'd slept with him. He couldn't believe that either, but she had not denied it. She had in fact, confirmed it in no uncertain way. Yet . . .

Damn it, Logan. Why?

He paused in his thoughts. He was being ridiculous again. Logan was nothing to him. What was he going on about? Whom she slept with, when and where, was no concern of his. She belonged to Fowler . . . to be ordered to do as Fowler thought fit. No, no. She belonged to Fowler; once.

Pross found a gap in the peaks and, like a speckled fish, the Lynx swam between them.

He had entered Tibet.

"They've got something, Comrade Colonel!" the trooper with the manpack said. He listened intently as Anakov and Kachuk drew closer. "A helicopter, coming this way. No other aircraft."

Chernskiy had seen their sudden attentiveness and hurried up to find out what was going on.

Anakov said, "Warn everyone to be alert."

"At once, Comrade Colonel." The trooper commenced relaying the orders.

Anakov said to Chernskiy, "You appear to have been correct so far, Comrade Chernskiy. There is only one aircraft: a helicopter."

Chernskiy had a smile on his round face. "An operation that has been most brilliantly planned is coming to its successful conclusion.

Anakov said nothing, scanned the sky anxiously.

Chernskiy noted the action and said, "I trust you will not launch a 24? I should hate to have to report that you caused the failure of a KGB operation when it was close to its conclusion. It would be a very difficult time for you after that."

Anakov looked at him bleakly. "I will not launch a 24,

315

Comrade Chernskiy. I assure you."

Chernskiy switched his smile on again. "I knew we would find agreement, Comrade."

"The helicopter is now five kilometres out," the trooper announced in a flat tone. "Four . . . three . . . two . . . It is here, Comrade Colonel."

Pross did not like what he saw as he came over the range of hills and dropped down towards the camp in response to Logan's directions. It was the first time she'd said anything since they had left, and her voice carried no emotion. He wished she had put the wretched gun away.

He saw the *Hinds,* the Mi-8s and the *Hellhound.* His eyes were drawn to it like a magnet attracting iron filings. God, but it was an evil-looking beast.

He had seen the radars too, and the missiles. He had flown into a hornets' nest; all thanks to Logan. If he were to have any hope of getting out at all, he would have to take out the radars first; then the *Hinds* on the ground — he was certain the *Hellhound* would be the first in the air, once the first of his missiles left the rails — and then he'd have to face the monster itself. And that was not counting ground fire.

It was bloody hopeless. Besides, Logan was not going to give him the chance.

"Thank you, Logan," he said bitterly, "for all you've done for me. I'll think of you when I'm taking it easy in Siberia."

"Just keep going down nicely and easily, Pross," she said coldly. The gun was pointing unerringly at him.

"*Bitch,*" he said savagely.

Her eyes showed no emotion.

Anakov, Kachuk, and Chernskiy were in a little group watching the Lynx come in, while the trooper continued to keep his respectful distance.

Anakov said to the trooper, "Tell everyone to be on their toes, and ask the radars to keep a continuing lookout for aircraft."

The trooper did as he was told.

"No aircraft at all, Comrade Colonel," he reported.

"Tell them not to relax for a second, or I shall personally tear them to pieces if anything gets through."

The trooper relayed the good news.

Chernskiy was saying, as the Lynx came slowly closer, "Beautiful, beautiful!" He was almost laughing. "What secrets we shall find!"

Anakov and Kachuk were watching the aircraft with a more professional interest.

Kachuk said, "Very efficient-looking. Nasty gun. Comprehensive weapons fit." He spoke with a kind of reverence and appreciation for something which, to him, was an object of beauty.

Anakov said nothing, seeing at last the aircraft that had destroyed his first prototype, and which was the danger to his entire programme. He stared at it as it approached slowly and head-on, seeming to drift towards them. As yet, he could not quite see the pilot; the person responsible.

He felt a dryness on his tongue. He looked forward to meeting his adversary who had come so close to destroying his career. His eyes grew cold.

Kachuk was looking at him. "You'd like to kill him, wouldn't you?" he queried softly.

Anakov said, "Before, I wanted to. Yes. But now that he is here, within our power . . . I am not so sure. But I am curious to meet him."

The Lynx approached the little group, seeming to stalk them.

"Turn broadside on," Logan ordered, "then land."

Pross turned the Lynx slowly so that her side of the aircraft was facing the four Russians. He could imagine every weapon in the place pointing his way. It was not a

317

good feeling.

Behind the group of four men, four others were trotting up towards the Lynx. They carried assault rifles.

Armed guard for me, he thought grimly.

His mind was a jumble of contradicting thoughts. He wanted to hate Logan, and found to his self-disgust that he couldn't, despite what she had done to him.

The squad had almost reached the four waiting men. Pross gave them several glances as he manoeuvred the Lynx. It was easy to see which one was Anakov: the tall arrogant one in the fancy flightsuit. The stocky one was a pilot too. The soldier to the right of the group was obviously a radioman. Those missiles on the high ground, he thought. Probably a direct link with them.

He wondered who the fat little one was. He certainly didn't look like a soldier.

Pross brought the Lynx down to a featherlight landing, feeling thoroughly gloomy; yet he kept his hands ready at the controls. He might just have a chance. Hope sprang eternal.

When the chance did come, it was from a totally unexpected quarter. He had been staring across at Anakov, who had been staring back at him. The engines were still running, and his hands were still on the controls, as if glued there. Logan had opened her door, and had unclipped her mask. She had not yet released her seat harness. She was still holding on to the gun, in her right hand, which was not in view of those outside.

"Hullo, Geörgy," he heard her call.

He saw the startled unbelieving face of Anakov.

"Araminta?" he heard the Russian shout. Anakov took a few steps forward, paused uncertainly.

The radioman stared at his commander, then back at the Lynx. The stocky one was looking with interest at Anakov. The fat one seemed puzzled. The four-man squad came to an unsure halt. It all took fleeting seconds.

Having thus successfully sown confusion, Logan went into action.

318

Her right hand came up with the sudden lunge of a striking snake. It was gripped by the left, and the magnum was pointing squarely at Anakov. There was barely the time for the horror to register on the faces of the watching men before the magnum barked twice, in rapid succession. She didn't miss.

The heavy bullets slammed into Anakov's chest, flinging him backwards, a look of astonishment and pain upon his face. He arched once as he fell, then lay still. Kachuk stared wide-eyed at his fallen comrade; but Kachuk also had fast reactions. He flung himself to the ground, using Anakov's body as a shield.

Even as Anakov was falling, Logan was tracking towards her next target: the radioman. One shot took him in the head. It was enough. The startled man crumpled as if someone had chopped his legs from beneath him. Then it was the turn of the fat little man who stood gaping, and was only belatedly attempting to draw his pistol.

The magnum barked once.

Chernskiy flung his arms outwards as if for balance. He trotted backwards, did a bizarre hop into the air, then fell heavily as he seemed to trip over one of his boots. He didn't get up.

Logan then squeezed her last shots at the four-man squad who were now diving in all directions. She got one in mid-flight, one as he hit the ground.

Then she had thrown the gun out, was shutting the door, and screaming, *"It's all yours now, Pross! Take us up. Up, up! Get me out of here!"*

He needed no further encouragement. Primed as he had been for any chance, he was ready when it came. His whole being was now swiftly assimilating itself with the aircraft. All thoughts not specifically concerned with the impending combat were ruthlessly crowded out. His mind began assessing the threats facing him.

Seconds. Seconds was all it had taken. Logan's shots had sounded like automatic fire. God. She was bloody brilliant. He found himself grinning in his mask. It was more of a muscular spasm than an expression of humour.

Think of the missiles, and those bloody radars. Get them first.

He raised the collective, hit the button for the downward-pointing nozzle briefly, felt a sudden upward surge as the neat fuel ignited. Christ. It was a mini-afterburner. The Lynx nearly ran away with him as it shot upwards; but he held it. Control was his. The Lynx was his, to do his bidding.

Seconds. Seconds evaporating. They would be getting over the shock soon; then hell would break loose, unless he did something bloody sharpish. He could sense Logan's eyes upon him.

Trust Logan. Trust Logan. Now it was trust Pross.

Displace, displace. Keep low. Don't give them a target. *Hit those bloody radars!*

Pross had selected the radar killers. Now he fired. Twin glows at the rails. Twin streaks curving to each hilltop. Twin crowns of flame erupting. Men, missiles, and radar, gaining sudden flight in the thin air.

Thank you, Mabel. Remind me to give you a hug when we get back. If we get back.

Ground fire. Where? *Where?* Christ. That was quick. They're bloody awake now. Give them something to think about.

Pross kept the Lynx low, dancing it erratically, never giving an aiming point. The ground fire was coming from near the Mi-8s. The Lynx cockpit was armoured, but it would only be a matter of time before something unpleasant happened.

Logan was still looking at him, willing him, he knew, to make it.

He went over to rockets. He needed to suppress the ground fire before he could run out of the valley. One way was home, the other, deeper into Tibet; and there was still the *Hellhound*. He could not get at it. A *Hind* was parked in the way, and going round would expose him to the concentrated ground fire.

He fired the HE rockets. The salvo tore into the two

transport helicopters, hitting tanks and fuel stores. An explosion like a massive thunderstorm rolled across the valley, throwing machinery and men into the cold air for a second time. Rotors wheeled free, achieving lift as they spun, scything across the ground. A tail rotor decapitated a soldier who had been running for cover.

Sympathetic explosions followed. Blazing fuel fell upon tents which caught fire, incinerating anything within them.

Kachuk watched the wheeling, speckled tormentor with an all-consuming hatred as he lay on the ground. *He had to move!*

He had known something was wrong as soon as the door to the helicopter cockpit had opened. There had been no attempt to climb down. But then, the woman . . . *A woman.*

Even now, Kachuk found it difficult to accept.

The woman had known Alex. She had called to him; and that, of course, had been the start of the trouble. Everyone had been taken by surprise Something you don't expect. The one that kills you.

Kachuk remembered his friend's words with bitterness. He inched his head round to look at Chernskiy's body. His hatred for the dead man was as strong as that which he felt for the British pilot.

Chernskiy had interfered, and now Alex was dead, killed by that woman. It had been a treacherous attack. He would derive great satisfaction from sending her flaming out of the sky with the British pilot to keep her company. But to do that, he had to get to the gunship.

He crawled toward Chernskiy's body, spat in its face. "That is for your operation; your successful operation." He found himself staring into the startled eyes of one of the survivors of the squad. *"What are you doing on the ground!"* he bawled. "Get up! Try and bring that thing down!" Then he was up and running, trying to make it to the prototype.

The attacking helicopter was preoccupied with keeping ground fire down, but it would soon be turning its attention to the 24s and the gunship. Why weren't the 24s up anyway? Two of them were crewed.

Then he saw that one of them was burning. It had been hit, it seemed, by a piece of blazing wreckage. The other was completely without a tail rotor. Something had sliced it away.

Kachuk felt despair. How could this have happened? Why hadn't Chernskiy left Anakov to do the job he knew best?

"You interfering bastard! he yelled in rage, thinking of Chernskiy. *"Fuck your operation!"*

He was nearly at the gunship. He saw Piotr Vanin running towards him. "Piotr! Get my ship going. I'm taking the prototype. We'll bracket the English bastard and his bitch."

"Bitch?" Vanin queried as they ran.

"Yes. There's a woman in that cockpit. She shot Alex. Two bullets. Right in the heart. Bang, bang. And Alex was dead. So easy. We were taken completely by surprise. What I'll never understand, was how Alex knew her. She called him by a funny name; but he knew her. He answered."

They ran on, reached the gunship.

"Where's your gunner?" Kachuk asked.

Vanin's eyes grew dark. "Dead. I got out in time. It's my ship that's burning."

"Find Nikolai Dznashvili." Kachuk opened the canopy and began to climb in.

Vanin said, "He was not on stand-by so he was by the 8s. The rockets got him."

Kachuk slammed a fist against the bodywork. "We must have another gunner somewhere!"

"I'm a gunner."

They looked. A smallish man had run up to them.

Kachuk was doing his straps swiftly. "Who are you?"

"The Comrade Lieutenant Voronov's gunner. Sergeant Mashyev. The Lieutenant is dead. He was hit by a splinter."

Kachuk closed his eyes briefly. Most of the air arm of the force wiped up before one aircraft had got into the air; and all because of Chernskiy. In his mind, Kachuk wished the soul of Colonel Chernskiy all kinds of terrible hell. But he did not believe in souls. The thought left him feeling dissatisfied.

"Get into my ship with Comrade Vanin," he ordered Mashyev, and began to put on Anakov's helmet. It was a little tight, but it would do. He felt his hand close round the side-stick controller that was the cyclic. "I'll get them for you, Alex." The canopy began to descend as he started the first of the two powerful engines.

He glanced to his right, and saw two things: Vanin and Mashyev were climbing into his 24 . . . and the British gunship was coming. So far, no one had asked how they were going to get home . . .

Pross brought the Lynx fast and low down the valley, wondering why the *Hinds* and the *Hellhound* had not lifted off. He was not complaining. Every piece of good fortune was a bonus. Whatever the reasons, he was very glad indeed, thank you, that they were still deck-bound.

"That's our way out," he said to Logan. He had taken the Lynx a couple of miles down the valley, away from what remained of small-arms fire. There did not seem to be any portable SAMs; something he considered unlikely. Perhaps they had been destroyed during his rocket bombardment; he hoped. A locked-on SAM could turn them into a spinning fireball if the radar did not warn him in time. But nothing was showing on the CRT. So far so good.

"Pross! Logan said in a hushed voice. "Those two!"

"I see them." Two sets of rotors. So, at last, someone was coming up to play. Hard cheese. They were not going to make it. "Don't worry," he said to her. "We'll catch them with their pants still down; just as you did earlier on."

He intended to use the *Hellfires*, the anti-tanks. On the ground, for his purposes, the *Hind* was a tank. Ditto for the *Hellhound*. One *Hellfire* to blow the *Hind* out of the way, with the second following close behind to take out the then exposed *Hellhound*. Off-load the remaining rockets at the camp to finish off whoever was till firing the Ak-74s and then off home.

That was how it was supposed to work.

Pross sent the first *Hellfire* streaking on its way. The *Hind* simply exploded in a billowing mass of flame that expanded outwards, spreading horizontally and rising skywards at the same time. The entire main rotor assembly detached itself completely from the flames, flipped into the verticle, and landed on its tips. It walked under its continuing momentum, chewings its way into two of the remaining tents before wheeling across the valley until its weight became greater than its forward motion. Then it simply fell, still intact, with slightly bent tips.

Immediately after the first missile had gone, Pross triggered the second, intending it to go straight through where the *Hind* had been, to make impact with the *Hellhound*.

Nothing happened.

He hit the trigger again and again. Still nothing. They flew past, the *Hellhound* quite unscathed.

"Shit, shit, shit!"

"What's wrong?"

Visored helmet looked at visored helmet. "The missile went on strike," Pross said. "It's still on the rail. The command link may be gone. We might have caught small-arms fire." He hoped everything else had not gone as well. They'd be sitting ducks for the *Hellhound* otherwise.

Just to test, he off-loaded the rockets. They went streaking away nicely, tearing the valley with the sound of their explosions. At least those worked.

Then the radar shrieked. The *Hellhound* was in the air, and looking for revenge.

324

Kachuk had watched as Vanin and Mashyev had been roasted where they sat, before they had even got off the ground. He had fully expected the next missile to have his name on it, and when it did not come, had scarcely been able to believe his luck.

"A hang-up!" he shouted into his mask exultantly.

On such small things did the outcome of a battle turn. He did not waste time. He pulled the stubby collective lever back; a touch of cyclic, and the *Hellhound* seemed to throw itself into the air. It wanted blood.

Kachuk armed the gun. There were no missiles; but he didn't care. He wanted to kill the pilot who had done so much damage, and his bitch who had killed Alex. He wanted to kill them with the gun.

He took the gunship high. He was going to swoop down on the speckled thing that had come into the valley to cause so much destruction. Like an avenging hawk— he did not believe in angels—he was going for the kill.

Pross knew the *Hellhound* had gone high. The radar told him all about it.

Logan said, "Will we know if he sends a missile?"

"We'll know alright."

"What do you think he's going to do?"

"Who knows? I would have expected a missile by now."

It was curious. Why no missiles? Did the *Hellhound* want a close-in fight?

Pross kept the Lynx close to the ground. On their way out of the valley, they had collected a few small-arms hits; but nothing to worry about. He had been terrified for Logan. Mercifully, nothing had come through anywhere vulnerable to hit her.

He felt pleased that Clara had been the turned agent, and not Logan; pleased that he had trusted her in the end . . . well, almost.

He had his own plans for the *Hellhound;* his own amphitheatere where he would take it on. He continued towards Nepal, conscious that the image on the screen was not closing range.

Follow me, Pross thought. *Follow me.*

He was now about a mile from the border, and still the hostile aircraft did nothing. He began lifting the Lynx to a higher altitude to clear a 14,500 foot peak. He was running into cloud again as the border approached.

Suddenly, the radar image began to close, doing so very fast. The *Hellhound* was diving onto the Lynx.

Pross did nothing. He wasn't going to telegraph his move.

The gunship continued to fall.

Pross selected a *Stinger.* The monitor told him the missile was ready for a shoot. He waited until the *Hellhound* was committed, did a quick stop, pivoted round 180 degrees. The HUD framed itself before him in the missile mode. He saw the *Hellhound* suddenly begin to reverse its own turn to regain position for a shoot.

A gun shoot, Pross thought. *That's what he wants.*

But why? It didn't matter now. The *Hellhound* was finished. The missile had a good lock-on.

He squeezed the trigger, began his turn away, to steer well clear of the expected blast.

Nothing happened!

"Not a bloody second time!" he fumed. *"Bloody hell, Mabel!"* he yelled into his mask and hit the button for the lateral manoeuvre nozzle.

Just as well that he did.

The nozzle roared sharply for a brief moment. The Lynx darted to the left in a flat displacement. A curve of tracer passed where it had been moments before, to be followed by the predatory shape of the *Hellhound.*

"Will you look at that," Pross said softly.

The gunship, sleek and black, its stub swept wings making it seem like a falcon swooping down on prey, shot past, and fell into a skidding, diving turn to the left.

"It looks even better in real life," he went on. "Anakov really did do his job." Pross glanced at Logan as he mentioned Anakov, but she seemed to be staring ahead.

The dark visor effectively hid her face behind its gleaming surface.

She said, "It didn't look as if it had any missiles. And what happened to our own missiles?"

"That's what I'd like to know. It gave me a good lock-on. I don't bloody understand what could have happened. There's no malfunction warning. I'll try for another. See what happens."

The *Hellhound* seemed to have gone. There was nothing on the radar, either from behind, or in front. He took the Lynx straight up, hugging a perpendicular ice wall for 1000 feet. He rose above the peak, and crossed into Nepal.

They were now within a great horseshoe of mountains whose vertical distance between the peaks and the river at the bottom was 7500 feet. But the bottom could not be seen. It was sealed by cloud that stretched for miles. This was to be the battleground.

Pross brought the Lynx to the hover just above the surface, and did a 360-degree slow pivot. The radars showed nothing.

"He's behind one of those peaks," Pross said. "He's got to come out. His fuel's not going to last for ever."

Pross lowered the Lynx slowly into the cloud, like someone sinking cautiously into a bath. Gradually, the helicopter immersed itself, until only the mast sensor remained. From above, its white camouflage made it disappear completely. It scanned the peaks.

Inside the Lynx, the world beyond the windscreens was a soft whiteness that seemed safe, and cosy. Pross held the aircraft steady for five minutes. Nothing showed on the monitors.

And then, something swift darted down from one of the peaks; something swift and shark-like, nosing in for a kill.

Pross took the Lynx right down through the cloud. Now thermal imaging took over. He went in a wide circle, knowing the *Hellhound* had him on radar. He towed it down for several thousand feet; and still the cloud continued. The *Hellhound* kept coming.

Then Pross turned, and went straight at him. The move startled the other pilot who began a climbing turn to Pross's right. Pross did a tight left pivot, reversed, found himself in a tail chase.

The *Hellhound* tightened its climbing turn, trying to gain a position on the Lynx's tail. They spiralled upwards in the cloud, not seeing each other, in their mad dance of death. It was as if someone had stuck a pole in the air, and they were doomed to whirl madly round it, sliding upwards or downwards as the mood took them. It was a catfight.

The two helicopters erupted out of the cloud, snarling tightly about each other as they went high. At times they were so close, it seemed as if their blades must touch.

Then Pross changed the game. He suddenly kicked the Lynx round in an opposite turn, went down to the cloud surface. Taken by surprise, the *Hellhound* continued upwards for two complete revolutions. By then, a good 2000 feet of vertical distance separated the two aircraft. Pross went for another *Stinger* shoot. He got a good lock-on. He squeezed the trigger.

Nothing.

"I don't bloody believe it!" he screamed in frustration. "What the hell have they been doing with these weapons?"

But there was no time to rage uselessly. The *Hellhound*, having survived a second faulty shoot, was on its way back down in a wide dropping turn, curving to get behind. Pross selected gun shoot, and watched the IFFC come on. It showed him that he had a full load of ammunition.

"I hope you're telling the truth," he said to it. All they needed now was a dead bloody gun.

He glanced at Logan. He hoped she was alright. He appreciated her silence. She was letting him get on with it. It was his province now.

He waited until he judged the *Hellhound* was again lining itself up to shoot, then he dropped swiftly and suddenly. The descent took him back into the cloud; but he brought the Lynx back up almost immediately.

And there was the *Hellhound* framed nicely in the HUD. Pull tightly into a left turn. Gunship moving to the right, drifting straight into the zone . . .

No go.

The other aircraft had rolled suddenly left, then right again, turning impossibly tightly and accelerating head-on.

Pross did a lateral shift to the right, gave the collective a gentle pull, cyclic back a shade and went into an inclined ascent which he halted suddenly, pivoted, climbed in the opposite direction, rolled almost onto his back, pulled the Lynx back down.

The *Hellhound* had misjudged his response and was caught out presenting a beautifully naked flank.

Again, the slab-sided black shape swam into the HUD; but just as Pross was about to fire, the shape flicked out of the zone.

Shit.

The workload was beginning to tell. But it would be working on the other pilot in a worse manner, Pross thought. He had nowhere to go. *If I keep him up here long enough,* Pross told himself drily, *he'll probably fall out of the sky through lack of fuel.*

But the gunship was not having any of that. It was coming back to kill, vengeance in its heart.

The fight had now taken them to the edge of the cloud. It was like the edge of a precipice. Ahead, mountains gleamed, their savage flanks coated a brilliant white. Behind, an apparently solid wall of cloud dropped down, almost to the valley floor.

Pross took the Lynx close to the walls of ice and rock, knowing it would be a difficult target optically. The *Hellhound* was now coming in for a flank attack. Pross decided to keep going, allowing the other to become mesmerised by having to pick out the speckled shape against the streaked background. He could imagine the pilot of the gunship, even with various aids, trying to get a good solution.

The *Hellhound* came closer.

Now.

Pross dropped again without warning, shifted laterally *towards* his attacker who began to correct by bringing his nose down, steepening his descent sharply. Pross went back up, forcing the *Hellhound* to try and come after him. The stub wings worked, giving the gunship a nicely tight turn that would have brought it close to Pross's tail. The only trouble was, a great flying buttress of rock, 6000 feet above the valley floor, was in the way.

With commendable agility, the *Hellhound* pulled itself clear. But the manoeuvre had left it with a severe loss of speed. There had been no room to drop into a fast descent, and the overhang made a rapid direct climb suicidal. The *Hellhound* seemed to wallow for vital, fleeting seconds.

Pross was waiting. Even as the *Hellhound* had come up against the buttress, he had dropped back down, and had shifted into a good gun position. The two aircraft were almost hovering in the clear emptiness of the mountains, when the HUD on the Lynx pulsed.

Pross squeezed the trigger, mentally crossing his fingers. What happened next took his breath away. The gun did not fire.

It roared. It bellowed. It spewed a deluge of massive rounds at the helplessly wallowing *Hellhound*. The Lynx was in the grip of a vibration whose frequency was so high, it did not feel like a shake at all. It was a smooth tremor that seemed to ooze its way into the senses. The accuracy of the gun was deadly. It literally tore the gunship apart. Pieces flew off it, darting from the centre of each explosive strike until, as if someone had cut its string from above, it abruptly plummeted to the far valley below. Before it got there, it exploded in a vivid sheet of flame that was starkly reflected upon the white flanks of the mountain, for the most fleeting of moments.

Pross felt a dryness in his mouth as he held the Lynx at the hover, a mottled speck against the vastness of the mountain. There was no sense of elation. A wind, coming off the mountain, tugged at the helicopter. Pross continued to hold it there. It was something of a salute to whoever had taken Anakov's place.

Logan raised her visor. The green eyes looked at Pross. "I want to tell you about Anakov," she said.

"You don't have to. It's none of my business."

"I want to tell you," she insisted.

And as they flew slowly back to the site, she told him about the fireball.

Epilogue

Pross entered the concert auditorium of St. David's Hall in Cardiff with a certain amount of wariness. He made his way along the green seats of the balcony, towards the lone man sitting in the front row.

"Hullo, Pross," Fowler said. "None the worse for wear, I see."

"Dodgy weapons systems permitting."

"Ah that wit of yours, Pross. You'll be pleased to know that your rather forceful recommendations are being acted upon. I suspect much of the problems were caused by finger trouble on the part of those who fitted them. Still, you did the job, and that, after all, is what really matters.

Pross stared at him. "Fowler, you're so devious that believing you is a high-risk occupation."

Fowler smiled. "Flattery."

"You knew all along that Logan would take off on her own."

"Yes," Fowler admitted shamelessly. "It was the only way to get Anakov. Be grateful. She saved your life. Anakov was good. I do think you would have met your match in him."

"You risked her, Fowler. Suppose she hadn't made it?"

"Oh do let's not be negative, Pross. She did."

Pross looked at Fowler with exasperation. Nothing seemed to shake the bastard. Fowler was staring at the small organ, built high into the right-hand corner of the stage area.

"Do you play, Pross?"

332

"No," Pross answered shortly. "Who was Clara Saxby, and all those other people I met in Europe?"

Fowler looked thoughtful, as if deciding whether to make reply. "Clara Saxby," he began after a while. "Not Department, but attached. We knew she was bent. That's why we used her; and there are others. You see, we knew the KGB were mounting their elaborate screen. We've got our own people over there, after all. Hansen, for example. Not his real name, of course. Good man. East German. Others were . . . er, loaned to us, so to speak. Saxby tried to discredit Logan by shooting the dead Telford. It failed because I know Logan. She didn't. Don't look so scandalised, Pross. The KGB kept many of their own people in the dark too."

"That's supposed to make me feel better?"

Someone else entered before Fowler could make comment. Pross turned and saw Logan, dressed in tight jeans and a floppy sweater, coming toward them. She smiled with pleasure at seeing him. It was the first time he had seen her since Nepal; since in fact, their return to the site after the destruction of the *Hellhound*. The BK117 had still been there, and it had whisked her away.

"Well, Pross," she said. The green eyes looked at him impishly.

"Well yourself. Three bloody weeks, Logan. A card would have been nice."

"I'm here. Isn't that better than a card?"

Fowler said, mildly, "That's her way of apologising."

Pross looked at him. "Why have you brought me here, anyway? Cryptic messages to my secretary. She thinks you're some kind of villain."

"Do I detect some pleasure in your voice, Pross? Have no fear," Fowler went on. "I'm here to say thank you; personally. I have not seen you since your return. How's business? Some nice new contracts?"

Pross nodded slowly, resigned to the fact that his life was becoming more and more entwined with Fowler's. There had indeed been some lucrative new contracts waiting when he'd got back. But Fowler was not going to have it all his own way.

"Don't think this buys me," he said.

"I would not dream of it."

"Of course you wouldn't."

Logan said, "Mr. Fowler, I've been wanting to say something to you for some time." She went on, as he looked at her with mild curiosity, "I happen to agree with the women at the peace camp."

"So do I."

She stared at him. "I actually believe you're serious."

"Of course." He smiled at her. "But don't tell anyone I said so. I shall quite naturally deny it."

She took Pross by the arm. "Come on, Pross. You're buying me lunch."

"I am?"

"Yes." She began to lead him away. At the exit, she turned to glance back at Fowler, who had remained where he was. As they later stepped out into the cloudy, but mild day, she said, "Fowler always manages to surprise me. I would never have believed that of him." She tucked her arm in his. "Forget Fowler. Let's eat. I hope your wife won't mind me hijacking you like this."

The word brought back memories, and they both began to laugh.

Fowler came out of the building and watched as they walked away. It occurred to him that Logan had a jaunty step as she talked and laughed with Pross. Every so often, it appeared that her head briefly rested upon his shoulder. Accident? Or design?

Fowler continued to gaze after them, and smiled. He seemed pleased about something.

THE FINEST IN SUSPENSE!

THE URSA ULTIMATUM (2130, $3.95)
by Terry Baxter

In the dead of night, twelve nuclear warheads are smuggled north across the Mexican border to be detonated simultaneously in major cities throughout the U.S. And only a small-town desert lawman stands between a face-less Russian superspy and World War Three!

THE LAST ASSASSIN (1989, $3.95)
by Daniel Easterman

From New York City to the Middle East, the devastating flames of revolution and terrorism sweep across a world gone mad . . . as the most terrifying conspiracy in the history of mankind is born!

FLOWERS FROM BERLIN (2060, $4.50)
by Noel Hynd

With the Earth on the brink of World War Two, the Third Reich's deadliest professional killer is dispatched on the most heinous assignment of his murderous career: the assassination of Franklin Delano Roosevelt!

THE BIG NEEDLE (1921, $2.95)
by Ken Follett

All across Europe, innocent people are being terrorized, homes are destroyed, and dead bodies have become an unnervingly common sight. And the horrors will continue until the most powerful organization on Earth finds Chadwell Carstairs—and kills him!

DOMINATOR (2118, $3.95)
by James Follett

Two extraordinary men, each driven by dangerously ambiguous loyalties, play out the ultimate nuclear endgame miles above the helpless planet—aboard a hijacked space shuttle called DOMINATOR!